The Ethnic Detectives

The Ethnic Detectives

Masterpieces of Mystery Fiction

Edited by

Bill Pronzini and Martin H. Greenberg

DODD, MEAD & COMPANY

New York

6954

Copyright © 1985 by Bill Pronzini and Martin H.
Greenberg

All rights reserved
No part of this book may be reproduced in any form
without permission in writing from the publisher.
Published by Dodd, Mead & Company, Inc.
79 Madison Avenue, New York, N.Y. 10016
Distributed in Canada by
McClelland and Stewart Limited, Toronto
Manufactured in the United States of America
Designed by K. Parker
First Edition

Library of Congress Cataloging in Publication Data

Main entry under title:

The Ethnic detectives.

    1. Detective and mystery stories.   I. Pronzini, Bill.
II. Greenberg, Martin Harry.
PN6120.95.D45E89   1985   808.83'872   84–24638
ISBN 0–396–08545–8

ACKNOWLEDGMENTS

"The Coffins of the Emperor," by Robert van Gulik. From *Judge Dee at Work*. Copyright © 1967 by Robert van Gulik. Used by permission of Charles Scribner's Sons.

"A Star for a Warrior," by Manly Wade Wellman. Copyright © 1946 by The American Mercury, Inc. First published in *Ellery Queen's Mystery Magazine*. Reprinted by permission of Kirby McCauley, Ltd.

"The Case of the Emerald Sky," by Eric Ambler. Copyright © 1940 by Eric Ambler. Reprinted by permission of the author.

"The Black Sampan," by Raoul Whitfield. Copyright © 1932 by Blazing Publications, Inc. All Rights Reserved. Originally published in *Black Mask*, June 1932, under the pseudonym "Ramon Decolta." Copyright © 1932 by The Pro-Distributors Publishing Company, Inc. Copyright © 1960 by Popular Publications, Inc. Reprinted by special arrangement with Blazing Publications, Inc., proprietor and conservator of the respective copyrights and successor-in-interest to Popular Publications, Inc.

"Mom Makes a Wish," by James Yaffe. Copyright © 1955 by Mercury Publications, Inc. First published in *Ellery Queen's Mystery Magazine*. Reprinted by permission of the author.

"Inspector Ghote and the Test Match," by H. R. F. Keating. Copyright © 1969 by H. R. F. Keating. Reprinted by permission of Literistic, Ltd.

"The Most Obstinate Man in Paris," by Georges Simenon. Copyright © 1947 by Georges Simenon. Reprinted by permission of the author.

ACKNOWLEDGMENTS

"The Hair of the Widow," by Robert Somerlott. Copyright © 1964 by Robert Somerlott. First published in *Ellery Queen's Mystery Magazine*. Reprinted by permission of McIntosh and Otis, Inc.

"White Water," by W. Ryerson Johnson. Copyright © 1941 by This Week Magazine. First published in *This Week Magazine*. Reprinted by permission of the author.

"Inspector Saito's Small Satori," by Janwillem van de Wetering. Copyright © 1978 by Davis Publications, Inc. First published in *Alfred Hitchcock's Mystery Magazine* under the pseudonym "Seiko Legru." Reprinted by permission of the author.

"One for Virgil Tibbs," by John Ball. Copyright © 1977 by John Ball. First published in *Ellery Queen's Mystery Magazine*. Reprinted by permission of the author.

"The Luck of a Gypsy," by Edward D. Hoch. Copyright © 1985 by Edward D. Hoch. An original story published by permission of the author.

"Goldfish," by Hayford Peirce. Copyright © 1985 by Hayford Peirce. An original story published by permission of the author.

"The Witch, Yazzie, and the Nine of Clubs," by Tony Hillerman. Copyright © 1981 by the Swedish Academy of Detection. Reprinted by permission of the author.

"The Beer Drinkers," by Josh Pachter. Copyright © 1984 by Josh Pachter. First published in *Ellery Queen's Mystery Magazine*. Reprinted by permission of the author.

"The Sanchez Sacraments," by Marcia Muller. Copyright © 1985 by Marcia Muller. An original story published by permission of the author.

"J," by Ed McBain. Copyright © 1961 by Ed McBain. First published in *Ellery Queen's Mystery Magazine*. Reprinted by permission of the author and John Farquharson, Ltd.

CONTENTS

INTRODUCTION

There are all sorts of fictional detectives, as any reader of mystery fiction well knows. Some are self-employed, the famous (and occasionally infamous) "private eyes"; some work for police departments, insurance companies, and similar institutions; while others are amateurs for whom crime solving is merely a hobby—murder and mayhem seem to intrude with frightening regularity on their otherwise rather mundane lives. The amateur detectives (or ADs, as they are fondly known among the cognoscenti) come from all walks of life: doctors, lawyers, merchants, thieves, newspaper reporters, poets, playwrights, fiction writers, salesmen, bankers, artists, magicians, priests, rabbis, gamblers, teachers, scientists, sports figures, publicans, and a hundred more. Whether amateur or professional, the fictional investigator may be male or female, straight or gay, young or old, fat or thin, active or sedentary; he/she may be hardboiled, soft-boiled, half-baked, well-pickled, sugar-coated, and either a wit or a half-wit. He/she may even be handicapped in some way, one of those characters sometimes referred to as the "defective detectives"—blind persons, persons confined to wheelchairs, persons missing limbs, midgets, individuals with uncommon phobias or medical problems.

And then, of course, there are the ethnic detectives.

The ethnic sleuth emerged in crime fiction for two distinct reasons. One is a combination of expediency and ingenuity: mystery writers are forever searching for a "handle," something unique that differentiates *their* work from that of the multitude of other stories and novels published in the genre past and present; an ethnic detective allows for the introduction of exotic characters, interesting cultural backgrounds, and sometimes unusual crimes. The second reason is an abiding interest by many writers in the various ethnic cultures, especially those writers who themselves are members of a specific ethnic group. So much nonsense has been published about blacks and Orientals, for instance, that some blacks and Orientals have taken to writing crime fiction in sheer self-defense.

Defining what makes a detective ethnic is not always simple, however. In one sense, the very first fictional detective, Edgar Allan Poe's C. Auguste Dupin, qualifies. Although he was a Frenchman working in France, and therefore not a member of a minority, it was the English and Americans who were the primary audience for his cases; *for them*, Dupin was an ethnic investigator. So it is certainly possible for a Filipino such as Raoul Whitfield's Jo Gar, a Pakistani such as Josh Pachter's Mahboob Ahmed Chaudri, a Romanian Gypsy such as Edward D. Hoch's Michael Vlado, or another Frenchman, Simenon's Inspector Maigret—each working in his native land—to be seen as an ethnic detective by people of a different culture.

The most accepted definition requires the sleuth to be a member of a minority group within a dominant culture, one whose mannerisms, world view, and approach reflect his or her ethnic origins. John Ball's Virgil Tibbs and Chester Himes's Coffin Ed Johnson and Gravedigger Jones (black), Tony Hillerman's Joe Leaphorn and Jim Chee (Navajo), Marcia Muller's Elena Oliverez (Chicana), James Yaffe's "Mom" and Harry Kemelman's Rabbi David Small (Jewish), and of course Earl Derr Biggers's Charlie Chan are among the best examples.

Pursuant to the above, there is also the question of just how ethnic a detective must be in order to qualify. The mere possession of an Hispanic, Italian, or Jewish surname is not enough; the character's ethnicity should ideally play an important role in his/her life, and frequently play an important role in a crime and/or its solution. The detectives represented in this anthology, both the native variety and those who are members of minorities within the United States, are among the most authentic of all ethnic investigators.

Overall, a great many groups and cultures are represented in crime fiction—the larger percentage of all such groups and cultures, in fact. Among them are detectives who are black, Chinese, Japanese, Hawaiian (before Hawaii became a state of the union), Irish, Scotch, Swedish, Norwegian, Danish, Italian, German, Dutch, Belgian, Czechoslovakian, Russian, Gypsy, Turkish, Spanish, Greek, Jewish (both in a cultural and a religious sense), Israeli, Iraqi, Pakistani/Bahrainian, Indian, Tibetan, Bantu, Filipino, Malaysian, Tahitian, Australian, Brazilian, Jamaican, Mexican, and Native American (and one could reasonably ask why the first Americans should be considered a "minority"). There is also the sub-category of crime solvers of mixed background, such as Spanish/Nez Percé Indian (Bill S. Ballinger's Joaquin Hawks), Greek/Swedish (Dorothy Uhnak's Christie Opara), and Norwegian/Japanese (Poul Anderson's Trygve Yamamura). These are particularly interesting characters because their adventures frequently concern problems of identity, of the search for one's roots, and of reconciling different heritages—problems that are the stuff of emotion and high drama.

We might also add yet another sub-category, that of the gay detective, since the existence of a homosexual culture in American and non-American societies makes members of this group similar to ethnics, even though they may also be members of *other* ethnic groups (George Baxt's gay black detective, Pharaoh Love, for instance). Indeed, the interplay of culture and ethnicity is one of the attractive features that have made the ethnic detective so popular for so many years.

Mention should be made, too, of the ethnic villains—in particular, the Oriental villain—whose fictional history is unfortunate but nonetheless important in the early development of the genre. Dr. Fu Manchu and the other Oriental supercriminals were a product of the "Yellow Peril" hysteria of the first quarter of this century, and certainly do not bring credit to writers such as Sax Rohmer and M. P. Shiel, who saw little except evil in ethnic and racial groups different from their own. More recently, the depiction of Italian-American culture, beginning with W. R. Burnett's *Little Caesar* (1929) and extending to such contemporary novels as Mario Puzo's *The Godfather* (1969), has created a false impression that violence and gangsterism are inherent traits in the Italian nationality.

In this connection, it is interesting to note the ethnic backgrounds of those writers who have created ethnic detectives. On the one hand there are numerous examples of members of a particular group writing about their own: Harry Kemelman, Henry Klinger, and James Yaffe have created Jewish sleuths; Chester Himes and Percy Spurlark Parker have created black detectives; Ed McBain and Bill Pronzini have created Italian-American detectives. On the other hand there are even more examples of one group (generally white Anglo-Saxons) writing about a detective of another group; among these are Robert van Gulik, Earl Derr Biggers, and Janwillem van de Wetering on Orientals; Elizabeth Linington, the Lockridges, and Julie Smith on Jews; Ed Lacy, A. H. Z. Carr, Ernest Tidyman, John Ball, Veronica Parker Johns, Octavus Roy Cohen, and John Wyllie on blacks; and Marcia Muller, Rex Burns, Dell Shannon (Elizabeth Linington), and Robert Somerlott on Mexicans and Mexican-Americans. For the most part, owing to a genuine interest and feeling for a specific culture, these "outsiders" have been equally successful in capturing an honest ethnic flavor with their characters.

This book is a tribute to all ethnic detectives: a stalwart bunch, many of whom, as John Ball has ironically pointed out in an essay, were accepted by modern society long before real-life members of the ethnic groups they represent. It is also a celebration of detective fiction in general and at its best—an art form that has provided countless readers with countless hours of pleasure for well over a century.

Vive le roman policier!
Vive la différence!

Bill Pronzini and Martin H. Greenberg
August 1984

The Ethnic Detectives

Judge Dee

THE CHINESE DETECTIVE

THE COFFINS OF THE EMPEROR

Robert van Gulik

The most famous Chinese detective, of course, is Earl Derr Biggers' immortal Charlie Chan, who appears in six novels (but no short stories), over 40 films, and numerous radio and TV shows. Next in line is surely Robert van Gulik's Judge Dee Jen-djieh, the seventh century (T'ang Dynasty) magistrate whose celebrated cases have been called "the finest ethnographic detective [stories] in English."

The Judge Dee novels and novelettes are classic puzzles, exercises in ratiocination and deduction in which Dee works strictly within the historical parameters of Chinese administrative and criminal law. But they are also superb historical set pieces, offering graphic portraits of daily life in medieval China. "The Coffins of the Emperor" takes place in the year A.D. 672, and presents two distinct problems for Dee to solve with his usual élan.

Robert van Gulik (1910–1967) was a Netherlands diplomat who possessed a lifelong fascination for ancient China. He spent most of his adult years in the Near and Far East, where in his spare time he wrote numerous scholarly volumes (on such subjects as ancient Chinese pictorial art, jurisprudence, and sexual practices), as well as the Judge

1

Dee series. Among the Judge Dee books are the novels The Phantom of the Temple *(1966) and* Necklace and Calabash *(1967); and the collections of novelettes* The Chinese Maze Murders *(1957),* The Chinese Bell Murders *(1958),* The Haunted Monastery *(1963), and* The Monkey and the Tiger *(1965). Van Gulik's only non-Oriental novel,* The Given Day *(1964), has recently been published in the United States for the first time in a limited edition.*

·   ·   ·

The *events described in this story took place when Judge Dee was occupying his fourth post as magistrate, namely of Lanfang, an isolated district on the western frontier of the mighty T'ang Empire. Here he met with considerable trouble when taking up his duties, as described in the novel* The Chinese Maze Murders. *The present story tells about the grave crisis that threatened the Empire two years later, in the winter of the year* A.D. *672, and how Judge Dee succeeded in solving, on one and the same night, two difficult problems, one affecting the fate of the nation, the other the fate of two humble people.*

As soon as Judge Dee had entered the dining room on the restaurant's top floor, he knew that the banquet would be a dismal affair. The light of two large silver candelabras shone on the beautiful antique furniture, but the spacious room was heated by only one small brazier, where two or three pieces of coal were dying in the embers. The padded curtains of embroidered silk could not keep out the cold draught, reminding one of the snowy plains that stretched out for thousands of miles beyond the western frontier of the Chinese Empire.

At the round table sat only one man, the thin, elderly magistrate of Ta-shih-kou, this remote boundary district. The two girls who were standing behind his chair looked listlessly at the tall, bearded newcomer.

Magistrate Kwang rose hastily and came to meet Judge Dee.

"I profoundly apologize for these poor arrangements!" he said with a bleak smile. "I had invited also two colonels and two guildmasters, but the colonels were suddenly summoned to the Marshal's headquarters, and the guildmasters were wanted by the Quartermaster-General. This emergency . . ." He raised his hands in a helpless gesture.

"The main thing is that I shall now profit from your instructive conversation!" Judge Dee said politely.

His host led him to the table and introduced the very young girl on his left as Tearose, and the other as Jasmine. Both were gaudily dressed and wore cheap finery—they were common prostitutes rather than the refined courtesans one would expect at a dinner party. But Judge Dee knew that all the courtesans of Ta-shih-kou were now reserved for the high-ranking officers of the Marshal's headquarters. When Jasmine had filled Judge Dee's wine beaker, Magistrate Kwang raised his own and said:

"I welcome you, Dee, as my esteemed colleague of the neighbor-district and my honored guest. Let's drink to the victory of our Imperial Army!"

"To victory!" Judge Dee said and emptied his beaker in one draught.

From the street below came the rumble of iron-studded cartwheels on the frozen ground.

"That'll be the troops going to the front at last for our counteroffensive," the judge said with satisfaction.

Kwang listened intently. He sadly shook his head. "No," he said curtly, "they are going too slowly. They are coming back from the battlefield."

Judge Dee rose, pulled the curtain aside and opened the window, braving the icy wind. In the eerie moonlight he saw down below a long file of carts, drawn by emaciated horses. They were packed with wounded soldiers and long shapes covered with canvas. He quickly closed the window.

"Let's eat!" Kwang said, pointing with his chopsticks at the silver bowls and platters on the table. Each contained only a small quantity of salted vegetables, a few dried-out slices of ham and cooked beans.

3

"Coolie fare in silver vessels—that sums up the situation!" Kwang spoke bitterly. "Before the war my district had plenty of everything. Now all food is getting scarce. If this doesn't change soon we'll have a famine on our hands."

Judge Dee wanted to console him, but he quickly put his hand to his mouth. A racking cough shook his powerful frame. His colleague gave him a worried look and asked, "Has the lung epidemic spread to your district too?"

The judge waited till the attack had passed, then he quickly emptied his beaker and replied hoarsely, "Only a few isolated cases, and none really bad. In a milder form, like mine."

"You are lucky," Kwang said dryly. "Here most of those who get it start spitting blood in a day or two. They are dying like rats. I hope your quarters are comfortable," he added anxiously.

"Oh yes, I have a good room at one of the larger inns," Judge Dee replied. In fact he had to share a draughty attic with three officers, but he didn't like to distress his host further. Kwang hadn't been able to accommodate him in his official residence because it had been requisitioned by the army, and the magistrate had been obliged to move with his entire family into a small ramshackle house. It was a strange situation; in normal times a magistrate was well-nigh all-powerful, the highest authority in his district. But now the army had taken over. "I'll go back to Lan-fang tomorrow morning," the judge resumed. "There are many things to be attended to, for in my district also food is getting scarce."

Kwang nodded gloomily. Then he asked: "Why did the Marshal summon you? It's a good two days' journey from Lan-fang to here, and the roads are bad."

"The Uigurs have their tents on the other side of the river that borders my district," Judge Dee replied. "The Marshal wanted to know whether they were likely to join the Tartar armies. I told him that . . ." He broke off and looked dubiously at the two girls. The Tartar spies were everywhere.

"They are all right," Kwang said quickly.

"Well, I informed the Marshal that the Uigurs can only bring two thousand men in the field, and that their Khan went on a prolonged hunting trip to Central Asia, just before the Tartar emissaries arrived at his camp to ask him to join forces with them. The Uigur Khan is a wise man. We have his favorite son as hostage, you see, in the capital."

"Two thousand men won't make any difference either way," Kwang remarked. "Those accursed Tartars have three hundred thousand men standing at our frontier, ready to strike. Our front is crumbling under their probing attacks, and the Marshal keeps his two hundred thousand men idle here, instead of starting the promised counteroffensive."

For a while the two men ate in silence, while the girls kept their cups filled. When they had finished the beans and salted vegetables, Magistrate Kwang looked up and asked Tearose impatiently, "Where is the rice?"

"The waiter said they don't have any, sir," the girl replied.

"Nonsense!" the magistrate exclaimed angrily. He rose and said to Judge Dee: "Excuse me a moment, will you? I'll see to this myself!"

When he had gone downstairs with Tearose, the other girl said softly to Judge Dee, "Would you do me a great favor, sir?"

The judge looked up at her. She was a not unattractive woman of about twenty. But the thick layer of rouge on her face could not mask her sallow complexion and hollow cheeks. Her eyes were unnaturally wide and had a feverish glow.

"What is it?" he asked.

"I am feeling ill, sir. If you could leave early and take me with you, I would gladly receive you after I have rested awhile."

He noticed that her legs were trembling with fatigue. "I'll be glad to," he replied. "But after I've seen you home, I shall go on to my own lodging." He added with a thin smile: "I am not feeling too well myself, you know."

She gave him a grateful look.

5

When Magistrate Kwang and Tearose came back, Kwang said contritely, "I am very sorry, Dee, but it's true. There is no rice left."

"Well," Judge Dee said, "I enjoyed our meeting very much. I also think that Jasmine here is quite attractive. Would you think it very rude if I asked to be excused now?"

Kwang protested that it was far too early to part, but it was clear that he too thought this the best solution. He conducted Judge Dee downstairs and took leave of him in the hall. Jasmine helped the judge don his heavy fur coat, then they went out into the cold street. Sedan chairs were not to be had for love or money; all the bearers had been enlisted for the army transports.

The carts with the dead and wounded were still filing through the streets. Often the judge and his companion had to press themselves against the wall of a house to let dispatch riders pass, driving their weary horses on with obscene curses.

Jasmine led the judge down a narrow side street to a small hovel, leaning against a high, dark godown. Two struggling pine trees flanked the cracked door, their branches bent low under the load of frozen snow.

Judge Dee took a silver piece from his sleeve. Handing it to her, he said, "Well, I'll be going on now, my inn . . ." A violent attack of coughing seized him.

"You'll come inside and at least drink something hot," she said firmly. "You aren't fit to walk about as you are." She opened the door and dragged the judge inside, still coughing.

The attack subsided only after she had taken his fur coat and made him sit down in the bamboo chair at the rickety tea table. It was very warm in the small dark room; the copper brazier in the corner was heaped with glowing coals. Noticing his astonished glance, she said with a sneer, "That's the advantage of being a prostitute nowadays. We get plenty of coal, army issue. Serve our gallant soldiers!"

She took the candle, lit it at the brazier, then put it back on the table. She disappeared through the door curtain in the back wall. Judge Dee surveyed the room in the flickering light of the candle. Against the wall opposite him stood a large bedstead; its curtains were drawn, revealing rumpled quilts and a soiled double pillow.

Suddenly he heard a queer sound. He looked round. It came from behind a faded blue curtain, which was covering something close to the wall. It flashed through his mind that this could well be a trap. The military police flogged thieves on the street corners till their bones lay bare, yet robbery and assault were rampant in the city. He rose quickly, stepped up to the curtain and ripped it aside.

He blushed despite himself. A wooden crib stood against the wall. The small round head of a baby emerged from under a thick, patched quilt. It stared up at him with its large wise eyes. The judge hurriedly pulled the curtain close, and resumed his seat.

The woman came in carrying a large teapot. Pouring him a cup, she said, "Here, drink this. It's a special kind of tea; they say it cures a cough."

She went behind the curtain and came back with the child in her arms. She carried it to the bed, pulled the quilts straight with one hand and turned the pillow over.

"Excuse this mess," she said as she laid the child on the bed. "I had a customer here just before the magistrate had me called to attend our dinner." With the unconcern marking women of her profession, she took off her robe. Clad only in her wide trousers, she sat on the bed and leaned back against the pillow with a sigh of relief. Then she took up the child and laid it against her left breast. It started drinking contentedly.

Judge Dee sipped the medicinal tea; it had an agreeable bitter taste. After a while he asked her: "How old is your child?"

"Two months," the woman replied listlessly. "It's a boy."

His eye fell on the long white scars on her shoulders; one broad weal sorely mutilated her right breast. She looked up and saw his glance. She said indifferently, "Oh, they didn't mean to do that, it was my own fault. When they

7

were flogging me, I tried to wrench myself loose, and one tongue of the scourge curled over my shoulder and tore my breast."

"Why were you flogged?" the judge asked.

"Too long a story to tell!" she said curtly. She concentrated her attention on the child.

Judge Dee finished his tea in silence. His breathing came easier now, but his head was still throbbing with a dull ache. When he had drunk a second cup, Jasmine carried the baby back to the crib and pulled the curtain shut. She came to the table, stretched herself and yawned. Pointing at the bedstead, she asked, "What about it? I have rested a bit now, and the tea hardly covers what you paid me."

"Your tea is excellent," the judge said wearily; "it more than covers what I gave you." In order not to offend her he added quickly, "I wouldn't risk infecting you with this accursed lung trouble. I'll have one more cup, then I'll be on my way."

"As you like!" Sitting down opposite him, she added, "I'll have a cup myself, my throat is parched."

In the street footsteps crunched in the frozen snow. It was the men of the night watch. They beat midnight on their wooden clappers. Jasmine shrank in her seat. Putting her hand to her throat, she gasped, "Midnight already?"

"Yes," Judge Dee said worriedly, "if we don't start our counteroffensive very soon, I fear the Tartar hordes will break through and overrun this area. We'll drive them back again, of course, but since you have that nice child, wouldn't it be wiser if you packed up and went east tomorrow morning?"

She was looking straight ahead, agony in her feverish eyes. Then she spoke, half to herself, "Six hours to go!" Looking at the judge, she added: "My child? At dawn his father will be beheaded."

Judge Dee set his cup down. "Beheaded?" he exclaimed. "I am sorry. Who is he?"

"A captain, name of Woo."

"What did he do?"

"Nothing."

"You aren't beheaded for nothing!" the judge remarked crossly.

"He was falsely accused. They said he strangled the wife of a fellow officer. He was court-martialled and condemned to death. He has been in the military jail now for about a year, waiting for the confirmation. It came today."

Judge Dee tugged at his moustache. "I have often worked together with the military police," he said. "Their judicial system is cruder than our civilian procedure, but I have always found them efficient, and very conscientious. They don't make many mistakes."

"They did in this case," Jasmine said. She added resignedly: "Nothing can be done; it's too late."

"Yes, since he is to be executed at dawn, there isn't much we can do about it," the judge agreed. He thought for a while, then resumed, "But why not tell me about it? You would get my mind off my own worries and perhaps it might help you to pass the time."

"Well," she said with a shrug, "I am feeling too miserable to sleep anyway. Here it is. About a year and a half ago, two captains of the garrison here in Ta-shih-kou used to frequent the licensed quarters. One was called Pan, the other Woo. They had to work together because they belonged to the same branch of the service, but they didn't get along at all; they were as different as can be. Pan was a milksop with a smooth face, a dandy who looked more like a student than an officer. With all his fine talk he was a nasty piece, and the girls didn't like him. Woo was just the opposite, a rough-and-ready boy, a good boxer and swordsman, quick with his hands and quick with a joke. They used to say that the soldiers would go through fire and water for him. He wasn't what you'd call handsome, but I loved him. And he would have no one but me. He paid the owner of the brothel I belong to at regular times so that I didn't have to sleep with the first comer. He promised to buy and marry me as soon as he got his promotion, that's why I didn't mind having his child. Usually we get rid of them when we are pregnant or sell them. But I wanted mine." She emptied her cup, pushed a lock away from her forehead, and went on, "So far so good. Then, one night about ten months ago, Pan came home and found his wife lying there strangled to death, and Woo standing by her bed, looking dazed. Pan called in a passing patrol of the military police, and accused Woo of having murdered his wife. Both were brought before the military tribunal. Pan said that Woo kept bothering his wife, who wouldn't have him. The slimy bastard said he warned Woo many times to leave her alone; he hadn't wanted to report him to the colonel because Woo was his fellow officer! Well, Pan added that Woo knew that Pan was on night duty in the armory that evening, so he had gone to Pan's house and again tried to bed with his wife. She had refused, and Woo had flown into a rage and strangled her. That was all."

"What did Woo have to say to that?" Judge Dee asked.

"Woo said that Pan was a dirty liar. That he knew that Pan hated him, and that Pan himself had strangled his wife in order to ruin him."

"Not a very clever fellow, that captain of yours," the judge remarked dryly.

"Listen, will you? Woo said that when he passed by the armory that night, Pan hailed him and asked him to go round to his house and see whether his wife needed anything, for she had felt indisposed that afternoon. When Woo got there, the front door was open, the servants gone. No one answered his calls, so he went into the bedroom where he found her dead body. Then Pan came rushing inside and started hollering for the military police."

"A queer story," Judge Dee said. "How did the military judge formulate his verdict? But no, you wouldn't know that, of course."

"I do. I was there myself, sneaked in with the others. Wet all over with fright, I tell you, for if they catch a whore in a military establishment she gets scourged. Well, the colonel said that Woo was guilty of adultery with the wife of a fellow officer, and sentenced him to have his head chopped off. He said he wouldn't say too much about murder, for his men had found out that Pan himself had sent his servants away after dinner that night, and as soon as he had gone on duty at the armory, he had told the military police that he had been warned about thieves in his neighborhood, and asked them to keep an eye on his house. The colonel said that it was possible Pan had discovered that his wife was carrying on with Woo, and that he had therefore strangled her. That was his right; according to the law, he could have killed Woo too, if he had caught them in the act, as they call it. But maybe Pan had been afraid to tackle Woo, and had chosen this roundabout way of getting at him. Anyway that was neither here nor there, the colonel said. The fact was that Woo had played games with the wife of a fellow officer, and that was bad for the morale of the army. Therefore he had to be beheaded."

She fell silent. Judge Dee caressed his sidewhiskers. After a while he said, "On the face of it I would say that the colonel was perfectly right. His verdict agrees with the brief character sketch you gave me of the two men concerned. Why are you so sure that Woo didn't have an affair with Pan's wife?"

"Because Woo loved me, and wouldn't even look at another woman," she replied promptly.

Judge Dee thought that this was a typical woman's argument. To change the subject, he asked: "Who flogged you, and why?"

"It's all such a stupid story!" she said in a forlorn voice. "After the session I was furious with Woo. I had discovered that I was pregnant, and the mean skunk had been carrying on with the Pan woman all the time, behind my back! So I rushed to the jail and got inside by telling the guards I was Woo's sister. When I saw him I spat in his face, called him a treacherous lecher, and ran off again. But when I was so far gone I couldn't work any more, I got to thinking things over, and I knew I had been a silly fool, and that Woo loved me. So eight weeks ago, after our child had been born and I was a little better, I again went to the military prison to tell Woo I was sorry. But Woo must have told the guards how I fooled them the time before—and he was right, too, the way I had shouted at him! As soon as I was inside they lashed me to the rack and gave me a flogging. I was in luck, I knew the soldier who handled the scourge; he didn't hit too hard, else the army would have had to supply a coffin then and there. As it was, my back and shoulders were cut to ribbons and I was bleeding like a pig, but I am no weakling and I made it. As strong as a farmhand, father used to say of me before he had to sell me to pay the rent for our field. Then there came rumors about the Tartars planning an attack. The garrison commander was called to the capital, and the war started. What with one thing and another Woo's case dragged on. This morning the decision came, and at dawn they'll chop his head off."

Suddenly she buried her face in her hands and started to sob. The judge slowly stroked his long black beard, waiting till she had calmed down. Then he asked:

"Was the Pans' marriage a happy one?"

"How do I know? Think I slept under their bed?"

"Did they have children?"

"No."

"How long had they been married?"

"Let me see. About a year and a half—I know that. When I first met the two captains, Woo told me that Pan had just been called home by his father to marry the woman his parents had got for him."

"Do you happen to know his father's name?"

"No. Pan only used to brag that his father was a big noise in Soochow."

"That must be Pan Wei-liang, the Prefect," Judge Dee said at once. "He is a famous man, a great student of ancient history. I have never met him, but I have read many of his books. Quite good. Is his son still here?"

"Yes, attached to headquarters. If you admire those Pans so much, you'd better go there and make friends with the mean bastard!" she added contemptuously.

Judge Dee rose. "I'll do that," he said, half to himself.

She mouthed an obscene word. "You are all the same, all of you!" she snapped. "Am I glad I am just an honest whore! The gentleman is choosy, doesn't want to sleep with a woman with half a breast gone, eh? Want your money back?"

"Keep it!" Judge Dee said calmly.

"Go to hell!" she said. She spat on the floor and turned her back on him.

Judge Dee silently put on his fur coat and left.

While he was walking through the main street, still crowded with soldiers, he reflected that things didn't look too good. Even if he found Captain Pan, and even if he succeeded in extracting from him the fact he needed for the testing of his theory, he would then have to try to obtain an audience with the Marshal, for only he could, at this stage, order a stay of execution. And the Marshal was fully occupied by weighty issues, the fate of the Empire was in the balance. Moreover, that fierce soldier was not notorious for his gentle manner. Judge Dee set his teeth. If the Empire had come to such a pass that a judge couldn't prevent an innocent man from being beheaded . . .

The Marshal's headquarters were located in the so-called Hunting Palace, an immense compound that the present Emperor had built for his beloved eldest son, who had died young. The Crown Prince had been fond of hunting on the western frontier. He had died on a hunting expedition there, and it had been his wish to be buried in Ta-shih-kou. His sarcophagus had been placed in a vault there, and later that of his Princess beside it.

Judge Dee had some trouble in getting admitted by the guards, who looked with suspicion on every civilian. But at last he was led to a small, draughty waiting room, and an orderly took his red visiting card to Captain Pan. After a long wait a young officer came in. The tight-fitting mail jacket and the broad swordbelt accentuated his slender figure, and the iron helmet set off his handsome but cold face, smooth but for a small black moustache. He saluted stiffly, then stood waiting in haughty silence till the judge addressed him. A district magistrate ranked much higher, of course, than an army captain, but Pan's attitude suggested that in wartime things were different.

"Sit down, sit down!" Judge Dee said jovially. "A promise is a promise, I always say! And better late than never!"

Captain Pan sat down on the other side of the tea table, looking politely astonished.

"Half a year ago," the judge continued, "while passing through Soochow on my way to Lan-fang, I had a long conversation with your father. I also am a student of history, you know, in my spare time! When I was taking my leave, he said: 'My eldest son is serving in Ta-shih-kou, your neighbour-district. If you should happen to pass by there, do me a favor and have a look how he's doing. The boy had awfully bad luck.' Well, yesterday the Marshal summoned me, and before returning to Lan-fang I wanted to keep my promise."

"That's most kind of you, sir!" Pan muttered, confused. "Please excuse my rudeness just now. I didn't know . . . and I am in a terrible state. The bad situation at the front, you see . . ." He shouted an order. A soldier brought a pot of tea. "Did . . . did my father tell you about the tragedy, sir?"

"Only that your young wife was murdered here last year. Accept my sincere . . ."

"He shouldn't have forced me to marry, sir!" the captain burst out. "I told him . . . tried to tell him . . . but he was always too busy, never had time . . ." With an effort Pan took a hold of himself, and continued, "I thought I was too young to marry, you see. Wanted my father to postpone it. For a few years, till I would've been stationed in a large city, for instance. Give me time to . . . to sort things out."

"Were you in love with another girl?"

"Heaven forbid!" the young officer exclaimed. "No sir, it was simply that I felt I was not the marrying kind. Not yet."

"Was she murdered by robbers?"

Captain Pan somberly shook his head. His face had gone a deadly pale. "The murderer was a fellow officer of mine, sir. One of those disgusting woman chasers; you could never have a decent, clean conversation with him. Always talking about women, women, always letting himself be caught in their filthy little games . . ." The young man spat out those last words. He quickly gulped down the tea, then added in a dull voice, "He tried to seduce my wife, and strangled her when she refused. He'll be beheaded at dawn." Suddenly he buried his face in his hands.

Judge Dee silently observed the stricken youngster for a while. Then he said softly: "Yes, you had very bad luck indeed." He rose and resumed in a businesslike manner, "I must see the Marshal again. Please take me there."

Captain Pan got up quickly. As he conducted the judge down a long corridor where orderlies were rushing to and fro, he said: "I can take you only as far as the anteroom, sir. Only members of the High Command are allowed beyond.'

"That'll do," Judge Dee said.

Captain Pan showed the judge into a hall, crowded with officers, then said he would wait outside to lead the judge back to the main gate. As soon as the judge had entered, the hubbub of voices ceased abruptly. A colonel stepped up to him. After a cursory glance at Judge Dee's cap he asked coldly: "What can I do for you, Magistrate?"

"I have to see the Marshal on urgent business."

"Impossible!" the colonel said abruptly. "The Marshal is in conference. I have strict orders to admit nobody."

"A human life is at stake," the judge said gravely.

"A human life, you say!" the colonel exclaimed with a sneer. "The Marshal is deliberating on two hundred thousand human lives that are at stake, Magistrate! May I lead the way?"

Judge Dee grew pale. He had failed. Piloting the judge politely but firmly to the exit, the colonel said: "I trust that you'll understand, Magistrate. . . ."

15

"Magistrate!" shouted another colonel who came rushing inside. Despite the cold his face was covered with sweat. "Do you happen to know where a colleague of yours is, called Dee?"

"I am Magistrate Dee," the judge replied.

"Heaven be praised! I have been looking for you for hours! The Marshal wants you!"

He dragged the judge by his sleeve through a door at the back of the anteroom into a semi-dark passage. Thick felt hangings dampened all sound. He opened the heavy door at the end, and let the judge go inside.

It was curiously still in the enormous palace hall. A group of high-ranking officers in resplendent armor stood round a monumental desk, piled with maps and papers. All were looking silently at the giant who was pacing the floor in front of it, his hands clasped behind his back.

He wore an ordinary mail jacket with battered, iron shoulderplates and the baggy leather trousers of a cavalry man. But on top of his high helmet the golden marshal's dragon raised its horned head. As the Marshal walked to and fro with heavy tread, he let the point of the broad sword that was dangling from his belt clatter carelessly on the delicately carved, marble floor tiles.

Judge Dee knelt down. The colonel approached the Marshal. Standing stiffly at attention, he said something in a clipped voice.

"Dee?" the Marshal barked. "Don't need the fellow anymore, send him away! No, wait! I still have a couple of hours before I order the retreat." Then he shouted at the judge: "Hey there, stop crawling on the floor! Come here!"

Judge Dee rose hurriedly, went up to the Marshal and made a deep bow. Then he righted himself. The judge was a tall man, but the Marshal topped him by at least two inches. Hooking his thumbs in his swordbelt, the giant glared at the judge with his fierce right eye. His left eye was covered by a black band—it had been pierced by a barbarian arrow during the northern campaign.

"You are good at riddles, they say, eh, Dee? Well, I'll

show you a riddle!" Turning to the desk, he shouted: "Lew! Mao!"

Two men wearing generals' armor hurriedly detached themselves from the group round the table. Judge Dee recognized the lean general in the shining golden armor as Lew, commander of the left wing. The broad-shouldered, squat man wearing a golden cuirass and a silver helmet was Mao, commanding general of the military police. Only Sang, the commander of the right wing, was missing. With the Marshal these three were the highest military leaders; in this national crisis the Emperor had placed the fate of the Chinese people and the dynasty in their hands. The judge made a low bow. The two generals gave him a stony look.

The Marshal strode through the hall and kicked a door open. They silently passed through a number of broad, empty corridors, the iron boots of the three officers resounding hollowly on the marble floor. Then they descended a broad staircase. At the bottom two palace guards sprang to attention. At a sign of the Marshal they slowly pushed open a heavy double gate.

They entered a colossal vault, dimly lit by tall silver oil lamps, placed at regular intervals in recesses in the high, windowless walls. In the center of the vault stood two enormous coffins, lacquered a bright red, the color of resurrection. They were of identical size, each measuring about ten by thirty feet, and over fifteen feet high.

The Marshal bowed, and the three others followed his example. Then the Marshal turned to Judge Dee and said, pointing at the coffins, "Here is your riddle, Dee! This afternoon, just when I was about to order the offensive, General Sang came and accused Lew here of high treason. Said that Lew had contacted the Tartar Khan and agreed that as soon as we would attack, Lew would join the Tartar dogs with his troops. Later Lew would get the southern half of the Empire as a reward. The proof? Sang said that Lew had concealed in the coffin of the Crown Prince two hundred suits of armor complete with helmets and swords, and marked with the special sign of the traitors. At the right moment Lew's confederates in the High Command would break the coffin open, don those marked suits of armor and massacre all the staff officers here who aren't in the plot."

Judge Dee started and looked quickly at General Lew. The lean man stood there stiffly erect, staring ahead with a white, taut face.

"I trust Lew as I trust myself," the Marshal went on, aggressively thrusting his bearded chin forward, "but Sang has a long and honorable career behind him, and I can't take any chances. I must verify the accusation, and quick. The plans for our counteroffensive are ready. Lew will head a vanguard of fifteen thousand men and drive a wedge into the Tartar hordes. Then I'll follow up with a hundred and fifty thousand men and drive the dogs back into their own steppes. But there are signs that the wind is going to shift; if I wait too long we'll have to fight with snow and hail blowing right into our faces.

"I have examined the coffin of the Crown Prince for hours, together with Mao's best men, but we can find no sign that it has been tampered with. Sang maintains they excised a large section of the lacquer coating, made a hole, pushed the stuff inside and replaced the section of coating. According to him, there are experts who can do this without leaving a trace. Maybe there are, but I must have positive proof. But I can't desecrate the coffin of the Emperor's beloved son by breaking it open—I may not even scratch it without the special permission of His Majesty—and it'll take at least six days before I can get word from the capital. On the other hand I can't open the offensive before I have made sure that Sang's accusation is false. If I can't do that in two hours, I shall have to order a general retreat. Set to work, Dee!"

The judge walked around the coffin of the Crown Prince, then he also examined cursorily that of the Princess. Pointing at a few long poles that were lying on the floor, he asked, "What are these for?"

"I had the coffin tilted," General Mao said coldly, "in

order to verify whether the bottom hadn't been tampered with. All that was humanly possible has been done."

Judge Dee nodded. He said pensively, "I once read a description of this palace. I remember that it said that the August Body was first placed in a box of solid gold, which was then placed in one of silver, and that in turn in a case of lead. The empty space around it was filled up with the articles of adornment and court costumes of the Crown Prince. The sarcophagus itself consists of thick logs of cedarwood, covered on the outside with a coat of lacquer. The same procedure was followed two years later, when the Princess died. Since the Princess had been fond of boating, behind the palace a large artificial lake was made, with models of the boats used by the Princess and her court ladies. Is that correct?"

"Of course," the Marshal growled. "It's common knowledge. Don't stand there talking twaddle, Dee! Come to the point!"

"Could you get me a hundred sappers, sir?"

"What for? Didn't I tell you we can't tamper with that coffin?"

"I fear the Tartars also know all about these coffins, sir. Should they temporarily occupy the city, they'll break the coffins open to loot them. In order to prevent the coffins from being desecrated by the barbarians, I propose to sink them to the bottom of the lake."

The Marshal looked at him dumbfounded. Then he roared: "You accursed fool! Don't you know the coffins are hollow? They'll never sink. You . . ."

"They aren't meant to, sir!" Judge Dee said quickly. "But the plan to sink them provides us with a valid reason for deplacing them."

The Marshal glared at him with his one fierce eye. Suddenly he shouted: "By heaven, I think you've got it, Dee!" Turning to General Mao, he barked: "Get me a hundred sappers here, with cables and rollers! At once!"

After Mao had rushed to the staircase, the Marshal started pacing the floor, muttering to himself. General Lew covertly observed the judge. Judge Dee remained standing there in front of the coffin of the Crown Prince, staring at it silently, his arms folded in his long sleeves.

Soon General Mao came back. Scores of small, squat men swarmed inside behind him. They wore jackets and trousers of brown leather and peaked caps of the same material, with long neck- and ear-flaps. Some carried long round poles, others rolls of thick cable. It was the sappers corps, expert at digging tunnels, rigging machines for scaling city walls, blocking rivers and harbors with underwater barriers, and all the other special skills used in warfare.

When the Marshal had given their commander his instructions, a dozen sappers rushed to the high gate at the back of the vault, and opened it. The bleak moonlight shone on a broad marble terrace. Three stairs descended into the water of the lake beyond, which was covered by a thin layer of ice.

The other sappers crowded round and over the coffin of the Crown Prince like so many busy ants. One heard hardly a sound, for the sappers transmit orders by finger-talk only. They are so quiet they can dig a tunnel right under a building, the occupants becoming aware of what is happening only when the walls and the floor suddenly cave in. Thirty sappers tilted the coffin of the Crown Prince, using long poles as levers; one team placed rollers under it, another slung thick cables round the huge sarcophagus.

The Marshal watched them for a while, then he went outside and on to the terrace, followed by Dee and the generals. Silently they remained standing at the water's edge, looking out over the frozen lake.

Suddenly they heard a low rumbling sound behind them. Slowly the enormous coffin came rolling out of the gate. Dozens of sappers pulled it along by thick cables, while others kept placing new rollers underneath it. The coffin was drawn across the terrace, then let down into the water as if it was the hulk of a ship being launched. The ice cracked, the coffin rocked up and down for a while, then settled with about two-thirds of it under water. A cold wind blew over the frozen lake, and Judge Dee started to cough violently. He pulled his neckcloth up over the lower part of his face, beckoned the commander of the sappers and pointed at the coffin of the Princess in the vault behind them.

Again there was a rumbling sound. The second coffin came rolling across the terrace. The sappers let it down into the water where it remained floating next to that of the Crown Prince. The Marshal stooped and peered at the two coffins, comparing the waterlines. There was hardly any difference; if anything the coffin of the Princess was slightly heavier than that of the Crown Prince.

The Marshal righted himself. He hit General Lew a resounding clap on his shoulder. "I knew I could trust you, Lew!" he shouted. "What are you waiting for, man? Give the signal, go ahead with your troops! I'll follow in six hours. Good luck!"

A slow smile lit up the general's stern features. He saluted, then turned round and strode off. The commander of the sappers came and said respectfully to the Marshal: "We shall now weigh the coffins with heavy chains and rocks, sir, then we . . ."

"I have made a mistake," the Marshal interrupted him curtly. "Have them drawn on land again, and replace them in their original position." He barked at General Mao: "Go with a hundred men to Sang's camp outside the West Gate. Arrest him on the charge of high treason, and convey him in chains to the capital. General Kao shall take over his troops." Then he turned to Judge Dee, who was still coughing. "You get it, don't you? Sang is older than Lew, he couldn't swallow Lew's appointment to the same rank. It was Sang, that son of a dog, who conspired with the Khan, don't you see? His fantastic accusation was meant only to stop our counteroffensive. He would have attacked us together with the Tartars as soon as we started the retreat. Stop that blasted coughing, Dee! It annoys me. We are through here, come along!"

The council room was now seething with activity. Large maps had been spread out on the floor. The staff officers were checking all details of the planned counteroffensive.

A general said excitedly to the Marshal: "What about adding five thousand men to the force behind these hills here, sir?"

The Marshal stooped over the map. Soon they were deep in a complicated technical discussion. Judge Dee looked anxiously at the large water clock in the corner. The floater indicated that it would be dawn in one hour. He stepped up to the Marshal and asked diffidently: "May I take the liberty of asking you a favor, sir?"

The Marshal righted himself. He asked peevishly: "Eh? What is it now?"

"I would like you to review a case against a captain, sir. He's going to be beheaded at dawn, but he is innocent."

The Marshal grew purple in his face. He roared: "With the fate of our Empire in the balance, you dare to bother me, the Marshal, with the life of one wretched man?"

Judge Dee looked steadily into the one rolling eye. He said quietly: "A thousand men must be sacrificed if military necessity dictates it, sir. But not even one man must be lost if it's not strictly necessary."

The Marshal burst out in obscene curses, but he suddenly checked himself. With a wry smile he said: "If ever you get sick of that tawdry civilian paperwork, Dee, you come and see me. By God, I'll make a general officer out of you! Review the case, you say? Nonsense, I'll settle it, here and now! Give your orders!"

Judge Dee turned to the colonel who had rushed towards them when he heard the Marshal cursing. The judge said, "At the door of the anteroom a captain called Pan is waiting for me. He falsely accused another captain of murder. Could you bring him here?"

"Bring also his immediate superior!" the Marshal added. "At once!"

As the colonel hastened to the door, a low, wailing blast came from outside. It swelled in volume, penetrating the thick walls of the palace. It was the long brass trumpets, blowing the signal to assemble for the attack.

The Marshal squared his wide shoulders. He said with a broad smile: "Listen, Dee! That's the finest music that ever was!" Then he turned again to the maps on the floor.

Judge Dee looked fixedly at the entrance. The colonel was back in a remarkably short time. An elderly officer and Captain Pan followed him. The judge said to the Marshal, "They are here, sir."

The Marshal swung round, put his thumbs in his swordbelt and scowled at the two men. They stood stiffly at attention, with rapt eyes. It was the first time they had ever seen the greatest soldier of the Empire face to face. The giant growled at the elderly officer: "Report on this captain!"

"Excellent administrator, good disciplinarian. Can't get along with the men, no battle experience . . ." The officer rattled it off.

"Your case?" the Marshal asked Judge Dee.

The judge addressed the young captain coldly: "Captain Pan, you weren't fit to marry. You don't like women. You liked your colleague Captain Woo, but he spurned you. Then you strangled your wife, and falsely accused Woo of the crime."

"Is that true?" the Marshal barked at Pan.

"Yes, sir!" the captain replied as if in a trance.

"Take him outside," the Marshal ordered the colonel, "and have him flogged to death slowly, with the thin rattan."

"I plead clemency, sir!" Judge Dee interposed quickly. "This captain had to marry at his father's command. Nature directed him differently, and he couldn't cope with the resulting problems. I propose the simple death penalty."

"Granted!" And to Pan: "Can you die as an officer?"

"Yes, sir!" Pan said again.

"Assist the captain!" the Marshal rasped at the elder officer.

Captain Pan loosened his purple neckcloth and handed it to his immediate superior. Then he drew his sword. Kneeling in front of the Marshal, Pan took the hilt of the sword in his right hand and grabbed the point with his left. The sharp edge cut deeply into his fingers, but he didn't seem to notice it. The elder officer stepped up close to the kneeling man, holding the neckcloth spread out in his hands.

Raising his head, Pan looked up at the towering figure of
the Marshal. He called out:

"Long live the Emperor!"

Then, with one savage gesture, he cut his throat. The
elder officer quickly tied the neckcloth tightly round the
neck of the sagging man, staunching the blood. The Marshal
nodded. He said to Pan's superior, "Captain Pan died as
an officer. See to it that he is buried as one!" And to the
judge: "You look after that other fellow. Freed, reinstated
to his former rank, and so on." Then he bent over the map
again and barked at the general: "Put an extra five thousand
at the entrance of this valley here!"

As the four orderlies carried the dead body of Pan outside,
Judge Dee went to the large desk, grabbed a writing brush
and quickly jotted down a few lines on a sheet of official
paper of the High Command. A colonel impressed on it
the large square seal of the Marshal, then countersigned
it. Before running outside Judge Dee cast a quick look at
the water clock. He still had half an hour.

It took him a long time to cover the short distance between the Palace and the Military Jail. The streets were
crowded with mounted soldiers; they rode in rows six
abreast, holding high their long halberds, so greatly feared
by the Tartars. Their horses were well fed and their armor
shone in the red rays of dawn. It was General Lew's vanguard, the pick of the Imperial army. Then there came
the deep sound of rolling drums, calling up the Marshal's
own men to join their colors. The great counteroffensive
had begun.

The paper with the Marshal's seal caused Judge Dee to
be admitted at once to the prison commandant. A sturdily
built youngster was brought in by four guards; his thick
wrestler's neck had been bared already for the sword of
the executioner. The commandant read out the document
to him, then he ordered an adjutant to assist Captain Woo
in donning his armor. When Woo had put on his helmet,
the commandant himself handed him back his sword. Judge
Dee saw that although Woo didn't look too clever, he had

a pleasant, open face. "Come along!" he said to him.

Captain Woo stared dumbfounded at his black judge's cap, then asked: "How did you get involved in this case, Magistrate?"

"Oh," Judge Dee replied vaguely, "I happened to be at Headquarters when your case was reviewed. Since they are all very busy there now, they told me to take care of the formalities."

When they stepped out into the street Captain Woo muttered: "I was in this accursed jail almost a year. I have no place to go."

"You can come along with me," Judge Dee said.

As they were walking along the captain listened to the rolling of the drums. "So we are attacking at last, eh?" he said morosely. "Well, I am just in time to join my company. At least I'll die an honorable death."

"Why should you deliberately seek death?" the judge asked.

"Why? Because I am a stupid fool, that's why! I never touched that Mrs. Pan, but I betrayed a fine woman who came to see me in jail. The military police flogged her to death."

Judge Dee remained silent. Now they were passing through a quiet back street. He halted in front of a small hovel, built against an empty godown.

"Where are we?" Captain Woo asked, astonished.

"A plucky woman, and the son she bore you are living here," the judge answered curtly. "This is your home, Captain. Good-bye."

He quickly walked on.

As Judge Dee rounded the street corner, a cold blast blew full into his face. He pulled his neckcloth up over his nose and mouth, stifling a cough. He hoped that the servants would be on hand already in his inn. He longed for a large cup of hot tea.

David Return

THE NATIVE AMERICAN DETECTIVE ("Tsichah")

A STAR FOR A WARRIOR

Manly Wade Wellman

David Return is the very first American Indian detective in crime fiction: "A Star for a Warrior," his only recorded case, appeared in Ellery Queen's Mystery Magazine *in 1946 (and was the recipient of first prize in the first annual best short story of the year contest sponsored by EQMM). Like the Amerind series characters later created by Tony Hillerman (Joe Leaphorn and Jim Chee) and Brian Garfield (Sam Watchman), Return is a tribal policeman whose beat is a large reservation—in his case, the land belonging to the "Tsichah," an imaginary tribe based mainly on the Cheyenne and somewhat on the Pawnee.*

As Ellery Queen wrote on the initial publication of "A Star for a Warrior," David Return "investigates not as a white man but as an Indian steeped in Red Man's lore; and his deductions arise out of deep understanding of Indian character, tradition, and ceremonials. Indeed, David Return is the first truly American detective to appear in print."

It is a pity that Manly Wade Wellman chose not to bring Return back in other stories; he would have made an even greater contribution to detective fiction if he had. But Well-

*man is primarily a writer of science fiction and fantasy,
genres in which his work has achieved a high level of popu-
larity and critical respect. His criminous output is com-
prised of only a few short stories, one mystery novel*—Find
My Killer *(1947)—and a science-fiction Sherlock Holmes
pastiche in collaboration with his son Wade Wellman,* Sherlock Holmes's War of the Worlds *(1975).*

.   .   .

Young David Return half-ran across the sunbright plaza
of the Tsichah Agency. He was slim everywhere except
across his shoulders, his tawny brow, his jaw. For this occasion he had put on his best blue flannel shirt, a maroon
scarf, cowboy dungarees, and on his slim toed-in feet,
beaded moccasins. Behind his right hip rode a sheath knife.
His left hand carried his sombrero, and his thick black hair
reflected momentary blue lights in the hot morning. Once
he lifted the hat and slapped his thigh with it, in exultation
too great for even an Indian to dissemble. He opened the
door of the whitewashed cabin that housed the agency police detail, and fairly bounded in.

"*Ahi!*" he spoke a greeting in Tsichah to the man in the
cowskin vest who glanced up at him from a paper-littered
table. "A writing from the white chiefs, grandfather. I can
now wear the silver star."

The other lifted a brown face as lean, keen, and grim
as the blade of a tomahawk. Tough Feather, senior lieutenant of the agency police, was the sort of old Indian that
Frederic Remington loved to paint. He replied in English.
"Reports here," he said austerely, "are made in white man's
language."

David Return blinked. He was a well-bred young Tsichah,
and did his best not to show embarrassment. "I mean,"
he began again, also in English, "that they've confirmed
my appointment to the agency police detail, and—"

"Suppose," interrupted Tough Feather, "that you go outside, and come in again—properly."

Some of the young man's boisterous happiness drained

27

out of him. Obediently he stepped backward and out, pulling the door shut. He waited soberly for a moment, then re-entered and stood at attention.

"Agency Policeman David Return," he announced dutifully, "reporting for assignment as directed."

Tough Feather's thin mouth permitted a smile to soften one of its corners. Tough Feather's deepest black eyes glowed a degree more warmly. "Your report of completed study came in the mail an hour ago," he told David, and picked up a paper. "They marked you 'excellent' everywhere, except in discipline. There you're 'qualified.' That's good, but no more than good enough."

David shrugged. "The instructors were white men. But you'll not have any trouble with me. You're my grandfather, and a born chief of the Tsichah."

"So you are a born chief," Tough Feather reminded him, "and don't forget it. This police work isn't a white man's plaything. We serve the government, to make things better for all Indians. *Ahi,* son of my son," and forgetting his own admonition, Tough Feather himself lapsed into Tsichah, "for this I taught you as a child, and saw that you went to school and to the police college. We work together from this day."

"*Nunway,*" intoned David, as at a tribal ceremony. "Amen. That is my prayer."

From a pocket of the cowskin vest Tough Feather drew a black stone pipe, curiously and anciently carved. His brown fingers stuffed in flakes of tobacco. He produced a match and struck a light. Inhaling deeply, he blew a curl of slate-colored smoke, another and another and others, one to each of the six holy directions—north, west, south, east, upward and downward. Then he offered the pipe to David.

"Smoke," he invited deeply. "You are my brother warrior."

It was David Return's coming of age. He inhaled and puffed in turn, and while the smoke-clouds signalized the directions, he prayed silently to the Shining Lodge for strength and wisdom. When he had finished the six ritualistic puffs, he handed the pipe back to Tough Feather, who shook out the ashes and stowed it in his pocket. Then from the upper drawer of the desk Tough Feather produced something that shone like all the high hopes of all young warriors. He held it out, the silver-plated star of an agency policeman.

Eagerly David pinned it to his left shirt pocket, then drew himself once more to attention. "I'm ready to start duty, grandfather," he said.

"Good." Tough Feather was consulting a bit of paper with hastily scribbled notes. "David, do you remember an Indian girl named Rhoda Pleasant, who came to the agency last week with letters of introduction?"

"I remember that one," nodded David. "Not a Tsichah girl. A Piekan, going to some university up north. She's pleasant, all right," and he smiled, for Indians relish puns as much as any race in the world.

"Not pleasant in every way," growled Tough Feather, not amused. "She's been here too long, and talked too much, for a stranger woman. Plenty of young Tsichah men like her even better than you do. They might finish up by not liking each other."

"Then she's still here on the reservation? I met her only the one time, and the next day she was gone."

"But not gone away," Tough Feather told him. "Gone in. She borrowed a horse and some things to camp with. You know why, don't you? She wants to learn our secret Tsichah songs." The hard-cut old profile shook itself in conservative disapproval.

"*Ahi*, yes," said David. "She talked about that. Said she was getting her master's degree in anthropology, and she's hoping for a career as a scholar and an Indian folklore expert. She told me she'd picked up songs that Lieurance and Cadman would have given ten years of their life to hear and get down on paper. But I couldn't tell her about our songs if I wanted to. We hear them only about once or twice a year, at councils and ceremonies."

"The songs are like the chieftainships, passed from father

to son in one or two families," reminded Tough Feather. "Right now only three men really know them—"

"And they're mighty brash about it," broke in David, with less than his usual courtesy. "I know them. Dolf Buckskin, Stacey Weed, John Horse Child. All of them young, and all of them acting a hundred years old and a thousand years smart, out there in their brush camp with a drum— the kind with a pebble-headed stick—and a flute. They think we others ought to respect them and honor them."

"And you should," Tough Feather rejoined stiffly. "They're young, but their fathers and grandfathers taught them songs and secrets that come down from our First People. Those three young men are important to the whole Tsichah nation. Too important to be set against each other by Rhoda Pleasant."

"You mean she's out there seeing them?" David was suddenly grave, too. "I see what you're worried about. They'd not pay any attention to a man who asked rude questions, but a young woman as pretty as that Piekan—*ahi!* She'd give anybody squaw fever if she tried."

"Go to their camp," commanded Tough Feather. "It's off all the main trails, so you'll have to ride a pony instead of driving a car. Tell the girl to report back here and then go somewhere else."

David frowned. This was not his dream of a brilliant first case for his record. Then he smiled, for he reflected that the ride back from the camp of the singers would be interesting, with a companion like Rhoda Pleasant. "Where is that camp, grandfather?"

Tough Feather pointed with the heel of his hand. "Southwest. Take the Lodge Pole Ridge trail, and turn at the dry stream by the cabins of old Gopher Paw and his son. There's no trail across their land, but you'll pick one up beyond, among the knolls and bluffs. That branches in a few miles, and the right branch leads to where the singers are camped. Take whatever pony you want from the agency stable."

"The paint pony?" asked David eagerly.

"He's not the best one," and Tough Feather eyed his grandson, calculatingly. "Not the best traveler, anyway."

"Now about a saddle," went on David, "will you lend me the silvermounted one that Major Lillie gave you ten years ago?"

Tough Feather smiled, perhaps his first real smile in twenty or thirty days. "All right, take it and take the prettiest bridle, too. You're probably right, David. You'll have less trouble bringing that girl back if you and your pony are good to look at."

The paint pony was not the best in the agency stables, but he was competent on the narrow rough trail David had to take. His lightshod feet picked a nimble way through the roughest part of the reservation, over ground even less fit for farming than the poor soil of prairie and creek bottoms. It was rolling and stony, grown up here and there with cottonwood scrub and occasional clumps of willow or Osage orange. Once or twice rabbits fled from the sound of the hoofs, but not too frantically: animals felt safe in the half-cover of this section; long ago they had escaped here from the incessant hunting enthusiasm of Tsichah boys with arrows or cheap old rifles. David followed the right branch of the trail his grandfather had described and went down a little slope, across an awkward gully where he had to dismount and lead the pony, and beyond among scattered boulders, rare in this country.

He felt that he was getting near his work, and in his mind he rehearsed the words, half-lofty and half-bantering, with which he would explain to Rhoda Pleasant that she must cease her troublesome researches and head back with him. She was a ready smiler, he remembered, both bolder and warmer in manner than any Tsichah girl he knew. And she wore her riding things with considerable knowledge and style, like a white society girl. Suppose she elected to be charmingly stubborn, to question his authority? He decided to stand for no nonsense and to admit no dazzlement from her smile and her bright eyes. He would be like the old warriors who had no sense of female romance or glamor, who took sex, like all important things, in their dignified stride.

Then he rode around a little tuft of thorn bushes and

saw that Rhoda Pleasant was beyond hearing arguments or considering authorities.

Here by the trailside was her little waterproofed tent, with a canvas ground cloth and a mosquito bar. Near it was picketed the bay horse she had borrowed at the agency. A fire had burned to ashes, and a few cooking utensils lay beside it. On the trail itself lay Rhoda Pleasant, grotesquely and limply sprawled with her face upward. Her riding habit was rumpled, her smooth-combed black hair gleamed in the sunlight like polished black stone. She looked like a rag doll with which some giant child had played until it was tired and dropped its plaything. Thrown away, that was how she looked. David Return knew death when he saw it.

He got off his pony and threw the reins over its head, then squatted on his heels beside the body. Rhoda Pleasant's neck-scarf had been white. Now it was spotted with stale blood, dark and sticky. David prodded her cool cheek with a forefinger. Her head did not stir on her neck. That was *rigor mortis.* She had been dead for hours, probably since before dawn. Fully dressed as she was, she might have died before bedtime the night before.

David studied her clay-pale face. The dimmed eyes were open, the lips slack, the expression—she had no expression, only the blank look he had been taught to recognize as that of the unexpectedly and instantly stricken. Gingerly he drew aside the scarf. The throat wound was blackened with powder but looked ragged, as if a bullet and a stab had struck the same mark. Someone had shot Rhoda Pleasant, decided David, then had thrust a narrow, sharp weapon into the bullet hole.

Rising, David turned his attention to the trail. Its earth was hard, but not too hard to show the tracks of moccasins all round the body, moccasins larger than David's. More tracks were plain nearer the tent and the fire, of the large moccasins and of a companion pair, long and lean. Here and there were a third set of moccasin-prints, this time of feet almost as small as Rhoda Pleasant's riding boots.

Three men had been there, apparently all together. And there were three tribal singers camped not far away.

David broke bushes across the trail on either side of the body, and from the tent brought a quilt to spread over the calm dead face. Mounting again, he forced the paint pony off the trail and through thickets where it would disturb no clues. When he came to the trail beyond, he rolled a cigarette and snapped a match alight. Before he had finished smoking he came to another and larger camp.

In a sizable clearing among the brush clumps, by a little stream undried by the summer heat, stood an ancient Sibley tent like a square-bottomed teepee. Behind it was a smaller shelter, of bent sticks covered thickly with old blankets in the shape of a pioneer wagon cover. It was big enough for a single occupant's crouching or lying body, and entrances before and behind were tightly lapped over. Near one end burned a small hot fire, with stones visible among its coals. As David watched, a hand poked out with rough tongs made of green twigs, lifted a stone and dragged it inside. Strings of steamy vapor crept briefly forth.

"Sweat lodge," said David aloud. The old Tsichah had built and used sweat lodges frequently, but he himself had seen only a few and had been in one just once in his life, as part of the ceremony of joining the Fox Soldier society two years back. He called in Tsichah: "*Ahi*, you singing Indians! Someone has come to see you!"

From the Sibley tent came Stacey Weed. He was taller than David, and leaner, with hair cut long for a young Indian. All that he wore was a breechclout and moccasins. In one hand he carried a canvas bucket, and he turned at first toward where the camp's three horses were tethered on long lariats downstream from the tent. Then he pretended to notice David, and lifted a hand in a careless gesture of greeting. "*Ahi*, nephew," he said, also in Tsichah.

To be called nephew by a Tsichah can be pleasant or unpleasant. An older man means it in friendly informality; a contemporary seeks to patronize or to snub or to insult, depending on the tone of his voice. Stacey Weed was perhaps two years older than David, not enough seniority to make for kindliness in the salutation.

"John," called Stacey back into the tent, "we must be important. A boy with a new police star has ridden in."

John Horse Child followed Stacey into the open. He too was almost naked, powerfully built and just under six feet tall. His smile was broad but tight. "I heard that David Return had joined the police," he remarked to Stacey, as though discussing someone a hundred miles away.

David kept his temper. He spoke in English, as he judged his grandfather would do. "I suppose," he ventured, "that Dolf Buckskin's in the sweat lodge."

John and Stacey gazed at each other. Their eyes twinkled with elaborate and unpleasant mockery. "They say that policemen get great wisdom with those stars they wear," said John, carefully choosing the Tsichah words. "They can tell who's in a sweat lodge and who is not. It's a strong medicine. They learn things without being told."

"Then why tell them things?" inquired Stacey brightly.

The two squatted on the earth, knees to chin. John began to light a stone pipe, older and bigger and more ornate than the one Tough Feather had shared with David earlier that morning. It was part of the ceremonial gear these tribal singers used in the rites they knew. John smoked a few puffs, passed it to Stacey, who smoked in turn and handed it back. Neither glanced at David, who got quickly out of his saddle and tramped toward them. He still spoke in English, which he knew they understood, but he used the deep, cold voice of unfriendly formality.

"I'm as good a Tsichah as either of you ever dared to be," he told them. "I'm a good American citizen too, and whether you like it or not this ground is part of a government reservation, under police authority. If we're going to have trouble, it will be your starting. I want to ask—"

A wild yell rang from the sweat lodge. Out scuttled Dolf Buckskin, slimmer and shorter and nuder than either of his friends. He shone with the perspiration of the lodge's steamy, hot interior. Even as David turned toward him, Dolf threw himself full length into the widest part of the stream and yelled even louder as the cold water shocked his heated skin. He rolled over and over, then sat up and slapped the streams out of his shaggy hair.

"Come here, Dolf," called David, and Dolf pushed his slim feet into moccasins, tied a clout about his hips and stalked over, with a grin as maddening as either of his fellows.

"Rhoda Pleasant," began David, "came and camped near by, with the idea of teasing or tricking you into teaching her our tribal songs."

"We know that, nephew," said Dolf.

David decided to go back to the Tsichah tongue, since they refused to drop it. "She made eyes and smiles at all of you," he went on. "She half-promised all sorts of things if you would tell her your secrets."

"We know that," Stacey echoed Dolf, and the three of them looked at each other knowingly, like big boys teasing a little one.

Dolf sat down with his friends, and David stood looking down at the three. He pointed trailward with his lifted palm.

"Rhoda Pleasant lies dead back there," he went on, "within a little walk from here."

Then he reflected silently that it is not good to stretch your face with a mocking grin, because when something takes the grin away you look blank, almost as blank as somebody who has been suddenly killed. The three singers betrayed no fear or shock, for they were Indians and steeped from boyhood in the tradition of the stoic; but they succeeded only by turning themselves stupidly expressionless.

John Horse Child broke the silence finally. "We know that, too," he said.

Stacey offered David the ceremonial pipe. It was still alight.

"Smoke," urged Stacey. "We will joke with you no more."

David squatted down with the three, puffing as gravely as when he had smoked with Tough Feather. Then he handed back the pipe and cleared his throat. He spoke in Tsichah:

"First, let me tell what I know already. You're all tribal

35

singers, medicine men, and when you think your knowledge is big and your position strong, you think the truth. Nobody among the Tsichah can replace any one of you very well. You are keepers of knowledge that should live among the people. You," he tilted his chin at John Horse Child, "play the flute. You," and he indicated Dolf Buckskin, "beat the drum with the pebble-headed drumstick. And Stacey, you are the singer and dancer. Without one, the other two are not complete. Besides, you are close friends, like three brothers."

"*Yuh,*" assented Stacey. "That is true."

"I know things about the girl too. A small bullet was fired into her throat, and then a thin knife was stabbed into the same place. She died, I think, not too late last night. And all three of you have been at her camp."

"All three of us have been there several times," said John quietly. "Do you think, David, that all three of us killed her?"

"I think one went alone to her and killed her and made both the wounds," replied David. "I think that one hid his tracks, and that you went together and found her dead this morning. I think the killer has not told his two good friends what he did.

"If these things are true we can believe more things. Of you three, one knows who killed Rhoda Pleasant because he is the killer. Of the other two, each knows that one of his two friends killed her, and he wants to help whichever of the two it may be. I can see that much, because I know who you are and what you do, and what Rhoda Pleasant was trying to do here."

"She came smiling and flattering and asking for our songs," Dolf Buckskin admitted.

"*Ahi,*" went on David, "she was a pretty girl, prettier than any on this reservation. Three men, living alone together, find it easy to look at that sort of girl and to like her. Now I come to the place where I am not sure what to think. I cannot say surely which of several reasons the killer had to do that thing."

"Every killer has a reason," said John weightily, handing the pipe along to Stacey.

"It was about the songs, anyway," David ventured.

Stacey smoked the pipe to its last puff, tapped out the ashes, and began to refill it. "Perhaps it was none of us, David. Perhaps some other man, someone who wanted to rob her or steal her."

"No," said David emphatically. "Her face showed no fear or wonder. She had no trouble with the one who came to kill her, and she must have seen him, for the wounds were in front. Nobody else lives near here, anyway. I think the killer is right here."

John's grin of mockery found its way back. "Why don't you arrest the guilty man?" he challenged. "Nobody will stop you."

"But," added Stacey, rekindling the pipe, "you can't take the wrong man. The government courts would set him free, and pay damage money for false arrest. Probably the policeman who guessed so foolishly would be discharged."

"I'll get the right one," promised David bleakly. "The two innocent men won't be bothered."

"*Ahoh*—thanks," said Stacey deeply, and passed the pipe to Dolf.

"*Ahoh* from me, too," echoed Dolf.

"And from me *ahoh,*" chimed in John. The pipe traveled around the circle again, David smoking last. Finally he rose to his feet.

"If you don't hinder me, I want to search the tent," he said.

"What you wish," granted Stacey, receiving the pipe from him.

David went to the tent and inside. Sunlight filtered brownly through the canvas. Three pallets, made up of blankets spread over heaps of springy brush, lay against the walls. David examined with respectful care a stack of ceremonial costumes, bonnets and parcels in a corner, then turned to the personal property of the three singers.

John's bed could be identified by three flutes in a quiver-like buckskin container, slung to the wall of the tent. David pulled out the flutes one by one. Each was made of two wooden halves, cunningly hollowed out and fitted together in tight bindings of snakeskin. Each had five finger holes and a skillfully shaped mouthpiece. At the head of the pallet lay John's carving tool. David slid it from its scabbard, an old, old knife, its steel worn away by years of sharpening to the delicate slenderness of an edged awl. It showed brightly clean, as from many thrustings into gritty soil. Someone had scoured it clean of Rhoda Pleasant's blood.

On another cot lay Dolf's ceremonial drum, of tight-cured raw buckskin laced over a great wooden hoop and painted with berry juices in the long ago—strange symbols in ochre and vermilion. David looked for the drumstick, that he had often seen at public singings, a thing like a little war club with an egg-sized pebble bound in the split end of the stick. It was not in sight, and he fumbled in the bedclothes. His fingers touched something hard and he brought it to light; not the drumstick, but an old-fashioned pocket pistol barely longer than his forefinger. David broke it and glanced down the barrel, which was bright and clean and recently oiled.

His exploration of Stacey Weed's sleeping quarters turned up a broad sheath knife, but no gun. He emerged from the tent with John's slender carving tool and Dolf's pistol.

"You found them," said Stacey, hoisting his rangy body from its squat. "Which killed her?"

"Both," volunteered John, but David shook his head.

"Either wound would have been fatal," he said, "but the bullet went in first, and the knife followed. That changed the shape of the round bullet hole. As I say, she was struck down from in front, and she knew her killer and had not feared or suspected him."

"That bullet must have struck through her spine at the back of the neck," said Stacey at once, "or she would have looked surprised, at least, before she died."

"*Ahoh*, Stacey," David thanked him. "That is a helpful thought. Now, Rhoda Pleasant smiled on you all, but who did she like best?"

"She wanted only the songs," replied Dolf.

"And did she get any of them?" demanded David quickly.

Stacey shook his head. "I don't think so, David. We sang when she first came, but when we saw her writing on that paper lined out to make music signs on, Dolf said to stop singing. That was the first day she visited us, and cooked our noon dinner."

David tried from those words to visualize the visit. Rhoda Pleasant had tried to charm and reassure the three by flattery and food. She had almost succeeded; they had begun to perform. When they grew suspicious and fell silent, had she concealed her disappointment and tried something else? He hazarded a guess, though guessing had been discouraged by his instructors.

"Then she tried paying attention to one of you alone. Which?" He waited for an answer, and none came. "Was it you, John, because you could play the songs on the flute?"

John shook his head, and Stacey spoke for him. "It was I. She wanted both words and music, and I knew them. She whispered for me to visit her camp. That was two days ago.

"I went," Stacey continued, "but she tricked no songs out of me. She tried to get me off guard by singing songs she had heard on other reservations, and the best of them was not as good as our worst. I sang nothing in exchange. Yesterday she came back and tried her tricks on John instead."

"We went riding together," supplied John. "She talked about songs to me, too, but I only said I had forgotten to bring my flute."

"Then she hunted out Dolf?" suggested David.

"*Wagh!*" Dolf grunted out the Tsichah negative like an ancient blanket Indian, and scowled more blackly still. "Why should she pay attention to me? I am a drummer, and drum music is easy. The one time she heard us all together was enough to teach her what she wanted to know about my drum."

More silence, and David examined these new grudging

admissions. Rhoda Pleasant had, very practically, concentrated on the two singers whose secrets were hardest to learn. On their own showing, John and Stacey had kept those secrets loyally. "This brings us to last night," said David at last.

"I will say something," John spoke slowly. "You think the pistol killed her, and it's Dolf's pistol. But perhaps he didn't use it. Perhaps Stacey did, or I, to make it look like Dolf."

"Perhaps," granted David. "Perhaps not. I think the stab in the wound was to change the shape of the bullet hole. It covered the killer's trail, as the scratching away of the tracks at her camp did."

"But it hid nothing," reminded John.

"Perhaps it *pretended* to hide something," pursued David. "The killer might have thought that he would give the wound a disguise—but one easy to see through."

"*Ahi,*" rejoined Stacey gravely. "You mean that the bullet hole would mean Dolf's pistol and make him guilty—because the knife is John's and the pistol is Dolf's. Perhaps you want to say that I stole them both and killed Rhoda Pleasant."

"Perhaps he wants to say that I used my own pistol to kill," threw in Dolf, "and did the other things to make the pistol-wound look like a false trail."

"There is a way to show who fired the shot," David informed them. "A white man's laboratory trick, with wax on the gun hand and then acid dripped on to show if there was a fleck of powder left on the hand from the gun going off."

"My hand would show flecks like that," Dolf said readily. "I fired the gun for practice yesterday."

"I saw him," seconded John. "Anyway, David, you promised that you would take only the guilty man. That means you must find him here and now, without going to the agency for wax and acid."

"It was a promise," David agreed, "and the Tsichah do not break their promises to each other." He held out the thin-ground knife. "This was bloody, and now it is clean. Who cleaned it?"

"Whoever used it," said Stacey.

David put the knife on the ground. "You were telling me a story, John. You stopped at the place where you and Rhoda Pleasant went out riding and came back yesterday."

"She left me here at camp and rode on alone," John took up the account. "Dolf and Stacey saw her go away. We three were here together for supper, and together we went to sleep early. Then—"

"Then, this morning, I went to her camp alone," said Stacey. "Last night, when she came back past here with John, she made me a sign, like this." He demonstrated, a scooping inward to beckon Indian fashion, then a gesture eastward. "Come after sunrise, she told me by that sign. I thought she would beg again for the music. I would let her beg, then laugh at her and say she was wasting her time with us. But I found her lying face up in the trail."

"As I found her," finished David for him. "Well, you probably are telling the truth. If you were questioned long in this way, any lies in your stories would trip each other up. This much is plain as your tracks at her camp: The killer went to her alone, with the knife and the pistol. He did not want his friends to know—"

"His friends do not ask to know," said Dolf, with an air of finality.

"Because," amplified John, hugging his thick knees as he squatted, "his friends know, like him, that Rhoda Pleasant was a thief of secrets. Nobody here is sorry she died, though we would be sorry if one of us suffered for killing her."

"Nobody is sorry she died?" repeated David, and tried to study all three of their faces at once. They stared back calmly.

"But all three went to her camp," said David again. "Not Stacey alone."

"I came and got them to see her," Stacey told him. "We had to decide what to do. We saw everything there you saw. We talked as we waited there. Finally we agreed we must carry the news, after we all took sweat baths."

"Sweat baths?" echoed David. "Why?"

"We are medicine men, and we had all touched a dead body," John answered him coldly. "Sweat baths are purification; or have you forgotten the Tsichah way since you learned the policeman's way?"

"I have forgotten neither way," was David's equally cold rejoinder. "Who said to carry the news, and who said to take the sweat bath?"

"I thought of both those things," Dolf volunteered.

"No, I think I did," argued Stacey. "I built the fire anyway, and gathered the rocks to heat."

"But I took the first bath," resumed John, "for I touched her first when we saw her together. Then Stacey took his, and then Dolf, who had not finished when you first came."

David pointed to the slim knife he had brought from the sleeping tent. "This went to the lodge with you, John?"

"If you expect to find prints of guilty fingers, you will not," said John. "Yes, I took the knife into the sweat lodge— to purify it from the touch of that dead Piekan squaw, *Ahi,*" and he put out his palm and made a horizontal slicing motion. "I finish. That is the end of what I will say."

There was silence all around. David stooped and took the knife, wedging it into the sheath with his own, then put Dolf's pistol into his hip pocket.

"Something here I have not yet found," he announced. "And I have wondered about it all the time we were talking. I think I know where it is now. I, too, am going into your sweat lodge. Can any of you say why I should not?"

They stared, neither granting nor denying permission. David walked past the Sibley tent to the close-blanketed little structure, pulled away the blanket that sealed the door, and peered in through the steam that clung inside. It billowed out, grew somewhat thinner, and he could see dimly. Under his breath he said a respectful prayer to the spirit people, lest he be thought sacrilegious in hunting there for what he hoped to find. Then he dropped to all fours and crawled in.

On the floor stood an old iron pot of water, still warm. In it were a dozen of the stones that had been dropped in at their hottest to create the purifying steam. David twitched up his sleeve and pulled out one stone, then another and another. They were like any stones one might find in that part of the reservation. He studied the ground, which was as bare and hard as baked clay, then rose from all fours and squatted on his heels. His hands patted and probed here and there along the inner surface of blankets, until he found what he was looking for.

He seized its little loop of leather cord and pulled it from where it had been stuck between the blankets and one of the curved poles of the framework. A single touch assured him, and he edged into the open for a clear examination of it.

The thing was like a tiny war club of ancient fashion. A slender foot-long twig of tough wood had been split at the end, and the two split pieces curved to fit around a smooth pebble the size of an egg. Rawhide lashings held the stone rigidly in place. It was the ceremonial drumstick he had missed when searching Dolf Buckskin's bed in the tent, the absence of which he had been trying to fit into the story of Rhoda Pleasant's death. He balanced it experimentally, swung it against his open hand, carefully bent the springy wooden handle.

Then he thrust it inside his shirt, standing so that the three watching singers could be sure of what he handled and what he did with it. He walked over to where his pony cropped at some grass.

"I'm going to look at Rhoda Pleasant once more," he announced. "That look will be all I need to tell me everything."

Mounting, he rode slowly up the trail to the silent camp of the dead girl. He dismounted once again and took the cover from the expressionless face.

Again he put out a finger to touch, this time at the side of the head, where Rhoda Pleasant's hair was combed smoothly over the temple. He felt the other temple, and

43

this time his finger encountered a yielding softness.

"*Ahi,*" he grunted, as if to confirm everything. "The thin bone was broken."

He returned to his horse and lounged with his arm across the saddle, quietly waiting.

Hoofbeats sounded among the brush in the direction of the singers' camp. After a moment, Dolf Buckskin rode into sight. He had pulled on trousers and a shirt, as though for a trip to the agency.

"I am waiting for you," called David to him.

"I knew you would be," replied Dolf, riding near. "Maybe I should have told you all about it when you brought my drumstick out of the sweat lodge, but it was hard to speak in front of my two friends who were trying to help me."

"You need not tell me much," David assured him, as gently as he could speak. "I knew the answer when John told of purifying his carving knife in the sweat lodge because it had touched the dead body of Rhoda Pleasant. Your drumstick was missing. I reasoned that if the drumstick was also in the sweat lodge, all was clear. And it was. Why should you have taken the drumstick into the lodge? Only to purify it, as you yourself must be purified. Why should it need purifying? Only if the drumstick too had touched the dead body. Why should it have touched the dead body? Only if the drumstick were the true weapon."

David paused. "You're a good drummer, Dolf. By long practice you can strike to the smallest mark—even the thin bone of the temple—swiftly and accurately, with exactly the strength you choose. That pebble-head is solid, the handle is springy. It was a good weapon, Dolf, and easier to your hand than any other."

"She did not even hear me as I came up behind her," Dolf said with something like sorrowful pride. "You were wrong about her seeing the killer and not fearing him. She never knew."

"You used your own gun and John's knife to hide the real way of killing. They were the false trails. But you could not break the old ceremonial rites. The true weapon had to be purified—and so I knew."

Dolf raised his head and looked at the still form. "It's strange to think of what I did. I wanted her so much."

"*Yuh,*" and David nodded. "You wanted her. She would not look at you, only at John and Stacey. You were left out, and your heart was bad. Perhaps if you explain to the court that for a time your mind was not right, you will not be killed, only put in jail."

"I don't think I want to live," said Dolf slowly. "Not in jail, anyway. Shall I help you lift her and tie her on her horse's back?"

"*Ahoh,*" said David. "Thank you."

When the three horses started on the trail back, David glanced down at his silver-plated star. It was dull and filmy— from the steam of the sweat lodge. An agency policeman's star should not be dull at the end of his first successful case. It should shine like all the high hopes of all young warriors. Proudly David burnished the metal with his sleeve—until it shone with the wisdom of the Shining Lodge and the strength of the white man's star.

Dr. Jan Czissar

THE CZECHOSLOVAKIAN DETECTIVE

THE CASE OF THE EMERALD SKY

Eric Ambler

*Eric Ambler is best known, of course, for his superb novels
of espionage and foreign intrigue. But there is another fictional side to Ambler, as evidenced by his stories featuring
Czechoslovakian refugee Dr. Jan Czissar; these are much
lighter in tone, deliberately mannered, with emphasis on
deduction instead of thrills and suspense. There is also a
strong ethnic flair to Dr. Czissar, late of the Prague police,
who fled to London to escape the Nazis in the late 1930s
and who delights in exasperating Scotland Yard by solving
crimes before they can.*

*"The Case of the Emerald Sky" and five other stories fea-
turing Czissar originally appeared in* The Sketch (*London*)
*in 1940—not quite enough to fill a book, or they would
surely have been collected by now. Perhaps* The Complete
Short Stories of Eric Ambler *will one day be assembled
for publication, so that American readers will have the pleasure of following the good doctor through all six of his
cases.*

*Eric Ambler's writing career has spanned five decades,
beginning with the novel* The Dark Frontier *in 1936.
Among his other novels are* Cause for Alarm (*1938*), *the*

classic A Coffin for Dimitrios (*1939*), Judgment at Deltchev (*1951*), Dirty Story (*1967*), *and* Doctor Frigo (*1974*). *He has also written numerous screenplays, a nonfiction book,* The Ability to Kill and Other Pieces (*1963*), *and several thrillers with Charles Rodda under the pseudonym Eliot Reed.*

. . .

Assistant Commissioner Mercer of Scotland Yard stared, without speaking, at the card which Sergeant Flecker had placed before him.

There was no address, simply:

DR. JAN CZISSAR
Late Prague Police

It was an inoffensive-looking card. An onlooker, who knew only that Dr. Czissar was a refugee Czech with a brilliant record of service in the criminal investigation department of the Prague police, would have been surprised at the expression of dislike that spread slowly over the assistant commissioner's healthy face.

Yet, had the same onlooker known the circumstances of Mercer's first encounter with Dr. Czissar, he would not have been surprised. Just one week had elapsed since Dr. Czissar had appeared out of the blue with a letter of introduction from the mighty Sir Herbert at the home office, and Mercer was still smarting as a result of the meeting.

Sergeant Flecker had seen and interpreted the expression. Now he spoke.

"Out, sir?"

Mercer looked up sharply. "No, sergeant. In, but too busy," he snapped.

Half an hour later Mercer's telephone rang.

"Sir Herbert to speak to you from the Home Office, sir," said the operator.

Sir Herbert said, "Hello, Mercer, is that you?" And then, without waiting for a reply: "What's this I hear about your refusing to see Dr. Czissar?"

Mercer jumped but managed to pull himself together. "I did not refuse to see him, Sir Herbert," he said with iron calm. "I sent down a message that I was too busy to see him."

Sir Herbert snorted. "Now look here, Mercer; I happen to know that it was Dr. Czissar who spotted those Seabourne murderers for you. Not blaming you, personally, of course, and I don't propose to mention the matter to the commissioner. You can't be right every time. We all know that as an organization there's nothing to touch Scotland Yard. My point is, Mercer, that you fellows ought not to be above learning a thing or two from a foreign expert. Clever fellows, these Czechs, you know. No question of poaching on your preserves. Dr. Czissar wants no publicity. He's grateful to this country and eager to help. Least we can do is to let him. We don't want any professional jealousy standing in the way."

If it were possible to speak coherently through clenched teeth, Mercer would have done so. "There's no question either of poaching on preserves or of professional jealousy, Sir Herbert. I was, as Dr. Czissar was informed, busy when he called. If he will write in for an appointment, I shall be pleased to see him."

"Good man," said Sir Herbert cheerfully. "But we don't want any of this red tape business about writing in. He's in my office now. I'll send him over. He's particularly anxious to have a word with you about this Brock Park case. He won't keep you more than a few minutes. Good-bye."

Mercer replaced the telephone carefully. He knew that if he had replaced it as he felt like replacing it, the entire instrument would have been smashed. For a moment or two he sat quite still. Then, suddenly, he snatched the telephone up again.

"Inspector Cleat, please." He waited. "Is that you, Cleat? Is the commissioner in? . . . I see. Well, you might ask him as soon as he comes in if he could spare me a minute or two. It's urgent. Right."

He hung up again, feeling a little better. If Sir Herbert

could have words with the commissioner, so could he. The old man wouldn't stand for his subordinates being humiliated and insulted by pettifogging politicians. Professional jealousy!

Meanwhile, however, this precious Dr. Czissar wanted to talk about the Brock Park case. Right! Let him! He wouldn't be able to pull that to pieces. It was absolutely watertight. He picked up the file on the case which lay on his desk.

Yes, absolutely watertight.

Three years previously, Thomas Medley, a widower of 60 with two adult children, had married Helena Merlin, a woman of 42. The four had since lived together in a large house in the London suburb of Brock Park. Medley, who had amassed a comfortable fortune, had retired from business shortly before his second marriage, and had devoted most of his time since to his hobby, gardening. Helena Merlin was an artist, a landscape painter, and in Brock Park it was whispered that her pictures sold for large sums. She dressed fashionably and smartly, and was disliked by her neighbors. Harold Medley, the son aged 25, was a medical student at a London hospital. His sister, Janet, was three years younger, and as dowdy as her stepmother was smart.

In the early October of that year, and as a result of an extra heavy meal, Thomas Medley had retired to bed with a bilious attack. Such attacks had not been unusual. He had had an enlarged liver, and had been normally dyspeptic. His doctor had prescribed in the usual way. On his third day in bed the patient had been considerably better. On the fourth day, however, at about four in the afternoon, he had been seized with violent abdominal pains, persistent vomiting, and severe cramps in the muscles of his legs.

These symptoms had persisted for three days, on the last of which there had been convulsions. He had died that night. The doctor had certified the death as being due to gastroenteritis. The dead man's estate had amounted to, roughly, £110,000. Half of it went to his wife. The remainder was divided equally between his two children.

A week after the funeral, the police had received an anonymous letter suggesting that Medley had been poisoned. Subsequently, they had received two further letters. Information had then reached them that several residents in Brock Park had received similar letters, and that the matter was the subject of gossip.

Medley's doctor was approached later. He had reasserted that the death had been due to gastroenteritis, but admitted that the possibility of the condition having been brought by the willful administration of poison had not occurred to him. The body had been exhumed by license of the home secretary, and an autopsy performed. No traces of poison had been found in the stomach; but in the liver, kidneys and spleen a total of 1.751 grains of arsenic had been found.

Inquiries had established that on the day on which the poisoning symptoms had appeared, the deceased had had a small luncheon consisting of breast of chicken, spinach (canned), and one potato. The cook had partaken of spinach from the same tin without suffering any ill effects. After his luncheon, Medley had taken a dose of the medicine prescribed for him by the doctor. It had been mixed with water for him by his son, Harold.

Evidence had been obtained from a servant that, a fortnight before the death, Harold had asked his father for £100 to settle a racing debt. He had been refused. Inquiries had revealed that Harold had lied. He had been secretly married for some time, and the money had been needed not to pay racing debts but for his wife, who was about to have a child.

The case against Harold had been conclusive. He had needed money desperately. He had quarreled with his father. He had known that he was the heir to a quarter of his father's estate. As a medical student in a hospital, he had been in a position to obtain arsenic. The poisoning that appeared had shown that the arsenic must have been administered at about the time the medicine had been taken. It had been the first occasion on which Harold had prepared his father's medicine.

The coroner's jury had boggled at indicting him in their verdict, but he had later been arrested and was now on remand. Further evidence from the hospital as to his access to supplies of arsenical drugs had been forthcoming. He would certainly be committed for trial.

Mercer sat back in his chair. A watertight case. Sentences began to form in his mind. "This Dr. Czissar, Sir Charles, is merely a time-wasting crank. He's a refugee and his sufferings have probably unhinged him a little. If you could put the matter to Sir Herbert, in that light . . ."

And then, for the second time that afternoon, Dr. Czissar was announced.

Mercer was angry, yet, as Dr. Czissar came into the room, he became conscious of a curious feeling of friendliness toward him. It was not entirely the friendliness that one feels toward an enemy one is about to destroy. In his mind's eye he had been picturing Dr. Czissar as an ogre. Now, Mercer saw that, with his mild eyes behind their thick spectacles, his round, pale face, his drab raincoat and his unfurled umbrella, Dr. Czissar was, after all, merely pathetic. When, just inside the door, Dr. Czissar stopped, clapped his umbrella to his side as if it were a rifle, and said loudly: "Dr. Jan Czissar. Late Prague Police. At your service." Mercer very nearly smiled.

Instead he said: "Sit down, doctor. I am sorry I was too busy to see you earlier."

"It is so good of you . . ." began Dr. Czissar earnestly.

"Not at all, doctor. You want, I hear, to compliment us on our handling of the Brock Park case."

Dr. Czissar blinked. "Oh, no, Assistant Commissioner Mercer," he said anxiously. "I would like to compliment, but it is too early, I think. I do not wish to seem impolite, but . . ."

Mercer smiled complacently. "Oh, we shall convict our man, all right, doctor. I don't think you need to worry."

Dr. Czissar's anxiety became painful to behold. "Oh, but I do worry. You see—" he hesitated diffidently, "—he is not guilty."

51

Mercer hoped that the smile with which he greeted the statement did not reveal his secret exultation. He said blandly, "Are you aware, doctor, of all the evidence against him?"

"I attended the inquest," said Dr. Czissar mournfully. "But there will be more evidence from the hospital, no doubt. This young Mr. Harold could no doubt have stolen enough arsenic to poison a regiment without the loss being discovered."

The fact that the words had been taken out of his mouth disconcerted Mercer only slightly. He nodded. "Exactly."

A faint, thin smile stretched the doctor's full lips. He settled his glasses on his nose. Then he cleared his throat, swallowed hard and leaned forward. "Attention, please," he said sharply.

For some reason that he could not fathom, Mercer felt his self-confidence ooze suddenly away. He had seen that same series of actions, ending with the peremptory demand for attention, performed once before, and it had been the prelude to humiliation, to . . . He pulled himself up sharply. The Brock Park case was watertight. He was being absurd.

"I'm listening," he said.

"Good." Dr. Czissar wagged one solemn finger. "According to the medical evidence given at the inquest, arsenic was found in the liver, kidneys and spleen. No?"

Mercer nodded firmly. "One point seven five one grains. That shows that much more than a fatal dose had been administered. Much more."

Dr. Czissar's eyes gleamed. "Ah, yes. Much more. It is odd, is it not, that so much was found in the kidneys?"

"Nothing odd at all about it."

"Let us leave the point for the moment. Is it not true, Assistant Commissioner Mercer, that all post-mortem tests for arsenic are for arsenic itself and not for any particular arsenic salt?"

Mercer frowned. "Yes, but it's unimportant. All arsenic salts are deadly poisons. Besides, when arsenic is absorbed by the human body, it turns to the sulphide. I don't see what you are driving at, doctor."

"My point is this, assistant commissioner, that usually it is impossible to tell from a delayed autopsy which form of arsenic was used to poison the body. You agree? It might be arsenious oxide, or one of the arsenates or arsenites, copper arsenite, for instance; or it might be a chloride, or it might be an organic compound of arsenic."

"Precisely."

"But," continued Dr. Czissar, "what sort of arsenic should we expect to find in a hospital, eh?"

Mercer pursed his lips. "I see no harm in telling you, doctor, that Harold Medley could easily have secured supplies of either salvarsan or neosalvarsan. They are both important drugs."

"Yes, indeed," said Dr. Czissar. "Very useful in one-tenth of a gram doses, but very dangerous in larger quantities." He stared at the ceiling. "Have you seen any of Helena Merlin's paintings, assistant commissioner?"

The sudden change of subject took Mercer unawares. He hesitated. Then: "Oh, you mean Mrs. Medley. No, I haven't seen any of her paintings."

"Such a chic, attractive woman," said Dr. Czissar. "After I had seen her at the inquest I could not help wishing to see some of her work. I found some in a gallery near Bond Street." He sighed. "I had expected something clever, but I was disappointed. She paints what she thinks instead of what is."

"Really? I'm afraid, doctor, that I must . . ."

"I felt," persisted Dr. Czissar, bringing his cowlike eyes once more to Mercer's, "that the thoughts of a woman who thinks of a field as blue and of a sky as emerald green must be a little strange."

"Modern stuff, eh?" said Mercer shortly. "I don't much care for it either. And now, doctor, if you've finished, I'll ask you to excuse me. I . . ."

"Oh, but I have not finished yet," said Dr. Czissar kindly. "I think, assistant commissioner, that a woman who paints a landscape with a green sky is not only strange, but also interesting, don't you? I asked the gentlemen at the gallery about her. She produces only a few pictures—about six a year. He offered to sell me one of them for 15 guineas. She earns £100 a year from her work. It is wonderful how expensively she dresses on that sum."

"She had a rich husband."

"Oh, yes. A curious household, don't you think? The daughter Janet is especially curious. I was so sorry that she was so much upset by the evidence at the inquest."

"A young woman probably would be upset at the idea of her brother being a murderer," said Mercer dryly.

"But to accuse herself so violently of the murder. That was odd."

"Hysteria. You get a lot of it in murder cases." Mercer stood up and held out his hand. "Well, doctor, I'm sorry you haven't been able to upset our case this time. If you'll leave your address with the sergeant as you go, I'll see that you get a pass for the trial," he added with relish.

But Dr. Czissar did not move. "You are going to try this young man for murder, then?" he said slowly. "You have not understood what I have been hinting at?"

Mercer grinned. "We've got something better than hints, doctor—a first-class circumstantial case against young Medley. Motive, time and method of administration, source of the poison. Concrete evidence, doctor! Juries like it. If you can produce one scrap of evidence to show that we've got the wrong man, I'll be glad to hear it."

Dr. Czissar's back straightened, and his cowlike eyes flashed. He said, sharply, "I, too, am busy. I am engaged on a work on medical jurisprudence. I desire only to see justice done. I do not believe that on the evidence you have you can convict this young man under English law; but the fact of his being brought to trial could damage his career as a doctor. Furthermore, there is the real murderer to be considered. Therefore, in a spirit of friendliness, I have come to you instead of going to Harold Medley's legal advisers. I will now give you your evidence."

Mercer sat down again. He was very angry. "I am listening," he said grimly; "but if you . . ."

"Attention, please," said Dr. Czissar. He raised a finger.

"Arsenic was found in the dead man's kidneys. It is determined that Harold Medley could have poisoned his father with either salvarsan or neosalvarsan. There is a contradiction there. Most inorganic salts of arsenic, white arsenic, for instance, are practically insoluble in water, and if a quantity of such a salt had been administered, we might expect to find traces of it in the kidneys. Salvarsan and neosalvarsan, however, are compounds of arsenic and are very soluble in water. If either of them had been administered through the mouth, we should *not* expect to find arsenic in the kidneys."

He paused; but Mercer was silent.

"In what form, therefore, was the arsenic administered?" he went on. "The tests do not tell us, for they detect only the presence of the element, arsenic. Let us then look among the inorganic salts. There is white arsenic, that is arsenious oxide. It is used for dipping sheep. We would not expect to find it in Brock Park. But Mr. Medley was a gardener. What about sodium arsenite, the weed-killer? But we heard at the inquest that the weed-killer in the garden was of the kind harmful only to weeds. We come to copper arsenite. Mr. Medley was, in my opinion, poisoned by a large dose of copper arsenite."

"And on what evidence," demanded Mercer, "do you base that opinion?"

"There is, or there has been, copper arsenite in the Medleys' house." Dr. Czissar looked at the ceiling. "On the day of the inquest, Mrs. Medley wore a fur coat. I have since found another fur coat like it. The price of the coat was 400 guineas. Inquiries in Brock Park have told me that this lady's husband, besides being a rich man, was also a very mean and unpleasant man. At the inquest, his son told us that he had kept his marriage a secret because he was afraid that his father would stop his allowance or prevent his continuing his studies in medicine. Helena Medley had expensive tastes. She had married this man so that she could indulge them. He had failed her. That coat she wore, assistant commissioner, was unpaid for. You will find, I think, that she had other debts, and that a threat had been made by one of the creditors to approach her husband. She was tired of this man so much older than she was—this man who did not even justify his existence by spending his fortune on her. She poisoned her husband. There is no doubt of it."

"Nonsense!" said Mercer. "Of course we know that she was in debt. We are not fools. But lots of women are in debt. It doesn't make them murderers. Ridiculous!"

"All murderers are ridiculous," agreed Dr. Czissar solemnly; "especially the clever ones."

"But how on earth . . . ?" began Mercer.

Dr. Czissar smiled gently. "It was the spinach that the dead man had for luncheon before the symptoms of poisoning began that interested me," he said. "Why give spinach when it is out of season? Canned vegetables are not usually given to an invalid with gastric trouble. And then, when I saw Mrs. Medley's paintings, I understood. The emerald sky, assistant commissioner. It was a fine, rich emerald green, that sky—*the sort of emerald green that the artist gets when there is aceto-arsenite of copper in the paint!* The firm which supplies Mrs. Medley with her working materials will be able to tell you when she bought it. I suggest, too, that you take the picture—it is in the Summons Gallery—and remove a little of the sky for analysis. You will find that the spinach was prepared at her suggestion and taken to her husband's bedroom by her. Spinach is *green* and *slightly bitter* in taste. *So is copper arsenite.*" He sighed. "If there had not been anonymous letters . . ."

"Ah!" interrupted Mercer. "The anonymous letters! Perhaps you know . . ."

"Oh, yes," said Dr. Czissar simply. "The daughter Janet wrote them. Poor child! She disliked her smart stepmother and wrote them out of spite. Imagine her feelings when she found that she had—how do you say?—put a noose about her brother's throat. It would be natural for her to try to take the blame herself."

The telephone rang and Mercer picked up the receiver.

"The commissioner to speak to you, sir," said the operator.

"All right. Hello . . . Hello, Sir Charles. Yes, I did want to speak to you urgently. It was—" He hesitated. "—it was about the Brock Park case. I think that we will have to release young Medley. I've got hold of some new medical evidence that . . . Yes, yes, I realize that, Sir Charles, and I'm very sorry that . . . All right, Sir Charles, I'll come immediately."

He replaced the telephone.

Dr. Czissar looked at his watch. "But it is late and I must get to the museum reading-room before it closes." He stood up, clapped his umbrella to his side, clicked his heels and said loudly: "Dr. Jan Czissar. Late Prague Police. At your service!"

Jo Gar

THE FILIPINO DETECTIVE

THE BLACK SAMPAN

Raoul Whitfield

Jo Gar is the only Filipino detective in crime fiction, and a memorable character he is. "The little Island detective" made his first appearance in the pages of the pioneering pulp, Black Mask, *in 1930; a total of twenty-four of his cases were published in that magazine over the next three years, all under the pseudonym Ramon Decolta. Two more Gar adventures appeared in* Cosmopolitan.

The Jo Gar series is among the best work of Raoul Whitfield (1897–1945), who was born in New York but who grew up in the Philippines. Whitfield, a former newspaperman, was a prolific writer during the 1920s and early 1930s, until illness forced him to abandon fiction. In addition to scores of shorter works, he published three crime novels: Green Ice (*1930*), Death in a Bowl (*1931*), and The Virgin Kills (*1932*). *He also wrote four young-adult novels and the screenplay for an obscure crime film,* Private Detective 62, *during that same period.*

*Tough and leanly told, "The Black Sampan" offers a vivid portrait of Manila and of life (and death) in the Philippines in the early '30s. It appears here for the first time since its original magazine publication more than half a century ago (*Black Mask, *January 1932).*

It was nearing the hour of the swift tropic twilight; a warm breeze blew in from Manila Bay and stirred the palm trees in the fringe of almost jungle growth between the narrow white beach and the low, straggling Spanish house. There had been a pink, fan-shaped sunset in the sky, but most of the light had faded now. Gulls screamed over the water and somewhere on the opposite side of the house a parrot shrilled monotonously.

Jo Gar stood near the black shape of the sampan, which rested in a cleared space about fifty yards from the house and towards the fringe of jungle growth. His gray-blue eyes were frowning. The sampan was like hundreds of others drifting on the water of the *Pasig*, the narrow curve of water that twisted through the City of Manila and emptied into the Bay. That is, it was like others in size and shape. But there were differences. This particular sampan rested on earth. And all the wood of it was black. The mast was black, and the drooping canvas of the sail had been painted black. Not a dull color, but a rich, almost glossy black. There was something funereal in the appearance of the craft, resting on land, with the palm trees swaying slightly between it and the water of the Bay. The color was funereal, and even the shape added to the effect.

Beside him, Harvey Wall said slowly and in his deep voice:

"I heard one terrible, shrill cry—I was in my study. I got a gun and came right out. My Chinese cook was upstairs, in his quarters. He came out behind me. We found Vincente as you see him now, but not until we'd searched quite a bit. You see, we didn't think to look in the sampan immediately."

The Island detective moved closer to the sampan, and Wall moved almost silently behind him. The American was a tall, lean man with gray eyes and slightly gray hair. There was a stoop to his narrow shoulders and his face was well browned. His voice was extraordinarily deep for a man of his build.

The dead figure of Vincente was lying sprawled on the

deck of the sampan, the left arm flung out so that the hand almost touched the base of the mast. In the breeze the rings of the sail made faint scraping sound against the mast-wood. Vincente's dark eyes were opened wide—he seemed to be staring in painful surprise at the darkening sky, as he lay on his back. There was blood on his throat, and more on his white shirt, over the heart. He was a small, wiry Filipino, and even the pain of his death had not robbed him completely of a dark handsomeness.

Jo Gar said softly: "You were not aware that he had enemies?"

Wall said with decision: "I do not think Vincente had an enemy. I can't understand it, unless robbery was the motive, and he surprised thieves who were waiting in the palm growth, for darkness to come."

Jo Gar leaned down and his gray-blue eyes searched the deck of the sampan, which was fairly small, near the body. He moved around the craft slowly, examining the ground, which was hard and dry from months without rain. Then he came close to the sampan and looked at the dead man again. The swift, tropical twilight came and was gone—it was suddenly dark.

Wall said in a steady, low voice: "Vincente has been with me for five years. He was more than my house-boy. I trusted him completely. Sometimes he did business for me. I live more or less of a secluded life, since I sold out my plantations up the river and on the other side of Luzon. Only Vincente and the cook, Sarong, live with me."

Jo Gar nodded. "Sarong is not a Chinese name," he observed. "Malay, perhaps?"

Wall said: "There may be Malay blood, but the man is Chinese. He was upstairs in his quarters when I heard the one scream. My study is on the second floor, and the servants have small rooms above, in the one high portion of the house. I called to Sarong as I came down, and he answered me."

The Island detective used the beam of a small flashlight on the ground around the sampan.

"What did this Sarong answer, when you called, Señor Wall?" he asked quietly.

Wall said: "He replied—'I come, Señor.' That was all. And I could hear him moving hurriedly."

Jo Gar nodded again. He snapped off the beam of the flash, so that they were in darkness. There was a short silence, then the parrot shrilled again. Jo spoke thoughtfully.

"If he had been knifed in the throat first—I do not think the scream would have been shrill. He was struck over the heart first, then in the throat. The Filipino cry of surprise or pain is most always shrill. As it is in anger."

Harvey Wall swore very grimly. "There was just the one scream, very high—of pain. It was terrible. I'll hear it at night—forever."

Jo Gar said quietly: "I think not. One forgets these things in time. You have notified the police?"

Wall spoke a little huskily. "I told Sarong to notify them, after you had arrived. I wanted you here first. I think that perhaps you work more slowly and more thoughtfully."

The Island detective bowed a little. "You are kind," he replied.

There was the sound of a car arriving at the far side of the house. A car door slammed. Harvey Wall said:

"Sarong will bring them here."

Jo Gar looked towards the sky and his eyes were almost closed. He spoke in a gentle voice.

"I think I shall take a short walk through the palms and along the beach," he said very softly. "The sampan here— it has been painted recently?"

Harvey Wall spoke in a toneless voice. "I am a sentimental man. When I came to the Islands, fifteen years ago, I was broke. I had to borrow the money to start in business, and my first business was hauling stuff down the river. I had two sampans—this is the first one I bought. I have always kept it, and when I sold that fleet of mine—I brought it over here. That was about a year ago. The ants were getting at it—it's had several coats of paint."

Jo Gar nodded slowly. "The color is peculiar," he said quietly. "Any particular reason for the color?"

Harvey Wall turned so that he faced the house. There were the sounds of voices, growing louder.

"Vincente painted it, and this time he said he had bought a new kind of paint. It was supposed to be thick and it contained a great deal of lead. He thought that would do for the ants and protect the wood."

The Island detective spoke very softly. "You suggested the color?"

Harvey Wall shook his head. "I was away at the time. But I do not object to the color. Why?"

Jo Gar shrugged and moved away from the sampan and the dead man, towards the fringe of palm trees that swayed in the breeze.

"It is a strange color for a sampan," he said.

There was irritation in Wall's voice. "It's a strange place for a sampan, too," he said. "But neither of those facts is helping us to find Vincente's murderer."

The Island detective paused for a few seconds. "Often one can never tell *what* is helping in the search for a murderer," he observed.

Harvey Wall said: "Well, you know more about this sort of thing than I do. But I think Vincente surprised thieves and they—or one of them—knifed him. Perhaps it was only one thief that he surprised."

The voice of Lieutenant Sadi Ratan sounded more clearly, and a flashlight beam cut through the darkness, near a side of the house. Jo Gar said:

"Why should Vincente have surprised a man lying in wait to enter the house, after darkness? Why should the man have been waiting? Why couldn't he come here after dark? But if he *was* here—why should he be surprised?"

Irritation was again evident in Harvey Wall's tone.

"I merely advanced my theory, Señor Gar. *I* would prefer to ask the questions, and have *you* answer them."

The Island detective moved in the darkness. "I shall do my best, Señor Wall," he said tonelessly. "But it is almost always simpler to ask questions than to answer them."

Lieutenant Sadi Ratan straightened up and faced the door as Jo Gar entered the library of the Wall house. There was perspiration on Ratan's handsome face, his dark eyes were frowning.

"The Chinese is either a fool or a murderer," he announced in his loud, sure voice.

Jo Gar smiled a little and said: "Good evening, Lieutenant. It has been cooler today."

Harvey Wall was pouring himself a drink of whiskey from a decanter. He said suddenly:

"Good ———! To think that my two servants hated each other! I never suspected—"

The Chinese sat impassively in a small wicker chair, and the light from a lamp struck full on his face." It was a round, brown face. His eyes were black and very small and they held no expression.

Sadi Ratan said: "He admits he hated Vincente, and he says Vincente hated him. The hatred was very strong. But he knows nothing whatever about the knifing of the house-boy."

Jo Gar inspected the brown paper of his cigarette. "What is it that makes him a fool, Lieutenant?" he asked slowly.

Sadi Ratan swore in Spanish. He wiped his forehead with a brown colored handkerchief.

"I said he was *either* a fool or a murderer," he corrected. "If he is not a murderer—he is a fool for telling me he hated the dead man."

The Chinese said in a flat voice: "I not a fool."

He said it as though he were patiently correcting some slight error. Jo Gar's gray-blue eyes were on the dark ones of the lieutenant of Manila police.

"Perhaps the Chinese believes that even if he *does* admit that he hated Vincente—that does not make him a murderer," he said gently.

Harvey Wall downed his whiskey and turned towards Sadi Ratan.

"How could Sarong have done this thing?" he demanded impatiently. "I have told you he was in his room, above my study. I called to him, just after the scream, and he answered me. He came from the house behind me, and we searched together."

The Chinese closed his eyes. Ratan looked at him with a peculiar expression in his dark ones.

"His room has a small balcony—it faces the sampan," he said simply.

Jo Gar smiled a little. "It would be remarkable knife throwing, Lieutenant," he said.

Sadi Ratan shrugged again, and Harvey Wall blinked at him.

"Good ———! What stupidity!" he breathed. "You mean to tell me you think this cook killed Vincente by throwing a knife from his balcony? How about the two wounds? And where would the knives have gone? And how could any person throw so accurately at such a distance? And what—"

He groaned and broke off suddenly, appealing with his eyes to Jo. The Island detective was looking at a wicker floor lamp and the light it cast on the waxed floor of the library. He was thinking about Sadi Ratan. The man was not a fool—he was trying to get at something, and was using his apparent stupidity as a mask.

The Chinese said impassively: "I no—kill Vincente."

Sadi Ratan spoke in a rising voice. "You hated him, and he's dead, murdered. Señor Wall called to you, and he *thought* he heard you answer."

Harvey Wall sucked in a noisy breath. "You mean—Sarong *wasn't* in his quarters?" he muttered. "You mean—"

He checked himself. There was a little silence and then Jo Gar said quietly:

"If I cared to believe that the cook murdered Vincente— I would prefer the lieutenant's theory. That Sarong was not in his quarters. You did not actually *see* him leave the house behind you, Señor Wall?"

Harvey Wall's eyes were wide. "No," he admitted. "I was

in too much of a hurry to get outside. I didn't wait for him. But I heard footfalls, and the voice that answered me sounded like Sarong's. When I got around the house, near the sampan, he came around—"

Sadi Ratan kept his eyes on the half-closed ones of the Chinese.

"He could easily have done that—and still have murdered the man he hated," he said grimly.

Jo Gar nodded his head. "Quite easily," he agreed. "And the one who answered for him and made the footfall sounds could have gone from the house and vanished."

Harvey Wall swore softly. The Island detective smiled.

"But it did not happen that way," he said quietly.

Sadi Ratan frowned at the diminutive detective, his fine figure very straight. The Chinese said slowly and with little tone in his voice:

"I in my room. I hear scream. Master—he call and me call back. I come down quick. It is so."

Sadi Ratan said in a hard voice: "It is so now, but I do not think it will be so in a short time. You are lying, Sarong, and it will not be easy for you to continue lying."

Jo Gar lighted another of his brown-paper cigarettes and spoke to Lieutenant Ratan.

"You have so often jumped at conclusions in the past, Lieutenant—and so often you have been mistaken. A man is dead, murdered, and a man that hated him is alive. Does that make him the murderer?"

Sadi Ratan smiled coldly at the Island detective. "It so happens that the Chinese is an expert with knives," he said evenly. "Perhaps you were not aware of that fact, Señor Gar?"

Jo Gar shrugged. "Many Chinese are experts with knives," he said.

The lieutenant of police continued to smile. "While you were strolling about the beach my men have been busy. I think that Sarong is both a fool and a murderer. They have found a palm that is scarred by the blades of thrown knives. There is a cleared spot near it. In the next house there is a house-boy named Carinto. He has seen the Chinese at practice."

Harvey Wall swore again, softly. Jo Gar said nothing.

The Chinese smiled impassively. "I know—Carinto see me," he said. "He no good. He hear knife strike tree. One time me miss."

Jo Gar grinned, showing his white, even teeth. He chuckled softly. Harvey Wall grunted. Sadi Ratan frowned at the Chinese.

Jo said: "You have an accommodating murderer, Lieutenant. He even admits that there are times when he misses a throw."

The Chinese smiled at the Island detective, then suddenly his eyes held a worried expression. He spoke very rapidly in Chinese, and Jo saw that even Sadi Ratan did not understand.

Jo replied to the cook, and Sarong smiled again. Ratan said in a cold voice:

"What did he say, Señor Gar?"

Jo said: "He said that he did not murder the man that he hated, and that he did not wish to die because some other one *did* murder him. He trusts that I will be able to find this other one, because he thinks that I am an honest man and he thinks that you do not like him."

Sadi Ratan scowled at the Chinese, whose eyes again held no expression. Jo Gar asked:

"Why, Sarong, did you hate Vincente?"

The Chinese started to speak in his native tongue, but Jo shook his head.

"In English, Sarong," he said. "Señor Wall should be able to understand."

The cook turned his eyes towards Harvey Wall, then looked at Jo.

"He want to kill me," he said simply. "He no like me. He talk to himself—I hear him say some day he kill me. And I no like him."

Jo Gar chuckled again. "That is a good reason for disliking a man," he agreed. "A very good reason."

Sadi Ratan muttered something under his breath, then said coldly:

"It is not even funny. He is lying. Why did you hate Vincente, Sarong? Why did you murder him with a knife— with one of your knives, and then hide the knife, perhaps throw it into the Bay? Why did you place the body in the black sampan? What was the real reason?"

Jo Gar said dryly: "And why did you spend all this time in practicing *throwing* knives when you are supposed to have murdered Vincente *without* throwing one?"

Sadi Ratan swung his body towards Jo Gar's. "You will please remain silent," he said grimly. "*I* am questioning this man."

Jo Gar turned his back, shrugging slightly. Ratan spoke in a hard, loud tone.

"Was it because of a woman? Because he owed you money?"

The Chinese sighed heavily. He half closed his eyes again. One of Lieutenant Ratan's men came into the library, almost silently. He went to Ratan's side.

"We have found the woman, Lieutenant," he said in precise Spanish. "It is the kitchen maid of the Dutch family in the adjoining house—Herr Saaden."

Lieutenant Ratan stood very erectly, and when Jo Gar faced him again he was smiling in a satisfied manner.

"A woman or money," he announced. "It is almost always one or the other."

"Or both," Jo added. "What about the woman?"

Sadi Ratan looked at the khaki-clad police officer who had come in.

"What about the woman?" he asked. "Tell us."

The officer was short and chesty. He stood very stiffly and said that as ordered he had gone to the nearest house to make inquiries. He had talked with the house-boy, one named Carinto, and had learned that the Chinese and the Filipino of the American señor, Harvey Wall, hated each other. He had learned that the house-boy of the Dutch family had watched the Chinese throwing knives at a palm tree. He had brought this information to Lieutenant Ratan and had then sought a reason for the hatred. And he had now learned that both Sarong and the dead Filipino had been in love with this Filipino maid of the family in the nearest house. Her name was Maria Tondo, and she was a half-breed of Spanish-Filipino parentage.

Sadi Ratan gestured with spread hands, brown palms upturned, when the policeman had finished.

"That is good," he said. "We will go with the Chinese to the woman—"

The officer interrupted to state that the woman was now outside. Sadi Ratan said sharply:

"Bring her in."

He faced the Chinese and spoke coldly. "You will be wise to confess. We know that you hated the dead man, and that you are an expert with knives. You will confess and tell us who it was that you sent to your room, in case your master should call. The one who was to answer in your tone of voice, while you crept through the palm growth and knifed Vincente to death, because you wanted this Maria Tondo, and because perhaps you feared that she preferred Vincente."

The Chinese said flatly: "I no kill Vincente—I no want Maria."

Lieutenant Ratan slapped a fist against a palm of his left hand and swore in Spanish. The policeman came in behind a slim, short girl of perhaps seventeen. She was pretty in a dark, graceful way. Her eyes were very black.

She stopped several feet from the Chinese, and her breath was drawn in in a sharp hiss. Then she raised both arms above her head and cried out shrilly. She moved towards Sarong, who was watching her with narrowed eyes. Sadi Ratan caught her by an arm, held her firmly. But he let her talk.

She said that Sarong was the son of a dog; she cursed him, waving her one free arm about. Her eyes were flashing and she was breathing heavily. She said that he had murdered the man she loved, and that he would die for it.

He deserved to die for it, a thousand times. She had told Vincente only this very morning that she would marry him, and he had told Sarong, of course. And therefore the Chinese had murdered the man she loved.

When she quieted, Sadi Ratan looked at Harvey Wall and smiled a little proudly. Then he turned towards Jo Gar, who had been smoking and watching the Chinese.

"It is finished," he said. "We now have the motive."

The Island detective smiled back at Lieutenant Ratan, while Harvey Wall was repeating that he could hardly believe it—he had never noticed any hatred between his two servants. But then, he had been very busy with his monthly accounts of late. Perhaps he had not paid much attention to matters between the two.

Jo Gar said suddenly: "You do not find it strange, Lieutenant, that the body was found in the black sampan?"

The lieutenant shrugged. "He was murdered perhaps alongside of it," he suggested. "No—I do not find it strange."

The girl, still breathing heavily, said that she often met Vincente beside the sampan. Because Sarong was a devil, he had deliberately placed the body of the man she loved in it.

Sadi Ratan smiled more broadly. "You see?" he said. "It is all very simple."

There was a little silence and then the lieutenant went close to the seated Chinese.

"Who was the one you had in your room, to answer Señor Wall?" he demanded.

The Chinese raised his eyes and looked at the lieutenant of Manila police. He shook his head slowly from side to side, then looked at Jo Gar.

"I did not—kill him," he said very steadily and tonelessly. "This girl—she lie."

The girl shrilled words at him again, in her native tongues—a mixture of Low Spanish and Filipino. Sadi Ratan interrupted her.

"In prison it will be different," he said. "We will have his confession there."

Jo Gar spoke softly. "I do not think it will be different.

It is not easy for one to confess to a murder not committed."

Sadi Ratan smiled nastily, then sighed. "Confession will hardly be necessary," he said. "The evidence is very strong against the Chinese."

Harvey Wall came over near Jo Gar and looked at him with wide eyes.

"You are not satisfied that Sarong is guilty?" he asked.

Jo smiled a little. "I certainly am not," he replied. "On the contrary, I am quite sure he is innocent."

Sadi Ratan gestured towards the girl and then motioned for her to be taken out. Two more policemen came into the room, and the lieutenant pointed at Sarong.

"He is arrested for the murder of Señor Wall's houseboy, Vincente," he said slowly. "Take him away, and guard him carefully."

The Chinese stood up, raised his hands slightly and let them fall at his sides. Jo Gar smiled at him.

"It will be for only a short time, Sarong," he said. "Perhaps only for hours."

The Chinese lifted his shoulders, let them fall, and was led from the room. Sadi Ratan went to a small wicker table and placed his pith helmet on his head, adjusting it carefully. Jo Gar spoke quietly.

"You have probably worked more rapidly on this case than on any other, Lieutenant," he said. "Unfortunately, I do not think you have the right person."

Sadi Ratan smiled at Harvey Wall, as though in sympathy.

"It was your wish to call in Señor Gar," he said. "I regret that he was of so little use to you."

Harvey Wall looked at Jo Gar. "I think the lieutenant is right, Señor Gar," he said. "It is a surprise—but I think Sarong killed Vincente. The girl is sure of it, and the evidence is all against him."

Jo Gar narrowed his gray-blue eyes on the gray ones of the American. He let his gaze flicker to Sadi Ratan, and then come back to the American again.

"But you still wish to find the murderer of your houseboy?" he asked pleasantly.

Harvey Wall frowned. "Certainly," he said.

The Island detective nodded his head and looked towards the screened windows that faced in the direction of the Bay.

"In that case," he said very tonelessly, "I shall wander about a bit."

Sadi Ratan sighed again. "While I am getting a confession from the Chinese," he said.

Jo Gar bowed slightly. "While you are *attempting* to get a confession from the Chinese," he corrected placidly.

A half hour or so before dusk, on the next day, Jo Gar stood near the desk of Lieutenant Ratan, at police headquarters, just off the *Escolta*. The creak of carriage wheels and the chug-noise of small machines on Manila's main business street came through the screened windows of the room. Sadi Ratan sat behind his desk and seemed very pleased with himself.

"He has not confessed," he said, "but these things take some time, as you know. Because you are interested in the case, and appear to sympathize with this Chinese, I shall be severe but not at all brutal with him!"

The Island detective nodded. "It is kind of you," he returned. "You are dealing with a very clever murderer. He could not have been at all certain that Señor Wall would call for him, nor could he have been certain that Vincente would cry out. Yet he went to great trouble in putting a substitute in his quarters, in case of such a circumstance."

The lieutenant frowned. He tapped the desk surface with his right-hand fingers.

"You think that Sarong would not have planned so carefully," he said slowly. "I disagree—the Chinese are very shrewd."

Jo Gar nodded. "Sarong was the cook," he said. "Ground glass in food would have been much more simple."

Sadi Ratan shook his head. "In the autopsy it would have been discovered. Instantly Sarong would have been caught—just because he *was* the cook."

The Island detective was silent for several seconds. "In the tropics one can hardly help but notice servants," he said. "Yet Señor Wall failed to notice that they hated each other. That is unnatural."

Sadi Ratan made a gesture that was broad and dismissing. "He was busy with his monthly accounts. And it is very possible that Sarong and Vincente were careful."

Jo Gar frowned slightly. "There is the matter of the sampan," he said. "The body being placed on the wooden deck would make sound. Or if it fell there it would make sound. And yet it was found there."

The police lieutenant smiled coldly. "You are growing old, Señor Gar," he observed viciously. "The sampan was the love spot of the house-boy and the girl. Sarong had discovered that—it pleased him to deposit Vincente's body there."

Jo Gar said: "This Maria has told you that Sarong loved her, as well as Vincente?" he asked.

Sadi Ratan nodded. "Naturally, and that she refused him, even laughed at him. There is no Chinese blood in her veins. She would not marry him. Vincente was a Filipino."

Jo Gar looked at the ceiling fan. "The girl is here?" he asked.

The police lieutenant shook his head. "I released her this afternoon. She is needed at the Saaden house. She will not go away. She hates Sarong. She says there is bad Malay blood in him. She will stay, and if he does not confess— her word will be enough to convict him."

Jo Gar placed his soiled Panama on top of his head and turned towards the office door.

"The newspapers are complimenting you, Lieutenant," he stated pleasantly. "But then, they have done that before."

Sadi Ratan frowned. "I have made mistakes," he said. "They have complimented me too soon. But this time I am right. Sarong was the murderer. You arrived on the scene ahead of me, Señor Gar, but you reasoned poorly. I regret that, sincerely."

Jo Gar smiled and bowed. "I would regret it also, Lieutenant," he replied cheerfully, "if I believed it was so."

The Island detective drove through the *Luneta,* between the Manila Hotel and the Army and Navy Club, while the Constabulary Band was playing its final number. The sun was very low, beyond the Island of Cavite, but tonight there were no clouds in the sky and the sunset was not beautiful. The driver of the *caleso* made low, clucking sounds to his thin horse, and Jo Gar smoked a brown-paper cigarette.

Near the Army and Navy Club he told the driver to stop, and descended from the carriage. He walked slowly along the avenue that wound nearest the Bay and when he was within five hundred yards of the Wall house it was almost dark.

When he reached the gate on the avenue frontage of the place the twilight was rapidly fading; it was gone as he used the key he had obtained from Wall an hour ago, in the city. There were no lights showing; Harvey Wall was staying with friends for the night. Jo Gar moved very quietly through the foliage just off the cinder path, circled the house and approached the spot where the black sampan rested, from the far side.

He stood motionless for almost five minutes, listening carefully. Gulls were crying, over the water, but the parrot did not make sound. The Island detective raised his eyes and saw the dark shape of the house rising beyond the sampan. He smiled faintly, waited another five minutes. There were no alien sounds to be heard; his smile became a frown.

And then, as he bent down and got first on his knees, then flat on the ground, he heard the light noise of footfalls. They seemed to be coming from the direction of the Bay. At intervals they ceased completely, then he would hear them again. And they increased in sound—the one who was making them was coming nearer.

The light from the stars was brighter tonight, but Jo Gar did not move his head as the person who was making the footfall sounds passed within ten yards of him. He waited for almost a minute, and when the sounds were very light he looked up. The black sampan was only a shape in the semi-darkness—a coffin-like shape, with the mast a tombstone.

But near it stood a small figure—and as his eyes became accustomed to the light Jo saw that it was the girl, Maria Tondo. She was standing motionless, near the sampan, but her head was thrown back. She was looking, Jo realized, not at the craft but at the house.

For several seconds she stood without making any movement. Then she turned and moved back towards the Bay, passing so close to him as he lay flat among the dried palm leaves and shrubbery that he could hear her even breathing.

After another thirty seconds or so he raised his head. He got very slowly to his feet, moved carefully through the fringe of palms towards the beach and the water of the Bay. When he reached the Bay side of the palm thicket he could see her walking along the beach. Near the end of the Wall property line there was an outrigger that Harvey Wall sometimes used for swimming. The girl went straight to it, seated herself on it. Her back was to Jo Gar—she was facing the beach of Herr Saaden.

Jo Gar straightened and smiled grimly. He worked his way slowly along the edge of the palm fringe, getting nearer the outrigger. It was slow work, and once he halted for seconds and fingered the Colt in the right-hand pocket of his lightweight suit, getting the safety lock off.

When he reached a spot almost opposite the beached outrigger he crouched low and waited. The figure of the girl was very still. And then, from some spot farther along the fringe of palms, he heard a long, low whistle.

The girl's body moved. She stood up, but did not go away from the outrigger. She turned her head slightly and whistled as the other had whistled—long and softly.

Jo Gar's gray-blue eyes were expressionless as he waited. When the figure of the man came along the sand he drew in a short breath. He slipped his right hand into the right pocket of his coat and closed his short fingers over the grip of the gun.

When the man reached the girl's side he took her in his arms. Their bodies were close together for seconds. They stood facing the water, after a time, and Jo could hear the low murmur of their voices.

He stepped out from the fringe of palms, moved as quietly as he could across the pebbles and sand of the narrow beach. His eyes were on the two figures; they had stopped talking now. When he was within twenty-five feet of them, directly behind them, his right shoe struck against a piece of drift-wood. The sound was sharp, and they both swung around.

Jo Gar walked forward, a smile on his face. The sand gave light to the scene, and he watched their hands care-fully. The man's breath was coming sharply. The girl's eyes were wide. She said in a half whisper:

"Señor—Gar!"

Jo Gar smiled more broadly. He nodded his head, and stopped within ten feet of them. The man was a Filipino— he had a sharp face and a small mustache. His hair was very black and clipped short. He wore a white shirt and white trousers, and his feet were bare. There was a red sash around his waist.

The Island detective said: "Yes, it is Señor Gar. And this is the house-boy, Carinto, I suppose? The house-boy of Herr Saaden."

The Filipino's thick lips parted; he half muttered some-thing, nodding his head jerkily. Jo Gar continued to smile. His eyes flickered to the eyes of the girl.

"You do not grieve long," he said with faint mockery. "One love is dead—only a short time. Yet already you have another."

The girl's body stiffened, and the man made a slight move-ment with his left hand.

Jo Gar said sharply: "No! My fingers hold a gun!"

There was silence except for the short breathing of the two. Jo Gar looked at the Filipino and said softly:

"The house-boy of Herr Saaden—and the murderer of Vincente!"

The girl screamed and raised her hands to her face. The Filipino ripped at the left side of his red scarf and the blade of the knife shone in the beach light. But he did not throw it. Instead he leaped forward, the knife held low in his hand. His arm was moving upward as he leaped.

Jo Gar twisted to one side and squeezed the trigger of the Colt. The Filipino groaned as the shot crashed; he fell heavily to the sand near the feet of the Island detective. The girl screamed again, took her hands away from her face and rushed at him. Jo Gar lifted his gun again, let his hand drop. The girl was tearing at him with her fingers, when he got a grip on her throat. His skin was ripped twice before she was quiet, relaxed in his arms.

He let her slip to the sand, turned the house-boy over on his back. The knife he twisted from his weak grip. There were cries from the direction of the Saaden house, and the beams of flashlights were showing.

Jo Gar straightened up and looked down at the Filipino. The girl stirred in the sand and moaned. Jo Gar said heavily:

"The bullet is in your shoulder—you won't die—yet. Why did you—murder Vincente?"

Carinto cursed in his native tongue. The girl pulled herself to her knees and faced Jo.

"If we tell the truth—will it help?" she asked.

Jo Gar nodded. "The truth always helps," he said a little grimly. "How much, I cannot say."

The girl said: "We'd saved money—to get married. Vincente did not want it. He saw that Juan drank, and then he gambled with him. He won all of his money. Juan did not think it was honest, and he knew why Vincente had done it. He caught him near the black sampan—and killed him. Vincente screamed, but Juan did not care. He put him on the sampan. He said it looked like a coffin—and he got away. He thought that Sarong would be suspected, because he knew the Chinese hated Vincente. He had lost money to him also—and the two had quarreled much. Juan thought that Señor Wall knew that, but he did not. I went to the house tonight; it was dark and I thought we were safe—"

Her voice broke. The thick voice of Herr Saaden was calling, and Jo Gar answered him. On the sand Juan Carinto was groaning. Jo Gar held his Colt low at his side; his eyes were expressionless. He nodded his head very slowly.

"It will interest Lieutenant Ratan to know that he was correct in *one* thing," he murmured tonelessly. "He said that murder was almost always for a woman or money."

The flashlight beams were moving nearer and the voices were growing louder. Jo Gar looked out over the water and sighed.

"And Vincente spent so much time painting the spot where his body was to rest," he said with irony. "He even chose the proper color—"

Herr Saaden came limping up and asked questions. Jo Gar answered them, and after a short silence he said:

"We will take the wounded man to your house, and from there I will call Lieutenant Ratan."

The Dutchman nodded his head. "He will be pleased," he said seriously.

Jo Gar smiled a little grimly. "He will be delighted," he said. "When he realizes that he did not recognize what a poor actress your kitchen maid is, and that he thought Sarong was much more clever than I did, and that he failed to wonder why your house-boy, Carinto, was so eager to come forward and state that he had seen the Chinese practicing with knives—he will be delighted."

Herr Saaden looked puzzled, but Jo Gar only smiled very faintly. He was not very concerned—whether Herr Saaden understood or not.

"Mom"

THE JEWISH DETECTIVE

MOM MAKES A WISH

James Yaffe

Crime fiction's most famous Jewish detective is certainly Harry Kemelman's Rabbi David Small, hero of such best-selling novels as Sunday the Rabbi Stayed Home (*1969*), Tuesday the Rabbi Saw Red (*1974*), *and* Thursday the Rabbi Walked Out (*1979*); *but as is the case with many other well-known ethnic detectives, Rabbi Small appears only in novels.*

This is not to imply that James Yaffe's quintessential Jewish mother, "Mom," is an unknown character (and she is a character), or that she is second best to anyone, including Rabbi Small, when it comes to detective work. Indeed not. Mom, a Bronx housewife whose son is a homicide detective and who discusses his cases with him, is as good (and as ethnic) as they come—and a joy to watch in action. As James Yaffe himself has written, "It is 'Mom's' wise, kindly, shrewd, slightly cynical attitude towards life which enables her to penetrate to the truth of the mysteries which confront her son."

The first of the "Mom" stories was published in Ellery Queen's Mystery Magazine *in 1952; four others followed it over the next three years, after which she was retired*

*until a brief three-story comeback in the late 1960s. Her
cases have yet to be collected, and more's the pity. Modern
readers would surely delight in such a book-length gathering.*

James Yaffe sold his first short story to EQMM *in 1943,
at the tender age of fifteen—"Department of Impossible
Crimes," which began another series, this one about a non-
ethnic detective, Paul Dawn, who specializes in solving "impossible" mysteries. He has published one criminous novel,*
Nothing But the Night *(1957), but is perhaps best known
for his mainstream novels and such collections as* Poor
Cousin Evelyn *(1952).*

· · ·

Ordinarily my wife Shirley and I have dinner in the Bronx
with my mother on Friday nights. This is the most convenient night for me, because Saturday is my day off from
the Homicide Squad. Once a year, though, we show up
even if it isn't Friday—since the night of December 18 is
Mom's birthday.

Another hard-and-fast custom gets upset on this night.
Mom doesn't do any of the work on the dinner. Shirley
cooks it, and I wash the dishes, so that Mom can sit back
in her easy chair and relax and enjoy the television or gossip
with her friends over the telephone. She does this relaxing,
of course, under protest. Her suspicion of Shirley's abilities
as a cook is deep-rooted. "So where did you learn how to
cook anyway?" Mom invariably demands. "Nowadays, the
way they bring up the young girls, if she knows how to
boil an egg she considers herself a regular Oscar of the
Walgreen." And when Shirley explains about the Home
Economics course she took at Wellesley, Mom simply gives
one of her magnificent snorts. "Wellesley yet! So answer
me please, how good was the *gefilte* fish at Wellesley?"

As for my dish-washing, Mom's opinion of it couldn't be
lower. All she can do is throw up her hands and bemoan,
"Once a *schlimazl* always a *schlimazl!*"

But Shirley and I have a stubborn streak of our own, so

inevitably we win out over Mom's protests. And she usually has a pleasant birthday party in the end.

At last year's celebration there was a special treat. I brought along Inspector Millner. Inspector Millner is my superior, and also the most eligible bachelor on the Homicide Squad. He's a short heavy man in his fifties, with grayish hair, a square tough jaw, and a curiously delicate melancholy look in his eyes which makes him very attractive to motherly ladies of his own age. For a while now, Shirley and I have been trying a little mild matchmaking between Inspector Millner and Mom.

She was delighted to see him. She clapped him on the back and brought out all her heartiest jokes about policemen. He smiled sheepishly, enjoying his own embarrassment. And then, towards the middle of the meal, Mom suddenly gave him a shrewd sharp look.

"So why don't you finish your chicken leg?" she said. "It's a nice chicken—considering it wasn't cooked, it was home-economized. You got some worry on your mind, don't you?"

Inspector Millner attempted a smile. "You see right inside of a man, as usual," he said. "Okay, I admit it. David can tell you what it is."

"It's this new case we're on, Mom," I said. "A pretty depressing business."

"A mystery?" Mom said, cocking her head forward. The keen interest that Mom takes in my cases is surpassed only by her uncanny talent for solving them long before I can.

"No mystery," I said. "It's a murder, and we know who did it, and we'll probably make the arrest before the end of the week."

Inspector Millner heaved a long sad sigh.

"So come on, come on," Mom said, with extra cheerfulness. "Tell me all about this, spit it out of your chest!"

I took a breath, hitched up in my chair, and started in:

"First of all, you have to know about this college professor. This *ex*-professor, that is. Professor Putnam. He's a man over fifty now, and he lives in a small three-room walk-up apartment near Washington Square with his daughter Joan. Ten years ago Putnam used to teach English Literature at the college downtown. He was considered quite a brilliant man. Then his wife died, and he seems to have gone almost completely to seed. He would sit in his room for long periods of time, just staring at the ceiling. He showed up late for his classes—and after a while he stopped showing up at all. He wouldn't read his students' essays, and he began to skip his conferences with graduate students. He was warned several times by the Dean about his conduct, and because of his fine record and the tragedy in his life great allowances were made for him. But finally, after two years of this, the college decided that they couldn't keep him on. So the Dean told him he was dismissed."

"And this daughter that you mentioned?" Mom said. "She was what age at this time?"

"She was seventeen," I said, "just starting at college herself. But when her father lost his job, she had to quit school. And since he wasn't doing anything to help himself, she found that she had the responsibility of supporting both of them. She learned typing and shorthand, and got a job as secretary in a law office, and she's been doing nicely ever since. They don't live in luxury, you understand—but at least they live."

"And the old man," Mom said, "he never snapped himself up again?"

With another long sigh, Inspector Millner took the story over from me. "He went from bad to worse, I'm afraid. Shortly after he lost his job, he took to drinking. Twice a week—every Thursday and Monday night—he left the apartment after dinner and didn't come home till after midnight, reeking of whiskey, so drunk that he could hardly walk. Joan Putnam was always waiting up for him to put him to bed. Several times in the last ten years she's tried to break him of the habit, but with no success. Because in addition to his twice-a-week binges, he keeps bottles of whiskey hidden around the house. Every so often she finds one, big full bottle of the cheapest stuff, and she throws it away.

But he always manages to think of a new hiding place."

"And that's not the worst of it," I broke in. "When Professor Putnam lost his job, he blamed the Dean for it. Dean Duckworth was about his own age—the two men had started at the college together as young instructors and had been friends for many years. When Dean Duckworth told him he was dismissed, Professor Putnam made a terrific scene—it's still remembered by other people on the faculty. He accused the Dean of forcing him out of his job because of jealousy, of ruining his career, of bringing about his wife's death—of all sorts of things. He threatened to get even with him some day. And ever since, old Professor Putnam has gone on hating Dean Duckworth just as loudly and publicly as he did ten years ago. Recently, though, the whole business came to a head—"

"I think I can guess this head," Mom said. "Dean Duck-soup has got a young bachelor son, am I wrong?"

"Amazing," Inspector Millner murmured, under his breath. "We could use a brain like that on the Homicide Squad."

"For all practical purposes," Mom said, "you're already using it."

"Well, to get on with the story," I said quickly—because even Inspector Millner doesn't know exactly to what extent Mom helps me out with my knottier cases. "You're absolutely right, Mom. Dean Duckworth's son Ted is an instructor at the college. He's in his early thirties and still unmarried. And a few months ago he became engaged to Joan Putnam. The engagement was perfectly satisfactory to Dean Duckworth. But Putnam raised a terrific row. He told his daughter that he refused to let her marry the son of the man who had ruined his life. He wouldn't let the boy set foot in his apartment when he came to make friends. And one night, a week ago, he stormed right into Dean Duckworth's home—the Dean has a two-story house off Washington Square—and made a scene in front of a room full of guests. He yelled out that Dean Duckworth had taken his job away from him, his wife away from him, his self-respect away from him, and now he was trying to rob him of the only thing he had left in the world, his daughter. He told the Dean that he was going to kill him for that. 'And it won't be murder,' he said, 'it'll be an execution.' The upshot of it all was that his daughter Joan told young Ted Duckworth that she couldn't go through with the marriage right now—she insisted on postponing it until her father sees reason."

"Which will be never," Shirley put in. "The case is really quite a common one. He justifies his neurotic dependence upon his daughter by transferring his feelings of guilt to a third party—"

"Very common," Mom put in, with that edge that always comes into her voice when Shirley pops out with her Wellesley Psychology course. "What a big help to the people that's involved, to tell them that they're really quite a common case."

"Anyway, you can guess what happened, Mom," I went on. "Last Monday night after dinner, Professor Putnam left his apartment for his regular drunken bout. Joan waited up for him as usual. Only he wasn't in by midnight. He didn't get in till 1:30. He was staggering and reeking with whiskey, of course. And around the same time a policeman in the Washington Square area found Dean Duckworth's body. He was lying on the sidewalk about a block from his own house. He had been brutally beaten to death, and the weapon was right by the body—a broken whiskey bottle.

"Well, we were on the job all morning. We found out from his son and his wife that he had left his house around 12:30 to buy a late newspaper at the subway station. But he had no paper on him, and the news vendor didn't remember seeing him, so he must have met his murderer on the way. Mrs. Duckworth and Ted were together all night, incidentally, waiting for him to come home, so they alibi each other. We also found out, in no time at all, the whole background of his feud with Professor Putnam. By 6 o'clock in the morning we were at Professor Putnam's door, to question him about his whereabouts all night."

"The poor fellow," Inspector Millner said, shaking his head. "He was completely muddled and bleary-eyed. His daughter had a lot of trouble waking him up. When we told him what had happened to Dean Duckworth, he blinked at us for a while as if he couldn't understand what we were saying. Then he started crying. And then he started talking about the old days, the days when Duckworth and he were idealistic young men, starting off in the teaching profession together. And all the time his daughter, that poor kid, was staring back and forth from us to her father, with a kind of horror in her eyes because she knew what was coming."

"It was terrible, Mom," I said, shuddering a little at the memory. "Finally we had to interrupt him and ask him pointblank to account for his actions that night. Well, he refused to do it."

Mom narrowed her eyes at this. "He refused? Or he couldn't remember because he'd been drinking so much?"

"He refused. He didn't even claim he couldn't remember. He just said that he wouldn't tell us. We warned him how incriminating it looked, and his daughter pleaded with him. She said that he didn't have to be ashamed if he was in a bar drinking somewhere, because everybody knew about his habit anyway. But he still refused. Well, what could we do, Mom? We didn't exactly charge him with murder yet, but we took him down to headquarters for questioning."

Mom nodded wisely. "Third degree."

"No, not third degree," I answered, a little annoyed. Even though she knows better, Mom likes to pretend that the police department is still using the methods they used a hundred years ago. This is Mom's idea of making fun of me. "Nobody laid a finger on him. But we did question him pretty thoroughly, on and off, for over twelve hours."

"We have to do it that way," Inspector Millner put in apologetically. "Murderers are pretty jumpy usually, right after their crime. The sooner we get to them and work at them, the better chance there is of getting a confession. Don't think I enjoyed it," he added hastily. "That poor old man—really old, though he's actually the same age as I am—God knows I didn't enjoy it."

Mom's voice and face softened immediately. "Of course you didn't enjoy it," she said to Inspector Millner. "I'm a dope if I even hinted that you did."

"And the point is," I said, "Professor Putnam *didn't* confess. He insisted he hadn't committed the murder, but he refused to tell us where he was at the time. Well, we didn't really have enough evidence yet to hold him, so we took him back to his home and his daughter."

Inspector Millner reddened slightly. "She had some pretty strong things to say to us, I'm afraid." He sighed. "Well, a policeman gets used to it—"

"We were pretty sure Putnam was guilty," I said, "so our next step was to find witnesses who could place him in the neighborhood that night. Naturally it wasn't hard. When a man goes out on a drunk—even if he's like Putnam, and prefers to do it alone, without drinking companions— sure enough somebody is bound to notice him. We went to all the bars in the vicinity of the house and showed Putnam's photograph around. Finally we got results at a bar only three blocks from the Duckworth house. Harry Sloan, the bartender and also the owner of the place, remembered Putnam. He'd seen Putnam in his place off and on during the last few years. And the night of the murder, he saw Putnam again. It was around a quarter of 1 in the morning. Harry and his wife were closing the place up—they do their business mostly with the college kids, and since this is vacation time they take the opportunity to close up shortly after midnight and get some sleep. Well, Putnam came knocking on the door, making a terrible ruckus. They opened the door and told him they were closed, but he insisted he had to have a drink, and he showed them the money to pay for it. Harry figured it would be easier to give him what he wanted and then send him away. So he let Putnam in, and Harry and his wife say that the old man killed nearly half a bottle of bourbon before they could get rid of him at a quarter past 1. He wasn't just drinking for the pleasure of it, they say. He really seemed to have something on his mind. Mrs. Sloan says he looked scared of something to her."

"So this don't prove he committed a murder."

"No. But along with everything else it's pretty strong evidence. First of all, he had the motive. Second of all, he had the opportunity. The time schedule is just right. Duckworth leaves his house at 12:30 to get a paper. On the way—by accident or on purpose—he's met by Putnam. Putnam is carrying a bottle, which he uses to hit Duckworth. That's around a quarter of 1. Putnam is then so upset and scared at what he's done that he makes for the nearest bar, desperate for a drink. He leaves the bar at a quarter past 1, and gets home, by his daughter's own testimony, at 1:30. Third of all, his behavior fits in perfectly with this theory—his urgent need for a drink in Sloan's bar, his refusal to tell us what he was doing all night. It's an open-and-shut case, Mom."

And Inspector Millner joined in mournfully. "Open-and-shut. There's no other way to look at the evidence."

There was a long silence, and then Mom produced a snort. "There's *one* other way," she said. "The *right* way!"

We all lifted our heads and stared at her. How many times has Mom done this to me—but every time it takes me by surprise!

"Really, Mother," Shirley was the first one to react, "you *can't* mean that you've got some *other* solution—"

"Now you're kidding, Mom," I said.

"Impossible, impossible," said Inspector Millner, shaking his head. "I wish it could be—that poor old man—but it's impossible."

"We'll see how impossible," Mom said. "Only first I'd like to ask three simple questions."

I tightened up a little. Mom's "simple questions" have a way of confusing things beyond all understanding—until Mom herself shows how simple and relevant those questions really are. "Go ahead and ask them," I said, in a wary voice.

"Question One: A little bit of information please about this Dean Duckpond. What was his opinion of Professor Putnam being such a big drunk? Of drunkenness did he approve or disapprove?"

I had been afraid the question wouldn't make any sense, but I answered patiently all the same. "He didn't approve at all," I said. "Dean Duckworth was a big teetotaler—he was running a crusade against college students drinking, and trying to pass rules, and so forth. He used to tell his wife and his son that Putnam's taking to drink was proof of his weak moral character. It showed how right Duckworth had been to fire him from his job ten years ago."

Mom beamed with satisfaction. "That's a good answer," she said. "Question Two: When you got through giving Professor Putnam his third degree down at police headquarters and you then took him home to his daughter, what did he do?"

"What did he do, Mom?"

"*I'm* the one that's asking."

Again it didn't seem to make any sense, but again I was patient. "As a matter of fact, we know what he did, Mom, because we kept a man in the apartment to make sure Putnam didn't try to skip out. He went to sleep on the couch, right in front of his daughter and our man. The next morning he woke up and had breakfast. Orange juice, toast, and coffee. Two lumps of sugar. Is that an important clue?"

Mom ignored my sarcasm and went on beaming. "It's a clue if you got the brains to see it. Final Question: Is it possible that one of the movie houses in the neighborhood was playing *Gone With the Wind* on the night of the murder?"

This was too much for me. "Honestly, Mom! This is a murder investigation, not a joke!" And Shirley and Inspector Millner also made sounds of bewilderment.

"So who's joking?" Mom answered serenely. "Do I get my answer, or don't I?"

It was Inspector Millner who answered, in a voice of respect. "I don't see how it fits in," he said, "but as a matter of fact, the neighboring Loew's *was* playing *Gone With the Wind*. I remember passing it on my way to question Professor Putnam for the first time."

"Exactly like I thought," Mom said, with her nod of triumph. "The case is now sewed in the bag."

"That's very interesting, Mother," Shirley said, as sweet as she could. "But of course, David and Inspector Millner *already* have the case sewed in the—sewed up, that is. They know who the murderer is, and they're ready to arrest him."

"Whether we like it or not," Inspector Millner muttered.

But Mom's look of triumph wasn't disturbed a bit. She simply turned it on Inspector Millner, and a touch of tenderness mingled in it. "Maybe you'll end up liking it," she said. "Professor Putnam didn't do the murder."

Again we all stared at her.

Inspector Millner blinked uncertainly—half relieved, and half unwilling to believe in his relief. "Do you—do you honestly have some proof of that?"

"It's such a simple thing," Mom said, spreading her hands. "It's my cousin Millie the Complainer all over again."

"Your cousin Millie—?" Inspector Millner's relief began to waver.

"The Complainer," Mom said, with a nod. "Never did she stop complaining, that woman. Always about her health. Her heart was weak. Her legs hurt. She had a pain in her back. Her stomach wasn't digesting. Her head was giving a headache. A physical wreck she was—every year a *different* kind of a physical wreck. She wasn't married either, and her poor brother Morris, her younger brother, he lived with her and supported her. He never got married either. If he so much as looked once at a girl, cousin Millie's aches would start aching separate and all together, harder than ever. One day she died. She was climbing on a chair up to the kitchen cupboard to get for herself a piece of cheesecake, and she lost her step, and hit her head on the floor, and the concussion killed her. When the doctor examined her, he told her brother Morris that, except for the bump on her head, she was absolutely the healthiest corpse he ever saw. Only by that time poor Morris was already fifty-seven years old, with a bald head and a pot belly that no woman would look at."

Mom stopped talking, and we all thought hard.

Finally Shirley said, "Mother, I just don't see the connection."

"The connection," Mom said, "it's right in front of your nose. It was the timing that gave me first an inkling of it."

"The timing, Mom?"

"The timing of this Professor Putnam. He's a drunk, you told me, who goes out every Thursday night and every Monday, always at the same time, always after dinner, and always he comes in at the same time, around midnight, staggering a little and smelling from whiskey. Right away this to me is peculiar. A drunk who keeps such regular hours, on a schedule almost, like a businessman. When a man gets drunk—extra special drunk like this Professor— he don't look at his watch so careful. Chances are he couldn't see his watch even if he looked at it. Besides which, this timing of his—Thursdays and Mondays from after dinner to midnight—this reminds me of something else. This reminds me of the schedule at a movie house. On Thursday and Monday the picture changes, and the complete double bill runs from after dinner till before midnight."

"Mom," I broke in, "do you mean—?"

"Quiet," Mom said. "You didn't see it from the beginning, so you got to give me the pleasure of telling it at the end. The timing makes me suspicious, so I ask you a question: After he left the police headquarters, where he was questioned for twelve hours, what did this Professor Putnam do? He went home, he went to bed and slept, he woke up and had breakfast. He didn't have a single drink! Not once even did he *ask* for a drink! A man who's supposed to be a regular drunk, and who's just been twelve hours with the third degree—and he isn't even interested in taking a drink afterwards? Excuse me, this isn't sensible. So my original suspicion is positively proved—"

"He wasn't a drunkard at all," said Inspector Millner in a voice of wonder.

"Absolutely," Mom said. "Chances are he didn't even like the stuff. He was only *pretending* at being a drunk. Every Thursday night and Monday night for ten years, out he goes to the new show at the neighborhood movie house. He stays there till the show is over. Then he buys himself a bottle of whiskey maybe, he soaks his collar and his hands with it, he comes home and staggers for his daughter's benefit. Add on to this—he hides whiskey bottles around the house—always *full* whiskey bottles; his daughter, you notice, don't ever find any half-empty whiskey bottles. Also add on to this that he's very careful to explain that he's a lonely drunk, he don't ever have any companions to drink with."

"But why?" I said. "Why did he fool his daughter that way all these years?"

"My cousin Millie the Complainer," Mom said, with a smile. "This Professor loses his job, also he loses his manliness, he loses his grip on life. His daughter comes to take care of him, and he's happy to let her. But always he's afraid some day she'll get married and leave him. He needs something besides his own weakness to keep her with him. So he turns himself into a drunk. How can a nice kindhearted affectionate daughter go away and leave a poor drunk father all by himself? And it works. It works with poor Joan just like it worked with my poor cousin Morris. Only this time maybe it's not too late."

We were all silent for a while. In our minds we saw the picture of that broken old man, with still enough craftiness in him to plot holding on to his daughter. "And he was so ashamed of himself," Inspector Millner said, "that he preferred to face a murder charge than to admit that he *hadn't* been out drinking on Monday night."

"Just a minute," Shirley spoke up sharply. "You said he always went to the movies on Monday night, Mother, and that's why he always got home around midnight—the length of a double feature, you said. But on the night of the murder he didn't get home till 1:30. Now doesn't that prove that he committed the murder after all?"

Mom laughed. "You don't remember my final question. It proves only what I thought—that *Gone With the Wind* was playing at the neighborhood movie house. And *Gone With the Wind* takes a good hour longer than the average double feature."

Shirley subsided, looking rather squelched.

"And now," Mom said, "we're all finished with the main course. So isn't somebody going to bring in the dessert? If I'm not running things myself—"

"I'll get it, Mom," I said. I rose to my feet and started to the kitchen door. But I was stopped by Shirley's voice.

"Wait!" Shirley turned to Mother with satisfaction. "You haven't really given us a solution to the crime at all. So Professor Putnam wasn't really a drunk. That doesn't tell us who *did* commit the murder."

"Don't it?" Mom smiled slyly. "It tells us absolutely and positively. Professor Putnam wasn't a drunk. We know this for a fact. So how, please, could he go into Harry Sloan's bar after closing time and drink up half a bottle of bourbon? And how, please, could Harry Sloan and his wife have seen him in that bar off and on for the last few years?"

Inspector Millner and I looked up sharply at this. And a determined, grim look came over the Inspector's face. "Sloan and his wife were lying?" he said.

"What else? This Sloan, he killed Dean Duckling himself. You told me his motive yourself. The Dean was a big crusader against drinking. He was trying to pass rules that college students couldn't drink. This meant that the college students would go to bars that were far away from the college, so the Dean wouldn't catch them. And like you told me, this Sloan did most of his business with college students. The Dean was going to ruin his business—a pretty good motive to kill somebody in this day and age. Even so, in my opinion he didn't plan it out. He was on the street Monday night, and the Dean came by, going for his newspaper. And Sloan was maybe a little drunk himself and had a bottle with him. So he stopped the Dean and he tried to argue him out of his crusade maybe, and one word led to another, and all of a sudden he's killed him. So back he goes and tells his wife—"

"And the next night," I said, with a groan, "*we* came along and gave him his big opportunity. We showed him Putnam's picture, and told him that Putnam had no alibi for the time of the murder—so Sloan and his wife thought it was safe to be the witnesses against him."

"And they would've got away with it," Inspector Millner said solemnly, "if it hadn't been for—" He broke off in a small flurry of embarrassment and admiration.

Shirley and I exchanged our usual significant glance.

Shortly after, Inspector Millner got up and phoned headquarters to pick up Sloan and his wife. And I went out to the kitchen and lit the candles on Shirley's cake. Three candles—one for Mom's real age, one for the age she admitted to, and one for good luck. Then I marched the cake in, and we all sang "Happy Birthday to You," and Mom blushed as prettily as a schoolgirl.

Then the cake was put in front of her, and Shirley and I shouted for her to make a wish and blow out the candles.

But she hesitated, with a look at Inspector Millner. "You're still feeling bad about something," she said.

"I'm sorry," he said, looking up and grinning. "I just can't seem to stop thinking about that poor old man. His daughter will find out the truth now, and then she'll be leaving him to get married. What will happen to him when he's all alone?"

There was a touch of urgency in Inspector Millner's voice. And Mom's reply was curious. She ignored his question completely, and said in her most positive voice, "Old! Who's old?"

Then, as if she had said something a little too revealing, she turned quickly to the cake. "First a wish, and then a blow," she said. So she shut her eyes tightly, and her lips moved soundlessly for a moment. Then she opened her eyes, leaned over the cake, and gave a blow.

Whatever it was that Mom wished, she wasn't talking about it—not that night, anyway.

Inspector Ganesh Ghote

THE INDIAN DETECTIVE

INSPECTOR GHOTE AND THE TEST MATCH

H. R. F. Keating

Inspector Ganesh Ghote of the Bombay C.I.D. is India's foremost fictional detective. He has appeared in more than a dozen novels over the past twenty years, among them such acclaimed works as The Perfect Murder *(1965), which won awards from both the British Crime Writers Association and the Mystery Writers of America, and the recent titles* Filmi, Filmi, Inspector Ghote *(1976) and* Inspector Ghote Draws a Line *(1979). He is also featured in a number of short-shorts published in* Ellery Queen's Mystery Magazine, *one of which is this clever and ironic little tale of robbery at a cricket match.*

Ghote has been called "one of the few classical creations" among modern detectives, while his cases have been referred to in toto as "an acute and sympathetic picture of India, Indians, and foreigners in India." The vivid depiction of local color, as well as an accurate portrayal of the many facets of Indian culture, make the Ghote books and stories much more than just good mysteries. About them Keating himself has said, "I like to think they chiefly put a recognizable human being into broad general situations likely to happen to any one of us. Ghote has had to decide how far he should try to be perfect, just where his loyalties should lie, etc." In this, too, the author has been quite successful.

In addition to the Ghote series, H. R. F. Keating has written nonseries mysteries, mainstream novels, nonfiction books, radio plays, and reviews of crime fiction for the London Times (he has been that newspaper's resident mystery reviewer since 1967). He has also edited several books on the crime fiction genre, among them an appreciation of the works of Agatha Christie.

. . .

From the very beginning Inspector Ghote had doubts about Anil Divekar and the Test Match. Cricket and Divekar did not really mix. Divekar's sport was something quite different. He was a daylight-entry ace. Excitement for him lay not in perfectly timing a stroke with the bat that would send the ball skimming along the grass to the boundary, but in the patient sizing up, "casing," of a big Bombay house—the layout of its rooms, the routine of its servants—and then choosing the right moment to slip in and out carrying away the best of the portable loot.

But here he was, as Ghote on a rare free day stood with his son Ved outside the high walls of Brabourne Stadium, ticketless and enviously watching the crowds pouring in for the start of the day's play. Divekar even came up to them, smiling broadly.

"Inspector, you would like seats?"

At Ghote's elbow Ved's face lit up as if from a sudden inward glow. And Ghote nearly accepted the offer. Ved deserved the treat—he was well-behaved and worked hard at school. And it was only a question of a pair of tickets. Some of the Inspector's colleagues would have taken them as a right.

But Ghote knew all along that he couldn't do it. Whatever the others did he had always kept his integrity. No crook could ever reproach him with past favors.

He tugged Ved angrily off. But marching away from the

stadium he could not help speculating as to why Divekar should have been there at all. Of course, when every two years or so a team from England or Australia or the West Indies came to Bombay, Test Match fever suddenly gripped the most unexpected people. But all the same . . .

Yet the crowd outside the stadium had not all been the college students and excited schoolboys you might expect. Smart business executives had jostled with simple shopkeepers and grain merchants. The film stars' huge cars had nosed their way past anxious, basket-clutching housewives, their best saris already looking crumpled and dusty.

Fifty thousand people, ready to roast all day in the sun to watch a sedate game that most of them hardly understood! Waiting for someone to "hit a sixer" so that they could launch into frenzied clapping, or for someone to drop a catch and give them a chance to indulge in some vigorous booing, or—the height of heights!—for a home player to get a century and permit them to invade the pitch with flower garlands held high to drape their hero.

Where did they all get the entrance money? Ghote wondered. With even eighteen-rupee seats selling for a hundred, getting in was way beyond his own means. Little Ved's treat would have to be, once more, a visit to the Hanging Gardens.

But when they reached this mildly pleasurable, and free, spot, everywhere they went transistor radios were tuned teasingly to the Test Match commentary, and nothing Ghote offered his son was in the least successful.

He bought coconuts, but Ved would not even watch the squatting naralwallah dexterously chop off the tops of the dark fruit. He held out the gruesome spectacle of the vultures that hovered over the Towers of Silence where the Parsis laid out their dead, but Ved just shrugged. Ghote purchased various bottled drinks, each more hectically colored and more expensive than the previous one; but Ved drank them with increased apathy.

At last Ghote gave up in a spasm of irritation.

"If that is all you care, we will go home."

Ved made no reply.

They set off, Ghote walking fast and getting unnecessarily hot. And still, going down Malabar Hill with its huge garden-surrounded mansions and great shady trees, there were passers-by with transistors and the unwearying commentator's voice.

"What a pity for India. A glorious captain's knock by the Rajah of Bolkpur ends in a doubtful decision by Umpire Khan."

Ved swung round on him with an outraged glare. Whether this was because of the umpire's perfidy or because of not being there to judge the matter for himself it was hard to tell.

And then Ghote saw him. Anil Divekar. At least the figure that he half glimpsed ahead, sneaking out of a narrow gate and cradling in his arms a heavy-looking, sack-wrapped object, looked remarkably like Divekar. Ghote launched himself into the chase.

But the sound of running steps alerted the distant figure and in moments the fellow had disappeared altogether.

Ghote went quickly back to the house from whose side entrance he had seen the suspicious figure emerge. And there things began to add up. The big house had been rented temporarily to none other than the Rajah of Bolkpur himself and a few minutes' search revealed that all the Rajah's personal jewelry had just been neatly spirited away.

Ghote got through to C.I.D. Headquarters on the telephone and reported. Then he and Ved endured a long wait till a squad arrived to take over. But he did get away in time to go down to the stadium again to see if Ved, his autograph book ready, could catch a glimpse of the departing players.

And no sooner had they arrived at the stadium, just as the crowds were beginning to stream out, when there was Anil Divekar right in front of them. He made no attempt to run. On the contrary he came pushing his way through the throng, smiling broadly.

No doubt he thought he had fixed himself a neat alibi.

But Ghote saw in a flash how he could trap Divekar if he had slipped away from the game just long enough to commit the robbery. Because it so happened that Ghote knew exactly what had been occurring in the stadium at the moment the thief had slipped out of that house on Malabar Hill.

"A bad day's play, I hear," he said to Divekar. "What did you think about Bolkpur?"

Divekar shook his head sadly.

"A damn wrong decision, Inspectorji," he said. "I was sitting right behind the bat, and I could see. Damn wrong."

He looked at them both with an expression of radiant guiltlessness. "That was where you would have been sitting also," Divekar added.

You win, Ghote thought and turned grimly away. But on his way home he stopped for a moment at Headquarters to see if anything had turned up. His Deputy Superintendent was there.

"Well, Inspector, they tell me you spotted Anil Divekar leaving the house."

"I am sorry, sir, but I do not think it was him now."

He recounted his meeting with the man at the stadium a few minutes earlier. But the Deputy Superintendent was unimpressed.

"Nonsense, man, whatever the fellow says, this is Divekar's type of crime, one hundred percent. You just identify him as running off from the scene and we've got him."

For an instant Ghote was tempted. After all, Divekar was an inveterate thief: it would be justice of a sort. But then he knew that he had not really been sure who that running man was.

"No, sir," he said. "I am sorry, but no."

The Deputy Superintendent's eyes blazed, and it was only the insistent ringing of the telephone by his side that postponed his moment of wrath.

"Yes? Yes? What is it? Oh, you, Inspector. Well? What? The gardener? But —oh. On him? Every missing item? Very good then, charge him at once."

He replaced the receiver and looked at Ghote.

"Yes, Inspector," he said blandly, "that chap Divekar. As I was saying, he wants watching, you know, close watching. I'll swear he's up to something. Now, he's bound to be at the Test Match tomorrow, so you'd better be there too."

"Yes, sir," Ghote said.

A notion darted into Ghote's head.

"And, sir. For cover for the operation should I take this boy of mine also?"

"First-rate idea. Carry on, Inspector Ghote."

THE FRENCH DETECTIVE

THE MOST OBSTINATE MAN IN PARIS

Georges Simenon

It may be argued, of course, that Inspector Maigret of the Paris police is not truly an ethnic detective. But we are staunch defenders of the opposite view. Maigret is certainly a most Gallic sleuth, epitomizing the best (and occasionally the worst) qualities of the French character. He is, as Ellery Queen has written, "patient, persevering, painstaking; a bulldog in tenacity, a bloodhound on the hunt with his pipe puffing incessantly, with his placid exterior concealing a shrewd, observant, and highly intelligent brain; often surly as a bear (or as the Seine itself), often peevish and resentful, perplexed and irritable and grumbling, with a heart as big as Paris herself."

And in the best of his cases—"The Most Obstinate Man in Paris" is definitely one of them—there is a unique ethnic flair, a capturing of the je ne sais quoi *of the French lifestyle and of that one-of-a-kind city, Paris. What could be more ethnical in flavor, after all, than Paris in the springtime?*

Georges Simenon, like his most famous creation, is a complex and Gallic figure—a phenomenon who has published well over two hundred novels, collections, and nonfiction books over the past fifty years, a good percentage of them featuring Maigret. (The first Maigret novel, The Strange

Case of Peter the Lett, *appeared in 1933.*) *He has led a controversial life, the basic facts of which can be found in his recent autobiography,* Intimate Memoirs *(1984); and his public statement that during his eighty years of life he has had intimate relations with some 10,000 women has provoked as much argument and speculation as any of his books. But there can be no argument that he is a consummate craftsman in the art of fiction, or that his work in general and the Maigret series in particular has been applauded by readers and critics in every corner of the globe.*

·   ·   ·

In all the annals of Paris police no one had ever posed so long or so assiduously for a *portrait parle*. For hours on end—sixteen, to be exact—he seemed so stubbornly intent on attracting attention that Inspector Janvier himself came in to look him over at close range. Yet when it was necessary to detail his description, the outlines were blurred and inexact. And some of the dozen witnesses, none of them regularly given to flights of imagination, were sure that the stranger's ostentation was nothing less than a skillful trick.

It all happened on May 3—a warm, sunny day with the special feel of a Parisian spring in the air. The chestnut trees of the Boulevard Saint-Germain were in full bloom and their delicate, faintly sweet fragrance drifted into the cool interior of the cafe from morning till night.

As he did every day, Joseph opened the doors of the cafe at eight in the morning. He was in vest and shirtsleeves. The sawdust he had scattered on the floor the night before at closing time was still there and the chairs were piled high on the marble-topped tables. For the Cafe des Ministeres, at the corner of the Boulevard Saint-Germain and the Rue des Saints-Peres, was one of the rare old-fashioned cafes still left in Paris. It had resisted the influx of the hurried drinkers who had only time for a quick one. And it had resisted the rage of gilt fixtures, indirect lighting, mirrored pillars, and flimsy plastic taborets.

It was a cafe of regulars, where every customer had his

own table in his own corner and his own cards or chess set. Joseph the waiter knew them all by name—most of them bureau chiefs and government clerks from neighboring ministries.

Joseph himself was something of a personage in his own right. He had been a waiter for thirty years and it was difficult to imagine him wearing street clothes. Most of his regular customers would probably not recognize him if they met him on the street or in the suburbs where he had built himself a little house.

Eight o'clock was the hour of cleaning up and setting to rights. The double door was wide open on the Boulevard Saint-Germain. There was sunshine on the sidewalk, but inside the cafe there was only cool, bluish shadow. Joseph smoked as he went about the ritual of getting ready for the day's business. It was his only cigarette of the day. First he lit the gas under the coffee boiler, then polished the nickel until it shone like a mirror. Next he put the bottles on the shelves behind the bar, the aperitifs first, then the spirits. After that he swept up the sawdust and finally he set the chairs around the tables.

The man arrived at exactly ten minutes past eight. Joseph was busy at the coffee boiler and did not see him come in, a fact which he afterward regretted. Had the man rushed in furtively like someone being pursued? And why had he chosen the Cafe des Ministeres, when the bar across the street was already bustling with customers drinking their morning coffee and eating croissants and rolls.

As Joseph later described it: "I turned around and saw somebody already inside—a man wearing a gray hat and carrying a small valise."

The cafe was really open without being open. It was open because the doors were not closed, but nobody ever came in at this hour. The water was barely warm in the coffee machine and some of the chairs were still piled on the tables.

"I won't be able to serve you for at least half an hour," Joseph said.

He thought that settled matters, but the man merely

lifted a chair from a table and sat down, still holding tight to his traveling bag.

"It really doesn't matter," said the stranger calmly, with the air of a man who is not easily dissuaded.

His tone was enough to put the waiter in bad humor. Joseph was like a housewife who hates to have people around at cleaning time. He had a right to be alone while he was doing his housework. He grumbled:

"You'll have a long wait for your coffee."

He continued his daily routine until nine o'clock, favoring the stranger with an occasional glance. Ten times, twenty times, he passed very close to the man, brushed against him, even jostled him a few times while he was sweeping up the sawdust and taking down the remainder of the chairs.

At a few minutes past nine he reluctantly brought the man a cup of scalding coffee, a small pitcher of milk, and two lumps of sugar on a saucer.

"Don't you have any croissants?"

"The place across the street has croissants."

"It really doesn't matter," the stranger said.

It was a curious thing, but this man who must know he was in the way, who must know that he was in the wrong cafe at the wrong time, had a certain humility about him that made him rather likable. And there were other things which Joseph noted with appreciation. During a whole hour the man did not take a newspaper from his pocket, nor did he ask for a paper, nor did he consult the directory or the telephone book. Nor did he try to engage the waiter in conversation. And that was not all: he did not smoke, he did not cross and uncross his legs, he did not fidget. He merely sat.

Not many people could sit in a cafe for an hour without moving, without looking at the time every few minutes, without showing their impatience in one way or another. If this man was waiting for someone, he was certainly waiting with extraordinary equanimity.

At precisely ten o'clock Joseph finished his housework. The man was still there. Another curious detail struck Joseph: the stranger had not taken a chair by the window, but sat at the rear of the cafe near the mahogany stairway that led down to the washrooms. Joseph would be going downstairs soon himself to spruce up a little, but first he cranked down the orange-colored awning which gave a faint tint to the shadows inside.

Before going downstairs the waiter jingled a few coins in his vest pocket, hoping the man would take the hint, pay his bill, and leave. The man did nothing of the kind. Joseph left him sitting alone as he went down to change his starched collar and dickey, comb his hair, and put on his worn alpaca jacket. When he came back, the man was still there, still gazing into his empty coffee cup.

Mademoiselle Berthe, the cashier, had come in and was sitting at her desk, taking things out of her handbag. Joseph winked at her. The cashier winked back and started arranging the brass checks in regular piles. She was plump, soft, pink, and placid, and her hair was bleached. When she had finished with the checks, she looked down at the stranger from her throne-like perch.

"He gave me the impression of being a very gentle, very respectable person," she said later. "And I could have wagered he dyed his mustache, like the Colonel."

It was true that the blue-black tint of the man's little mustache suggested hair dye, just as the turned-up ends suggested the curling iron and wax.

Another part of the daily routine was the delivery of the ice. A giant with a piece of sacking on his shoulder carried in the opaline blocks, dripping a limpid trail as he put them away in the ice chest. He, too, noticed the solitary customer.

"He made me think of a sea lion," he said later.

Why a sea lion? The iceman couldn't say exactly.

As for Joseph, he kept strictly to his timetable. It was now time to remove yesterday's newspapers from their long-handled binders and to replace them with today's editions.

"Could I trouble you to pass me one of those?"

Well, well! The customer spoke at last—timidly, softly, but he spoke.

"Which paper do you want? *Le Temps? Le Figaro? Les Debats?*"

"It really doesn't matter."

That was another thing that made Joseph think the man was not a Parisian. He was not a foreigner either, for he had no accent. Probably just off the train from the provinces. And yet there was no railway station in the immediate vicinity. Why would a man come halfway across Paris to sit in a strange cafe? And it was a strange cafe, because Joseph, who had a memory for faces, was certain he had never seen the man before. Strangers who entered the Cafe des Ministeres by chance knew at once they did not belong there and promptly went away.

Eleven o'clock—the hour of the boss's arrival. Monsieur Monnet came downstairs from his apartment, freshly shaven, his cheeks aglow, his gray hair neatly slicked down, his perennial patent leather shoes gleaming below his gray trousers. He could have retired from business long ago. He had bought a provincial cafe for each of his children, but he himself could live no other place in the world than this corner of the Boulevard Saint-Germain where all his customers were his friends.

"Everything all right, Joseph?"

The boss had spotted the stranger and his coffee cup immediately. His eyes asked questions. Behind the counter, Joseph whispered: "He's been here since eight this morning."

Monsieur Monnet walked back and forth in front of the stranger, rubbing his hands as if to invite conversation. Monsieur Monnet was used to talking to his customers. He played cards and dominoes with them. He knew their family troubles, their office gossip. But the stranger did not open his mouth.

"The man appeared very tired, like someone who had spent a sleepless night in a train," the boss said later.

And very much later Inspector Maigret asked the three of them, Joseph, Mademoiselle Berthe, and Monsieur Monnet: "Did he seem to be watching for somebody in the street?"

Their answers were different.

"No," said Monsieur Monnet.

"I got the impression he was waiting for a woman," said the cashier.

"Several times I caught him looking toward the bar across the street," said Joseph, "but each time he lowered his eyes almost immediately."

At twenty past eleven, the stranger ordered a small bottle of Vichy. Several of Joseph's customers drank mineral water, and for reasons which Joseph knew. Monsieur Blanc, for instance, of the War Ministry, was on a strict diet. Joseph noted that the stranger neither drank nor smoked, which was most unusual.

For the next two hours he lost track of the man, for the regulars had begun to swarm in for their before-lunch aperitifs. Joseph knew in advance what each would drink and to which tables he should bring playing cards.

"Garcon!"

It was past one. The stranger was still there. His valise had been pushed under the red-plush banquette. Joseph pretended he thought the man was asking for the check, and he made his calculation half aloud.

"Eight francs fifty," he announced.

"Could you serve me a sandwich?"

"I'm sorry. We have none."

"Haven't you any rolls, either?"

"We don't serve any food here."

Which was both true and false. Sometimes in the evening a bridge player who had missed his dinner could get a ham sandwich, but it was not usual.

The man shook his head and murmured: "It really doesn't matter."

This time Joseph thought the man's lips trembled slightly. He was struck by the resigned, sorrowful expression on the stranger's face.

"Could I serve you something?"

"Another coffee, please, with plenty of milk."

The man was hungry and the milk would be a little nourishment. He did not ask for other newspapers. He had had time to read the first one from first line to last, including the classified ads.

The Colonel arrived and was distinctly unhappy because there was someone seated at his table. The Colonel was afraid of the slightest draught—spring draughts were the most treacherous of all—and always sat far back in the cafe.

Armand, the second waiter—he had been a waiter only three years and would never look like a real *garcon de cafe* if he remained a waiter all his life—came on duty at one thirty. Joseph immediately went behind the glass partition to eat the lunch brought down from the second floor.

Why did Armand think the stranger might have been a rug seller or a peanut vender?

"He gave me the feeling of not being frank and open," said Armand later. "I didn't like the way he looked at you from under his eyelids. There was something oily, something too sweet in his face. If I had my way I'd have told him he was in the wrong pew and thrown him out on his ear."

Others noticed the man, particularly those who came back in the evening and found him sitting in exactly the same place.

True, all these witnesses were amateurs, but the professional who was to come upon the scene later was just as vague and full of contradictions.

For the first ten years of his career Joseph had been a waiter at the Brasserie Dauphine, a few steps from the Quai des Orfevres, which was frequented by most of the inspectors and detectives of the Police Judiciaire. He had become a close friend of Inspector Janvier, one of Maigret's best men, and in time married Janvier's sister-in-law.

At three o'clock in the afternoon, seeing the man still in the same place, Joseph began to get really irritated. He formulated a hypothesis, to wit, that if this fellow stubbornly clung to his banquette it was not for love of the atmosphere inside the Cafe des Ministeres but for fear of what lay outside. When he got off the train, Joseph reasoned, the man must have felt that he was being followed, and had come to the cafe to avoid the police. So Joseph telephoned the Quai des Orfevres and asked for Inspector Janvier.

"I've got a funny customer here who's been sitting in his corner since eight this morning and who seems determined not to budge," he said. "He hasn't eaten anything all day. Don't you think you ought to come over and take a look at him?"

The meticulous Janvier packed up a collection of the latest "Wanted" notices and headed for the Boulevard Saint-Germain. By a curious chance, at the very moment he stepped into the Cafe des Ministeres, the place was empty.

"Flown the coop?" he asked Joseph.

The waiter pointed to the basement stairs. "Gone to telephone."

What a pity! A few minutes sooner and Janvier could have had the call monitored. As it was, the Inspector sat down and ordered a Calvados.

The stranger came back to his table, still calm, perhaps a trifle worried, but certainly not nervous. Joseph, who was getting to know the man, thought him rather relaxed.

For the next twenty minutes Janvier scrutinized the stranger from head to foot. He had plenty of time to compare the plump, rather vague features with the photos of the criminals.

"He's not on our lists," Janvier told Joseph. "He looks to me like some poor guy who's been stood up by a woman. He's probably an insurance agent or something of the sort." He chuckled. "I wouldn't be surprised if he turned out to be a coffin salesman. Anyhow, I don't see that I have any right to pick him up. There's no law against a man going without lunch, if he wants to, or sitting all day in a cafe as long as he pays his tab."

After chatting with Joseph a while longer, Janvier returned to the Quai des Orfevres for an appointment with Maigret. The two Inspectors were so engrossed in a gambling case that Janvier forgot even to mention the man of the Boulevard Saint-Germain to Maigret.

The dying rays of the sun slanted so low that they slid under the awnings of the Cafe des Ministeres. At five o'clock three tables were taken by *belote* players. Monsieur Monnet himself took a hand at a table just opposite the stranger. From time to time he glanced at the man who still sat motionless.

By six o'clock the cafe was jammed. Joseph and Armand hurried from table to table, their trays loaded with bottles and glasses. The aroma of Pernod soon overpowered the delicate scent of the blossoming chestnut trees on the boulevard.

Each of the two waiters, during the rush hour, had his own tables. The man was sitting at a table in Armand's section. Not only was Armand less observant than his colleague, but he occasionally slipped behind the counter to toss off a glass of white wine. It was understandable, therefore, that the events of the evening may have seemed somewhat blurred to him.

All he could say for sure was that a woman finally came in.

"She was a brunette, well-dressed, respectable looking, not at all one of these women who sometimes drop in to a cafe and try to strike up a conversation with strangers."

She was, according to Armand, a woman who would wait in a public place only because she had a date with her husband. There were several vacant tables, but she sat down at the table next to the man.

"I'm sure they didn't speak to one another," Armand said later. "She ordered a glass of port. I think I remember that besides her handbag—a brown or black leather bag— she was carrying a small package in her hand. I noticed it on the table when she ordered the port. It was tied up in paper. But when I brought her order, the package was no longer on the table. She had probably put it on the banquette beside her."

Too bad that Joseph did not see the woman more clearly.

Mademoiselle Berthe saw her all right, from her high-perched desk.

"Rather nicely turned out," the cashier said later. "She wore a blue tailored suit, a white blouse, and almost no makeup. I don't know why I say this, but I don't think she was a married woman."

There was a constant flow of customers in and out of the cafe until eight o'clock, the dinner hour. Then the vacant tables began to be more numerous. At nine o'clock only six other tables were occupied, two by bridge players who never missed a daily session, and four by chess players.

"One thing is certain," Joseph said later, "the man knew bridge. And chess, too. I'd say he was a demon at both. I could tell by the way he was watching the games around him."

So he was not at all preoccupied? Or was Joseph mistaken?

At ten o'clock only three other tables were occupied. The man from the ministeres went to bed early. At half-past ten, Armand went home. His wife was expecting a baby and he had arranged with the boss to leave early.

The man was still there, still sitting quietly.

Since ten minutes past eight that morning he had drunk three cups of coffee, a split of Vichy, and a bottle of lemon pop—nothing stronger. He had not smoked. He had read *Le Temps* during the morning and late in the afternoon he had bought an evening paper from a news vendor who passed through the cafe.

At eleven o'clock Joseph started piling the chairs on the tables, as he did every evening, although two tables were still occupied. He also scattered the sawdust on the floor, as usual.

A little later one game broke up. Monsieur Monnet shook hands with his partners, one of whom was the Colonel, went to the cashier's desk for the little canvas bag into which Mademoiselle Berthe had stuffed the sheafs of banknotes and the small change, and climbed the stairs to his apartment.

Before leaving he glanced once more at the obstinate customer who had been a topic of general conversation that evening and said to Joseph:

"If he makes any trouble, ring me."

There was a push-button behind the bar which set off an alarm in Monsieur Monnet's private apartment.

And that was the whole story. When Maigret started his investigation next day, there was little more to be learned.

Mademoiselle Berthe had left at ten minutes to eleven to catch the last bus for Epinay. She, too, had looked at the stranger one final time before leaving.

"I can't say that he was nervous, exactly, but he wasn't exactly calm either. If I'd met him in the street, for instance, he would have scared me, if you know what I mean. And if he'd got off the bus at my stop in Epinay, I wouldn't have dared walk home all alone."

"Why?"

"Well, he had one of those inward looks."

"What do you mean by that?"

"He didn't pay attention to anything that was going on."

"Were the shutters of the cafe closed?"

"No. Joseph doesn't lower them until the last minute."

"From your desk you can see the street corner and the bar across the street. Did you notice any suspicious movements in either place? Did you see anyone who might have been watching for him, waiting for him?"

"I wouldn't have noticed. As quiet as it is on the Boulevard Saint-Germain side, there's quite a bit of traffic on the Rue des Saints-Peres. And there's always people coming in and going out of the bar across the street."

"You didn't notice anyone outside this cafe when you left to go home?"

"Nobody. No, wait. There was a police officer at the corner."

The statement was confirmed by the district police station. Unfortunately the policeman was to leave his post a few minutes later.

Only two other tables were now taken, one by a couple who had dropped in for a drink after the movies, a doctor and his wife who lived a few doors down and often had a nightcap on their way home. They were considered regulars of the Cafe des Ministeres. They had paid their check and were leaving.

The doctor said, "We were sitting just opposite him, and I observed that he was not a well man."

"In your opinion, Doctor, what was wrong with him?"

"His liver, no doubt about it."

"How old would you say he was?"

"It's hard to say. I'm sorry now that I didn't pay more careful attention. In my opinion he was one of those men who look older than their age. Some people would say he was forty-five or even more because of the dyed mustache."

"He did dye his mustache, then? You're sure of that?"

"I think he did. However, I've known patients of thirty-five with the same flabby, colorless flesh, the same lifeless air . . ."

"Don't you think the fact that he had nothing to eat all day may have given him his lifeless air?"

"Possibly. Nevertheless, that would not change my diagnosis. The man had a bad stomach, a bad liver, and, I may add, a defective intestinal tract."

The bridge game at the last occupied table—the last except the stranger's—went on and on. Every time game and rubber seemed on the point of ending the contest, the declarer failed to make his bid. At last a contract of five clubs, doubled and redoubled, was miraculously made, thanks to the nervous error of a tired player who unintentionally established the dummy's long side suit.

It was ten minutes before midnight when Joseph piled the last chairs on a table and announced: "We're closing, *messieurs.*"

The stranger did not move while the bridge players were settling their bill, and Joseph would have admitted that at the moment he was frightened. He was on the point of asking the four regulars to wait while he put the man out, but somehow he didn't dare. The regulars filed out, still talking about the last hand. They continued arguing for a moment on the street corner and then separated.

"Eighteen francs seventy-five," Joseph said, a shade too

loudly. He was now alone with the stranger. He had already extinguished half the lights.

"I had my eye on an empty siphon of seltzer left over on the corner of the bar," he confessed to Maigret afterward. "One move and I would have bashed his head in."

"Did you put the siphon bottle there for that express purpose?"

Obviously he had. Sixteen hours had put Joseph's nerves on edge. The man had become a personal enemy, almost. Little by little Joseph had practically convinced himself that the man was there on the waiter's account exclusively, that he was waiting only for a propitious moment, a moment when they would be alone, to attack and rob him.

And yet Joseph made one mistake. While the man was fumbling in his pockets for change, still seated at his table, the waiter had gone out to crank down the iron shutters. He was afraid of missing his bus. True, the door was still wide open and there were still pedestrians on the boulevard, taking advantage of the midnight coolness.

"Here you are, *garcon.*"

Twenty-one francs! Two francs twenty-five tip for a whole day! Joseph was furious. Only his professional composure of thirty years kept him from throwing the change back on the table.

"And maybe you were a little afraid of him, too?" Inspector Maigret suggested.

"I really don't know. Anyhow, I was in a hurry to be rid of him. In all my life I've never been infuriated by a customer like that. If I'd only foreseen that morning that he was going to stay all day!"

"Where were you at the exact moment he left the cafe?"

"Let me see . . . First I had to remind him that he had a valise under the banquette. He was going off without it."

"Did he seem annoyed that you reminded him of it?"
"No."

"Did he seem relieved?"

"He didn't act pleased or displeased. Indifferent, I would

say. If I was looking for a cool customer, this was a cool customer. I've seen all kinds and shapes in the thirty years I've been a waiter, but I've never seen one who could sit behind a marble-topped table for sixteen hours straight without getting ants in his legs."

"And where were you standing?"

"Near the cashier's desk. I was ringing up the eighteen francs seventy-five. You've noticed there are two entrances here—the big double door that opens on the boulevard and the little one on the Rue des Saints-Peres. When he headed for the side door, I was going to call him back and show him the main entrance, but then I thought, *What's the difference? It's all the same to me.* I was through for the night, except to change my clothes and lock up."

"In what hand was he carrying his valise?"

"I didn't notice."

"And I suppose you didn't notice either if he had one hand in his pocket?"

"I don't know. He wasn't wearing a topcoat. I didn't actually see him go out on account of the chairs piled on the tables. They cut off my view."

"You kept standing in the same place?"

"Yes, right there. I was taking the ticket out of the cash register with one hand, and with the other I was fishing in my pocket for the last of the day's brass checks. Then I heard an explosion—like a motor backfiring. Only I knew right away it wasn't a car. I said to myself, 'Well, well! So he got it after all!'

"You think very fast at a time like that. You have to in my line of business. I've seen some pretty tough brawls in my life. I'm always amazed at how fast a man thinks.

"I was mad at myself. After all, he was just a poor guy who had hid out here because he knew he'd get knocked off the minute he stuck his nose outside. So I was sorry for him. He didn't eat anything all day, so maybe he didn't have the money to call a taxi and make a getaway before he got ambushed."

"Did you rush right out to help him?"

"Well, as a matter of fact . . ." Joseph was embarrassed. "I think I probably hesitated a moment. I've got a wife and three children, you know. So first I pushed the button that rings in the boss's bedroom. Then I heard voices outside, and the sound of people running in the street. I heard a woman say, 'You stay out of this, Gaston.' Then I heard a police whistle.

"I went out. I saw three people standing in the Rue des Saints-Peres, several metres from the door."

"Eight metres," said Inspector Maigret, consulting the police report.

"Possibly. I didn't measure. A man was lying in the street and another man was stooping over him. I found out afterwards it was a doctor who was on his way home from the theatre and who just happens to be a customer of ours. We have quite a few doctors among our regulars.

"The doctor stood up and said, 'He's had it. The bullet entered the back of his neck and came out through the left eye.'

"Then the police officer arrived and I knew I'd be questioned. Believe it or not, I just couldn't look at the ground. That business about the left eye made me sick to my stomach. I didn't want to look at my customer in that shape, with his eye shot out. I told myself that it was partly my fault, that perhaps I should have— But what could I have done?

"I can still hear the voice of the police officer, standing there with his notebook in his hand, asking: 'Doesn't anybody know this man?' And I answered automatically, 'I do. At least I think I—'

"Finally I forced myself to bend down and look. I swear to you, Monsieur Maigret—and you know me well enough, what with all the thousands of glasses of beer and Calvados I used to serve you over at the Brasserie Dauphine, Inspector, to understand I'm not given to exaggerating—I swear to you I never had such a shock in my life.

"*It was not the man!* It was not the stranger who had sat all day in the cafe.

"It was somebody I didn't know, somebody I never saw before—a tall skinny man in a raincoat. On a fine spring day, a night warm enough to sleep under the stairs, and he was wearing a tan raincoat.

"I felt better. Maybe it's silly, but I was glad it wasn't our customer. If my customer had been the victim instead of the murderer, I would have felt guilty about it all my life. You see, since early morning I felt there was something not quite right about my man. I would have put my hand in the fire, that he was a wrong one. It wasn't for nothing that I phoned Janvier. Only Janvier, even if he is practically my brother-in-law, always does everything according to the rules. When I called him, why didn't he ask to see the man's identity papers? They would have told him something, certainly. A decent law-abiding citizen doesn't sit all day in a cafe and then go out and shoot somebody on the sidewalk at midnight.

"Because you'll note that he didn't loiter after the shot was fired. Nobody saw him. If he wasn't the one that pulled the trigger, he would have stayed right there. He couldn't have walked more than a dozen steps by the time I heard the gun.

"The only thing I don't understand is about this woman— the one that ordered a glass of port from Armand. How does she fit into this? Because there's no doubt she had something to do with this man. We don't get many unescorted women in our cafe—it's not that kind of a place."

"I thought," Inspector Maigret objected, "that the man and the woman did not speak to each other."

"Did they have to speak? Didn't she have a little package in her hand when she came in? Armand saw it, and Armand is not a liar. He saw it on the table and then he saw it wasn't on the table any more and he supposed she'd put it on the banquette. And when this lady left, Mademoiselle Berthe watched her go out because she was admiring her handbag and wishing she had one like it. Now Mademoiselle Berthe didn't notice that she was carrying a package then, and you must admit that women do notice such things.

"You can say what you like, but I still think I spent the whole day with a murderer. And I think I got off very lucky."

Dawn brought one of those perfect spring days such as Paris manages to produce about every third year, a day meant for nothing more strenuous than nibbling at a sherbet or remembering the carefree days of childhood. Everything was good, light, heady, and of rare quality: the limpid blue of the sky, the fleecy whiteness of the few clouds, the softness of the breeze that kissed your cheek as you turned a corner and that rustled the chestnut trees just enough to make you raise your eyes to admire the clusters of sweet flowers. A cat on a window sill, a dog stretched out on the sidewalk, a shoemaker in his leather apron leaning in his doorway for a breath of air, an ordinary green-and-yellow bus rumbling by—they were all precious that day, all designed to instill gaiety into the soul.

That is probably why Inspector Maigret has always kept such a delightful memory of the corner of the Boulevard Saint-Germain and the Rue des Saints-Peres. It is also the reason he was later to stop frequently at a certain cafe for a spot of shade and a glass of beer. Unfortunately, the beer never tasted quite the same after that day.

The case he was investigating was destined to become famous, not because of the inexplicable obstinacy of the stranger in the Cafe des Ministeres, or of the midnight shooting, but because of the strange motive for the crime.

At eight the next morning, Inspector Maigret was at his desk in the Quai des Orfevres, all of his windows open on the blue-and-gold panorama of the Seine. He smoked his pipe with small, gluttonous puffs as he skimmed through the reports—and thus made his first contact with the man of the Cafe des Ministeres and with the death in the Rue des Saints-Peres.

The police of the district Commissariat had put in a good night's work. Dr. Paul, the medical examiner, had finished his autopsy by six in the morning. The bullet and the empty shell case, which had both been found on the sidewalk, had already been submitted to Gastinne-Renette, the ballistics expert, and a report was expected shortly.

The dead man's clothes, together with the contents of his pockets and several photographs of the scene made by Identification, were on Maigret's desk. Maigret picked up his phone.

"Would you step into my office, Janvier? According to the report, you seem to be somewhat involved in this case."

And so on that beautiful spring day Maigret and Janvier were once again teammates.

Maigret studied the clothing while he waited. The suit was of good quality and less worn than it seemed. It was the suit of a man who lived alone, without a woman to brush it off occasionally or to make him send it to the cleaners before it looked as though he had slept in it—which perhaps he had. The shirt was new and had not yet been to the laundry, but it had been worn for at least a week. The socks looked no better.

There were no papers in the pockets, no letters, no clues to the man's identity. The usual miscellany had some unusual additions: a corkscrew; a pocketknife with numerous blades; a dirty handkerchief; a button off his jacket; a single key; a well-caked pipe and a tobacco pouch; a wallet containing two thousand three hundred and fifty francs and a snapshot of a half a dozen bare-bosomed native girls standing in front of an African straw hut; a piece of string; and a third-class railway ticket from Juvisy to Paris, bearing yesterday's date. And finally there was a toy printing set, the kind with which children could fit rubber letters into a small wooden frame and make their own rubber stamps.

The rubber letters in the frame formed the words:

I'LL GET YOU YET.

The medical examiner's report contained several interesting details. The shot had been fired from behind at a distance of not more than ten feet. Death had been instantaneous. The dead man had numerous scars. The ones on his feet were obviously caused by chigoes, African jiggers which burrow under the skin and have to be dug out with the point of a knife. His liver was in pitiful condition, a real drunkard's liver. And finally the man killed in the Rue des Saints-Peres had been suffering from a bad case of malaria.

"Here you are!" Maigret reached for his hat. "Let's go, Janvier, old man."

They walked to the Cafe des Ministeres. Through the window they could see Joseph busy with his morning housework. But curiously enough, Maigret was more interested in the cafe across the street.

The two cafes were opposite in more ways than geographically. Joseph's domain was old-fashioned and quiet. The bar on the opposite corner—the sign read Chez Leon—was aggressively and vulgarly modern. At the long bar two waiters in shirtsleeves worked busily behind pyramids of croissants, sandwiches, and hard-boiled eggs. Now they were serving little but coffee and white wine. Later it would be red wine and anise-flavored aperitifs.

At the far end of the bar the proprietor and his wife alternated at the tobacco counter. Beyond was the back room, garish with its red-and-gold pillars, its one-legged tables in rainbow plastic, and its chairs covered with plush of an incredible red hue.

All the bay windows opened on the street and crowds swarmed in and out of the Chez Leon from morning to night—masons in powdery smocks, clerks and typists, delivery boys rushing in for quick ones before reclaiming their parked tricycle carriers; people in a hurry, people looking for a phone, and most of all, people who were thirsty.

"One up! . . . Two Beaujolais! . . . Three bocks!"

The cash register played a continuous tune. The waiters and barmen sweated as they worked, sometimes mopping their brows with bar towels. Dirty glasses, dipped in murky water, did not even have time to dry before they were refilled with red or white wine.

"Two dry whites," Maigret ordered. He loved the din and tumult of the morning rush. And he liked the rascally after-taste of the white wine which he never found anywhere but in bistros of this sort.

"Tell me, *garcon*, do you remember this man?"

Identification had done a good job. Photographing a dead man may be an ignoble way of earning a living, but it is an essential and delicate art. The inexpert result is often hard to recognize, especially if the face has been damaged. So the gentlemen from Identification first touch up the corpse, then retouch the negative so that the subject looks almost alive.

"That's him, all right. Isn't it, Louis?"

The other waiter looked over his partner's shoulder.

"Sure, that's the guy who bothered hell out of us all day yesterday. How could we forget him?"

"Do you remember what time he first came in?"

"Well, that's hard to say. He's not a regular. But I remember around ten o'clock this guy was all steamed up about something. He couldn't sit still. He came to the bar and asked for a slug of white. He gulped it down, paid, and went out. Ten minutes later he was back, sitting at a table, yelling for another slug of white."

"So he was in here all day?"

"I think so. Anyhow I saw him at least ten or fifteen times. He kept getting more and more jittery. He had a funny way of looking at you, and his hands trembled when he handed you the money. Like an old woman's. Didn't he break a glass on you, Louis?"

"He did. And he insisted on picking all the pieces out of the sawdust himself. He'd say, 'It's white glass. That's good luck. And do I need good luck, especially today. You ever been in the Gabon, lad?' he'd keep asking."

"He talked to me about the Gabon, too," said the other waiter. "He was eating hard-boiled eggs. He'd eaten twelve or thirteen in a row, and I thought he was going to bust, particularly as he'd had quite a lot to drink. So he said to me, 'Don't be afraid, lad. One time in the Gabon I made a bet I could swallow three dozen, with thirty-six beers along with the eggs, and I won.'"

"Did he seem preoccupied?" Maigret asked.

"Depends on what you mean by that. He kept going out and coming back. I thought he was waiting for somebody. Sometimes I caught him laughing all by himself, like he'd been telling himself jokes. And once he cornered an old man who comes in every afternoon for two-three slugs of red, a nice old man. He grabbed the old man's lapels and talked his ear off for an hour."

"Did you know he was armed?"

"How could I know that?"

"Because a man of this type is apt to show off his revolver in a bar."

It was indeed a revolver. The police had found it on the sidewalk beside the body. It was a large-caliber gun, loaded, but unfired.

"Let's have more of that white wine."

Maigret was in such high spirits that he could not resist the solicitations of a barefooted flower girl who came in at that moment. She was a skinny, dirty little elf with the most beautiful eyes in the world. Impulsively he bought a bouquet of violets which he then did not know what to do with, so he stuffed it into his coat pocket.

It must be said that this was a day for white wine. A little later Maigret and Janvier crossed the street and entered the savory gloom of the Cafe des Ministeres. Joseph rushed to meet them.

Here they tried to straighten out the blurred portrait of the man with the little valise and the blue-black mustache. Or perhaps "blurred" is not the word. The picture was rather one in which either the subject or the camera had moved, or had been developed from a film with double or triple exposure.

No two descriptions matched. Everyone saw the stranger in a different light. And now there was even one witness—the Colonel—who swore that the minute he saw the man he was sure he was up to no good.

Some remembered the man as terribly nervous, others as amazingly calm. Maigret listened to them all, nodding, stuffing his pipe with a meticulous forefinger, lighting it with great care, smoking with little puffs, narrowing his eyes like a man enjoying a wonderful day—a day on which heaven, in a fit of good humor, had decided to be generous to all mankind.

"About this woman—"

"You mean the girl?"

Joseph, who had only caught a glimpse of her, was convinced it was a girl—a pretty girl, distinguished and obviously of good family. He was sure she did not work for a living. He imagined her in comfortable bourgeois surroundings, baking pastry or making genteel desserts for her family.

Mademoiselle Berthe, on the other hand, had doubts.

"I for one," the cashier said, "would hesitate to give her absolution without confession. However, I do admit that she seemed a lot more decent than the man."

There were moments when Maigret wanted to yawn and stretch himself, as though he were in the country, laying in the sun. That morning he found life enchanting at the corner of the Boulevard Saint-Germain and the Rue des Saints-Peres. He was fascinated by the bus stopping and starting, by the passengers climbing aboard, by the ritual gesture of the conductor reaching for the bell. And what could be more lovely than the moving shadow patterns on the sidewalk, the leafy tapestry of the chestnut trees?

"I'll wager he hasn't gone very far," Maigret grumbled to Janvier, who was still vexed at not being able to give a more exact description of the man, after having looked him right in the face.

The two detectives left the cafe and paused a moment at the curb, staring at the bar across the street. Two men, two bars, one for each. It would appear that Fate had planted each man in his proper atmosphere: in one the calm man with the little mustache, the man who could sit all day without moving, who could live on coffee and soda, who did not even protest when Joseph told him there was nothing to eat. And across the street, in the noise and confusion of little people, of the press of secretaries and workmen and delivery boys, in the mad rush of white wine and hard-boiled eggs, the man who was too excited to wait, who popped in and out, button-holing people to talk to them of the Gabon.

"I'll wager that there's a third cafe," said Maigret, staring across the boulevard.

In that he was wrong. True, there was across the street a window that commanded a view of both corners and a window that obviously belonged to a public place of some kind. But it was neither bar nor cafe. It was a restaurant called A l'Escargot.

The restaurant consisted of one long, low-ceilinged room which was reached by two steps down from the street level. It was obviously a restaurant with a regular clientele, for along the wall there was a row of pigeonholes in which the diners could leave their napkins. The pleasant garlicky aroma of good cooking permeated the place. It was the proprietress herself who emerged from the kitchen to greet them.

"What is it, *messieurs?*"

Maigret identified himself. He then said, "I'd like to know if you had a customer here last night who lingered over his dinner much longer than is usual in your restaurant."

The woman hesitated. There was no one in the dining room. The tables were already set for lunch. At each place there were tiny decanters of red and white wine.

"I spend most of my time in the kitchen," she said. "My husband would know. He's usually at the cash desk, but he's out right now buying fruit. Our waiter, Francois, doesn't come on until eleven, but he won't be long now. May I serve you something while you're waiting? We have a little Corsican wine which you might like. My husband has it shipped direct."

Everybody was charming this fine spring day. The little Corsican wine was charming, too. And the low-ceilinged dining room where the two detectives waited for Francois was delightful. They watched the parade of pedestrians and the two cafes across the boulevard.

"You have an idea, Chief?"

"I've got several. But which is the right one, that's the question."

Francois arrived. He was a white-thatched old man who

would never be taken for anything but a restaurant waiter. He backed halfway into a closet to change his clothes.

"Tell me, waiter. Do you remember a diner last night who acted rather strangely? A girl with dark hair?"

"A lady," Francois corrected. "Anyhow, I noticed she wore a wedding ring, a red-gold band. I noticed it because my wife and I wear red-gold wedding rings, too. Look."

"Was she young?"

"I'd say about thirty. Quite a proper person, well spoken, with almost no makeup."

"What time did she come in?"

"At quarter-past six just as I finished setting the tables for dinner. Our regular clientele hardly ever gets here before seven. She seemed surprised by the empty room and started to turn around. 'Do you want dinner?" I asked, because sometimes people come in by mistake, thinking this is a cafe. 'Come in,' I said. 'I can serve you dinner in about fifteen minutes. Would you like something to drink while you're waiting?' And she ordered a glass of port."

Maigret and Janvier exchanged satisfied glances.

"She sat down near the window. I had to ask her to move because she was sitting at the table of the gentlemen from the Registry Office. They've been coming here regularly for ten years and they don't like to sit at any other table . . . Actually, she had to wait nearly half an hour because the snails were not ready. She wasn't impatient, though. I brought her a newspaper, but she didn't read it. She just sat quietly and looked out the window."

Just like the man with the blue-black mustache. A calm man and a calm woman. And at the other corner a madcap with nerves as taut as violin strings. Only at this point in the drama it was the madcap who had a rubber stamp in his pocket with the threat: *I'LL GET YOU YET.*

And it was the madcap who had died without firing his gun.

"A very gentle woman," Francois was saying. "I thought she must be somebody from the neighborhood who had forgotten her key and was waiting for her husband to come home. That happens oftener than people think, you know."

"Did she eat with good appetite?"

"Let me see . . . A dozen snails . . . Then some sweet-breads, some cheese, and some strawberries and cream. I remember because those dishes all cost extra on the menu. She drank a small carafe of white wine and then a cup of coffee.

"She stayed quite late. That's what made me think she was waiting for somebody. She wasn't quite the last to leave, but there were only two other people here when she asked for her check. It must have been after ten o'clock. We usually close at ten thirty."

"Do you know which direction she took when she left?"

"I hope you gentlemen don't mean any harm to this lady?"

The old waiter seemed to have an affection for his one-night customer. "Good. So then I can tell you that when I left here myself at quarter to eleven, I was surprised to see her across the street, standing near a tree. Look, it was the second tree to the left of the lamppost."

"Was she still waiting for someone?"

"She must have been. She's not the sort you're thinking of. When she saw me, she turned her head away, as if she was embarrassed."

"Tell me, waiter, did she have a handbag?"

"Of course."

"Was it big? Small? Did you see her open it?"

"Just a moment . . . No, she didn't open it. She put it on the window sill next to her table. It was a dark leather, rectangular, fairly large. It had a big letter on it—an *M*, I think, in silver or some other metal."

"Well, Janvier, old man?"

"Well, Chief?"

If they drank many more of these little glasses here and there, they would end up this fine spring day by acting like a couple of schoolboys on vacation.

"Do you think she killed him?"

"We know he was killed from behind, at not more than ten feet."

"But the man in the Cafe des Ministeres could have—"

"Just a moment, Janvier. Which of these two men was going to attack the other?"

"The dead man."

"Who was not yet dead, but who was certainly armed. So he was the menace, the ambusher. He was a threat to the other. Under these conditions, unless he was dead drunk by midnight, it is unlikely that the other could have surprised *him* and shot *him* from behind on emerging from the Cafe des Ministeres, especially at such short range. On the other hand, the woman—"

"What do we do now?"

If Maigret followed his inclination, they would have loitered a while longer in the neighborhood. He liked the atmosphere. He would go back for another white wine with Joseph. Then back to the bar across the street. Sniff around. Drink a little more wine. Play different variations on the same theme: a man with a waxed mustache here; a man across the street, rotten with fever and alcohol; and finally a woman so respectable looking that she had conquered the heart of old Francois, eating snails, sweetbreads, and strawberries and cream.

"I'll wager she's used to simple family cooking and eats out very rarely," said Maigret.

"Why do you say that, Chief?"

"The menu. She ordered three dishes that cost more than the regular dinner. People who eat out regularly don't do that, particularly two of the dishes which you rarely get at home—snails and sweetbreads. The two don't go together. The fact that she ordered them indicates she is something of a gourmand."

"You think a woman about to commit murder gives much thought to what she's eating?"

"First of all, my dear Janvier, we know nothing that *proves* she was going to kill anyone last night."

"If she did kill him, she must have been armed. Right? I got the drift of your questions about the handbag. I was waiting for you to ask the waiter if he thought it might be heavy."

126

"Second," Maigret went on, ignoring the interruption, "even the most poignant tragedy will not make most human beings unaware of what they are eating. You must have seen it as clearly as I have. Somebody is dead. The house is upside down. The place is filled with tears and wailing. Life will never resume its normal rhythm. Then somebody comes in to fix dinner—an old aunt, a neighbor, a neighbor's maid. 'I couldn't swallow a mouthful,' the widow swears. Everybody coaxes her. They make her sit down to the table. The whole family abandons the corpse and sits down with her. After a minute everybody is eating with gusto. And the widow is asking for the salt and pepper because the ragout needs seasoning . . . Let's go, my dear Janvier."

"Where to, Chief?"

"To Juvisy."

They really should have caught a suburban train at the Gare de Lyon, but Maigret was horrified at the thought of ending a perfect spring day by fighting crowds of commuters at the ticket windows and on the platforms, ending up either in a No Smoking compartment or standing in the corridor. So, refusing to envisage what the auditor at Police Judiciare might say about his expense account, Maigret hailed a taxi—an open car, almost brand-new—and spread himself luxuriously on the cushions.

"Juvisy," he told the driver. "Drop us across from the railway station."

He half closed his eyes and spent the journey in a delicious trance, only the trail of smoke from his pipe indicating that he was not asleep.

For a long time, whenever he was asked to tell the story of one of his most famous cases, Inspector Maigret used to describe some investigation in which his stubborn persistence, his intuition and his sense of human values literally forced the truth to surface.

Nowadays, however, the story he likes to tell is the case of the two cafes in the Boulevard Saint-Germain, even though his own part in it was a rather slim one. And when he finishes with a satisfied smile that is almost a smacking of the lips, someone inevitably asks, "But what is the true story?"

Maigret smiles even more and says, "It's up to you. Pick the one you like best."

For on at least one point the whole truth was never discovered by Maigret or by anyone else.

It was half-past twelve when the taxi dropped the two Inspectors opposite the suburban railway station of Juvisy. The detectives first entered the Restaurant du Triage, an undistinguished oasis with a terrace surrounded by bay trees in green tubs. They exchanged questioning glances. Could they enter a cafe—especially today—without taking a drink? Maigret shrugged. Inasmuch as they had devoted themselves so far to white wine, like the dead man of the Rue des Saints-Peres, they might as well continue.

Maigret produced his retouched photograph of the cadaver and showed it to the prizefighter-looking man who was operating behind the zinc bar.

"Tell me, *patron*," he said, "do you recognize this face?"

The man behind the bar held the picture at arm's length and squinted at it, as if he were farsighted.

"Julie, come here a minute," he called. "Isn't this the bird from next door?"

His wife came in, wiping her hands on her blue-denim apron. She took the photograph gingerly in her fingers.

"Why, sure it is!" she exclaimed "But he has a funny expression in this picture, hasn't he?" Turning to Maigret she added, "Probably stiff again. He's a great drinker. Just last night he kept us up past eleven o'clock, tossing them off."

"Last night?" Maigret was startled.

"No, wait a minute. It must have been the night before last. Yesterday I did my washing and last night I went to the movies."

"Can we have lunch here?"

"Sure you can have lunch. What do you want to eat? Veal fricandeau? Roast pork with lentils? And you can start with a good homemade pate."

They ate outside on the terrace, next to the taxi driver they had asked to wait. From time to time the tavern-keeper came out to talk to them.

"My neighbor next door can tell you a lot more than I can," he said. "He rents rooms. We don't. Your man has been staying there for the last month or two. When it comes to drinking, though, he drinks all over town. Why, just yesterday morning—"

"Are you sure it was yesterday?"

"Positive. I was just opening up at six thirty when he came in. He tossed off two or three glasses of white wine. 'To kill the worms,' he said. Then all of a sudden he grabbed his raincoat and ran for the station. The Paris train was just leaving."

The tavern-keeper knew nothing about the man except that he drank a lot of wine, that he talked about the Gabon with or without the slightest provocation, that he was contemptuous of anyone who had not lived in Africa, and that he bore a bitter grudge against somebody. Who? The tavern-keeper didn't know, but he repeated a speech the man with the raincoat had once made:

"Some people think they are very clever, but they're not clever enough. I'll get them in the end. Sure, anybody can be a skunk at times, but there's a limit on how much of a skunk a man can be."

Half an hour later Janvier and Maigret were talking to the proprietor of the Hotel de Chemin de Fer. It looked exactly like the place next door except that there were no bay trees around the terrace and the chairs were painted red, not green.

The proprietor had been behind the bar when they came in, reading a newspaper aloud to his wife and his waiter. When Maigret saw the likeness of the dead man on page one, he knew that the first editions of the evening papers had reached Juvisy. He himself had sent the photographs to the press.

"That your tenant?" Maigret asked.

The proprietor darted a suspicious glance. He put down the paper.

"Yes. So?"

"Nothing. I just wanted to know if he was your tenant."

"Good riddance, in any case."

Maigret hesitated. They were going to have to drink something again and it was too soon after lunch to drink any more white wine.

"Calvados," he ordered. "Two."

"You from the police?"

"Yes."

"I thought so. Your face is familiar. So?"

"I'm asking you what you think of the murder."

"I would have thought that he was the one to shoot somebody else, not to get shot himself. Although it wouldn't have surprised me if he'd got his face kicked in. He was impossible when he was drunk, and he was drunk every night."

"Do you have his registration blank?"

With great dignity, to show that he had nothing to hide, the proprietor went for his register which he offered to Inspector Maigret with just a touch of contempt. The entry read:

Ernest Combarieu. Age 47. Born at Marsily, La Rochelle arrondissement (Charente-Maritime). Occupation: wood cutter. Coming from: Libreville, French Equatorial Africa.

"I hear he stayed with you for six weeks."

"Six weeks too long."

"Didn't he pay his bill?"

"He paid regularly every week. But he was a lunatic—stark crazy. He used to stay in bed with the fever two or three days at a time, and he'd order rum sent up to cure him. He drank the rum right out of the bottle. Then he'd get up and make the rounds of every bistro in town. Sometimes he'd forget to come home, sometimes he'd wake us up at three o'clock in the morning to let him in. Sometimes I had to undress him and put him to bed. He used to vomit on the stairway carpet or on the rug in his room."

"Did he have any family here in town?"

Husband and wife looked at each other.

"He knew somebody here, that's certain. If it was a relative, our friend didn't like him, I can guarantee you that. He used to say to me, 'One of these days you're going to hear news about me and a scoundrel who everybody thinks is an honest man, but who is really a dirty hypocrite and the worst thief in the world.'"

"You never knew which man he was talking about?"

"All I know is that our tenant was unbearable and that when he was drunk he had the crazy habit of pulling out a big revolver, aiming across the room, and shouting, 'Bang! Bang!' Then he would burst out laughing and order another drink."

"You'll have a little drink with us, won't you?" said Maigret. "One more question. Do you know a gentleman in Juvisy who is medium height, plump but not fat, with a fine turned-up black mustache and who sometimes carries a small valise?"

The proprietor turned to his wife. "That mean anything to you, *bobonne?*"

The woman shook her head slowly. "No . . . Unless— No, he's shorter than medium and I never thought of him as plump."

"Who is this?"

"Monsieur Auger. He lives in a villa in the new subdivision."

"Is he married?"

"Oh, yes, to a very nice wife. Madame Auger is very pretty, very sweet—a homebody who almost never leaves Juvisy. *Tiens!* That reminds me—"

The three men looked at her expectantly.

"Yesterday while I was doing my laundry in the yard, I saw her walking toward the railway station. She must have been taking the four thirty-seven for Paris."

"She has dark hair, hasn't she? And she carried a black leather handbag?"

"I can't tell you the color of her handbag but she was

wearing a blue tailleur and a white blouse."

"What does Monsieur Auger do for a living?"

This time the woman turned to her husband.

"He sells postage stamps," the landlord said. "You've seen his name in the classified ads—*Stamps for Collectors*. An envelope of a thousand foreign stamps for so many francs. Five hundred assorted for so much. A mail-order business, C.O.D."

"Does he travel much?"

"He goes to Paris from time to time. On stamp business, I suppose. He always carried his little valise. Two or three times when his train was late he stopped in here for a cup of coffee or a split of Vichy."

It was too easy. This wasn't even an investigation any more. It was a day in the country, an outing enlivened by a laughing spring sun and an ever-increasing number of the cups that cheer. And yet Maigret's eyes sparkled as though he had already guessed that behind this apparently banal affair lay one of the most extraordinary human mysteries he had ever encountered in his long career.

They gave him the address of the Augers. The new subdivision was quite a distance away, near the Seine. Hundreds, perhaps thousands, of little villas had arisen there, each in its own little garden, some of stone, some of pink brick, others of blue or yellow stucco. The worst part of it was that the villas had names instead of numbers, and it took the two Inspectors a long time to find the villa *Mon Repos*.

The taxi rolled along new streets lined with half-finished sidewalks and newly planted trees as skinny as skeletons. Vacant lots separated many of the houses. They had to ask their way several times. After a number of wrong addresses, they finally reached their goal: a pink villa with a blood-red roof. A curtain in the corner window stirred slightly as Maigret and Janvier got out of the taxi. 'Should I wait outside, Chief?"

"Maybe you'd better. I don't expect any trouble, though. As long as there is somebody home."

He found the tiny bell-push in the too-new door. He heard

the ring inside. Then he heard other sounds—whispering, footsteps, a door closing.

At last the street door opened. Standing before Maigret was the young woman of the Cafe des Ministeres and the Escargot. She was wearing the same blue tailleur and white blouse she had worn the night before.

"I'm Inspector Maigret of the Police Judiciaire."

"I thought it might be the police. Come in."

He climbed a few steps. The stairway seemed to have just come from the carpenter's shop. So did all the woodwork. The plaster on the walls was scarcely dry.

"Come this way, please."

She signaled through a half-open door to someone Maigret could not see. Then she ushered the Inspector into the living room—the corner room with the curtains that had stirred a moment ago. There was a sofa with brightly colored silk cushions, books, bric-a-brac. On a coffee table there was the noon edition of a Paris newspaper with the dead man's photograph staring from the front page.

"Please sit down. Am I allowed to offer you something to drink?"

"Thank you, no."

"I should have suspected that it wasn't done. My husband will be here in a moment. You needn't worry. He won't try to run away. His conscience is clear. However, he has not been well all morning. We took the first train home today. He has a heart condition. He had a slight attack when we got home. He's up and dressed now, though. He's shaving."

Maigret nodded. He had heard the water running in the bathroom. The walls were not very thick in the new subdivision. He smiled at Madame Auger. She was quite pretty, in a wholesome, middle-class way. And she was quite calm.

"You must have guessed that I was the one who killed my brother-in-law," she said. "It was high time. If I had not killed him, my husband would be dead today. And after all, Raymond is worth a hundred Ernests."

"Raymond is your husband?"

"For the last eight years. We have nothing to hide, Monsieur l'Inspecteur. I know that we should have gone to the police with the whole story last night. Raymond wanted to do it, but I wouldn't let him. Because of his heart condition, I wanted him to get over the first shock before facing added complications. And I knew you would come here sooner or later."

"You mentioned your brother-in-law a moment ago. His name is different from your husband's."

"Combarieu was the husband of my sister Marthe. He used to be quite a nice fellow. Perhaps a little mad . . ."

"One moment. May I smoke?"

"Please do. My husband doesn't smoke because of his heart, but tobacco doesn't bother me a bit."

"Where were you born?"

"In Melun. We were sisters, Marthe and I, twin sisters. My name is Isabelle. We looked so much alike when we were tots that my parents—they're both dead now—used to put different colored ribbons in our hair so they could tell us apart. Sometimes we would play a joke on them and change the ribbons."

"Which one of you married first?"

"We were married the same day. Combarieu used to work at the Prefecture in Melun. Auger was an insurance broker. They knew each other because, as two bachelors, they used to eat in the same restaurant. My sister and I met them together. We even lived on the same street in Melun early in our marriage."

"During this time, Combarieu was still working at the Prefecture and your husband was still in the insurance business?"

"Yes. But Auger was already interested in philately. He started his own stamp collection for pleasure, but he realized that stamps could be a lucrative business."

"What about Combarieu?"

"He was ambitious. He was impatient, and he was always short of money. He met a man just back from the colonies who gave him the idea of going to Africa and making his fortune there. He wanted my sister to go with him, but she refused. She had heard that the climate was very unhealthy, particularly for women."

"So he went alone?"

"Yes. He was gone for two years. He came back with his pockets bulging with money. But he spent it faster than he had made it. He had already begun to drink. When he was in his cups he would proclaim to the world that my husband was a mouse instead of a man. A real man, he used to say, would not spend his life selling insurance or postage stamps."

"He went back to Africa?"

"Yes, but the second trip was less successful. His letters were as boastful as ever, but reading between the lines we could feel that things were not going too well for him. Then two winters ago my sister Marthe died of pneumonia. We wrote the bad news to her husband, who began drinking more than ever to drown his grief."

"A little later my husband and I moved here to Juvisy. For a long time we had been wanting to build our own home, and live closer to Paris. My husband had discovered he could make a comfortable living with his stamp business and had given up his insurance connections completely."

She spoke slowly, quietly, weighing every word. She seemed to be listening to the sounds from the bathroom.

"Five months ago my brother-in-law returned here without a word of warning." she continued. "Our doorbell rang one night and when I opened the door, there he was, weaving drunk. He gave me a funny look, and without even saying hello, how are you, he sneered and said, 'Just as I suspected.' "

"At that time I hadn't the slightest idea what he was talking about. He didn't look well, and from the way he was dressed, he didn't seem too prosperous. In other words, it was not the brilliant homecoming he had enjoyed before, even if he had not been so drunk."

"He came in and for a few minutes talked a lot of incoherent nonsense. Neither of us could make out what he meant.

Suddenly he got up and said to my husband, 'You're not only a scoundrel but you're the king of scoundrels. Admit it, now.' Without another word he left. We had no idea where he went."

"A few weeks later he returned, still drunk. He said to me, 'Well, well, my little Marthe.' 'You know very well I'm not Marthe,' I told him; 'I'm Isabelle.' He put on his best sneer. 'We'll see about that some day, won't we?' he said. 'As for your blackguard of a husband who sells postage stamps—' "

"I don't know if you understand what was happening, Monsieur l'Inspecteur, but we didn't at first. He wasn't crazy, exactly, although he certainly drank too much. But he had this fixed idea which we were slow to grasp. For weeks we didn't understand his threatening gestures, his sardonic smiles, his insinuations. Then my husband began to get threats by mail. Just one phrase: I'LL GET YOU YET."

"In a word," Maigret interrupted quietly, "your brother-in-law Combarieu for one reason or another got it into his head that his wife was still alive and that it was Auger's wife who had died of pneumonia."

It was a startling idea: twin sisters so alike that their parents had to dress them differently to tell them apart . . . Combarieu far away in darkest Africa, learning that his wife was dead . . . imagining on his return—correctly or not— that there had been a switch, that it was Isabelle who had died and that his own wife Marthe had taken her place in Auger's bed.

Maigret's eyes were half closed as he considered the situation.

"Life has been a nightmare for us these past months," Madame Auger continued. "The menacing letters became more frequent. Combarieu would stagger in here at all hours of the day and night, draw his revolver, point it at my husband, then put it away again and laugh. 'No, not yet,' he would sneer; 'It would be too good for you.' "

"Then he took a room here in town so that he could

torment us more often. He's as sly as a monkey, even when he's drunk. He knows very well what he is doing."

"He knew," Maigret corrected her.

"I'm sorry." She colored slightly. "You're right. He knew. And I don't think he was too anxious to get into trouble. That's why we felt fairly safe here. If he had killed Auger here in Juvisy, everybody would know that he was the murderer."

"My husband hardly dared leave the house. Yesterday, however, he simply had to go to Paris on business. I wanted to go along but he wouldn't hear of it. He took the first train out, the early express, hoping that Combarieu would still be sleeping off his wine and wouldn't see him leave, even though Combarieu had a room just opposite the railway station."

"He was wrong. In the afternoon he telephoned me to come to Paris and bring his pistol to a cafe in the Boulevard Saint-Germain."

"I could see that my husband had come to the end of his rope, that he wanted to settle things once and for all. He told me on the phone that he would not leave the cafe before closing time. I brought him his Browning. I also bought a revolver for myself. You must understand, Monsieur l'Inspecteur."

"I understand that you had made up your mind to shoot before your husband was shot. Right?"

"I swear to you that when I pressed the trigger, Combarieu was raising his gun to aim at my husband . . . That's all I have to say. I'll be glad to answer any questions you want to ask me."

"How is it that your handbag is still marked with the initial *M?*"

"Because the handbag used to belong to my sister. If Combarieu was right, if there really had been this switch he was talking about so much, don't you suppose I'd have made sure to change the initial?"

"In a word, you are enough in love with a man to—"

"I love my husband."

"I was going to say you are enough in love with a man, whether he is your husband or not, to—"

"But he *is* my husband!"

"You are enough in love with this man, meaning Auger, that you would commit murder to save his life or to prevent him from committing murder?"

"Yes," she said.

There was a faint noise at the door.

"Come in," she said.

At last Maigret cast eyes on the man who had been described so differently by so many witnesses—the man with the blue-black mustache, the patience of an angel, and the obstinacy of a mule. In his domestic setting, he was a great disappointment. After the young woman's declaration of love, the man impressed Maigret as despairingly commonplace, the very quintessence of mediocrity.

Auger looked about him uneasily.

The woman smiled and said, "Sit down. I've told the Inspector everything . . . *Your heart?*"

Auger poked vaguely at his chest and said, "Seems all right."

A jury in the Court of Assizes for the Department of the Seine found Madame Auger not guilty on grounds of legitimate self-defense.

Every time Maigret has told about the case, he has always concluded with an ironic: "And that's the whole story."

"Does that mean," someone would always ask, "that you have reservations?"

"It means nothing at all—except that it is not impossible for a very commonplace little man to inspire a very great love, a passion of heroic proportions, even if he has a weak heart and sells postage stamps for a living."

"What about Combarieu?"

"Well, what about him?"

"Was he crazy when he imagined that his wife was not dead at all but was passing herself off as Isabelle?"

Maigret would shrug and mockingly declaim: "A very great love! A grand passion!"

And sometimes when he was in particularly good humor, perhaps sipping some fine old Calvados that he had warmed gently by holding the inhaler between the palms of his hands, he would continue:

"Is it always the husband who inspires these great loves and mad passions? And don't sisters often have the grievous habit of swooning over the same man? Remember that Combarieu was far away . . ."

Then, puffing great clouds of smoke from his pipe, he would conclude:

"Too bad the parents were dead, so we couldn't question them about the twins who couldn't be told apart. Anyhow, it was a fine day—the most beautiful spring day I ever saw. And I doubt if I ever drank so much on any one case. If you catch Janvier in an unguarded moment, he might even tell you we were surprised to find ourselves singing duets in the taxi coming back to Paris. And Madame Maigret has always wondered why I had a bouquet of violets in my pocket when I got home . . . What a Jezebel, that Marthe! Excuse me, I mean, that Isabelle!"

Sergeant Vincente Lopez

THE MEXICAN DETECTIVE

THE HAIR OF THE WIDOW

Robert Somerlott

There have been but a few native Mexican detectives, and none who has been featured in a series of novels. Robert Somerlott's Sergeant Vincente Lopez has appeared only in short stories published in Ellery Queen's Mystery Magazine; *and D. L. Champion's Meriano Mercado appeared only in a series of novelettes in the pulp magazine* Dime Detective *in the 1940s. (Of native Latin American and South American detectives, only Robert L. Fish's Captain Jose da Silva of the Brazilian constabulary has had a major impact on crime fiction; he appears in a total of ten novels but no short stories.)*

"The Hair of the Widow," set in an isolated Mexican village, is the perfect ethnic detective story: not only is the sleuth himself an ethnic character, but all the other principals and *the crime are ethnic in origin. There is even a Mexican superstition, that of the* divina, *which may or may not play an important role in the story, depending on what you choose to believe . . .*

Robert Somerlott knows whereof he writes, having traveled extensively in Mexico and having lived in the village of San Miguel de Allende. He has published criminous short fiction in EQMM, Cosmopolitan, *and other publications. He is also the author of "Eskimo Pies," a short story which won an* Atlantic *award in 1965 and which was included in the annual* Best American Short Stories *of that year; and of several mainstream novels under his own name and pseudonyms, among them* The Flamingos *(1967),* The Inquisitor's House *(1968), and the recent* Blaze.

. . .

Primitivo, the goatherd, lied to his wife and father that morning. He told them he was going up the mountain to search for a lost ram. The truth was that Primitivo wanted to find a secluded place where he could play with his yoyo.

The yoyo was a beautiful and fascinating object. Pierced with tiny holes, it whistled, giving forth wonderful, ear-puncturing squeals. But every time Primitivo took the yoyo from his pocket, his father would shout, "Out of my sight with your *gringo* extravagances! Wastrel! Playboy!"

Primitivo's wife wept at the idea of her husband's venturing up the mountain. "Bandits!" she cried. "You will be carried off. Only four days ago they seized Don Gregorio Martinez. Think of your children!"

"Go ahead," said Primitivo's father. "What would bandits want with you?"

"Nothing," said Primitivo innocently.

The barranca-slashed mountain towered over Tlaxtalapan, sealing the village off from the outside world. Its lower slope bristled with cactus and maguey, which slowly gave way to pinyon trees. Above these rose the cloud forest of 200-foot trunks whose branches disappeared into a perpetual mist.

After climbing for an hour, Primitivo sat on a fallen tree munching tortillas and cabbage. From here he could see far beyond Tlaxtalapan—almost to the town of Nexcotela where there was a post office and even telephone wires that stretched all the way to Guadalajara. Primitivo was utterly alone except for *Zopilote*, the vulture, who soared in narrowing circles above the pinyon trees.

141

It suddenly occurred to Primitivo that perhaps *Zopilote* had found the remains of the lost ram, which had probably been seized by a puma. Tucking the cabbage into the pocket of his bloomer-like trousers, Primitivo made his way across a gully toward the center of the vulture's circle. There the goatherd came upon a sight he would one day describe to his grandchildren.

In a clearing the naked body of a dead man was tied spread-eagled to a kapok tree. Primitivo stood transfixed by the horror of the blueish face. It took him a full minute to recognize the corpse.

With a wild yell Primitivo stumbled down the mountainside. Horrible! Don Gregorio Martinez, the richest man in Tlaxtalapan, coming to such an end! He would tell the police. He would tell everybody in the village!

Then in midst of his fright a wonderful thought struck Primitivo. Perhaps the police would take him to Nexcotela and he could repeat his story to important officials—speaking over the telephone wires that stretched all the way to Guadalajara.

Detective Sergeant Vincente Lopez of the Jalisco State Police sat uncertainly on a carved Spanish chair in the late Don Gregorio's house, wondering if its spindly legs would support his six-foot, 190-pound frame. The woven shutters darkened the room and muffled the wailing of mourners who were now in the 27th hour of their wake. Even at nine o'clock in the morning, the heat was stifling in the closed room.

Lopez blew a gust of air through his mighty mustachios, and mopped his brown forehead with a polka-dot handkerchief. How, he wondered, could the black-clothed woman sitting opposite him manage to look so cool and self-possessed?

"Now, señora," he said, "if you will tell me the whole story once more."

The widow's thin eyebrows lifted in undisguised contempt. "I have told you twice," she said. "Last night when you arrived in the village and again just now. That should be enough even for a policeman!"

Lopez controlled his temper. "Once more, señora."

The woman shrugged. "A week ago, in the night, there was knocking on our door. Everyone was asleep, so I went into the patio and asked who was there. A voice said, 'The police!'

" 'What police?' I asked.

" 'Fernando Bernal.' "

The widow's hands tensed, her knuckles turning to white spots. "I believed it was Fernando Bernal, Chief of the village police. So I unbarred the door. Two men plunged into the patio, carrying pistols and machetes. They seized me, dragging me to the bedroom where they woke my husband, slashing his face with a pistol barrel. I was tied to the bed, and rags were stuffed in my mouth. They forced my husband to go with them, prodding him with the point of a machete. An hour later I loosened the ropes and woke the servants who sleep at the rear of the house."

"Then you told the village police?"

She nodded. "Don Fernando Bernal was furious that a *bandito* should imitate his voice. But he would not go up the mountain at night—and who can blame him? Then a rock was thrown over our wall with a letter from my husband. The men demanded one hundred thousand pesos for his freedom."

One hundred thousand pesos! $8000, American. There was not so much money in the entire village of Tlaxtalapan.

"I gathered what pesos we had. I sold my earrings and my husband's horse. The next day I left nearly twelve thousand pesos under a rock, on the mountain. But did my husband come home?" The widow rose from her chair, pale eyes flashing. "At sunset he goes to the graveyard! May Jesus, Mary, and Joseph forgive my thoughts of vengeance."

The woman's thin nose and flaring nostrils revealed a strong strain of Spanish blood, unusual in this part of Mexico. A tiger, thought Lopez. Fiercer than any puma that stalked the mountain jungle. She stood tall and straight, her braided hair coiled high on her head.

"Everyone knows it was the Talamantes brothers," she said, spitting out the words. "They wore scarfs but I recognized them. They left Tlaxtalapan a year ago to live like mountain hawks."

She stepped close to Lopez, her voice shaking, her eyes dilated with hatred. "They have killed at least three men this year. The village police can do nothing. Detectives from Guadalajara have come and gone. Now the killers' hands drip with my husband's blood. And you, *Sargento,* like the others, will do nothing!"

Lopez stood up. "I will capture these murderers," he said.

"How?" The widow's voice brimmed with contempt. "Will you lead an army up the mountain? Or perhaps you will invite them to the village for a fiesta?" She sank into a chair, suddenly weary. "You talk bravely, *Sargento,* but you are a fool. Leave me to my prayers."

Lopez strode to the door. "Your grief has deranged your courtesy, señora!"

He clapped his sombrero on his head at a proud angle and marched through the cobblestone patio into the street. Leaning against an adobe wall, Lopez stared glumly at the vast slopes of the mountain. The widow, he thought bitterly, was right. How many men would be needed to comb that wilderness? A hundred? A thousand? And behind this mountain the whole range of the Sierra Madre Occidentals stretched for 200 miles. Hopeless!

As he walked toward the village police station, Lopez could almost feel the fierce glare of Captain Valles, who had sent him on this futile mission. The savage old captain, whose eyebrows grew so close that you couldn't put a thorn between them, had summoned Lopez to his office the previous morning.

"Get to the bottom of this scorpion's nest in Tlaxtalapan!" the Captain had shouted, pounding his desk. "Three citizens have been kidnaped and murdered in the past year."

No, Lopez could not borrow an official jeep to navigate the nearly impassable road to the village; his own Ford would do perfectly well. No, he could not have four men to help. "Call a few soldiers from Nexcotela if you need them," snarled the Captain. "And do better than you did in that affair of the three stolen burros last month, or you'll find yourself back where you were thirty years ago—guarding parked cars!"

Lopez was a married man with eleven children to support, and Captain Valles did not threaten idly. "Go to Tlaxtalapan!" said Valles. "Maybe this case will be more your style. Send an Indian to catch an Indian!"

Lopez sighed, his mustaches trembling. The Captain was a man of his word, and after eighteen hours in this village Lopez could see failure looming on the horizon like a black cloud.

The mud-walled police station squatted on a corner of the plaza. Although it was four hours before siesta, Chief Fernando Bernal was already asleep on the sunny steps, his great stomach heaving up and down like a hill in an earthquake. Lopez poked Don Fernando with the pointed toe of his boot, and the Chief opened a foggy eye.

"*Cómo esta?*" said Don Fernando, yawning. "How goes the investigation?"

"*Regular.*"

The Chief struggled to his feet.

"The papers to permit the burial await your signature," he said. "The relatives are anxious to end the wake. They have been wailing since yesterday morning. The women are tired, and the men are too drunk to go on much longer."

Lopez accompanied Don Fernando to a dark office where the air was rank with stale tequila and rotting limes. "The widow's story is unchanged," said Lopez, signing the release. "She opened the door thinking it was you."

"*Tragico!*" The Chief's jowls trembled. "It was bad enough when we just had bandits. Now they have become actors. *Que cosa!*" Leaning close to Lopez, Don Fernando spoke in a whisper. Lopez' nose wrinkled at the odor of tequila and garlic. "*Sargento,* I trust you did not remain in the room with the corpse?"

"A moment only. Why?"

"There are no onions!"

145

"What?"

"Under the coffin! There is no bowl of vinegar and onions. The widow has not placed them there. If the mourners catch cancer from the corpse it will be her fault. When I saw there were no onions, I ran out as though the devil had pinched me!"

"Very wise." Lopez headed for the door. The stench in the Chief's office was affecting his digestion.

Lopez strolled across the neglected plaza. Vinegar and onions! Memories of his childhood, of the village where he was born, came back to him. During his thirty years in Guadalajara, he had almost forgotten the ancient superstitions. Yet here, only sixty miles from the great city, the old beliefs lived on. To these people, devils and ghosts prowled the streets at night just as surely as pigs rutted in the plaza by day.

Lopez glanced at the crumbling walls of the church, built by the Spaniards two centuries ago, big enough to hold twice the population of the village. The massive doors were closed. There was no longer a padre in the town, but three times a year a priest came from Nexcotela to perform baptisms and solemnize marriages that had been consummated weeks or months before.

A block past the church the Señora Talamantes hunched in the doorway of a tumbledown house, a yellow cigarette clamped in her toothless gums.

"*Buenos dias,*" said Lopez, doffing his sombrero. The woman spat on the doorsill, the cigarette dangling precariously from her wet lips.

"You are the detective from Guadalajara," she said. "If you have come to ask about my sons, save your breath. Perhaps they are on the mountain—perhaps in hell. The whole village says they killed Don Gregorio, and I believe it."

"Why, señora?"

The woman spat again. "They were born with the devil's mark. The eldest was conceived in the dark of the moon— a time when God-fearing husbands let their wives alone.

146

The youngest was cursed by the priest for hiding idols in the church behind the statue of blessed St. Anthony."

"Have you seen them recently, señora?"

"Not since they fled to the mountain." The woman hurled her cigarette into the gutter. "They follow the devil's path, praying to the monkey-god, casting spells with goat's blood. Their mother's curse on them!"

There was nothing to be gained here. Lopez looked at the sun and reset his watch. It was noon. Time to go to the plaza for Coca-Cola.

The sidewalk café was empty except for a shirtless waiter and Primitivo, the goatherd, who sat dejectedly on the curb.

"Buenos dias," said the goatherd. "You are about to catch the bandits, no?"

"Who knows?"

Primitivo stared greedily at the Coca-Cola which the waiter placed in front of Lopez, his tongue running over his dry lips. "Two Cokes," said the sergeant.

"I, too, am faced with a mystery," said Primitivo. "A thief has stolen my yoyo."

"Madre de dios!" sighed Lopez.

"Last night I went to the cantina for a small glass. Afterwards, in the street, I felt the need of a short nap. This morning my yoyo was gone from my pocket."

"It is a local matter," said Lopez. "Don Fernando will investigate for you."

Primitivo looked doubtful. "There is a woman in the village called Doña Dolores," he said. "She has the second sight. A *divina*. If your Excellency would lend me two pesos, she would reveal the name of the thief to me."

Lopez stared fiercely at Primitivo. "Superstitious nonsense!" he said. "Useless!"

"Very true, your Excellency," agreed Primitivo. "But if you would lend me two small pesos . . ."

Lopez slapped the coins on the table. "Go with God," he said.

Primitivo leaped to his feet. *"Mil gracias!"* Running from the café, he turned at the first corner, racing toward the house of Doña Dolores, the witch who could locate missing keys, stolen chickens, and even tell you where to dig for water.

Lopez hissed sharply and the waiter brought him another Coca-Cola. The detective's eyes wandered to the distant mountain. How had the Talamantes brothers survived there? They had not stolen food from Don Gregorio's kitchen. Lopez drummed his heavy fingers on the table. Obviously the bandits were supplied from the village.

Leaving the restaurant, he walked slowly around the dusty plaza. He hesitated in front of the police station, inspecting the snoring Chief who was again stretched out on the steps. Lopez looked thoughtfully at Don Fernando's tooled leather boots and the ornate holster which revealed a silver-handled pistol.

Lopez sat on the curb beside a sleeping burro and pounded his forehead. *Madre de dios!* Although he knew the names of the killers, he was no further ahead than he had been last night. Lopez flexed his mustachios in helpless rage. His mind was blank, except for Captain Valles' taunting words, "Send an Indian to catch an Indian."

At that moment a flop-eared goat wandered past. Lopez looked at the goat and thought of Primitivo. When he thought of Primitivo, he thought of Doña Dolores, the witch who answered all questions for two pesos. Getting up, Lopez started toward the *divina's* house, glancing around to make sure nobody was watching him.

The murky room was bare except for a low table that held two stone images and the blackened horns of a ram. Sitting cross-legged on the floor, Lopez looked into the sunken face of the one-eyed hag who knelt opposite him. Skeletal and hunchbacked, she was a true witch. She could have no other profession.

"I seek guidance, señora. I will pay you."

The *divina's* left eye flickered with suspicion. "Ten pesos," she said.

"Two."

"Seven."

"Three."

"Very well," said the woman. "Five pesos. What do you seek?"

"The slayers of Don Gregorio."

The woman was silent, then her twisted body began to sway back and forth, her lips forming words in the guttural tongue of the Tarascans, one spidery hand fluttering above the horns and *idolatos* on the table. "I see two brothers," she moaned.

"Are they alone, *divina?*"

Dona Dolores hesitated, her eye flickering, then spoke softly. "There is a third in the shadows. He speaks to a woman behind a door—"

"Who speaks, *divina?*"

With a cry the woman flung herself onto the table, her body trembling. "I have no more!" Slowly she rose, her eye fixed unblinkingly on Lopez. "Why should I tell the señor a name he knows already?"

Lopez nodded silently. "How should I capture these killers, *divina?*"

"In November," she whispered, "on the Day of the Dead, the ghost of Don Gregorio will return. Rub your eyes with water from the eyes of a dog. You will see the ghost, and the ghost will lead you to the murderers."

"The Day of the Dead is almost a year away. I cannot wait."

"There are other ways. The hair of the widow is powerful in such cases. Also, it is said that if the corpse is buried with his legs bound together, the slayers cannot run away."

Lopez stared thoughtfully at the stone idols on the table. "I have heard this, *divina*," he said. "But I had forgotten." Lopez stood up suddenly, thrusting his hand into his pocket. He gave the woman ten pesos. *Mil gracias, divina.*"

Lopez hurried to the house of Don Gregorio, and there had a short but important conversation with the widow. A few minutes later he found Chief Fernando Bernal sitting barefoot on the steps of the station while a small boy was polishing his boots.

"Don Gregorio's funeral will be held in an hour," the Chief told Lopez. "Will the sergeant accompany me?"

"I must return to Guadalajara at once. My work here is finished."

"Finished?" The Chief's eyebrows rose in doubt.

"I will tell Captain Valles that the killers are known, but there is no way to capture them until hunger drives them from the mountain. Then, doubtless, you will arrest them yourself, Don Fernando."

"Assuredly," said the Chief. "You have a keen mind, *Sargento. Adios.*"

"Hasta la vista," said Lopez.

Two hours later Lopez crouched in a thicket of *capa del pobre* and watched the black-clad funeral procession move slowly into the Tlaxtalapan graveyard, the coffin borne by Don Gregorio's four brothers. Two cows, grazing among the slanting headstones, scarcely looked up as the weeping crowd made its entrance.

The mourners gathered near the newly dug grave, Chief Fernando Bernal conspicuous in his city-bought suit. The widow was not there, of course. It was customary for the wife to wait at home. Afterward, relatives would run to her house to report the details of the burial.

Beads of perspiration formed on Lopez' forehead. He parted the great leaves slightly and peered toward the cemetery gate. Then he heaved a great sigh of relief as Don Gregorio's widow, accompanied by the hunchbacked *divina,* entered the graveyard, walking silently toward the cluster of mourners, who suddenly turned toward the two women in surprise and shock.

Lopez leaned forward, straining to hear, but there was no need, for the widow's voice was firm and clear.

"Open the coffin!" she commanded, and when Don Gregorio's astonished brothers did not move, she strode to the grave and flung back the wooden lid. Hobbling to her side, the *divina* pulled the black *rebozo* from the widow's head, and two heavy braids dropped below her waist. With a sharp knife the *divina* cut first one braid, then the other from the widow's head, while the villagers gaped in amazement.

Bending over the coffin, the *divina* bound the legs of the corpse with ropes of black hair.

"Now," cried the widow, "let him be put in the ground." Under her cold eyes the brothers closed the coffin and lowered it into the waiting grave. She lifted her cropped head toward the twilight sky. "They cannot escape now," she said. "Now vengeance will come."

"It is so," cried the *divina* hoarsely. "Let all men who have forgotten this now remember!"

As the earth was heaped upon Don Gregorio's coffin, spadeful by spadeful, the two women walked triumphantly down the path toward the village.

Lopez and four soldiers from Nexcotela drove the last six kilometers without headlights, twice nearly hitting cows that slept in the road. Mist obscured the thin new moon as Lopez parked the Ford. For ten minutes the men moved toward the graveyard.

"Now," whispered Lopez, when they reached the thicket of *capa del pobre,* "we will wait."

The soldiers were nervous as the mist crept among the stone crosses, creating a wavering world of smoke and darkness. When a stray burro wandered into the thicket, one soldier leaped to his feet. Lopez clapped a heavy hand over the man's mouth. *"Silencia!"*

As the clock in the village church tolled the twelve lonely strokes of *media noche,* Lopez saw the gleam of a shrouded lantern. A moment later there was the clink of a spade striking a headstone. Lopez slowly counted to 200, then gestured for the soldiers to follow him. They were twenty paces from the grave of Don Gregorio when the mist parted and the moon filled the cemetery with pale light.

"Aiyaah!" Lopez plunged forward. The soldiers' flashlights pierced the dimness and Lopez fired his pistol in the air. Three men stood paralyzed near the half-opened grave. Then one flung down his spade and turned to flee, but Lopez' powerful arm locked around his throat.

"Ah, Don Fernando," said Lopez. *"Buenas noches!"*

*　　*　　*

After the Talamantes brothers and Don Fernando were bound and put under guard in the Chief's own jail, Lopez went to the cantina to celebrate. The whole village awoke as word passed from door to door that the *banditos* had been captured while digging up the coffin of Don Gregorio to cut the menacing ropes from his legs.

The dead man's four brothers ran to the cantina, bringing bottles of *pulque*. They drank toasts to Lopez, to the Jalisco police, to the President, and finally to the Revolutions of 1839 and 1910.

As Lopez leaned against the bar, picturing the astonished look that would be on Captain Valles' face the next day, he heard a high-pitched, whistling noise. Primitivo stood in the doorway, proudly spinning his yoyo.

"Ah, my friend," said Lopez. "I see the *divina* located your treasure."

Primitivo smiled happily. "No, señor. On my way to her house I thought about what you said. So I took the two pesos and went to Nexcotela to buy another yoyo. You are right about the *divina*. It is superstitious nonsense and quite useless."

"Yes," Lopez, reaching for the *pulque* bottle. "Useless."

Primitivo's new yoyo whistled beautifully.

Poleon Baptiste

THE MÉTIS DETECTIVE

WHITE WATER

W. Ryerson Johnson

*The word "métis" means one of mixed blood, a half-breed—
in the case of Poleon Baptiste, the protagonist of "White
Water," a mix of French-Canadian and Cree Indian. The
métis of the Canadian frontier have appeared often in
"Northern" adventure novels, in particular those featuring
the Northwest Mounted Police; but seldom has one of their
number been made the hero of a story. Poleon is not strictly
a detective, not yet; rather, he is a woodsman whose driving
desire is to become an official tracker for the Mounted Police.
But he is made of the stuff of all great detectives, as we
think you'll agree when you read this suspenseful account
of his wilderness race with another métis, Andre, in pursuit
of a madman.*

"White Water" was first published in This Week Magazine *in 1941 and is the only story featuring Poleon. As
with other "one-shots" in this book, we wish there had been
a good many more.*

*Born in 1901, Walter Ryerson Johnson has had a remarka-
ble literary career that spans more than half a century.
He wrote scores of stories for the Western and adventure
pulps from the late 1920s to the late 1940s; he has con-*

153

*tributed adult and juvenile fiction and fact articles to a
wide variety of publications (including a recent story to*
Ellery Queen's Mystery Magazine); *and he has published
several novels, among them the criminous paperback origi-
nals* Naked in the Streets (*1952*), Lady in Dread (*1955*),
*and in collaboration with Davis Dresser (Brett Halliday),
under the pseudonym Matthew Blood,* The Avenger (*1952*)
and Death is a Lovely Dame (*1954*). *He currently divides
his time between Chicago and Maine, and is working on
several projects, one of them being his autobiography,* We
Don't Want It Good, We Want It Wednesday.

 •   •   •

A rocky island loomed through the world's-end mist, and
Poleon checked the forward sweep of his canoe. By straining
his eyes he could make out the warning words of the sign:
Beware This Fork—Rapides du Mort.

Poleon beached his canoe, stepped out, climbed to the
sign. His stubby hands gripped it strongly, shook, noted
with satisfaction that the post was firmly embedded in its
cairn of rocks. Andre, he mused, would have taunted him
for his caution, arguing the sign was put here by the
Mounted Police. The mounties do not blunder. Therefore,
the sign continues to remain firm at its base and to point
the correct way.

But in the woods Poleon took nothing on trust. Here,
where the waters parted, a man had to choose which fork
he would take, and choose well, or else dip his way to death.
It was not true, as Andre charged and as the Mounted Police
most likely supposed, that Poleon was a timid man. Cautious
only, and rightly so. The animals, big and little—consider
them. They tread stealthily through the woods, sniffing everything, looking everywhere, listening. And the most cautious lived the longest.

Back at the water's edge, Poleon stopped short. His eyes
had perceived some minute displacement of gravel not
made by his own moccasined feet. He looked further for
telltale signs which might show where a man had driven

a canoe ashore. He found no signs. For a moment he stared broodingly into the waist-deep water while the witch-wind of early morning breathed about him.

He returned to the signpost. Dropping on his knees, he started removing the cairn rocks. He had to lift only a few before he could see that the rock moss had been previously broken. Not longer than yesterday, because the day before there had been rain, and the rain would have settled the sand and silt in the crevices.

There was but one thing to suppose. The mad killer whom he tracked had changed the sign to point to the wrong fork, cunningly thinking to lure his pursuers into those rapids of death.

The hair tugged at its roots on the back of Poleon's thick neck as he contemplated his narrow escape. It was known that somewhere ahead the two forks of this river joined again. It was said that the waters mated in black pools overlaid with lily pads and white lily flowers. Funeral flowers. From the time of the first fur *voyageurs* into this great lone land, no man had taken his canoe through the white-water gorge and lived to boast about it. For if by a miracle he escaped the grinding death of the rapids, he met death in the overfalls, a drop, it was said, the height of a valley spruce.

Poleon went swiftly to work again. If the madman had changed the sign to point down the wrong fork, the thing to do was change it back so that Andre and all who might come carelessly after him would not be guided down the wrong waterway.

Afloat again, Poleon paddled strongly to make up for his loss of time. It was Poleon's self-appointed chore to track down this madman, to apprehend him before Andre could. Yes, and to apprehend him before the Mounted Police could, to prove to those police that Poleon was—to use their quaint phrasing—a stout fellow, worthy of the job of tracker for the Fort Endurance post.

Almost since Poleon had been old enough to wrap chubby fingers around a brass button, wide eyes blinking at the scarlet uniform, it had been his unswerving ambition to become a tracker for the Mounted Police.

But they were so blind, these mounties. For their tracker they preferred a big man who, by making faces, could scare babies; one whose talk had the empty bluster of the wind which swept down from the Barren Grounds; one so lacking in woods lore that he could not track a caribou through snow.

That was to say, the police preferred Andre. They were going to make him official tracker for the Fort Endurance post. They were, unless Poleon Baptiste could prove to them what a bold heart beat within his stumpy frame; what firmness, what resolution, what woods-cunning lay behind his mild eyes, his cherubic, smoked-wood face.

In contemplating the changed sign, Poleon remained charitable in his feelings toward the madman. Under the weight of northern solitudes he had known men to break before. Poor shake-brains, they but followed the dictates of phantom voices they alone could understand.

But if the madman had no murder in his heart, he had it in his hands. The unhappy creature had struck first in the Sweetgrass Hills, felling his brother with a broadax. Seventy miles away, on Running Wolf Creek, he had struck again, his rifle dropping an Indian lad who was fishing from his canoe. The madman had stolen the canoe and thereafter his gibbering laughter—and his callous rifle—had sounded on many waterways.

Too inept to hold to the mad killer's trail, Andre had followed Poleon, clinging to him like a shadow through all the Big Thunder land, into the valley of the Okopotowee, and now at last into this muskeg region of interlaced thickets and spider-webbed waterways so remote that half the streams had never been named.

That big one had even lolled in his canoe and made taunting remarks when Poleon, at the portages, drew up and laboriously searched the landwash for signs of the mad killer's passing. In the end, Poleon had been forced to make an "arrangement," sharing his campfire with Andre. *Waugh,* but the arrangement was one of a bitter taste! However, two campfires winking side by side through the night were a great stupidity, surely, doubling the amount of smoke and fire for a warning to the killer.

This morning Andre had not arisen to follow Poleon. That of itself was not strange; the trail was now so hot Andre could follow it alone. The puzzling thing was that now, with every minute counting, Andre had so placidly allowed Poleon to gain this head start.

Mile after mile, he swept along through the clearing mist, and gave himself up to exultation. But as time went on and the canoe of Andre did not appear in sight, a disturbing thought kept crowding in the back of his mind. The thought pushed and swelled, grew finally into a monstrous thing . . . and Poleon drove his canoe ashore on a pea-gravel bar and sat there trembling, his soul sick from a horrible knowledge.

In the first place, there were all the little things of last night at their camp just above the signpost island: Andre's unnatural manner, his curious nervousness, his so-mocking prediction that Poleon would never get the tracking job. But most of all there was the lie he had told about his wet clothes. He had fallen in the water, he said. But when a man falls in water, the water splashes. It does not wet him evenly all around as when he wades. Andre had been evenly wet to the waist—the depth of the water between shore and signpost island.

The absence of canoe marks on the gravelly landwash had troubled Poleon from the first, because had the madman landed on the island he would almost certainly have left them. Yes, the pattern of guilt was clear. Andre's incredible failure to roll from his blanket this morning was incredible no longer. That big one had stayed behind, feigning sleep, expecting Poleon to float to his death down the wrong waterway. It was not the madman, but Andre who had changed the sign . . .

There had been always in Andre a streak of ruthlessness.

He was a man who, when he could not get what he wanted in one way, got it in another . . . Well, his so-diabolical plan to win for himself the tracking job had failed. Because of this very caution which they called timidity, he, Poleon Baptiste, was still alive. Alive and leading the chase. Andre had defeated himself . . .

Why, Andre had *killed* himself!

But yes! He would come along in his canoe, that careless one. In the mist, he would see little of the river or the shore. He would seek out the sign only, the sign which he himself had made to point the wrong way. And he would let himself be guided by the sign, not knowing that Poleon had changed it back. He would float to eternal darkness in the white waters of the *Rapides du Mort.*

He would . . . unless—

The water boiled as Poleon dug his paddle deep, savagely swerving the canoe. He started paddling—upstream. Half-way back to the water's parting, the police canoes passed him, scudding fast. Those policemen waved a tolerant greeting.

The Sergeant Altward cupped a hand to his mouth and shouted, "What's your hurry going back, Poleon? The loony chasing you?"

Poleon could see the flash of their teeth when they laughed. It was nothing new for them to laugh. He kept paddling.

Poleon found Andre. He found him beside the wreck of his canoe, far down the route to the *Rapides du Mort.* At the last moment, quite obviously, the half-breed had become alarmed at the swiftness of the water, at the deepening of the gorge in which these fierce rapids roared.

He had landed in a panic, running ashore on a shelf of rock which had ripped the whole bottom from his canoe. Now he stood there, as helplessly marooned in this land of interlaced waterways as though he had been wrecked on a South Sea island.

Poleon headed in, made the landing safely. He eyed Andre impassively. "Tak' your paddle an' get in my canoe."

158

Wheedling words jammed from Andre's lips as he bent in fumbling haste for his paddle. "Togedder, you and me, Poleon, we will get thees mad killer. An' when we have got him I will say to the p'lice: It mak's all the credit to Poleon!"

Poleon stared blankly. "Get in the canoe, liar—liar and sign-changer."

Andre's face turned white as the underside of an aspen leaf. He got in the canoe. Poleon made no threatening move, and then Andre's confidence flowed back as he counseled himself that this stumpy little man was, after all, a rabbit.

Poleon, being lighter, took the forward seat. With a single sweep of his paddle he sent the canoe into the slick of the current—*heading downstream.* Above the roar of those rapids ahead, he heard Andre's voice, ugly with fear, "This way brings death!"

Andre tried desperately to sprag with the flat of his paddle. But they were in the full grip of the current now and there was no perceptible slackening in their speed. Andre half stood up. The canoe wobbled.

Poleon looked around. "Sit down." He grinned thinly. "We will catch the madman togedder, Andre, like you have said."

"You are the madman!" Andre screamed crouching. "This way you will catch nothing but death for us bot'."

"It mak's ver' possible, yes." Then Poleon explained patiently, as to a child: "If we are to catch the mad killer, this is our single chance. The red-coat p'lice are tracking too, have you forgotten that? If we are to beat them, we have no time to fight the current all the way back to the safe fork. A half day I have wasted already, returning for you. Sit down, Andre—"

"I will not sit down!"

Poleon lifted his paddle from the water, raised it high. Then Poleon, who shrank from clubbing the live mink in his trap, brought the paddle down in a hard, swift blow against Andre's head. The half-breed slumped, unconscious, in the bottom of the canoe.

The canoe rocked . . . but remained afloat. They were in white water now. The canoe dipped and leaped like a bucking horse. But Poleon held it under the mastery of his paddle, gripping the handle so hard that his knuckles appeared as white bumps in the brownness of his hands.

Deep in the gorge now the cliffs reared high, enclosing the noonday sun. The water in its swift flow made white patches as it broke with a sullen roar against fangs of rock.

With eyes slitted against the glare, Poleon crouched and worked as never before in his toilsome life, fighting the white water with a paddle that was bent sometimes almost to breaking as he drove now under the loom of the cliff wall so close that he raked it, now out in the middle, drenched with spray and swerving in the boil of the current to miss outcropping boulders.

Death! So close and so long. Life! So good and so short. Wild geese honking high; the sun on an otter skin; winter air tanged with wood smoke; summer air made crisp and heady from the smell of pines . . . It would be sad to leave all this.

But he need not. Very nearly he had run the whole gantlet of these death rocks, with but one more washboard rapids to be traversed—

He was in it! Dipping down, tipping . . . he was out of it! So fast, like the blinking of an eye. He had run the *Rapides du Mort* and he floated free! Life—it was in his two hands . . .

No! No it was not. It was still on the lap of the white water. Because ahead, around this cliff bend, remained the great falls.

Around the bend the canoe sped, the rail sucking water. And at once there was a quickening, a sickening forward lurch, as the craft was gripped from underneath and hurled ahead faster than it yet had gone. Here, as the walls narrowed down, squeezing the sun from the gorge, there was a curious half-hush, more frightful than the water's roar in the upper rapids. It made a pressure against the ears as dead ahead—terrifyingly near—the river poured into the sky.

At the very brink of the falls, two upthrust rocks met the rush of water, forcing it in a swelling mound between them. Poleon made his choice. Between these rocks he would go, as though with the canoe he were threading a giant needle. That much he could accomplish with the deft use of his two strong hands. After that, it was the hands of *le bon Dieu* which must direct.

Below this thunder water was the place where lily pads lay flat on still black pools. No water breaking in white flashes, but only the tranquil loveliness of white lily blooms. Perhaps the lilies would soon become funeral flowers.

It was at the same time a few short seconds and several billion years—then the canoe came pouring with the river into the sky.

He was an eagle soaring.

Then he was tilting down, down, down, in sparkling spume, with the bow of his canoe overshooting the water into the sun. Down and down—a screaming eagle—dropping from the top of the world into tall spruces . . .

Into rocks also. He could see now. Below, through this trough of white foaming hell, were black snags of rock. Ah, but between the rocks there must be water. And the canoe still sailed right-side-up. So why should he die? All those who had come before had died. But that was because the water ran higher or lower in the gorge, or because their canoes had struck rocks, or overturned in the eddies, or—

He was in it. Out of the air and into the water. Into the rocks and the roar. The spray beat overhead as in a solid wave. A whirlpool rapids seized the canoe, spun it— flung it clear to bob among the lily pads in the still black pools below. He could see the lilies. No, funeral flowers they were.

The next instant the waterlogged canoe turned over, as Andre, stirring back to consciousness, thrashed in uncalculated effort. They splashed ashore together, Poleon and the revived Andre, virtually into the arms of the Mounted Police.

There was the whole patrol, the Sergeant Altward and all. For once, those red-coat police were not glib with words. They stood in the willow scrub and stared in frank jaw-dropping wonder.

Against his wet clothes Andre's chest was swelling, and with the fast returning of his wits he was talking in his accustomed wide way:

"T'rough the rapids an' over the falls we came Thees wan—" His hand waved out toward Poleon—"he object. But I tell him: these red-coat p'lice are trail the mad killer also. If we are to beat them, we have no time to go by the safe route. We mus' tak' our chance in the *Rapides du Mort* w'ere nevair man before has gone an' lived."

Poleon stumped forward unsteadily on his short legs. "Listen to me w'at I say—" But he was so choked with water and outraged anger that the words caught in his throat.

Andre, who was always so quick with the right words, said, "Don' pay him some attention. He shake han's wit' the willows from w'ere I have to hit him on head wit' my paddle. In great fear, he refuse to run the rapids. I have much trouble wit' him, *oui*. He has delay me greatly."

Poleon ground his teeth. To have earned that tracking job, only to have Andre snatch it from him at this last moment—

But then the hard flat voice of the Sergeant Altward cut through his despair, as the sergeant questioned Andre.

"If Poleon is the coward as you say, and you had to hit him on the head with your paddle, then why is the bump on *your* head instead of Poleon's? Why did we meet Poleon going in the opposite direction on the other branch of the river this morning? Wasn't it because Poleon tossed away his lead in the chase to go back and rescue you when you blundered down the wrong fork of the river? Are you such a clumsy tracker, Andre, that you cannot see a signpost on an island?"

Andre hung his head and said nothing. Poleon couldn't understand at first. But after a moment he did. What *could* Andre say without revealing that he was not only a liar but a sign-changer?

The Sergeant Altward was talking again, looking at Poleon with a sober smile. "The madman's slipped us," he said. "Can you put us back on his trail?"

"By the whiskers of a green musk ox," Poleon sputtered, "I can!"

"You're hired," the sergeant said, "as tracker for the Fort Endurance post."

Poleon swallowed, gasped, drew himself up in the manner of a veritable Bonaparte. "Official?"

"Official," the sergeant assured him.

Fiercely, Poleon frowned. "I accept," he said grandiloquently.

THE JAPANESE DETECTIVE

INSPECTOR SAITO'S SMALL SATORI

Janwillem van de Wetering

*Until recent years, the only Japanese detective of conse-
quence was John P. Marquand's enigmatic and wily Mr.
Moto, hero of such novels as* Thank You, Mr. Moto *(1936)
and* Stopover: Tokyo *(1957) and several 1930s films starring (ironically enough) Hungarian-born Peter Lorre. But
with the surge of interest in detective stories in Japan during
the past ten years, a growing fraternity of Japanese writers
have been producing important crime fiction that is only
just now finding publishers and readers in the United
States. And in this country, American writers have also created Japanese detectives: Nan Hamilton (John Ball's wife)
with Japanese-American police lieutenant Sam Ohara; and
Janwillem van de Wetering with Inspector Saito, a native
Japanese whose only recorded cases appeared in* Alfred
Hitchcock's Mystery Magazine *in the late 1970s, under the
pseudonym Seiko Legru.*

*At first it might seem odd that a Dutch writer, creator
of Amsterdam policemen Adjutant Grijpstra and Serjeant
De Gier, should choose to write stories about a Japanese
sleuth. Van de Wetering, however, is a former disciple in
a Zen Buddhist monastery who has traveled extensively*

in Japan and who understands the Japanese culture as well as any non-Oriental. The Inspector Saito stories are authentic in background and characterization (and expertly plotted and written mysteries as well).

Janwillem van de Wetering, a former businessman and member of the Amsterdam police force, has published several crime novels featuring Grijpstra and De Gier, beginning with Outsider in Amsterdam *(1974). He has also written two nonfiction books about his experiences in the Buddhist monastery,* The Empty Mirror *(1973) and* A Glimpse of Nothing *(1975). He presently makes his home in the United States, in the state of Maine, the setting of one of his procedurals,* The Maine Massacre *(1979).*

.   .   .

Inspector Saito felt a bit better when the constable had switched off the Datsun's siren, but just a trifle better for his headache throbbed on. Once more he felt sorry about having visited the Willow Quarter the night before, and about the sixth jug of sake. He should have remembered his limit was five jugs. But it had been a good bar and there had been good people in the bar. And the difference between six jugs and five jugs is only one jug, one small jug. But the headache, which had now lasted nearly sixteen hours, showed no sign of abating.

He forced himself to walk over to the uniformed sergeant, a middle-aged man in a crisp green uniform waiting under the large ornamental gate. The sergeant bowed. Saito bowed back.

"In that direction, sir, in the alley next to the temple."

Saito grunted. There was a corpse in the alley, a female corpse—a *gaijin* body, white, limp, and lifeless. This much he knew from Headquarters. It was all very unfortunate, a miserable conglomeration of circumstances, all of them bad. He shouldn't have a hangover, he shouldn't have been on the night shift, and he shouldn't be trying to solve a murder case. But he *had* had too much to drink the night before, his colleague *was* ill, and there *had* been a murder.

And the three events now met in the person of Saito, only a short distance from an alley between two temples in Daidharmaji, the most beautiful and revered of all temple complexes in the holy city of Kyoto.

Saito's foot stumbled over a pine root that twisted over the gravel of the path. He had to swing out his arms and then sidestep to regain his balance. He was dancing quite gracefully for a moment, but the effort exhausted him and he stopped and looked around. Daidharmaji, Temple of the Great Teaching. A gong sounded in the center of the compound and its singing metal clang filled the quiet path and was caught and held by the eight-foot-thick mud-and-plaster walls shielding the temples and their peaceful gardens.

Saito's brain cleared and he could think for a few seconds. The Great Teaching. He remembered that these temples had but one purpose: the teaching of the truth to priests, monks, and laymen. Right now monks were sitting in meditation after having chanted to the accompaniment of the bronze gongs of the main temple. In their minds insight was supposed to develop and this insight would, in time and after much effort, rise to the surface of their beings like bubbles, or flashes of light. Enlightenment, manifested in sudden outbursts of what the teachers called *Satori*.

He smiled unhappily. Satori indeed. He recollected what he knew about the term. Insight has to do with detachment, with the breaking of the shell in which ego hides and which it uses as a defense to hold on to its identity—to a name, to possessions, to having and being. Satori cracks the shell and explodes into freedom. By becoming less, one gains. The experience is said to be a release and leads to laughter. Monks who, through their daily discipline and meditation, manage to touch reality usually laugh or, at least, smile.

Saito sighed. All very interesting on some lofty level. Not his level, however. He was an ordinary dim-witted man, muddling about. He was muddling about now, and the sergeant, was waiting, a few steps ahead. Saito nodded and limped forward.

"Did you hurt yourself, sir?"

"Just a little. I didn't see the root."

"It's a bad root, sir, but it can't be removed, it belongs to that great pine over there, a very old tree, a holy tree."

Saito followed until the sergeant stopped and began to gesture. They had come to a narrow path with some shrubbery on each side, backed by temple walls.

The sergeant pointed and stepped back. Two uniformed constables were guarding two well-pruned cherry trees.

"In there?"

"Yes, sir. Another few yards, under a bush. We haven't touched the corpse, sir."

Saito walked on, protecting his face with an arm that felt as if it was made out of hard plastic. He didn't want a branch to snap against his head. One little blow and his skull would break.

He sat on his haunches and studied the corpse. It was a woman, still young, perhaps in her late twenties. She had long blonde hair and was dressed in white cotton trousers and a white jacket buttoned up to the neck, Chinese Communist style. A red scarf had been tucked into the jacket's collar. Its color matched the stains on the jacket. Saito produced a small flashlight and shone it on her face. It was the sort of face seen on models in expensive Western-style fashion magazines—beautiful, but cold, quite devoid of expression. Cool, impersonal, and dead. He studied the slack painted mouth. Very dead.

The sergeant was hissing respectfully just behind Saito's head. The inspector straightened up. "Yes, Sergeant. Please tell me all you know."

The sergeant checked his watch. "Ten fifteen P.M. now, sir. Young Tanaka reported the death at nine fifty-four. Young Tanaka lives nearby and he goes to drawing classes in the temple at the end of this alley on the left. He said he was going home and saw something white in the bushes. He investigated, saw the dead person, and came to tell us at the station."

"Person?"

"Yes, sir. He told us he had found a dead person."

"But this is a woman."

"Yes, sir. I came here with him, ran back and told my constables where the corpse was and ordered them to guard it, then I telephoned Headquarters."

Saito bent down and straightened up again, painfully. "The blood seems fresh, Sergeant. I hope the doctor is on his way. Do you know the lady?"

"Yes, sir. She studied meditation in the temple at the end of the alley, on the right, opposite the temple where young Tanaka learns how to draw. She is an American. Her name is Miss Davis and she stayed at the Kyoto Hotel. She came here most evenings, walked through this alley on her way in and out of the compound, and hailed a taxi from the main gate, opposite our station."

"Ah. And the priest who teaches her meditation?"

"The Reverend Ohno. He has several *gaijin* as disciples. They come every weekday, in the evening, and sit in meditation from seven to nine."

"Nine o'clock," Saito said, "and then they go home?"

"Yes, sir. But the others—there are two elderly ladies and a gentleman, also old—walk another way. They take a taxi from the west gate. They don't live in such an expensive hotel as the Kyoto Hotel. Miss Davis always walked by herself. It's only a short distance to the main gate and the compound is reputed to be safe."

Saito glanced down at the sprawling corpse. "Yes. Very safe. That's a knife wound, Sergeant. Do you know of anybody walking around here at night, anybody who carries a knife?"

At least two sirens tore at the quiet cool evening and Saito's hands came up and rubbed his temples. The sirens increased in volume and stopped. The sergeant barked at one of the constables and the young man saluted and jumped away.

"Anybody with a knife, Sergeant?"

The sergeant bowed and looked sad. "Yes, sir. There are street robbers, it is true. The compound is not safe any more. It used to be, and Miss Davis believed it to be. But . . ."

"But?"

"But there are young men, young men in tight trousers and leather jackets. They robbed an old man last week. The victim described the young men and I found the suspects and confronted them with the old man. He recognized the robbers but the suspects went free. There was only one witness, sir. To charge a suspect I need two witnesses."

"Were these robbers around tonight?"

"Probably, sir. When they aren't drinking or smoking the drug they roam about. They live close by. This is their territory. I will have them brought in for questioning."

"Good. And what about young Tanaka, where is he now?"

"At home, sir. I know his parents. I can call him to the station."

"Is he a good boy?"

The sergeant smiled his apology.

"Is he?"

"No, sir, and yes. We arrested him last year, and the year before. He is still young—sixteen years old. Indecent exposure, sir. But he is much better now. The priest who teaches him drawing says he has been behaving very well lately."

The constable had come back, leading a small party of men in dark suits, carrying suitcases. The men bowed at Saito and Saito returned the greeting, adjusting the depth, or lack of depth, of each bow to the colleague he was facing. The doctor grunted and asked for light. Several powerful torches lit up the grisly scene. A camera began to click. A light fed by a heavy battery was set up on a tripod.

Saito touched the sergeant's sleeve and they stepped back together. "Where is the hotel where these other Westerners stay?"

"The old *gaijin*, sir? They stay at the Mainichi."

Saito nodded. "I will go there now. And then I will come back to the station. Later on I will speak with the Reverend Ohno. Bring the young men and the boy Tanaka to the station so I can question them. Your information has been very clear. Thank you, Sergeant."

The sergeant bowed twice, deeply.

"I have served in this neighborhood for many years now, sir. I try to know what goes on."

"Yes," Saito said and closed his eyes. The sergeant had spoken loudly and he had a high voice.

"I see," the old gentleman in the bathrobe said. He had knelt down on the tatami-covered floor of the hotel's reception room and seemed quite at ease on the thick straw mat. Saito sat opposite the old gentleman, with the two elderly ladies on his right in low cane chairs. They were both dressed in kimonos printed with flowers. They weren't the right sort of kimonos for old ladies to wear. Flower patterns are reserved for young girls, preferably attractive girls.

"My name is McGraw," the old gentleman said, "and my friends here are called Miss Cunningham and Mrs. Ingram. They are spending a year in Japan and I have lived here for several years now. We are studying with the good priests of Daidharmaji."

Saito acknowledged McGraw's opening by bowing briefly.

Miss Cunningham coughed and made her thin body lean forward.

"Are you a follower of the way too, Inspector?"

"Yes, I am."

"Do you meditate?"

"No, Miss Cunningham, I do not practice. My family belongs to a temple in another part of the city. I go there with my parents on special days and the priests visit our home. That is all."

"What a pity," said Mrs. Ingram. "Meditation is such a marvelous exercise. It has done wonders for us. But you are very busy, of course. Perhaps later, when you retire?"

"Yes, Mrs. Ingram." He felt proud that he could remember the difficult names and that he was speaking English. He had studied English because he had wanted to be a police officer in Tokyo. There were many foreigners in the capital and English-speaking police detectives were rapidly promoted. But so far he had been confined within the limits of his home city, Kyoto, the city of temples.

He cleared his throat and addressed himself to McGraw. "Please, sir, what do you know about Miss Davis?"

McGraw's heavy-lidded pale-blue eyes rested on the neat impassive form of the inspector.

"May I ask, Saito-san, what sort of trouble Miss Davis is into?"

"She is dead."

While the two ladies shrieked, McGraw's eyes didn't change. They remained gentle and precise. "I see. And how did she die?"

"We are not sure yet. I would think she had been knifed."

The two ladies shrieked again, much louder. Saito closed his eyes with desperate determination.

When he left the small hotel a little while later Saito carried some information. Miss Davis had spent only two months in Japan. She was rich. Her father manufactured most of the shoe polish used in the United States. She could have lived a life of leisure, but she had not; she had been very diligent, never missing an evening's meditation at the priest Ohno's temple. She had managed to master the full lotus position, wherein both legs are crossed and the feet rest upside down on the opposite thighs. She had been in pain but she had never moved during the half-hour periods in which the two-hour sessions were divided. She had been very good indeed.

McGraw was most positive about the young woman's efforts. He himself, Miss Cunningham, and Mrs. Ingram couldn't be compared to Miss Davis. The three older students had some experience in the discipline, but even they still moved when the pain became too severe and they still fell asleep sometimes when they happened not to be in pain and Ohno-san often had to shout at them to make them wake up. Miss Davis never fell asleep. She had been an ideal student, yes, absolutely.

But McGraw knew little about Miss Davis's personal life. He didn't know how she spent her days. He had asked her to lunch once and she had accepted the invitation but never returned it. They had conversed politely but nothing of consequence. All he had learned was that she had lived in New York, held a degree in philosophy, and had experimented with drugs.

And tonight? Had he noticed anything in particular?

No. It had been an evening like the other evenings. They had sat together in Ohno's magnificent temple room. When the two hours were up and the sound of Ohno's heavy bell floated away toward the garden, they had bowed and left. McGraw had walked Miss Cunningham and Mrs. Ingram home and Miss Davis had left by herself, as usual.

Saito sat in the back of the small Datsun and asked the young constable to drive slowly. When he spied a bar, Saito asked him to stop. He got out and drank two glasses of grape juice and one glass of orange juice and swallowed two aspirin provided by the attractive hostess, who snuggled against his shoulder and smiled invitingly. But Saito thanked her for the aspirin and hurried back to the car.

The Datsun stopped under a blue sign with the neat characters that make up the imported word "police." Saito marched into the station. The sergeant pointed to a door in the rear and led the way. Saito sat at the desk. "I'll be with you in a few minutes. After a phone call."

The doctor's hoarse voice described what Saito wanted to know. "Yes, she died of a knife wound. A downward thrust, with considerable force. The blade hit a rib but pushed on and reached the heart. Death must have been almost immediate. The knife's blade was quite long, at least three-and-a-half inches. I can't say how wide for it was moved about when it was pulled free."

"Sexual intercourse?" Saito asked.

"Not recently, no."

"Thank you. Can you connect me with whoever went through her pockets? I noticed she had no handbag."

Another voice greeted the inspector politely. "No, Inspector, there was no handbag, but the lady carried her things in the side pockets of her jacket. We found a wallet with

172

some money, almost ten thousand yen, and a credit card. Also a key, cigarettes, a lighter, and a notebook—excuse me, sir, I have a list here. Yes, that's right, and a lipstick. That was all, sir."

"What's in the notebook?"

"Names and phone numbers."

"Japanese?"

"No, sir, American names. And the phone numbers begin with 212, 516, and 914."

Saito nodded at the telephone. "New York area codes. I have been there once. Very good, thank you."

The sergeant was waiting at the door and led Saito to a small room where two surly young men sat slumped on a wooden bench in the back. A chair had been placed opposite the bench. The sergeant closed the door and leaned against it. "The fellow on the left is called Yoshida, and the other one is Kato."

Saito was thirsty again and wondered whether he should ask the sergeant for a pot of green tea but instead he plunged right in. "O.K., you two, where were you tonight? You first—Kato, is it?"

The two young men were hard to tell apart in their identical trousers, jackets, and shirts. They even wore the same hairstyle, very short on top, very long on the sides.

"We were around."

"Where were you between nine and ten?"

They looked at each other and shrugged. "Around."

"That's bad," Saito said cheerfully. "Real bad. If no one saw you between nine and ten, you are in trouble. You may have to spend the night here, and many other nights besides. This is a nasty place, eh, Sergeant?"

"Yes, sir."

"Small cells, bad food, nothing to smoke. Do you fellows smoke?"

They nodded.

"You'll have to give it up for a while." He took out a cigarette. "But I'll smoke for you. Did you go through their pockets, Sergeant?"

"Yes, sir."

"Any knives?"

The sergeant stepped out of the room and came back carrying two yellow plastic trays, neatly labeled. There was a pack of cigarettes in each tray, plus a dirty handkerchief, a wallet, and a long knife sheathed in leather.

"Good. Please have one of your men have the knives checked for blood."

"Blood?" the young man called Yoshida asked. "What blood?"

"A lady's blood, a *gaijin* lady. Did you see her in the compound tonight?"

Kato answered, "An old lady or a young lady?"

"A young lady with long blonde hair, wearing white clothes."

"Not tonight, but we know her. She came every evening to Ohno-san's temple. She was a holy woman." He sniggered and nudged his friend.

Saito jumped up, leaped across the room, and grabbed Kato by the shoulders, shaking him vigorously. "What do you mean, you punk! What do you mean?" He pushed Kato back on the bench and stood over him, one hand balled up.

"Nothing."

"You meant something. Tell me, or . . ." He could feel the artificial rage turning into real rage. He would have to watch himself.

"I just mean that maybe the lady liked the priest. Me and Yoshida saw them together in the garden one afternoon last week, in the temple's garden."

"What were they doing?"

"Laughing, talking."

"That's all?"

"They weren't kissing," Yoshida said gruffly, "just enjoying a good conversation."

Saito turned to the sergeant, who had returned. "Would you ask somebody to make me a pot of tea, Sergeant? And bring a chopstick, just one."

The sergeant raised his eyebrows but bowed and left the room. He came back with the chopstick.

"Here," Saito said. "You, Kato. You are a knife fighter, eh? Here is a knife. Now attack me."

Kato hesitated and Saito waited. Kato got up and took the chopstick.

"Come on, attack me. Here I am, and you hold a knife. Show me that you can handle it."

Kato got up and the sergeant's hand dropped down and touched the revolver on his belt. The atmosphere in the room became tense. Kato spread his legs and hefted the chopstick. Saito waited, motionless. Then Kato yelled loudly and jumped. The hand holding the chopstick shot up. But Saito was no longer there—he had fallen sideways and his foot was against Kato's shin. Kato fell too. The chopstick broke on the floor. Saito helped the young man back on his feet. "Fine. Sergeant, may we have another chopstick?"

Yoshida's attack was more artful and took more time. He approached Saito, holding the chopstick low, but seemed to change his mind and feinted at the sergeant. The sergeant pulled his gun as the chopstick went for Saito's stomach, but Saito's arm effectively blocked it with a blow to Yoshida's arm, knocking it aside.

A constable brought a pot of tea. Saito poured himself a steaming cup of tea and sat sipping it, eyeing his opponents. Kato was rubbing his shin and Yoshida was massaging his wrist. "Did I hurt you?"

Both shook their heads and tried to smile.

"I didn't mean to hurt you. But carrying knives with blades longer than three inches is illegal. The sergeant will charge you and you will be kept here for the night. Perhaps I'll see you tomorrow. If you want to see me you can tell the sergeant. Good night."

He got up and went outside, beckoning the sergeant to follow him. "Now the other one, Tanaka, the boy who found the corpse."

"He is waiting in the other room, sir."

Saito smiled when he saw the boy. Young Tanaka was a

175

good-looking young man, with a childish open face but wide shoulders and narrow hips. He wore his school uniform, and his cap was on the floor under his chair. He got up when Saito entered and he bowed.

"Thank you for reporting to us tonight, Tanaka-san," Saito said, "that was very good of you. I am sorry to have you called in so late, but we have to work quickly. Did you know the *gaijin* lady at all?"

"Yes, sir, I have seen her many times. She studied at Ohno-san's temple. But I never spoke to her. And I didn't know the corpse was the *gaijin* lady's body. I was frightened, sir. I saw a body and there was nobody else around and I just ran to the police station."

"So that's why you said you saw a *person.*"

"Yes, sir. I just saw the legs and a hand."

Saito tried to remember the corpse. There had been no polish on the nails, no colored polish anyway. He lowered his voice. "Now tell me, Tanaka-san, tell me and be honest. I know you have been in trouble with the police before. You know what I am referring to, don't you?"

"Yes, sir. But I don't do that any more. I used to, but that has gone."

"What has gone?"

"The need to do that, sir."

"You are sure, are you? You were in the alley, and the lady was in the alley. You were facing her and she was coming closer . . ."

"No, sir. The body was in the bushes."

Saito turned to the sergeant. "May I have a chopstick, Sergeant?"

When the sergeant returned with the chopstick Saito gave it to the boy. "Imagine this is a knife. Can you do that?"

The boy held the chopstick. "Yes, sir. It is a knife."

"And I am your enemy. I am a burglar sneaking into your room. I am going to attack you and you must kill me. Stick the knife into me. It is very important. Please do it for me."

"Like this, sir?"

The boy raised his arm high, pointing the chopstick at Saito's chest.

"Yes, you are very angry, very frightened. All you know is that you have to kill me."

The chopstick hit Saito's chest with force and broke.

"Thank you. You can go home now. Sleep well . . ."

When Saito left the police station, his driver came to attention and opened the rear door. The inspector shook his head. "No, I am going into the temple compound. I may be a while. You can wait in the station if you like. The tea isn't bad."

He walked until he found Ohno's temple and stopped and looked about. He could feel the quietness of hundreds of years of solitude, of silent effort. The aspirin had dulled his headache, and his thoughts connected more easily.

The gate of the temple hadn't been locked and he walked through it.

"Good evening." The voice came from the shadows of the building.

"Good evening. My name is Saito. I am a police inspector. I have come to see the priest Ohno."

"I am Ohno. Walk up the steps and come and sit next to me."

Saito took off his shoes and walked across the polished boards of the porch. His eyes adjusted to the darkness and he could see the shape of a man sitting upright with his legs folded. Saito bowed and a cushion slid toward him. He took the cushion and sat down.

"Do you know that Miss Davis died tonight?"

"I heard."

"Who told you?"

"The old woman who cleans the temple. She heard a commotion in the alley and found out what had happened."

"The death of the *gaijin* lady is unfortunate. She was killed with a knife. We are holding several suspects."

He could see the priest's face now. Ohno was still a young man—thirty years old perhaps, or a little older. The priest

177

wore a simple brown robe. The faint light of a half moon reflected on his shaven skull.

"Who did you arrest?"

"Two young toughs, Yoshida and Kato. They have robbed in the Daidharmaji compound before but nothing could be proved. They couldn't explain their movements at the time of Miss Davis's death. They both carried knives. We are also holding a boy called Tanaka, who reported the crime. Excuse me, do you have a telephone?"

Ohno got to his feet and led his guest inside the temple. Saito dialed. A man in the laboratory answered.

"The knives? They both fit the wound but so would a million other knives. And they are both clean, no traces of blood."

"Whoever did it could have cleaned the knife afterward."

"He could. If he did, he did a good job."

"Thank you."

The priest invited Saito into his study and an old woman made them tea. Saito sipped slowly, enjoying the rich bitter taste.

"Very good tea."

"A present from Mrs. Ingram. I couldn't afford it myself."

"You have only foreign disciples?"

"Yes. When *gaijin* come to Daidharmaji, the chief abbot usually sends them to me. I am the only priest who speaks reasonably good English. I spent several years in a temple in Los Angeles as the assistant to the teacher there."

"I see. Did you get to know Miss Davis well?"

"A little. She was a dedicated woman, very eager to learn."

"Did she learn anything?"

Ohno smiled. "There is nothing to learn. There is only to unlearn."

Saito shook his head.

"You don't agree?"

"I have no wisdom," Saito said. "I am a policeman; my level of investigation is shallow. I have small questions and need small answers. Yoshida and Kato weren't helpful. The boy Tanaka tried, but he couldn't tell me much. Mr. McGraw and the old ladies who study with you tried to clarify my confusion. But I am still confused and now I have come to see you."

"I know the two young men, Yoshida and Kato," Ohno said. "I know their parents too—they often come to these temples. The boys have lost their way, but only for the time being. They will find the way again. They may have robbed people but they have never killed anyone. They watch movies and try to imitate images of what they think is admirable."

"In the movies many images get killed. Yoshida and Kato carry knives, killing knives with slits in the sides so that the blood will drain easily."

"They didn't kill tonight."

"And the boy Tanaka, do you know him too?"

"Very well. When his mind was sick, his parents came to see me. They live close by and they often bring gifts to this temple. They knew the priest who lived here before and now they come and visit me. The boy was mad, they said, but I didn't think so. The boy came too sometimes— he liked to help me in the garden. He placed the rocks and we planted moss."

"He would show himself when he met women, right here, in this holy compound."

"I know."

"You don't think that is a bad thing to do?"

"It is embarrassing, for the women and for the boy himself. But he had a need to reveal himself to that which he loved. I wanted to help him but I didn't know what to do and I spoke to the old priest in the temple next door. Young Tanaka likes to paint and draw, and the old priest is an accomplished artist. So we agreed that he would try to lead Tanaka away from his compulsion. Since then the boy's trouble has faded away. There have been no more complaints."

Saito got up. He wanted to say something noncommittal before he left. He looked around and saw several cameras

on a shelf and another on the floor. "Do you like photogra-
phy, Ohno-san?"

"Yes, it is my hobby." The priest picked up the camera.
"I use a new method now. I make instant photographs and
if I succeed in obtaining a well-balanced picture I try again
with a conventional camera that can be adjusted to a fine
degree of perception. One day when you have time you
should come and see some of my photographs—if you are
interested, that is."

"I would very much like to. Thank you."

Saito looked at his watch. It was past one o'clock but
he might as well go on. He was very close now, but there
were still important questions.

The temple next door was dark and the gate had been
locked, but he found a side door and made his way into
the courtyard, using his flashlight. He took off his shoes
and climbed the steps and knocked on the door of the main
building. Within seconds a light came on inside and shuffling
steps approached. The priest was old and bent—and sleepy.

"Yes?"

Saito showed his identification. "Inspector Saito, Criminal
Investigation Department. I am sorry, sir, but I have to
bother you for a few minutes. May I come in?"

"Of course. I heard about the lady's death. Most regretta-
ble. Please come in, Inspector-san."

In view of the late hour, Saito decided that it would be
impolite to be polite. He came to the point.

"You are teaching a boy called Tanaka?"

"That is correct."

"He draws and paints. Please tell me what his favorite
subjects are."

"Women. He only draws women. I don't allow him to
paint yet. He sketches. I showed him copies of famous paintings and he seemed most interested in portraits of Kwan-
non, the goddess of compassion. He has been drawing her
for months now and doesn't tire."

Saito smiled. "Tanaka-san is in love with the goddess?"

The priest looked serious. "Very much so. And that is

180

good for the time being. I want him to continue, to approach perfection. Later he will see that her real shape is truly perfect and then perhaps he will meet and know her. But first he must do this. He is talented. I am grateful he was brought to me."

"May I see the drawings?"

"Surely. Follow me, please."

The sketches were all in the same vein, although the postures and moods of the divine model were different. The boy clearly had only one type of woman in mind, and the woman was Japanese, with a long narrow face, thick black hair, a small nose, and enormous slanting eyes.

"Thank you."

"Not at all."

"One last question, sir. Do you know Ohno-san well?"

The old priest nodded.

"Does Ohno-san engage in any of the martial sports? Judo? Sword fighting? Bowshooting, perhaps?"

The old priest tittered. "Oh, no. Ohno-san likes to fuss in his garden, to make photographs, and to meditate, in that order. He once came to help me chop some wood for my bathhouse. He broke two axe handles in one hour. I had no more axes so we had tea instead. No, Ohno-san is, shall we say, a little clumsy?"

Nearly five minutes passed before Saito could bring himself to walk through Ohno's gate again. He found the priest where he had found him before, on the porch. Saito didn't say anything but sat down.

"Yes?"

"I am sorry, I have come to arrest you."

Ohno didn't reply. Saito sat quietly.

Several minutes passed.

"Please come with me, Ohno-san."

The priest turned and faced the inspector. "No. I will have to ask you a favor. Let me go inside and please wait half an hour. I will leave a confession and you can close your case."

Saito smiled, but the smile was neither positive nor negative. It was very quiet on the porch.

Ohno cleared his throat. "Would you mind explaining why you chose me?"

"Because you killed her. She was killed by an amateur, by someone who doesn't know how to handle a knife. A knife fighter will hold his weapon low and thrust upward, so that the knife pierces the soft skin of the belly and so its point will travel upward, behind the ribs. To stab downward is silly—the ribs protect the heart. Much unnecessary force is needed. And the attacker who holds his knife high has no defense, his own body is left open."

"Many people walk through this compound. Most of them do not know how to handle a knife."

"That is not true. There are very few people about after nine o'clock. Even when we found the dead woman a crowd didn't gather. And whoever killed Miss Davis either hated her or was frightened of her. To hate or to fear takes time. The feeling isn't born overnight. Miss Davis only spent a few months in Japan and kept herself apart. The only person she involved herself with was you. You were her teacher. She came here every night. But she also came during the day. Did you sleep with her, Ohno-san?"

The priest's head jerked forward briefly. "I did."

"She seduced you?"

The head jerked again.

"She was in love with you?"

Ohno's even white teeth sparkled briefly in the soft moonlight.

"No. To love means to be prepared to give. She wanted to have. And she wanted me to give to her. The way has many secrets, many powers. Our training, when practiced properly, is complete. It is also slow, unbearably slow. Miss Davis comes from a country that believes in quick results. Americans are capable of great effort, but they want rewards. She suspected that I knew something and she wanted what I knew."

"You were teaching her meditation. You were giving."

182

"Yes. But meditation takes forever, or so she began to believe. She wanted to be initiated, to be given powers. I told her my rank was too low, my development too minute. Only a true teacher can pass a student. This temple is a little school for beginners, for toddlers. The abbot knows I have disciples and he watches them. He will take over when he feels that the disciples are ready. Mr. McGraw is sometimes allowed to see the abbot. He has learned much— he has learned to be modest. Miss Davis had learned to be the opposite."

"She tried to force you?"

"Yes."

"How?"

"I am a weak man, a silly man. She began to visit me during the day. I have lived in America and I am very proud of my experience with foreigners. We flirted. Then we slept together."

"In the room where we were earlier on tonight?"

"Yes."

"The room where you have your cameras?"

"Yes. The camera can be set so that it goes off after several seconds. I showed her how. She laughed and set it and pressed herself against me. We had no clothes on. The camera clicked. She took the photograph with her. I didn't understand what she meant to do. I thought it was a joke."

"She threatened to show the photograph to the abbot?"

"Yes. Today. She came to see me this morning. She said she was prepared to continue her meditation practice for another year, but she wanted something right now. Some power. That was all she wanted—not insight, just power. She said I knew about the secret initiations and that I must make her break through. I told her we have no secret initiations. I told her that perhaps in Tibet they do, but not here."

"She planned to visit the abbot tonight?"

"Tomorrow. I had to stop her."

Saito waited. "And the abbot, what would he have done?"

"He would have sent me away. And rightly so, for I have failed. I am only a low-ranking priest. My training has hardly begun. That I am allowed to teach meditation to beginners is a great honor. I am not worthy of the honor."

Ohno's voice dropped and Saito had to strain his ears to hear the priest's words through the chirping of the cicadas.

"Tonight," Ohno said, "I watched her walk through the gate. I ran through the garden and climbed the wall so that I would be waiting for her when she turned the corner of the temple wall and the alley. I had taken a knife from the kitchen. I put myself in her way and showed her the knife. I asked her to give me the photograph. She laughed and tried to push me aside. I became very angry. I don't think I intended to kill her, I only meant to threaten. But her laugh infuriated me."

"Do you have the photograph?"

"Yes. I don't remember how I got it. I must have taken it from the pocket of her jacket."

"And now you plan to kill yourself," Saito said pleasantly.

"Yes."

"But how can you continue your training when you are dead? Isn't this life supposed to be the ideal training ground and isn't whatever comes afterward a period of rest in which nothing can be achieved? You may have to wait a long time before you are given another chance. Is this not so?"

The dark shape next to Saito moved. "Yes."

"I don't know anything," Saito said. "But priests sometimes come to our house to burn incense in front of the family altar and to chant the holy sermons. I have listened. Isn't that what they say? What you say?"

"Yes."

"And if you come with me, if you allow yourself to be arrested and to face the court and be convicted and spend time in jail, doesn't that mean that your training will continue? That you can go on with your practice? And won't the abbot, who is a master and your teacher, come and visit you or send messages, and help you along?"

"Yes."

"And isn't it true that we all fail? And that failure is never definite? That we can always correct our situation, no matter how bad it seems to be?"

"Yes."

Saito thought he had said enough. He was tired of listening to his own voice. He brought out a cigarette and lit it. Ohno's hand reached out and Saito gave him the cigarette and lit another. They smoked together. The two stubs left the porch at the same moment and sparked away as they hit the wet moss of the garden.

They walked to the gate slowly, two men strolling through the peaceful night.

"I was worried when you said you suspected Tanaka," Ohno said. "He is a nice boy."

"Yes," Saito said. "He was the most likely suspect, but something didn't fit. Indecent exposure is an act of surrender, not of aggression. I would have arrested him if he had drawn the face or body of Miss Davis. But his fantasies are centered on the beauty of our own women. I checked just now at your neighbor's temple. Miss Davis was beautiful, but not to young Tanaka. I don't think she was even female in his eyes."

"She was in mine."

Saito didn't answer. They had passed through the main gate and reached the car. Saito leaned inside and touched the horn. The driver appeared immediately from the station.

"Headquarters, please. This venerable priest is coming with us."

"Sir." The driver bowed to Ohno. Ohno bowed back.

Saito felt pleased. He had solved the case quickly, discreetly. This could be the credit that would get him transferred to the capital. He grinned but the grin froze halfway. He tried to analyze his state of mind but he was bewildered. The more he probed, the emptier his mind seemed.

He felt the priest's presence and then his own hand reached out and touched the wide sleeve of Ohno's robe.

"Yes," Ohno said, "you were right, Inspector-san. It was silly of me to consider my shame and to respond to that shame. I am what I am and I will continue from the point where I find myself. The point happens to be bad, that is all. There will be good points later on, and they won't matter so much either. *Ha!*"

Saito grinned. The priest's words had helped to make the grin break through, the priest's words and the strange power of quietness he had felt seeping into his being while he wandered among the temples of Daidharmaji. And he realized that he didn't care about his successful investigation or about the forthcoming praise of his superiors or about the possibility of a transfer to the capital. The priest's shame was as much of an illusion as his own fame. He felt much relieved, lightheaded. The grin spread over his face. *"Ha!"* The laugh was as carefree as Ohno's laugh had been.

"So . . ." Ohno said.

"So nothing!" Saito replied.

The car took a sharp turn and they fell into each other's arms. They laughed together while the embrace lasted.

At Headquarters, the priest was taken to a cell and Saito accompanied him. He waited while the constable locked the heavy door. Ohno bowed, Saito bowed. They straightened up and studied each other's smile through the bars of the cell door.

"You understood something, didn't you, Inspector-san?"

"Oh, yes," Saito said softly. "Yes, I think I did."

"Oh, yes," Ohno whispered. "And it had nothing to do with you or me or even poor Miss Davis."

"No, it didn't." Saito nodded and gazed at Ohno before turning and following the constable out of the cell block. He felt very tired, so tired that he was hallucinating. He wasn't walking through a dimly lit concrete corridor but floating in a lake of light. The light began to fade as he approached his house and he found that he was shaking his head and talking to himself.

ONE FOR VIRGIL TIBBS

John Ball

The first notable black detective is Octavus Roy Cohen's Florian Slappey, a Birmingham native transplanted to New York's Harlem who made his first appearance in the 1920s. The Slappey stories were intended as broad ethnic humor, but they are much less funny today than they were half a century ago, full as they are of stereotypical characters and painful Stepin Fetchit dialect. It wasn't until Veronica Parker Johns created Webster Flagg in her 1953 novel Murder by the Day *that the black sleuth was allowed to detect with dignity. (Even Flagg, however, had his drawbacks: he is a Harlem domestic who solves crimes in a mostly white milieu.)*

Ed Lacy's Toussaint Moore, hero of Room to Swing *(1957), which won the Mystery Writers of America Edgar as best novel of its year, is the first fully realized black detective. And he was followed shortly by two others: Chester Himes's Coffin Ed Johnson and Gravedigger Jones, a pair of Harlem policemen featured in such wild and woolly novels as* The Crazy Kill *(1959) and* Cotton Comes to Harlem *(1965). Both of these writers were much more qualified to write about blacks than their predecessors: Himes himself is black and Ed Lacy, though white, was married to a black woman.*

Numerous other black investigators have appeared over the past quarter-century, among the more notable of which are Ernest Tidyman's John Shaft, George Baxt's Pharaoh Love, Percy Spurlark Parker's Big Bull Benson, J. F. Burke's Sam Kelly, and Kenn Davis's Carver Bascomb in this country; Donald McNutt Douglas's Bolivar Manchenil and A. H. Z. Carr's Xavier Brooke in the Caribbean; and John Wyllie's Dr. Quarshie and James McClure's Bantu policeman, Detective-Sergeant Mickey Zondi, in Africa. No black detective has made more of an impact on crime fiction, however, than John Ball's redoubtable Pasadena cop, Virgil Tibbs.

Tibbs' first adventure, In the Heat of the Night *(1965), was not only a successful novel (it won an MWA Edgar and a British Golden Dagger) but an enormously successful film starring Sidney Poitier and Rod Steiger (in his Oscar-winning performance as a redneck Southern sheriff). Other Tibbs novels—*The Cool Cottontail *(1966),* Five Pieces of Jade *(1972),* The Eyes of the Buddha *(1975)—and films followed, firmly cementing Virgil Tibbs as the premier black detective.*

Tibbs has also appeared in a handful of short stories published in Ellery Queen's Mystery Magazine *in the 1970s, of which "One for Virgil Tibbs" is the first. It clearly demonstrates John Ball's first-hand knowledge of police work and sympathetic understanding of the black character and of other ethnic groups.*

A former pilot and world traveler, John Ball has written numerous other books, including such suspense tales as Mark One—The Dummy *(1974), such noncriminous novels as* Last Plane Out *(1970), such juveniles as* Arctic Showdown *(1966), and such nonfiction works as* Dragon Hotel *(1969). He has also created another detective character, Police Chief Tallon, protagonist of* Police Chief *(1977) and other titles; and has edited a collection of essays on mystery fiction,* The Mystery Story *(1976), as well as a volume of stories by members of the Mystery Writers of America,* Cop Cade *(1979).*

. . .

At 11:31 A.M. on an unusually fine morning in Pasadena, California, the operator of a power shovel swung a full load of soil over the top of a heavy truck and pulled the release. Since the truck was almost full, a small shower of stones rattled off the sides, some loose dirt, and one human skull.

Fortunately Harry Hubert, male, 31, was working close by. As he raised his arm to signal the truck driver to move on he looked down, then froze in his tracks. "Hold it!" he yelled.

He was not a superstitious man, but he did not want to handle the skull. He signaled the shovel operator to cease digging, pointed to what he had discovered, then waved his arms in the air to be sure that everyone understood that all work was to stop.

The shovel operator brought his machine to a halt and the truck driver shut off his engine.

Superintendent Angelo Morelli was sent for. Meanwhile, the truck driver got out of his cab and joined Hubert to find out what was wrong. He looked down at the object on the ground, bent over to examine it more closely, then spoke. "Alas, poor Yorick," he said.

He was an admirer of Sir Laurence Olivier.

Superintendent Morelli was a man accustomed to making decisions. It took him only seconds to assay the situation, then he sent for the police.

One of the all-white Pasadena patrol cars responded promptly. It arrived without lights or siren, and as the working officer driving it got out, Morelli wondered, What the hell. The officer was a woman and a comely one at that.

As soon as she was close enough, he read the nameplate over her right pocket. It said DIAZ.

Morelli checked her over. She was armed, of course; metal handcuffs were properly pouched on her belt, and there was even a small container of Mace visible.

The superintendent approached her. Although he was a rough-and-ready type, he also knew how to be diplomatic.

"I certainly appreciate your quick response," he said. "However, I'm not sure this is suitable for a policewoman."

"I'm not a policewoman," she answered. "I'm a cop. Where's the fight?"

Morelli was amused. "No fight this time," he reassured her. "Do you get many of those?"

"I broke one up last night—knives in a bar. I have a suspect in custody."

"Then kindly step this way."

Officer Marilyn Diaz spent three minutes in a careful survey of the situation. Then, despite her immaculate uniform, which was the same as the ones worn by the male members of the department, she explored the fresh excavation and the approximate spot where the skull had been unearthed.

She had one question for the shovel operator. "Is there any way you can tell," she asked, "how deeply that skull was buried when you dug it up?"

"No, ma'am, because I started my pass at the bottom of the cut and came up. I would guess that it was somewhere near to the top."

"So would I," Diaz agreed. "Hold everything, will you?"

"Right."

Officer Marilyn Diaz, who is one of the particular prides of the Pasadena Police, returned to her car and picked up the radio mike. Socially she was an attractive and charming young woman; on the job she did not waste words. "I've got one for Virgil," she reported. "At the Foothill Freeway construction site, near Raymond."

"Paramedics wanted?"

"No, human remains, but so far bones only."

"Anything else?"

"Yes," Diaz answered. "I've seen the skull. Unless I'm very wrong, the victim was an eight-to-ten-year-old child."

On the wall of the small office he shared with his partner, Bob Nakamura, Virgil Tibbs had a small sign posted. It read:

Write, for the night is coming. He was engaged in doing precisely that, presiding over a manual typewriter and punching out the words of a report that, by police tradition, would be hopelessly pedantic and at least twice the necessary length. He spent hours writing reports, as did practically everyone else in the department. It was the curse of the profession.

His phone rang. He took the call, listened, then got up and put on his coat. As the ranking homicide specialist of the Pasadena Police, the discovery of an unattached skull was referred to him automatically. Ray Heatherton could have handled it, but Ray was only too delighted to let Virgil Tibbs sit at the top of the death-by-violence totem pole. Virgil had earned the spot many times over.

Virgil picked up an unmarked car, drove to the location, parked behind Marilyn Diaz' unit, then walked over to where the people were gathered.

Superintendent Morelli saw him coming, noted that he was black, and remembered what he had read in the papers. "Is that Virgil Tibbs?" he asked Diaz.

"It is," she answered.

"He's good, I understand."

"The best."

Seconds later she made the introductions. Morelli shook hands, then got down to business. "As soon as the skull showed up, we stopped everything immediately." He motioned to a hardhat who was waiting close by. "This is Harry Hubert, he was the first to spot it."

Virgil listened to the man's account, then talked to the truck driver and the shovel operator. After that he addressed himself once more to Morelli. "I don't want to hold you up," he said. "I know that tying up men and equipment is costing you money and job delay. If you need the shovel somewhere else, I don't see any reason why you shouldn't move it. I'll need the truck until we can check the load in detail. Also, I want to go over the spot where the dirt is being dumped."

"I thought of that," Morelli said. "I stopped the unloading

immediately. I don't believe anything has been moved since Harry saw that skull come off the truck."

"For that I'll buy you your lunch," Tibbs said.

"You're on."

"Fine. While we're eating, there are a few questions you might be able to answer for me."

Sergeant Jerry Ferguson headed the investigation team that arrived almost immediately thereafter. Since there was obviously pick-and-shovel work to be done, Superintendent Morelli assigned a half dozen men to work under Ferguson's direction. With Agent Barry Rothberg three of them left for the fill area where the dirt from the excavation was being dumped. At a convenient spot the filled truck that had taken the last load from the power shovel spread out what it had on board as another police unit arrived headed by Lieutenant Ron Peron.

Under careful examination the load that had been on the truck yielded up three additional bones and part of a spinal column. That grisly discovery was made shortly before Captain Bill Wilson arrived to see how the investigation was progressing.

By nightfall a set of foot bones that was almost intact had been discovered *in situ.* Its position suggested that the body, which had presumably been buried not long after death, had lain approximately four feet, three inches below the surface of the ground, with the head in an easterly direction. After extensive photographs had been taken, and measurements made, the few recovered bones were turned over to the Los Angeles County coroner. Even careful sifting gave no hope of recovering the complete skeleton, a point that disturbed Virgil Tibbs.

Satisfied that for the moment no more evidence would be found at the location, he authorized Superintendent Morelli to resume the construction work. He did ask that careful watch be kept while the remaining digging was done in the immediate vicinity—unauthorized burials were not always single projects. After the amount of searching that had already been done, he did not feel he could halt the important and expensive project any further without something definite in the form of additional evidence.

In the morning Tibbs went to work with grim determination. From the real-estate maps he located the exact piece of property that had marked the spot where the remains had been uncovered. It had been a single-family dwelling on a medium-sized lot in a definitely lower-class neighborhood. There had been no basement.

By the time he had these facts, the coroner's office called: the bone specialist was on the line. Virgil talked to the doctor for several minutes and was not encouraged by the conversation. From the skull it had been determined that the deceased had been a child approximately eight years of age. But no information could be given either as to race or sex. "You mean you can't say whether it was a boy or a girl?" Tibbs asked.

"That's right. The indications simply aren't present at that age."

"Can you make an informed guess?"

"Not based on what I have here."

The black detective was patient. "What *can* you tell me?" he persisted.

"The individual is deceased. Beyond that, only what you already have."

"Any dental data?"

"I should have mentioned that, forgive me. So far as can be determined, and this is pretty definite, the deceased never had any dental work done. But this doesn't necessarily indicate neglect; the subject could have been seen by a dentist who found that no work was required."

"And the age of the remains?"

"Say from three years back. There are several reasons why I can't be more definite."

"I think I know what they are," Virgil said. "Thank you, Doctor."

"You're most welcome."

Virgil turned to Bob Nakamura. "All I have to worry about

now is a missing child, male or female, ethnic background unknown, who disappeared anytime from, say, three years ago to you-say-when. And the fact that all the bones were not located after very careful search suggests that the corpse may have been cut up and buried in various places."

Bob was sympathetic. "Tough case, but not impossible. You have the specific house to work with—that should tell you a lot. Better than that corpse in the nudist park."

"Hell, yes, that took weeks." And Virgil went back to work.

By noon he had the picture. The house had last been occupied by an elderly couple, Mr. and Mrs. Ajurian. Mrs. Ajurian was recently dead; her husband was in a nursing home in a senile condition. The Ajurians had no known living relatives. Before their occupancy the house had stood vacant for almost three years, tied up in litigation because the owner had been killed in a car accident.

Prior to that the house had been rented on a month-to-month basis, frequently to young people who had been required to pay in advance, and occasionally to transient farm labor. The house itself had been moved away when the area had been cleared for the freeway. It had been offered at auction, but no bids had been received.

Two hours after lunch the house itself was located. It stood, helpless and unwanted, in a row of similar derelicts that had been parked in an available open area. As Virgil explored it minutely, he could not escape a feeling of profound depression. It was in a wretched state of outside repair and, if possible, was even worse inside.

The single bathroom had been painted a particularly violent purple and despite long disuse, it still carried a faintly unpleasant odor indicative of bad sanitation. Where the telephone had been, the walls were covered with jottings in various hands; the smaller bedroom had children's crude drawings covering most of the wall space within their reach. None of the drawings revealed any talent either in art or draftsmanship.

The floor in one closet was missing; the rectangular open-

194

ing had the remains of a ledge that had once, obviously, held an unattached trap door. There was, of course, nothing unusual in that—it was a conventional access hole—but something else about the house interested Tibbs. When he had spent the better part of an hour examining the structure, he thanked the employee of the house mover who was serving as his guide.

"Did you find out anything?" the man asked, walking outside with Virgil.

"Yes, I think so."

"What?"

Virgil nodded down the long row of empty shells, the tombstones of what had once been homes. "Did you notice anything different about this one?" he asked.

"Not particularly. Most of them were in pretty bad shape when they came out here."

"It's at least two feet higher off the ground than any of the others," Tibbs said. "A little more than five feet between the surface of the ground and the bottom of the floor joists. Room enough for a man to work in, if he had to."

Meanwhile, Bob Nakamura determined, by interviewing some of their one-time neighbors, that the Ajurians had been a quiet elderly couple who had never entertained and seldom went out. They were judged to have been capable of only the simplest physical tasks. No children had ever been seen on their premises. The only criticism that the Nisei detective turned up was that they frequently cooked food so heavily spiced that the odor was objectionable. A check of the records revealed that they had been on welfare.

During the time the house had stood vacant, it had been frequently used as a juvenile and young-adult rendezvous; several arrests had been made, but there had never been any indications of violence.

One former long-time resident of the street recalled a Mexican family that had lived in the house. There had been eight or nine children; he did not remember the family name, but he did recall how the kids were incessantly running in and out and slamming the door each time. He had been glad when they moved away. He also remembered a group of six young people, three long-haired males and three females, who had taken up residence, but who had been surprisingly quiet and peaceful.

By the time all this information had been gathered, another day had gone by.

Most of the next day went into a careful examination of all available missing-juvenile reports that fell within the proper time frame. They added up to a heartbreaking number. Dental charts ruled out most of them, but Tibbs was left with over fifty possibles and sixteen that offered the best prospects of a make. When that tedious task had at last been completed, he sat back in his chair and began to think.

Bob Nakamura had seen him like that before, his eyes open but unfocused, his body relaxed. After half an hour, Virgil stirred and Bob was prepared. "It's a damn tough case," Bob said.

Tibbs nodded slowly. "Yes," he agreed, "but if I can put one or two more things together, I may have it."

"Accidental death?" Bob asked.

Virgil shook his head. "No—murder."

"The evidence of that is in the remains?"

"No."

"What else do you need?"

"I want to go back and re-examine that house. But before I do that, I've got some other work to do." He got up and stretched. "I'll see you after a while," he said, and left.

The voter-registration lists gave him some information, much of it quite old. He went over the available data carefully, but found little to excite his interest. The Mexican family that had lived in the house had never registered anyone, a fact that suggested they might have been illegal immigrants—a major problem in Southern California. On the other hand, it could have been indifference or an inability to understand English.

The welfare rolls were more productive. From them Virgil learned that Emilio and Rosa De Fuentes, plus their nine children, had been publicly supported at that address for some time.

That was a breakthrough. Knowing that welfare recipients often retained that status for years, he sent out a message through the network in California to learn if the same family was now being carried on the rolls elsewhere. That accomplished, Virgil once more took refuge in his second-floor office in the old part of the Pasadena Police building, leaned back, and went into another session of concentrated thought.

When he finally came up for air, Bob Nakamura was back and ready to play straight man. "Are you any nearer?" he asked.

"Yes."

"Fill me in."

Tibbs stirred. "A lot of things are beginning to fit together. My chief problem at the moment is the lack of hard data to back up some of my conclusions."

"Let's hear the conclusions."

"All right. We begin with the Ajurians, the Armenian immigrants."

"You dug that far back?"

"No, but I know they were immigrants because of the way they cooked their food. People direct from the old country tend to continue life as they knew it, particularly where diet is concerned. Second- and third-generation offspring from that part of the world prefer less spicy food. The Armenian part is easy because the name ends in *i-a-n*, something almost wholly Armenian."

"Go on."

"The evidence supports the fact that they were relatively feeble, and did not entertain, particularly children. Also, I'm inclined to rule out the hippie sextet who lived in the house for a while. I learned a lot from the drawings I found on the walls of one of the rooms."

"Explain."

Tibbs swung around to face his partner. "Obviously they weren't made during the time the elderly Ajurians were occupying the house. Yet they didn't remove them. They were on the wall of what would have been the second bedroom. The inference, therefore, is that they didn't remove the drawings because a fresh paint job was beyond their physical resources, or financial means. I suspect they closed off that room and used it only for storage.

"The hippie sextet also left the drawings alone—perhaps they found them amusing. It wasn't their house, they were simply living in it, and they probably favored self-expression. They weren't made during that period since I have statements that no children were seen around the house while the hippies were there."

"The drawings could have been faked—done by an adult."

Tibbs shook his head. "The only idea that holds water along that line would be an adult making them to entertain a child who used that room—but again, there were no children reported on the premises."

He stopped suddenly. For a moment or two he stared off into space with his lips held tightly together, then a whole new expression took over his face. "It's a long shot, but worth checking out." He got up once more.

"Where are you going this time?"

"I need a social worker and a grocery store," Virgil answered.

The social worker proved to be unavailable. After tracking her down, Tibbs learned that she had gone to Europe and was somewhere in Spain studying the guitar. He made a note of her name and background, then began his canvass of the grocery stores. That proved a much easier job; he hit paydirt within an hour.

Sam Margolis had operated his small market and liquor store at the same location for many years. He knew most of his customers well, and he recalled the De Fuentes family. "Too damn many kids," he declared. "She usually brought a lot of them with her and they couldn't keep their hands off anything. They even swiped ice cubes and sucked on them."

"They were on welfare, I believe."

"Yeah, they were. But the old man usually found enough money for a bottle. He wasn't a drunk, but he hit the cheap stuff a lot."

"Have you any idea where they went?"

Margolis shrugged. "Who knows? And to be honest, who cares? This is a cash business only—no checks except for welfare and payroll that I know. Two will get you five they were wetbacks, or whatever they call them now. And the woman—" He shook his head. "What he saw in her I'll never know. She was built like a pile of mashed potatoes."

"You've helped me a lot," Tibbs said. "More than you know. One thing more if you can remember. Were all the children that you saw normal, at least reasonably so?"

"All that I saw."

"And do you remember if they had a boy in his teen years, anywhere from about thirteen or fourteen up?"

Margolis was definite. "Sure, Felipe. He came to the store sometimes."

"What was he like?" Virgil asked.

"Another Mex kid," Margolis answered.

When Virgil Tibbs got back to his office, there was news for him: Mr. and Mrs. Emilio De Fuentes and their eleven children were on welfare in Modesto, California. In response Tibbs picked up his phone and called the police department there. When he had been put through to a detective sergeant, he made a request. He described the family and supplied the welfare case number to make things as easy as possible.

"What I need," Virgil said, "is some information on when they reached Modesto and precisely when they went on welfare. I'd like a copy of the original document accepting them as welfare clients. Then, if it isn't too much trouble, I'd like the birth records of any children added to their family since they arrived up there. Especially any evidence of twins."

"Can do," the Modesto sergeant said.

After he finished the conversation Virgil left his office and went out for one more look at the abandoned house. He stayed inside it for more than an hour, making an almost microscopic examination of the drawings that had first attracted his attention. He satisfied himself that three children, apparently of different ages, had made them.

Child number one had been the oldest, but the drawings, eight of them, were also the simplest and the most repetitive. Child number two had had a less steady hand, but more imagination. Tibbs traced six of the drawings to his or her hand, and no two of them were similar. Child number three appeared to have been the youngest since the drawings he or she had made were the lowest on the wall. They were also the most varied and showed, on Tibbs' second examination, evidence of talent.

Despite the crudity of the draftsmanship, the third child had painstakingly tried to add background, drawing a horizontal line to suggest ground level in one instance and adding what was obviously the sun in another. A third drawing showed experimentation; when a first attempt to draw a symmetrical figure had failed, the child artist had added lines until there were many arms and legs, and even the torso had a multiplicity of wavy outlines.

Virgil returned late to his office to find two messages. One of them was a report that had come in from Modesto by teletype, the other was a penciled note from Diane Stone, the chief's secretary, that Chief McGowan would like to see him when he came in.

He put in a call to the chief's office, but McGowan had already left. Virgil was glad of that because there were still some loose ends to tie up before he went upstairs. Since the chief had sent for him personally, it did not require much deductive ability to know what was on the chief's mind.

A welfare report he had been waiting for was on his desk. From it he learned that the De Fuentes family had come from a small village in Mexico. That was a setback since it meant that his chances of getting accurate birthdates and related information were close to nil. Fortunately, there were other routes of inquiry.

Tibbs went home to his apartment and stretched out to rest. He wanted an expensive dinner, but it was his superstition to hold off splurging while he was still closing a case. There was still one very sticky fact to be established and while he was by that time reasonably confident, it still had to be rated as a long shot.

In the morning he visited the public school where some of the De Fuentes children had been enrolled. He did not trouble the office for official records, interviewing instead some teachers who had been on the faculty when the Fuentes children had attended the school. The first three he spoke with could not help him much; one was resentful that he was there at all. "You haven't got any business prying into those peoples' lives," she told him. "You ought to be ashamed; you're a black man yourself and here you're trying to put down other people who have been discriminated against all their lives."

The gymnasium instructor was the one who came through. "I do remember the De Fuentes children very well," he told Virgil. "I was interested in them because one of the boys, Felipe, had remarkable athletic ability and exceptional reflexes. I think he could have made it all the way to the big time if he had really worked at it. But he showed no interest in baseball or basketball."

"Do you remember if he had any particularly close friends at school?" Tibbs asked.

"Yes, he did—several, as a matter of fact."

"May I have some names?"

"Yes, and you can get the addresses in the office if you need them. Willie Fremont, Cliff Di Santo, Trig Yamamoto, and—oh, yes, there was a girl too—Elena Morales."

By two in the afternoon Virgil Tibbs had determined that three of the families had moved away, but he had two forwarding addresses. He succeeded in locating the Yamamoto boy where he was working in the vegetable department of a supermarket. By a little after four he had found and also talked to the Morales girl, who was a winsome little beauty and highly intelligent. She supplied him with the final data that he needed.

He went back to the office and called Mrs. Stone, to say that he was in if the chief still wanted to see him.

McGowan did. Virgil walked into the boss's office and sat down. When Diane handed him a cup of coffee, with cream and sugar exactly to his taste, he understood that he might be there for a little while.

"Virgil," the chief said, "I have a rather personal interest in the case you're working on—the child remains found during the freeway construction. Have you been able to make any progress?"

"I believe so, sir."

Captain Wilson appeared at the door and the chief filled him in.

"How much have you got, Virgil?" the captain asked.

"Since I'm not in court yet, and I don't have to provide absolute proof," Tibbs answered, "I can tell you that it's a case of premeditated murder. So far I can name the victim, give the time of death, and supply the motive. If all goes well, by tomorrow night I should have enough solid evidence for an indictment."

"Virgil," the chief said, "you never cease to amaze me. Instead of waiting for your report, suppose you bring us up to date now."

"All right, sir." Tibbs relaxed and enjoyed a little of his coffee.

"The preliminary work was quite simple," he began. "I located the plot, got the history of the dwelling that had been on it, and inspected the house itself. Fortunately it hadn't been destroyed, because there was quite a bit of evidence there, notably a series of children's drawings which were especially helpful."

"Children's drawings?" the chief queried.

"Yes, in fact they provided the essential clue when I finally had sense enough to see it. I completely missed it the first time."

"You must be slipping," the chief said.

"Undoubtedly, sir. Anyhow, without going into unnecessary details, I checked out the history of the house and satisfied myself that the most recent residents had all had one thing in common—no children were ever known to be on the premises during their tenure. There was a period of vacancy when children might have gone into the house to play, but I couldn't find any evidence to support that idea. It was also possible that someone could have taken a child there with criminal intent, but the available missing-persons reports tended to reduce the odds on that.

"So I focused my attention on a large Mexican family that had occupied the house about five years ago. There were nine children, ranging from a boy of fourteen to a one-year-old infant. I'm now satisfied that three of these children made the drawings I found on the walls of the second bedroom. Offhand I would fix their ages at about ten, nine, and eight, with the youngest the most talented of the three."

"That's interesting, I'm sure," Wilson said, "but where is it leading us?"

"Into proof of murder."

"You have my attention," the chief said.

"Consider first the fact that there were nineteen drawings and that they were done by three different children. There you have definite evidence of lack of family discipline. It was a rental property, but no regard was given to the rights of the owner—otherwise the children would have been restrained from drawing all over the walls of what was evidently their bedroom. And there was no indication of any effort whatever to remove the drawings when the family left. So we may conclude that the family in question was at the best irresponsible."

"I think I'm beginning to see something coming," Chief McGowan murmured.

"When this family lived in Pasadena, shortly before their departure, they had nine children. The family is now in Modesto and the latest head count is eleven."

"Which is not surprising," Captain Wilson commented.
"That's the key to the whole thing," Virgil said.
"Eleven children?"
"Exactly."

It was silent in the executive office for a few moments.
Then Chief McGowan leaned forward in his chair. "I get
it," he said.

Tibbs nodded. "In a neighborhood like that, sir, with all
the constant comings and goings and the frequent turnover
in residents, hardly anyone, even the children's playmates,
can keep track of every child in a family. And I have now
learned that since the family moved to Modesto, three more
children have been delivered to them. The birth records
are on file and I have copies coming in the mail."

"Three more children. Nine plus three are twelve. But
you said the latest count was only eleven," Captain Wilson
noted.

"Yes, sir. Now add to that these facts: we have a set of
parents with a profusion of children. I'm not putting down
large families, but the De Fuentes family may have been
blessed with more than they actually wanted. They couldn't
possibly support them—they were on welfare, and the
mother was constantly pregnant.

"I was turning these thoughts over in my mind when
an idea hit me. What if one of those children had been
particularly unwanted, because of being retarded or otherwise afflicted? In most cases that wouldn't add up to murder,
not by a wide margin, but here we are faced with the undis-
putable fact that a child of approximately eight years of
age was buried under that house.

"If the child had died normally, since the family was already receiving assistance, some sort of funeral arrangements could have been made."

"Also," Captain Wilson added, "since they are Mexican,
there is a good chance the family is Catholic. The obvious
absence of birth-control measures would support that. If a
child of theirs had died under acceptable circumstances,
then they would want to have it buried in sanctified ground
with the proper religious rites."

204

Tibbs nodded agreement. "When I re-examined the house itself," he continued, "I checked carefully for any evidence that might reveal an abnormal child. It was entirely possible, with all those children, such an unfortunate individual could be kept effectively hidden from the casual observation of the neighbors. If the child's condition was bad enough, that would have been almost automatic.

"I found what I was looking for in the drawings I described. One of them in particular. It had been done by the youngest of the three child artists and this child, as I mentioned earlier, had some artistic ability. He, or she, added touches of background and tried to make an actual picture. One of these efforts showed a child with what at first appeared to be multiple arms and legs, and a torso of wavy outlines, drawn in apparently to get the right proportions. Then I realized it wasn't that at all. First, the other drawings done by the same child exhibited no such difficulty, in fact the proportions were quite good. What the child was actually drawing was another child—"

"Shaking!" the chief interjected. "A spastic!"

"That's it, sir. Now I was confident that I knew why a large family might willfully dispose of one of its children. Even death by accident wouldn't call for the extreme measure of burying a child under the house. The answer was painfully apparent—a too large family with a problem child might make the terrible decision to simply get rid of it before moving on. A family leaves one location with a large brood of children; it arrives at the next one, still with a large brood—who is going to notice that one is missing?"

"There are institutions," the chief said. "Surely they must have known that."

"Perhaps they did, but there is some indication that despite the fact the family had been on welfare for some time, it may have come to this country illegally. Also, unfortunately, there are many people to whom any kind of institution is terrifying. I believe they thought that what they planned would be simpler. Anyhow, the social worker's report on the family, which I dug out and read, lists a boy who would have been eight and a half when the family moved away. His name was Alberto. I checked with Modesto where the family is receiving assistance now. There is no Alberto. That is hard evidence. I suspect that if we confront the father with the facts we now have, he will admit to what he probably has rationalized as a mercy killing."

"I can't understand," Captain Wilson said, "how they expected to get away with it. What did they tell their other children?"

"Probably that Alberto had been taken away, or some other excuse. The older children might have been cautioned never to speak of their spastic brother in case it might harm their own images. They would understand that."

Tibbs stopped for a moment and locked his fingers tightly together as he frequently did when he was under mental stress. Then he looked up once more. "You see, sir, they *did* get away with it. The missing child died years ago—we know that—he was buried, and there he lay. No one ever raised a question so far as I have been able to learn, and I strongly doubt if anyone ever would. It was pure accident that the burial site was excavated for the new freeway, and even that could well have passed unnoticed if the skull had not rolled off the top of the load. If that truck had been half full or less when the bones were loaded, the chances are good they would never have been noticed."

Chief McGowan had one more question. "Did the social worker make any mention of an abnormal child in her report?"

Tibbs nodded. "Yes, sir, she did. But she called him an 'exceptional child,' which was the term just coming into use at that time. If the family saw the report, or was shown it, that phrase would probably not register with them, particularly since English is not their native language. I don't think, gentlemen, that we will have too much trouble in obtaining a confession."

And in that, too, he was right.

206

Michael Vlado

THE GYPSY DETECTIVE

THE LUCK OF A GYPSY

Edward D. Hoch

"The Luck of a Gypsy" is the first short story to feature a Gypsy detective—Michael Vlado, a native Romanian and head of a modern tribe living in a small village in the Transylvanian Alps. The only other Gypsy detective in crime fiction is New York-based Roman Grey, hero of two excellent novels by bestselling author Martin Cruz Smith, Gypsy in Amber *(1971) and* Canto for a Gypsy *(1972).*

The wily Vlado, who knows more than anyone the way of the Gypsy and the workings of the Gypsy mind, joins with Captain Segar of the Romanian government police to investigate the smuggling of gold ingots by Gypsy caravan from Yugoslavia—an investigation that soon turns into a murder case as well. A classic fair-play detective story, "The Luck of a Gypsy" is also rich in Gypsy lore and history. We hope it is but the first of many featuring Vlado and Segar.

Edward D. Hoch has created many series detectives, including such favorites as Captain Leopold, Simon Ark, Nick Velvet, and the retired spy, Rand. His short stories have appeared in every issue of Ellery Queen's Mystery Magazine *for more than a dozen years, as well as in numerous other periodicals—a total of more than 600 published pieces over the past thirty years. Hoch has also written five novels, among them* The Shattered Raven *(1967) and the science fictional mystery* The Transvection Machine *(1971); and he is the editor of the acclaimed annual* Year's Best Mystery & Suspense Stories.

. . .

In Romania, in the foothills of the Transylvanian Alps, men like Captain Segar no longer worried about vampires. Their concerns were the more mundane evils of life in the late twentieth century—gold smuggling, drugs, illegal border crossings and the like. And because Captain Segar could speak the Romany tongue so well, his special concern had become the Gypsies. In his region there were those who roamed in caravans and those who lived quietly in the little foothill villages like Gravita, with its dirt roads and grazing horses.

He had driven to Gravita that brisk May morning to confer with one man who knew more than he did about the way of the Gypsy and the workings of the Gypsy mind. In another time, another place, Michael Vlado might have been mayor of his village, or even an official of the central government. He was a wise man, a friendly man, and a natural leader among his people. The Gypsies of the area had gradually become farmers, toiling in the wheat fields in the shadow of the distant mountains. Romania was not an industrialized nation like the other members of the communist bloc, and it still depended heavily upon its annual crops of wheat and corn.

Even in such a setting, Michael Vlado was near the top, and as Segar left his dust-covered car in search of the dark-eyed Gypsy, the people of the village quickly informed him that Michael was presiding over a dispute involving a bride-price. Segar slipped into the back of the council hall to listen.

A number of Gypsy tribes, including the Rom of Eastern Europe and the Balkans, still maintained the institution of bride-price, whereby a payment was made by the family of the groom to the family of the bride, to indemnify them for the loss of a daughter. Captain Segar had always thought it an odd custom, the opposite of the dowry a bride's family supplied in some cultures. But while the dowry was generally a thing of the past, the bride-price was a matter of pride and honor among these Gypsy families. Here, in the informal court or *kris,* both sides had brought their dispute to be decided by Michael Vlado.

As Segar settled onto one of the hard wooden benches, a Gypsy named Ion Fetesti was arguing his case. "I appeal to this *kris* to find in my favor! I have paid a suitable sum as a bride-price to the family of Maria Malita, and my son should be allowed to marry her."

Behind the great oak judgment table, Michael Vlado turned his dark eyes to the other man who stood before him. "We have heard Ion Fetesti's side of the dispute. Now what do you have to say, Arges Malita?"

The bride's father was a slim, muscular Gypsy whom Segar knew slightly from previous visits. His clothes were not as expensive or colorful as Fetesti's, and he made that point at once. "My family is poor, as all of you know. Maria is our greatest asset, able to work long in the fields and still help her mother with the kitchen chores. To take her away from us for a few pieces of gold is an insult to the Rom tradition!"

"I have no—" Fetesti started to interrupt.

"You have everything!" Malita insisted. "You have a television, and tractors to pull your plows, and the only camping vehicle in the village! Your son will marry my daughter and both of them will work your fields. For this loss you offer a bride-price of a few gold pieces!"

Both men were stirred by emotion, and Michael Vlado must have felt it too. Instead of rendering an instant verdict, he announced, "I will take the matter under advisement. Return here tomorrow noon for my decision. The *kris* is adjourned until then."

There was grumbling from some of the spectators on both

sides, but they filed out peacefully. Captain Segar caught up with Michael as he exited by a side door. "Hold on there, Gypsy! I've driven a long way to speak with you."

Michael Vlado's weathered face relaxed into a smile. Though just past forty he had the commanding presence of an older man, and Segar often had to remind himself that they were contemporaries. "The government's police have arrived! Am I under arrest, good Captain? Is my village surrounded?"

"Hardly that. But all this talk of money and wealth in a communist state seems wrong."

Vlado smiled indulgently, as he often did at Segar's statements. "You forget that Gypsies do not live in a communist state. We are subject to our own laws and our own social structures."

They were strolling away from the village buildings, across a field where the first wildflowers of spring were just beginning to appear. "Let's not have the old arguments again," Segar told him. "You're citizens of Romania and you must obey Romanian laws."

"As we do, when they do not conflict with our own! Have I not directed the Gypsy energy into farming and away from our more traditional pursuits? A decade ago my people were blacksmiths and horse traders, peddlers and fortune-tellers."

"Many of them still are."

"Of course! But by the next generation it will be different. We will enter the mainstream of life while still clinging to the old customs. It can be done, Captain."

"Perhaps," Segar admitted. "But the renegades among you are still a problem. A problem for me, at least. That is why I'm here."

"What is it? An old Gypsy woman taking money for curing someone's arthritis?"

"A bit more serious than that. A Gypsy caravan crossed the border at Orsova, heading this way. You know the border there, at the Danube. The traffic from Yugoslavia is heavy with local people on weekends, and security is lax.

They checked one truck of the caravan and found several gold ingots hidden beneath it, taped to the frame and coated with grease. Unfortunately by that time the rest of the caravan had been allowed to pass through the checkpoint."

"Gypsies with gold! They are good people to know. Perhaps there is one among them who will offer a better bride-price for Maria Malita."

"This is nothing to joke about, Michael. The gold might be smuggled in to foment unrest. The Americans—"

Michael Vlado laughed. "Gypsies do not work for the Americans, any more than they work for the Russians."

"Still, there is fear of counterrevolutionary activities. I am to remain in this area for the next few days, in the event the caravan comes this way."

"And why should they?"

"To stay with fellow Gypsies."

"We are well integrated with the culture here, Captain, despite our clinging to the old ways. And we are sedentary. Only ten percent of Balkan and Eastern European Gypsies are nomadic, unlike our brothers in Western Europe. These people who cross the border will keep moving like the nomads they are. They will not seek out our village."

"We'll see," Segar told him. "Have you reached a decision yet in the matter of the bride-price?"

"I must sleep on it. Young Steven Fetesti is a fine lad, and it would make a good marriage. Still, the rights of the Malita family must be considered."

It was Steven Fetesti who brought them the news, an hour later, that a caravan vehicle carrying two strange Gypsies had arrived in the village.

There was a king of the Gypsies in Gravita, and it was to him that Michael Vlado carried word of the strangers' arrival. He was called King Carranza, and Segar had met him on previous visits. Once he'd been an active blacksmith, the strongest man in the tribe, but a runaway horse had crippled him ten years earlier. He was still the king, for what little the title meant, but it was Michael who exercised the power. Segar knew someday he would be a king like Carranza.

"Strangers?" the king said, lifting his mane of iron-gray hair. "Is that what brings the police?"

"It is," Segar replied, answering before Michael did. "We believe they smuggled gold ingots across the border. Now that they have reached the village I will have to stop and search them. I hope your people will cooperate."

King Carranza turned in his wheelchair. "Gypsies must stick together."

"These are strangers," Segar insisted. "You owe them nothing."

"We shall see."

Segar's hand dropped to the leather holster he wore on his belt. He had never drawn his weapon in the village of Gravita, but he was reminding them he still carried it. "I will search their vehicle," he said again.

The Gypsy king waved his hand. "So be it. Michael will assist you."

They left him in his room behind the blacksmith's shop and walked down the street together. In the distance they could see the shiny white vehicle where it had stopped. "It is nothing but a camper—identical to hundreds of others." Michael said it with a trace of scorn. "When I was a boy Gypsy caravans were pulled by horses, and each one was decorated in the manner of that family. They were colorful things of beauty, and no two were alike."

"Times change," Segar remarked. He was anxious to search the vehicle.

The two Gypsies who'd come in it—a young man and woman—stood by the side of the road talking to a beautiful young woman he recognized as Maria Malita, object of the bride-price dispute. Segar reflected again that Steven Fetesti was a very lucky man. A woman like Maria was worth any price.

Maria turned as they approached. "These strangers are on their way to Bucharest. They need directions."

"A bit out of your way, aren't you?" Segar suggested.

The two, who spoke a form of Romany mixed with some

Greek words, introduced themselves as Norn Tene and his sister Rachael. They claimed to have gotten lost on the back roads after crossing the border at Calafat. Captain Segar did not believe that any more than he believed they were brother and sister.

"You did not cross at Orsova?" he asked.

"Orsova?" Norn Tene repeated. "No, no. Calafat."

Segar studied the dust-covered Greek license plate on the back of the vehicle. "You came from Athens?"

"That's right."

"I must search your vehicle for illegal cargo."

"Search?" The young woman pretended not to understand.

Segar dropped his hand to his holster, and Michael Vlado spoke up. "He has the permission of King Carranza. I am to see that you cooperate." There was just a hint of a threat in his voice.

Norn Tene shrugged. "We have nothing to hide."

Segar crawled beneath the vehicle and inspected it with his flashlight. There was plenty of grease but no sign of any gold. Next he entered the camper with Tene and looked in any place large enough to hide gold ingots. Again there was nothing. "Are you satisfied?" the Gypsy asked.

Captain Segar studied him carefully. "I am never satisfied when I am outwitted by a Gypsy."

"In Greece there was no police harassment. Gypsies could move about with complete freedom."

"Then go back to Greece!" He stormed out of the camper.

"Did you find anything?" Michael asked.

"Nothing."

"Can they be on their way?"

"I suppose so." He would have to telephone back to headquarters and admit his failure.

"Perhaps only a few vehicles in the caravan were carrying gold," Michael suggested. "Or perhaps these two are telling the truth."

Segar had another thought. "You two—let me see your passports."

Norn Tene handed over two grimy Greek documents

of a sort easily forged. They were not stamped with the town of entry, but Segar knew the border guards were sometimes lax on weekends, especially with a large caravan traveling together. It proved nothing.

"May we go now?" the woman Rachael asked.

"Go!" Segar almost shouted.

He watched the vehicle pull away and then called out to young Steven Fetesti. "Where did you first see them coming into town? Were they traveling on the road from Calafat or from Orsova?"

"It was my father who first saw them, on the Orsova road. He sent me to tell you."

"The Orsova road," Segar repeated. He turned to Michael. "That gold is somewhere in the vehicle. I'm certain of it."

"But where? You searched it yourself, Captain." His tone of voice seemed to express little regret that Segar had been outwitted.

"I'm going after them," Segar decided. "Come along."

They went in the government car, going down the road in the direction the camper had taken. "I'm going with you only to protect you from harm," Michael assured him. "You must not do anything rash."

"I don't need protection. This is my lucky day."

"Of course," Michael agreed. "The luck of a Gypsy. The Rom have an old saying: *If in the morning a Gypsy you meet, the rest of your day will be lucky and sweet.*"

"And I've met plenty of Gypsies this day," Captain Segar agreed. He was keeping his eye on the road ahead, searching for a sight of the white camper. "Starting with you. How were you given a name like Michael, anyway?"

"After the last Romanian king. I was born in August of 1944, in the very month that he took power. Of course the Russians forced him to abdicate three years later, but he was a national hero for a brief time. He switched Romania to the Allied side, against Hitler."

"And Vlado is from Prince Vlad, the model for Count Dracula?"

214

Michael Vlado chuckled. "No, no—the legends of Transylvania are even more bizarre than those of the Gypsy. Vlado is a common family name among Gypsies, known even in America, where much of the Rom tribe has settled."

"Where are you from originally? India, as the legends say?"

"Northern India, most certainly. But we were as much outcasts there as we have been ever since."

"But now you wander no longer."

"Nine or ten centuries of wandering is enough for any tribe. Perhaps there is another saying: *The world shall know no peace, till the Gypsy's wanderings cease.*"

"There it is!" Segar said suddenly, catching sight of the white camper parked just off the road. He pulled in behind it and they got out.

The driver's door was standing open, and as they neared it Segar saw an arm dangling almost to the ground. He drew his pistol without a word. Norn Tene had toppled sideways from the driver's seat, and blood was running from two bullet wounds in his head, dripping onto the ground beside the car. In the passenger seat, the girl Rachael was crumpled and bleeding from wounds in her head and breast.

"They're both dead," Captain Segar said with something like awe in his voice.

This time Michael Vlado helped him search, but there was no sign of the gold. In fact there seemed to be no personal possessions at all in the camper except for some food and bedding. "Whoever killed them took it," Segar decided. "Do you agree?"

"There was no time for the killer to search the vehicle," Michael pointed out. "We were less than five minutes behind them. Besides, you'd already looked for the gold."

"I might have missed it," Segar said, though he didn't really believe that. He had not risen to the rank of Captain by missing something as large and obvious as gold ingots.

"The ingots might be of small size," the Gypsy pointed out.

"Those seized at the border were large enough. They were hidden beneath the camping vehicle, coated with grease."

"Perhaps there was some other motive for the killings." But Segar could tell that the words lacked conviction. They both knew the two had been killed for their gold, by one of the village Gypsies.

"There is no other motive," Segar said. "I want the killer, Michael, and I want the gold."

"I cannot give you what I do not have."

"I want the killer or I will have the militia up here, tearing apart every house in Gravita."

"You cannot do that."

Segar's temper boiled over. The killings seemed like a personal affront to him, and seeing the bodies not yet drained of their blood made him want to strike back. "I can do anything that I wish, Michael Vlado! You are nothing but a band of Gypsies, remember. You are beyond the protection of the law. I can have everyone in this town arrested if I wish."

"We have lived here all our lives. We are citizens."

"Then act like a citizen! Give me the killer of these two people."

"I cannot give you what I do not have," he repeated.

"I will call the authorities now to deal with these bodies. You have until morning to deliver the murderer to me. Otherwise you force me to take drastic action."

Michael Vlado merely shook his head and said nothing. Segar used the police radio in his car to summon assistance. Then he returned to the Gypsy, his temper calmed a bit, and attempted to show a degree of moderation. "You could start by listing for me those Gypsies known to possess guns."

"All of us possess guns, Captain. It is a farming and hunting community."

"And do all of you possess gold ingots?"

Michael Vlado sighed. "You must talk to King Carranza. If he approves, I will give you what help I can."

It was thirty minutes before the district police reached

the scene, and Segar saw at once that they had little knowledge or skill in dealing with the double killing. Some of his own men arrived soon after, and he ordered the government police under the Ministry of Justice to take jurisdiction in the matter. It was late afternoon before he was able to leave the scene and drive back to the village with Michael Vlado. At King Carranza's blacksmith shop they found they were not the only visitors. Steven Fetesti and Maria Malita had come with a special petition.

Steven, his young face troubled and intense, was pacing the floor of Carranza's living room while the crippled king sat hunched over in his wheelchair. He was obviously making a final plea that his marriage to Maria be allowed to proceed as scheduled. "It is our life, King Carranza, and a dispute over the bride-price should not be allowed to disrupt the ceremony!"

The king raised his hand for silence as Segar and Michael Vlado entered. "What new troubles do you bring me, Michael? I have already heard of the tragic killings on the north road."

"That is why I come. Captain Segar wants my cooperation. But tend to these young people first."

It was Maria who spoke next, and she addressed herself to Michael. "We know our fate is in your hands because you will rule on the bride-price controversy tomorrow noon. But we cannot accept a verdict that denies us the right to marry unless a few more *leu* or a few more gold necklaces are paid."

"You must abide by the ruling of the *kris*," the king told them. "That has always been the way of the Gypsies."

"Then it's time that way was changed," Steven told him. "If necessary we will leave Gravita. We will run away to Bucharest and be married there!"

Michael placed a hand on the young man's broad shoulders. "Wait until tomorrow, and see what happens. I urge you not to do anything rash that will bring shame on both your families."

Maria Malita seemed reassured by his words, and she took

Steven aside. Finally they promised not to do anything until the following day. When they had left, King Carranza said, "Your judgment in the matter must not be swayed by sentiment, Michael. If the bride-price is unfair, you must rule that way."

"Right now we have a more important matter before us."

"The killings? They were nomads, were they not?"

"They were Gypsies, from Greece. It seems obvious they headed in our direction because they sought safety with us. Instead they received bullets."

"From whom?"

"That we do not know."

"An outsider—"

"Not likely. One of our people saw the captain searching for smuggled gold. He—or she—waylaid them along the road and shot them both. The killer no doubt planned to search for the gold himself, but heard our approaching car and escaped into the woods. We were only minutes behind."

"Why do you say *she?*"

"We cannot rule out a woman," Michael said. "A woman would be more successful in getting them to stop in the first place, and she might have hidden a rifle under her full skirt."

But Captain Segar shook his head. "The murder weapon was more likely a pistol. The camper door was opened on the driver's side before the shots were fired, because there were no bullet holes in the glass. I think the killer was standing nearby, and at that range rifle bullets would have passed through the bodies. These bullets didn't. Also, a rifle or automatic pistol ejects its cartridge cases. There were none on the ground, and the killer wouldn't have had time to pick them up. I would guess a revolver was used."

Carranza's eyes twinkled. "You are a good detective."

"A detective, yes—but my knowledge of the Rom is limited. I speak your language, I know something of your customs, but for this investigation I need Michael here."

"You ask that he betray a fellow Gypsy?"

"The victims were Gypsies, and guests of this village."

"They were only passing through," Michael corrected. "But we had a responsibility for their safety."

The king nodded. "Perfectly true, and the Rom is a strictly moral society. We do have responsibility to uncover the killer if he is one of our people. Can we still insist that our unmarried girls be chaperoned when we let a double murder go unpunished?"

"I will help you," Michael told the captain, "if it is King Carranza's will."

"It is," the man in the wheelchair said.

"Tomorrow morning?" Segar asked.

"Tomorrow noon."

Captain Segar remained at the village overnight, sleeping at the Vlado home. Michael's wife Rosanna, whom Segar had not met before, proved to be a pleasant but withdrawn woman who took little interest in her husband's affairs. She carved little wooden animals which were sold in one of the village shops, and late in the evening warmed toward Segar enough to get out a deck of tarot cards and tell his fortune.

"She's good with those," Michael said, watching his wife with unconcealed admiration as she predicted a long and happy life, and many children, for Captain Segar.

"I have four children now," he told her. "Do you see more?"

"A fifth, at least. A girl."

Captain Segar smiled.

He slept downstairs on a worn sofa, and sometime past midnight awakened enough to see a shadow move across the front door of the little house. He started to reach for his gun but then he recognized Michael, slipping out of the house. Perhaps he was on his way to meet a woman or find a murderer. Either way, Segar knew he did not want company.

He woke at dawn, and saw that Michael was already sitting fully dressed at the kitchen table. Perhaps he had not slept at all. Segar rolled off the sofa, rubbing the sleep from his eyes. He went into the bathroom without speaking, and when he came out he said, "You promised me a murderer before noon."

"By noon, I think I said. First I must dispose of the matter of the bride-price."

"Never mind the bride-price. Do you know who killed those two people?"

"Yes."

"And where the gold was hidden?"

"Yes, that too."

"Where did you go during the night?"

"All in good time, Captain."

After breakfast they walked through the village and Michael Vlado spoke to everyone they passed. He wore a colorful new vest his wife had made, and seemed especially proud of it. "You are happy today," Segar observed.

"The weather is warming. Soon the crops will be planted. When my people have things to occupy them, there are not so many temptations about."

"You will lead them someday," Segar observed. "You will be their king."

"Carranza is their king. To go against his wishes would bring a curse upon the entire tribe."

"You still believe the old superstitions?"

But Michael did not answer.

When they reached the council hall, well before the time set for Michael to deliver his verdict, the rival fathers were already on the scene. Arges Malita was pacing back and forth, eying Ion Fetesti with open dislike. "Ah, Michael Vlado," he said as they approached, "do you have a verdict for me today?"

"I have. You will hear it at noon."

"Your daughter is not fit for my son!" Fetesti shouted suddenly, and Arges Malita hurled himself toward the other man. Segar moved quickly to keep them apart. Family members led them in separate directions, trying to calm them.

"I thought Gypsy marriages were arranged by the families," Segar said as they entered the building.

"Usually they are. But with Steven and Maria it is true love. The fathers were never friendly, and this business of the bride-price has driven them even further apart. I think Malita would have objected no matter what price the Fetesti family offered for Maria."

"Was there trouble when you and Rosanna married?"

Michael chuckled. "Nothing like this. But Gypsies are hot-blooded by nature. It is to be expected."

The spectators gradually filed in, taking their seats on opposite sides of the room. The families were divided, except that Steven and Maria sat together in the last row on his side. Just before noon Segar was surprised to see King Carranza wheeled in, his chair pushed by Michael's wife.

Segar stood at the back of the small room while Michael sat behind the judgment table. "This *kris* is now in session," he announced. "Although my judgment is informal, and has no legal sanction in the eyes of the state, it is binding in our community. Ion Fetesti and Arges Malita, please rise." When they had done so, he continued. "We find that the bride-price offered by the Fetesti family is a fair and reasonable one, and must be accepted by the family of Maria Malita."

There was cheering from the family of Steven Fetesti and silence from the Malita clan. Captain Segar glanced at King Carranza and thought he detected a slight smile. In the last row, Steven kissed Maria gently on the lips.

"There is one other matter," Michael announced as some of the family members began to file out. "Though it is not the official business of this *kris* to investigate crimes, we cannot let yesterday's terrible event pass without notice. Two travelers, Roms like ourselves, were brutally robbed and murdered while passing through the village. For this the killer must be brought to account. I have investigated the matter, and it is now my unpleasant duty to name the guilty party."

There was dead silence in the room as he spoke. Segar tensed, waiting for the next words.

"Ion Fetesti, you are the murderer!"

Fetesti, basking in the triumph of his victory on the bride-price, looked dumbfounded for just an instant. Then his hand streaked beneath his coat and came out holding a revolver. Segar's own shot was just a second too late, and he saw Michael topple as the killer's bullet struck him.

It was Rosanna who insisted that Michael be carried to their house, and it was she who worked on his shoulder, digging and probing until the bullet had been removed. Segar took it to match with the slugs from the other two victims, though the result would be of only academic interest. His own shot had blown off the back of Ion Fetesti's head.

When Michael could sit up and talk, there were questions from Rosanna and King Carranza, as well as from Segar. "It was a foolish thing, I suppose, announcing his name like that," Michael admitted. "But I had no way of knowing he'd be armed. I suppose he brought the weapon to protect himself from Maria's father."

"How did you know he killed those two?" Captain Segar asked. "You must have had some knowledge I lacked."

"No, no—you saw and heard all that I did. My midnight journey last night was only to confirm what I already knew. Our first sight of the victims' camper, parked in the village yesterday, showed that it was shiny—not dusty like your own car, Captain, after traveling these dirt roads. And yet the Greek license plate on the back was dusty. What does that suggest?"

"My God! They switched plates!"

"Or to be more exact, they switched campers. You did not find the gold ingots when you searched for them because you were searching the wrong vehicle. That camper came from this village, and they simply attached their plates to it. If you were listening during yesterday's *kris* testimony, you know that Ion Fetesti owned the only camping vehicle in the village. And I remarked myself how much alike they all looked. Is there confirmation of this theory? Yes, because young Steven told us his father first saw the visitors and sent Steven to tell us. While he was telling us, his father warned them the police were in the village and struck a deal with them. He emptied his own camper of his personal possessions, quickly switched license plates, and allowed them to drive it into the village. They did it in such a hurry, no one noticed the dusty license plates. Fetesti would have avoided getting his fingerprints on them as much as possible if he was planning a crime."

"He planned to kill them from the beginning?"

"Perhaps not. But while they were in the village with us he found the gold ingots fastened beneath the camper. He needed money—for his son's bride-price if nothing else—so he decided to keep that camper with its gold. He met Norn Tene and Rachael at the agreed-upon rendezvous outside the village, but instead of returning their camper he killed them."

"Where did you go during the night?" Segar asked.

"To Fetesti's house to look at his camper. I guessed he would leave the ingots safely where they were for the time being, and I found them just where you said, covered with grease."

"Why didn't those Gypsies simply remove the gold bars and leave them with Fetesti, rather than change campers?"

"They didn't trust him enough to show him what they were carrying. And when I examined them they were well hidden and difficult to remove from the camper's chassis."

Rosanna finished bandaging her husband, the rings on her fingers catching the light as she worked. "What about the wedding?" she asked, "now that Steven's father is dead?"

"Ion Fetesti must be buried first," Michael decided. "Then the wedding will go on as planned. A fair bride-price has been decided upon."

Gypsies, Captain Segar thought, remembering the young couple. There are good ones and bad ones. "I'll be going soon," he said. "Take care of yourself, Michael. That bullet might have killed you."

Michael Vlado smiled. "I have the luck of a Gypsy."

"It didn't help Fetesti today."

Commissaire Alexandre Tama

THE TAHITIAN DETECTIVE

GOLDFISH

Hayford Peirce

Commissaire de Police *Alexandre Tama is crime fiction's first Tahitian detective, and "Goldfish" is his first recorded case. Tama is cast in the mold of the classic "Golden Age" detective; in his size and prodigious appetite, in fact, he is reminiscent of John Dickson Carr's Sir Henry Merrivale and Dr. Gideon Fell. He has the same sort of gruff-and-bluster charm as Merrivale and Fell, as well—a welcome addition to the ranks of ethnic sleuths.*

"Goldfish" is rich in the sights, sounds, smells, and unique citizenry of Tahiti, the exotic island in French Polynesia whose allure drew painter Paul Gauguin and so many others since. Hayford Peirce among them: he is an American who has lived on Tahiti for the past twenty years, which accounts for the authenticity of the background, and of Tama, Inspector Opuu, and the other Tahitian characters.

Although he has sold a number of science fiction stories to such magazines as Omni, Analog, *and* Galaxy, *and two science-fiction novels—*The Thirteenth Death of Yuri Gellaski *and* In the Flames of the Flicker Man—*"Goldfish" marks Hayford Peirce's first sale in the detective field. We*

225

predict that it won't be his last, and that Commissaire *Tama* *will enjoy a long and illustrious career.*

. . .

Easter Sunday in Tahiti: hot, dry, and clear. A light breeze stirred the leaves of the trees that towered over the blacktop road that wound through the district of Tiarei: mangos and breadfruit, ironwood and mahogany, an occasional avocado or chestnut, and everywhere the graceful arc of the coconut palm. A pitiless sun lanced through the foliage to dapple the road, the Tahitian families on their way to church in long white dresses and dark blue serge suits with double-breasted lapels handed down from their grandfathers. Hedges of bougainvillea and hibiscus lined the road, their gaudy flowers lilac and orange, pale rose, deep red, creamy white, flaming yellow. Ginger, *opui,* frangipani, a dozen kinds of banana trees struggled for sunlight and survival. Even at nine in the morning heat waves shimmered on the road ahead, and over everything lay the scent of coffee beans and vanilla, mixed with the cloying odor of drying coprah.

Alexandre Tama, *Commissaire de Police* of the city of Papeete, reached forward over his belly to turn the air conditioning a notch higher, and mopped his mahogany-colored face with an enormous red handkerchief. He ran it through his thick black hair and around his neck. Sweat glistened and ran on his broad unwrinkled forehead, his puffed-out cheeks, his multiple chins, and stained the vastness of his light blue shirt in enormous dark half-moons. He sat back with a sigh in the specially reinforced seat of the long black Citroën and breathed deeply.

"It's a hot year, Marcel," he complained. "I've never known a hotter one."

"Not to mention the hurricanes, *M. le Commissaire,*" said the driver, a leathery-skinned Tahitian also clad in a light blue shirt and dark blue pants, but as short, thin, and wiry as Tama was tall, elephantine, and bloated. They spoke in French, though the one was as Tahitian as the other.

"Bof." Tama dismissed hurricanes with a wave of banana-

sized fingers. "No worry about hurricanes blowing *me* away. But heat though—heat can *melt* things."

The driver grinned and brought the Citroën to a smooth halt. "Here we are, sir. Shall I wait here?"

"Leave you in this cool air-conditioned car while I suffer in there? Not on your life!" Inspector Marcel Opuu sighed in mock dismay: he had been raised on the bleached wastes of a coral atoll in the remote Tuamotus and absorbed heat like a desert lizard; he hated air conditioning. Tama swung open the door and reached forward to grasp the six-inch length of steel tubing that had been bolted to the fender of the Citroën just to the front of the door. He pulled his vast bulk through the doorway and to his feet. He stood blinking owlishly in the sunlight, tugging at the wrinkles in his crumpled blue slacks.

Down the road Tama could make out hidden among the trees a large white church, a dilapidated Chinese general store, a school, a dozen houses. Bells pealed, calling the faithful to worship, roosters squawked, small brown children darted about, holiday traffic zipped by dangerously close. Before him the district *gendarmerie* nestled deep in the shade of a large chestnut tree whose branches extended as far as the road and a neatly painted cement-block wall. It was a small two-storied building painted a light tan, with a bright red galvanized tin roof. The blue, white, and red of the French tricolor flapped over the entrance. The front door, as well as the windows on either side, was open to the breeze, revealing a dark, cool-looking interior from which a sharp tang of fresh coffee wafted across the courtyard.

Commissaire Tama sniffed appreciatively, then eased himself through the gateway and marched up the pathway, his footsteps amazingly light and sure for a man of his colossal dimensions. Inspector Opuu hesitated a moment before following: the city police, of which Alexandre Tama was chief, had no jurisdiction beyond its limits. Law and order in the districts was left to the *Gendarmerie Nationale*. As far as the inspector knew, Tama's only business in the districts was at the lunch table of the Rotui Restaurant.

"M. le Commissaire!" A khaki-clad gendarme appeared from behind a curtain, stared in surprise, and sketched a vague salute. Alexandre Tama smiled and extended a massive hand. "Sergeant Croisie, I believe? My assistant, Inspector Opuu." He hooked his fingers together on the vast circumference of his belly and his black eyes twinkled behind the rolls of fat. *"I,* of course, am Commissaire *opu."* And he laughed immoderately, for in Tahitian *opu* means stomach.

Sergeant Croisie, a tall, thin Frenchman, grinned uneasily, aware that a joke had been made but unable to fathom it. He hid his discomfort by stepping past the curtain into the kitchen beyond and gesturing invitingly. *"M. le Commissaire:* Gendarmes Léogite and Harehoe; and my spouse, Mme. Croisie."

Two gendarmes, one French, one Tahitian, rose from the table and saluted stiffly. They were in khaki uniforms of short-sleeve shirts, knee-length shorts, and long tan stockings. Mme. Croisie, a rosy-faced dumpling in a bright printed dress, smiled and continued to pour coffee. A fan turned lazily overhead, circulating the smell of warm pastry.

"I've interrupted your breakfast," said Tama, his nostrils quivering delicately and his eyes darting about the kitchen.

"Not at all," protested Sergeant Croisie, pulling another two chairs up to the table. "Please join us, we were about to begin."

"Impossible," said Tama, his voice wavering only a little as he caught a glimpse of golden croissants being removed from the oven. "My inspector here is a man of almost no appetite at all, and I . . ." his voice trailed off and his head bobbed up and down piteously, *"I* am dieting."

Mme. Croisie pursed her lips in dismay: the commissaire and his appetite were a legend on the island.

"However," allowed Alexandre Tama judiciously, "I see no reason to deprive myself of at least one cup of coffee. . . ."

*   *   *

Twenty minutes later the remaining flakes of his fourth croissant were gathered up, slathered with Normandy butter, and carefully bound together with a last trickle of thick, wheat-colored honey poured from an old beer bottle.

"Ah," sighed Tama in appreciation, licking at his fingers. "Genuine Taravao honey: it's not often that I see it anymore. And superb croissants, Madame."

She flushed with pleasure.

"I won't disturb your Sunday any further," said Tama. "I was on my way elsewhere when I thought to stop for a moment's conversation."

Sergeant Croisie nodded solemnly.

"You've been here from France how long, Sergeant? Two years? Then you know the problems we have with teenage gangs, since they're in the districts as well as town. You've been told, I suppose, that they're a relatively new phenomenon of the last ten or fifteen years. This unfortunately is true. Ever since the Army arrived here for their H-bomb tests Tahiti has been living in the space age, and now we've got space-age problems, just like Paris or Marseilles."

"But surely the gangs are no great problem," said Sergeant Croisie, puffing clouds of blue smoke from his Gitane, "not the way they are in the *métropole*. A little petty theft, a little illegal entry—annoying to the people concerned, but not much more. Why, we broke up one gang six or seven months ago, after five months of work. Thirteen, fourteen, fifteen, none of them older than that. None living with his parents, just roaming around like wild animals, living in a deserted shack in the hills, coming out to steal a little food now and then."

"You sound like those soft-headed judges on the bench who give them a slap on the wrist and then send them off to rob some more," said Tama harshly.

Sergeant Croisie's shoulders straightened. "That is *not* what I said, *M. le Commissaire,*" he replied stiffly. "I merely—"

"Forgive me," said Tama. "It is inexcusable to abuse your hospitality by insulting you. I plead fatigue: I was up most of the night tidying up the mess one of these bands left. It was not pretty."

"I understand, *M. le Commissaire.* Eveline! More coffee for the commissaire."

"In general," Tama went on, "I know what you mean, Sergeant, and agree up to a point. In the old days—only a few years ago—the gangs were as you describe, and still are—in the districts. In town, however, they have become increasingly bold and rapacious. Petty theft of food has led inevitably to grand theft, complete with organizations for the distribution of stolen goods. Now it's no longer a loaf of bread but a stereo set, a television, jewelry stores, whatever isn't nailed down." He tapped the table lightly with an enormous fist. "Even I—I, Alexandre Tama!—now lock my house when I go out for the evening, and remove the keys from my car in town. In Tahiti! Can you imagine? We might as well be living in New York City!" He glared at Inspector Opuu and the three gendarmes as if the responsibility could be laid directly at their door.

"Moreover," said Tama, "these gangs now venture forth in the light of day. They harass passersby on the streets of town for money and cigarettes: soldiers, tourists, even other penniless Tahitians such as themselves. No money, no cigarette,"—he clenched a great fist—"bam! Right on the nose! At night, although I hate to say it, there are parts of town which are no longer safe, particularly if you're a French soldier or sailor, or a woman, or even a girl." His mouth tightened and he reached forward to clutch the sergeant's wrist in a grip of iron.

"You said they're like wild animals, Sergeant, these homeless waifs of yours. Well, I agree with you: they *are* wild animals!" His eyes closed and he spoke softly. "Last night, Sergeant, such a gang took possession of the old Chinese Consulate—you know it, don't you? It's on the waterfront across from the naval base, been deserted for years now. How many of them we don't know, but ten at least, possibly fifteen. Of all ages between ten and twenty. Vicious thugs, the lot of them!"

230

Tama removed his hand from the sergeant's wrist to jab an accusatory finger at each gendarme in turn. "They sauntered forth, did these thugs," he said between his teeth, "as if they were bandit chieftains from a mountain redoubt in Mexico or Corsica, abducted people from the street, one after the other, carried them back to the Consulate, and—do I have to tell you?"

Sergeant Croisie glanced at his plump little wife, sitting now pale and wide-eyed at the end of the table. "No," he said.

Alexandre Tama nodded. "There are five of them now in the hospital, three sailors—one of them Tahitian—and two girls. One of the girls is thirteen. Two are being evacuated on the military plane for France this morning. One will probably never walk again." He rose ponderously to his feet. "Inspector Opuu will leave you a circular with what details and descriptions we have. You'd have received it tomorrow morning in any case."

"You think this gang might be heading for the districts?" asked Sergeant Croisie.

Tama shrugged massive shoulders. "They might even *be* from the districts. We've never had a case like this before. Anything is possible." He sighed, and turned to Mme. Croisie to bow as low as his enormous belly would allow. *"Madame, mes hommages."*

At the doorway he halted and peered dubiously at the blazing sun. He pulled the red handkerchief from his pocket and dabbed at the back of his neck. "I nearly forgot," he murmured, turning back to Sergeant Croisie. "Join us in the shade of that chestnut for just a moment, would you? Ah, that's better. Two other matters, Sergeant, one of them rather delicate."

Sergeant Croisie's face grew solemn. "Sir!"

"Hrumph! Delicate is the word *he* used. Idiotic is the word *I* use." Tama scowled. "A certain high personage in the judiciary, one of the assistant prosecutors, is as human as the rest of us, it seems, no matter how fine the black robes and white lace he wears in court. He came to see

231

me at home last night, hush-hush, all very confidential, strictly off the record, personal favor, blah blah. You've heard such music."

Sergeant Croisie sniffed cynically. "Indeed I have."

"It seems our fine *procureur* has been keeping a *petite amie* on the side for almost a year now, something to distract himself with after those tedious hours in the courtroom. He even rented a little studio apartment in town to receive her. A young Tahitian girl named Hina Tevahine Terorotua. Calls herself Marie-Hélène when she feels like being fancy. A few days ago they had a spat and she walked out. The prosecutor had a few drinks to console himself before returning home to his wife, so it was some time before he noticed that Marie-Hélène had also walked off with his briefcase."

"Ah!" sighed Inspector Opuu.

"You can imagine the kind of papers a public prosecutor might be carrying around with him. And the embarrassment if they turn up missing. I'll let you fill in the rest."

Sergeant Croisie nodded dourly. "The girl is from the districts, he doesn't know how to find her, and he doesn't dare file a formal complaint."

"Exactly!" Commissaire Tama snorted. "So he comes to me, unofficially, to save his bacon. And fortunately for our friend, he's had one piece of luck. The girl's name rings a bell with me; I'm almost certain her father was a district policeman—a *mutoi*—in one of the districts here on this side of the island. André Terorotua, his name would be. I expect you've never heard of him personally, but you could ask some of your men." He scowled with comic ferocity. "Discreetly, of course. For the honor of the Republic!"

Sergeant Croisie struggled to keep a straight face. "Of course, sir. Right now?"

Commissaire Tama considered. "Inspector Opuu and I will be lunching at the Rotui. Why don't you telephone us there around one?"

"Certainly, sir. That should be plenty of time."

"Fine." Tama smiled. "Now: back to that fine air-conditioned car." He extended his hand, scowled, withdrew it.

"Dubreuil," he muttered. "That's the *other* matter. Paul-Emile Dubreuil. I believe he lives somewhere around here?"

"Dubreuil?" repeated Sergeant Croisie, a slow grin spreading across his face. "The man who was on television the other night? The man who finds gold in fishes' stomachs?"

"That's the one," said Tama heavily. "The man who finds gold in fishes' stomachs."

"Goldfish?" said Inspector Opuu as he maneuvered the Citroën around an ancient tractor chugging slowly down the road. "On television?"

"Disgraceful," muttered Tama. "The television shouldn't be allowed to show such things. No, Marcel, not goldfish, but a fine gentleman named Paul-Emile Dubreuil who claims to have a secret fishing hole where he catches fish with gold nuggets in their bellies."

"What!"

"Exactly," said the commissaire sourly. "It was on TV a couple of nights ago—I caught a minute or so of it on my way out. The kids were watching, and I was leaving for dinner with the secretary general. *Figure-toi*, Marcel, that here is a fellow, a Frenchman if you please, saying that in the last month he's found a kilogram of pure gold nuggets in the stomachs of *pahicheri*, which he's been catching with a special deep-line technique at 400 meters."

"*Pahicheri?* At 400 meters?" said Inspector Opuu, a noted fisherman. "Humph . . . Well, maybe . . ."

"They even showed him on his wharf cutting open three of these fish and finding a tiny nugget in the stomachs of two of them. Naturally the interviewer wanted to know where he was catching these remarkable fish, and naturally *M.* Dubreuil wasn't saying."

"You think it's possible?"

"Anything's *possible*," said Tama darkly. "After all, I'm not a marine biologist, just a dumb policeman. But I know a con man when I see one."

"Ahh," breathed Inspector Opuu.

"What else could he be? Those fools at the TV station let themselves be conned by this Dubreuil into showing his routine, and one of these days now we'll be getting a complaint from some poor imbecile that he's paid his life savings to this fellow to buy the map to the secret fishing grounds. And now he's complaining there aren't any fish, and if there are, they don't have any gold in their guts!"

"Pretty nervy," said the inspector. "And a pretty good swindle too. After all, I'm sure he wouldn't guarantee that *every pahicheri* would have a nugget in its belly."

Tama slammed the dashboard with the palm of his hand. "I don't care whether it's a good swindle or not," he roared, "I won't have it! Every con man in the Pacific seems to have been descending on Papeete lately, stuffing their pockets and making fools of the government. Do you realize how many millions of francs they've paid out to plausible-sounding scoundrels for so-called feasibility studies for oil refineries, thousand-room hotels with private landing strips, cold-water lobster farms—none of which are ever heard of again once the promoter's been wined and dined at our expense and caught the first plane out with the money in his pocket."

"What can you expect of politicians," asked Inspector Opuu, "common sense?"

"Agreed. It's our job to protect them from themselves." He stared out at a passing herd of black and white cows. "You know," he mused, "I may have been thinking too small-time about this goldfish business. Maybe Dubreuil's planning to sell his secret to the *government.* You can be sure *they'd* bite!"

Except for an old wooden house, clearly deserted and now falling to pieces some fifty meters away, Paul-Emil Dubreuil's was the only habitation for hundreds of meters in either direction. It sat on a muddy bit of waterfront pocked by the holes of scuttling landcrabs. Across the road was a magnificent view of the jagged peaks and tumbling waterfalls of the Tahitian interior, while to seaward a picture-book island with a single coconut palm on it lay a short

distance away on the placid blue waters of the lagoon. A
small wooden jetty poked into the lagoon, mooring an outrigger canoe and a white Boston Whaler.

"An attractive house," commented Alexandre Tama,
standing in the middle of the living room, his gaze moving
from the neat bamboo walls to the steeply pitched, coconut-
thatch ceiling to the many shelves of tightly-packed bookcases. "Modern, but with a certain *folklorique* charm."

"Just rented, I'm afraid," said Paul-Emil Dubreuil with
an easy smile. "Except for my books I like to travel light.
I expect I'll be moving on one of these days."

"I expect so. Along with your gold nuggets, of course."

"With my . . . oh, *those!* Of course! My gold nuggets."
Dubreuil's smile broadened. He was a darkly tanned
Frenchman of middle age, with cropped white hair, a guileless countenance, and bright blue eyes. He wore nothing
at all but a tiny red bathing suit and a gold coin which
dangled from his neck. His body was hard and muscled.
"You saw my little show."

"Parts of it," said Tama with ominous import.

Dubreuil blinked. "Oh?" His eyes moved from Tama to
Inspector Opuu and he smiled uncertainly. "I see. I think.
Could I . . . offer you a drink, *M. le Commissaire,* an aperitif,
or a beer perhaps?" He gestured. "Sit down, sit down."

"Thank you, no," said Tama coldly. "There are certain
types of people I prefer not to drink with."

Spots of red appeared in Dubreuil's sun-browned cheeks,
while his fists clenched at his side. "Exactly what do you
mean by that?"

"You can't guess?"

"I'm not in the mood for guessing. You come uninvited
to my home, you insult me for no reason which—"

"Come, come," chided Commissaire Tama. "I didn't expect to find a man of your profession as touchy as all that.
Speaking of which, *monsieur,* may one inquire as to what
exactly it *is?*"

Various emotions played across Dubreuil's face: stifled
rage, bafflement, caution. "What does it look like?" he
snapped, gesturing at the loaded bookcases, the crowded

worktables, the diagrams of fish tacked to the walls. "It's absolutely none of your business, but I'm a marine biologist and ichthyologist on a year's leave of absence, vacationing, and until now enjoying my—"

"Ichthyologist," repeated Tama slowly. "A fish expert, *hein?* Particularly of *pahicheri,* those curious Tahitian fish with gold in their bellies, *hein?"*

Dubreuil stepped forward, his clenched teeth gleaming white in his tanned face. "You great ninny, don't you realize—"

Commissaire Tama closed to meet him, and the thrust of his great belly drove Dubreuil back. "Maybe you even have a sea chart, or a map, that just before you leave our friendly islands you'll allow yourself to be persuaded to sell to—"

"Friendly islands! I . . . you . . ." he sputtered incoherently, then turned and sank onto a couch covered with gaudy *pareo* cloth. Tama watched impassively while Dubreuil fiddled with the sea shells that littered the coffee table before him, his eyelids hooded in thought.

"I see," he murmured at last, without looking up. "You think that *there"*—he sat up suddenly, flinging an arm towards a work table in the corner— *"there* I have a treasure trove of golden nuggets and a map ready for sale to some gullible local for millions of francs? Hence this impromptu visit of *M. le Commissaire* Tama, always alert to protect his guileless fellow citizens against the depredations of the wily Metropolitan, even on Easter Sunday." He rose briskly to his feet, a corner of his mouth twitching. A sneer? Or laughter?

Tama noticed that the sparkle had returned to his clear blue eyes and he frowned. "You take this very lightly," he growled. "Let me advise you that—"

"Come, come," said Dubreuil, as if humoring a child, "a commissaire of police, even a Tahitian one, attempting to advise an ichthyologist about fish? Are there not eels that generate their own electrical current? Do we not obtain silk from the lowly worm, and pearls from the humble oyster? Does not a cubic kilometer of ordinary sea water con-tain several tons of gold? Why should the mind boggle at the notion that Mother Nature with her infinite patience and diversity should not, over billions of years, evolve a fish capable of consolidating a tiny amount of gold from the waters of this modest lagoon? I assure you, my dear sir, that the oceans hold mysteries that will never be penetrated by the mind of man."

As Tama's scowl deepened Dubreuil grinned and spread his hands wide. "For instance . . ." He cocked his head to one side, as if in careful calculation. "I believe that in my refrigerator at this very moment is a delectable *ume*, a fish I am sure both of you are familiar with. Perhaps overfamiliar with," he added with a wry glance at the commissaire's girth. "I caught it early this morning in the lagoon and it awaits my dining pleasure. A banal and ordinary fish, you say? But who knows? It hasn't been gutted—I'm sure you recall an *ume* is cooked whole and then slathered with butter—would you care to join me in opening it up?" He gestured toward a doorway. "Who knows indeed what further mysteries the sea may reveal to us?"

The commissaire exchanged a sour glance with Inspector Opuu: the mockery in Dubreuil's voice was galling. Together they followed the nearly naked Frenchman into his small kitchen.

"Rather crowded in here," muttered Dubreuil with a pointed stare at Alexandre Tama's grotesquely rotund figure, and maneuvered the refrigerator door open to reveal a small *ume* lying on a plate, flat and grey.

Tightly hemmed by the two policemen, he laid the fish on a wooden cutting board, took a long thin knife from the drainboard, and with a single swift motion slit the fish open.

"Ah, the stomach," he said, prodding at the innards. "Let's just see now . . ." He slit the small pink sac, pulled it slightly open, and handed the knife to Commissaire Tama. "Perhaps you'd care to poke about inside."

"Hrumph," snorted Tama, handing the knife to Inspector Opuu, who stirred its tip through the sac.

Suddenly his eyes widened. "What . . ."

Tama saw it at the same time: a small irregular object, coated with slime, which nevertheless glinted brightly. . . .

"You're certain the oysters are fresh?" Tama asked the young Tahitian waitress. "Absolutely fresh? If someone like me gets a bellyache, you know, then it's an *enormous* bellyache."

"Oh yessir," she replied, trying to hide a giggle behind her hand.

"Humph. We shall see. Bring my abstemious friend here a large glass of *citronade,* and for myself a double whiskey in your biggest glass, a bowl of ice, and a litre bottle of Perrier. And with it kindly bring a single oyster on a plate."

"One oyster?"

"On a plate. You may put it on my bill."

When the bewildered waitress had left Inspector Opuu leaned forward. "You don't think . . . ?" he muttered softly. "I mean . . . *no one* keeps a fresh *ume* in the refrigerator with a nugget in its belly just on the off chance that someone might drop by. I mean, that fish was *fresh!"*

Commissaire Tama heaved a gigantic sigh and looked around him. They were sitting in a shady corner of the outside terrace at the Rotui Restaurant, a few miles down the road from Dubreuil's house. Even before noontime it was packed with holiday families clustered around the mounds of food on the buffet tables, and the din of laughter and shouting children was growing steadily. But for Tama the sound of Dubreuil's scornful laughter still rang in his ears.

"This has not been a successful morning," he conceded. "Perhaps I should have gone to lunch at my mother-in-law's after all, old hellion that she is. . . . Well, never mind. So the gold in the fish belly impressed you, did it?"

"Well . . ." Inspector Opuu had the grace to look abashed.

"Humph. It caught me by surprise too. But— Ah! the drinks. And my oyster. No, no, don't go away. First a little bread to clear the palate, then . . . hmmm, smells all right, down it goes . . . ah . . . hmmm." He smiled blissfully at the waitress. "You're right, it *was* fresh. Now that we've established that, why don't you bring, oh . . . these New Zealand oysters are so small, let's say a dozen for my friend and two dozen for me. Lots of brown bread, but none of that nasty vinegar that Frenchmen use to ruin their oysters."

"Yessir. As a first course. And then?"

Tama looked at her sternly. "First course? Certainly not! Just to nibble with our drinks. We'll be ordering the meal later on." He shook his head and swallowed a large portion of his whiskey. "Ah, that revives my spirits. Now look, Marcel, let me show you something. . . ."

He fumbled in his pants pocket and brought forth a fifty-franc piece. He placed it carefully in the middle of the white tablecloth. "It is heads, correct? Now watch closely. What I'm going to do is cover up that coin with this oyster shell, see? Now, while it's under that oyster shell I'm going to make it turn over from heads to tails. Go on, lift the shell, take a peek. Still heads? Good."

He leaned forward as much as the shape of his belly would allow. "You think that maybe I'll try to slip it out from under the shell? Well, let's cover the shell with this napkin so you can be certain I don't do that." Inspector Opuu frowned at the stiff linen napkin and the oyster shell bulging beneath it.

"Now," said Tama, grasping the napkin firmly around the shell with his right hand, "we'll just utter the magic spell"—he passed his left hand slowly back and forth over the napkin—"and the heads will have become tails! Look!" He lifted the napkin and pushed the coin forward for the inspector to examine.

"Sorry, still heads," he laughed.

Tama scowled. "So it is. We'll have to try again." He replaced the napkin, frowned in concentration, made signs with his left hand, and suddenly crushed the napkin flat with his right palm. "What?" he exclaimed. "Where did that oyster shell go to?" He lifted the napkin and shook it out. The bare coin lay on the table, still heads. The oyster shell was nowhere to be seen.

"That's strange," said Tama, "where could it have gone to? Humph, I feel something crawling up my arm!" He reached forward to scratch inside his left shirt sleeve and brought forth the missing oyster shell.

Inspector Opuu sighed. "I hate magicians," he said. "They never tell you how they do their tricks. I don't suppose—"

"No, no," said Tama, "I'm no exception. That was just a demonstration of the art of misdirection: you were expecting one trick, you got another. That is what Dubreuil did to us. He was sitting practically naked, remember, fiddling with things on the table in front of him. Suddenly he yelled 'There!', pointed to a corner, and palmed a so-called nugget that must have been lying among the rest of the junk. He must be good at manipulation though: he got it from there into the belly of that fish without my catching a glimmer of it. That is probably how he did the TV show as well."

"You could have just told me without all that oyster rigamarole," said Inspector Opuu peevishly. "What do we do now?"

"Now? We eat our oysters, order some wine, and get the menu so we can see about ordering a first course."

The phone call from Sergeant Croisie came just as they were finishing the platter of grilled *mahi-mahi* nestled on a bed of local *fafa* spinach. "Hmmph," said Tama when he had made his ponderous way back to the table. "He says one of his men *does* remember a *mutoi* named Terorotua. Retired now. He thinks he heard he was living here in Faaone."

"We could ask the waitress," suggested Inspector Opuu.

"Excellent idea. In fact here she is, with the lamb and lyonnaise potatoes, excellent girl." But the waitress had been raised in Punaauia and had only recently moved to this side of the island: she knew neither André Terorotua nor his daughter Hina Tevahine, *dite* Marie-Hélène. Commissaire Tama was pensive throughout the salad, cheese, and baked Alaska. As he finished his second glass of Otard brandy he grimaced in exasperation. "A fool's errand, Marcel, chasing after a man who turns fish into gold and a gold-digger who—"

"—turns the *procureur's* papers into gold, also?" suggested Inspector Opuu with a grin.

"That's what he's afraid of, all right," said Tama. "Where *is* that wretched girl? And don't ask how I got to be chief, either," he snapped.

"Oh, never, sir," said Inspector Opuu. "What I *was* going to say is this: Who is the last district chief for this area, before this Commune thing was organized?"

"Ah! The *tavana?* Hmmm. That would be old Georges Teinauri, I think. In fact, I'm certain of it. That's excellent, Marcel. We'll just stop off at his place for a moment on the way home."

The former *tavana* was a frail old man who blinked at Tama through thick spectacles as they spoke in Tahitian. He shook his head dolefully as Commissaire Tama regaled him with details of the iniquities of the goldfish man and of the gang in town. "Terrible," he muttered, bobbing his head up and down. "In *my* day we knew how to handle these problems." And he raised a clenched fist and shook it purposefully.

"Amen," said Tama, who agreed with him. "That's the only reasoning most of these people understand. It was a great mistake getting rid of the district chiefs. . . ."

The old man smiled wryly. "Just as well. I was growing too old to be chastising young thugs sixty years my junior."

"Never," said Commissaire Tama gallantly, and clambered to his feet. He wrapped his arms around the old man and hugged him. "We'll stop by again sometime. Ah, this talk of the old days reminds me . . . Whatever happened to André Terorotua, the *mutoi?* I might stop off to say hello if he's still in the district. . . ."

"Hmmph," groused the commissaire as the car moved slowly through the district of Faaone and into Papeari in the heavy Sunday afternoon traffic. "Why can't all these people stay at home, the way they used to? It used to be the roads were *empty* on Sundays."

"You mean former *mutois*," said Inspector Opuu. "Why can't *they* stay in one place?"

"Exact—slow! Isn't that the Chinese store? Yes, pull in here, Marcel." The long black Citroën nosed off the blacktop onto the dusty forecourt of a ramshackle old wooden building painted a faded green. Roosters scratched in the dust, while three emaciated dogs slept in the shade of the sagging wooden porch. The store was officially closed, but half a dozen near-naked Tahitians sat on the steps of the porch, drinking beer from frosty quart bottles and idly watching another group of Tahitians engaged in a traditional Sunday afternoon game of *pétanque*. Commissaire Tama waited until the last of the heavy metal balls had been tossed at a small stone to a chorus of shouts and groans before pulling himself laboriously from the car.

"*Hé, Chef!*" cried a Tahitian, raising a bottle in salute, while another nudged his neighbor in the ribs, then patted an imaginary belly.

"Hah!" rumbled Tama jovially. "Drinking beer on a public thoroughfare, eh? And on a Sunday afternoon, too. Most illegal; it'll be prison for all of you!"

Loud guffaws greeted this sally, and a dripping bottle was thrust at him. The commissaire examined it dubiously. "Well," he said, glancing over each shoulder, "just so long as that *mutoi* Terorotua isn't around to see me. Very strict, he is!"

"André?" scoffed an old Tahitian. "*Strict?* He was the biggest beer drinker on this side of the island!"

Tama swigged at the beer. "What? He doesn't live here anymore? Behind the Chinese store?"

"No, no, he moved to Papara."

"*Aita,* Punaauia!"

"Paea, stupid!"

"Hold it!" thundered Commissaire Tama, raising a massive hand. "You're trying to tell me Terorotua doesn't live

here anymore, and no one knows where he is? Is that it?"
He scowled darkly at the dozen brown faces that surrounded him. "Hrumph!" He lowered his great bulk to the
edge of the porch and thrust out a hand. "Maybe I'll have
some of that beer, after all." He drank deeply. "Ahhhh.
Now then: what do you rascals know about . . ."

"It'll be dinnertime when we get back if you don't stop
gossiping about the goldfish man and our precious gang
of *banditos* to every Tahitian you spy on the way around
the island," said Inspector Opuu towards the end of the
afternoon. They were in the district of Mataiea, inching
along in the home-going traffic, still twenty-odd miles from
Papeete.

"Dinner!" snorted Tama. "If I don't find this *mutoi* Terorotua it'll be my *head* someone will be having for dinner!"

Inspector Opuu restrained a smile. "We're really looking
for the *mahu* of Mataiea?"

"Might as well. They love to gossip: they know everything
that's going on. In fact, I'll bet he could tell us the names
of every single member of that blessed gang if he wanted
to."

Inspector Opuu pursed his lips. "Maybe twenty years ago,
yes. This *mahu* must be about the last of the real oldtime
district *mahus,* complete with beard and long red finger-
nails. All the young ones are at the Piano Bar dressed in
high drag these days. You patrol there on Saturday night,
and what with the sailors and tourists milling around on
the street in front of it you wonder if there are any *real*
men left on the island."

"A trifle exaggerated," said the commissaire, "but I know
what you mean. It was a lot simpler in the days when there
was one transvestite per district and everyone knew who
he was, particularly if he had a long white beard!"

"André Terorotua?" said the *mahu* of Mataiea. "Who
used to be a *mutoi* over in Tiarei? Of course. A dear boy,
very strong, very handsome." He waved a bony hand that

243

sparkled with rings and jewelry. The wrinkled old toothless face with its scraggly white beard was nearly hidden by the deep purple shadows cast by the thick strand of banana trees clustered about the small fiberboard shack. The old man's home was half a mile from the main road at the foot of the great mountains that thrust almost perpendicularly from the rich black soil. His gaudy red *pareo* was wrapped around his scrawny body woman-fashion, and to Tama's amusement he tugged at it constantly, pulling it up over nonexistent breasts.

Smiling a ghastly smile, he laid his hand on the commissaire's tree-trunk wrist. "Do sit down and tell me what you're doing out here in the districts, my dear Alexandre, and I'll tell you all you want to know about André Terorotua." His mouth twitched. "My, it's been *years* since I've seen you, Alexandre. How we've both changed. . . ."

They found the former policeman of the district of Tiarei coming out of church at the end of evening services, ten miles down the road in the district of Punaauia. "We've been all around the island looking for you," said Tama crossly. *"The wrong way.* If I'd known you were on *this* side I'd have gathered you up this morning and taken you to lunch."

"Lunch?" echoed André Terorotua, a solid Tahitian in his early sixties, neatly dressed in a long-sleeved white shirt and badly creased blue pants. "I may have missed lunch but I'm always ready for dinner." He poked a playful finger into the commissaire's colossal belly. "And it looks like you could do with some yourself, Alexandre. I'd say you've lost a good twenty pounds or so since I saw you last."

Commissaire Tama beamed, while Inspector Opuu rolled his eyes in despair.

"My daughter Hina?" said André Terorotua, two quarts of beer on the table before him, a foaming glass in his hand. "Haven't seen her for ages. Flighty little thing, always giving herself airs. Just because she's the *petite amie* of some government bigshot."

Commissaire Tama winced. "You know about that?"

André Terorotua looked startled. "Who doesn't? Except his silly wife. I've been telling her for years now she should settle down with some nice boy and raise a family."

"Sound advice," said Tama. "So you don't know where she is?"

"Don't know where she is?" André Terorotua gaped at his empty glass of beer as if it had spoken to him. "Of *course* I know where she is! Didn't she call me from the airport last week just before she flew off to Honolulu to get married? To some nice Hawaiian fella who has a chicken farm." He beamed proudly. "That's what I *told* her to do, you know. Settle down and raise a family."

Commissaire Tama looked up irritably from the dossier before him. "Well? Now what?"

Inspector Opuu cleared his throat. "You remember that goldfish fellow we talked to last week? Dubreuil?"

"Only too well." Dryly.

The inspector squirmed uneasily. "I went by the TV station a couple of days ago, just out of curiosity, you understand."

Tama nodded. "So?"

"They showed me a tape of the program where he was pulling gold from the fishes' bellies." He stopped to gaze pensively out the window, as if engrossed by the trees growing in the courtyard of the commissariat.

"Well, speak up, Opuu," thundered Tama. "What *about* this tape?"

Inspector Opuu drew a deep breath. "You see, sir, this Dubreuil really *is* a well-known marine biologist and ichthyologist. I . . . I checked with Paris on the Telex. He's here in Tahiti just as he said: on a year's sabbatical."

Commissaire Tama's face was like stone. "Go on," he muttered.

"Like you guessed, he's an amateur magician. Someone at the TV station thought it might be fun if he gave a series of little lectures about the marvels of the oceans, the wonders of the deep, eh? This goldfish thing was just his way

245

of dramatizing how much gold might pass through a fish in the course of its lifetime from the seawater it swallows." He blinked nervously. "At least I *think* that's what it was. It was sort of a . . . lead-in for the rest of the show."

"I see," said Commissaire Tama, his lips hardly moving. "Very well, Marcel. You've done a good job. Thanks for telling me before I—" He cut himself short. "Thanks." He nodded dismissal and Inspector Opuu escaped gratefully.

For a long time Commissaire Tama sat motionless at his desk, glaring at the tips of his fingers. At last he sighed and began to lift himself to his feet. "Well," he muttered, "if you're going to do it at all, you might as well do it now. How *humiliating!* I *hate* apologizing. How could I be so stup—"

He stopped short, then sagged back into his enormous *tau*-wood chair. "Oh no," he murmured, "oh *no!* I didn't think of *that,* either!" He reached hastily for the phone. "Damn, damn, damn, *damn!* Hello, hello? *Gendarmerie de Tiarei? Ici le Commissaire Tama. Passez-moi le Sergeant Croisie.*"

"They caught them *all?*" marveled Inspector Opuu. "The entire gang from the Chinese consulate?"

"Hah!" said Alexandre Tama grandly. "I *told* you that brains will always find a way. They've already confessed and been arraigned." Inspector Opuu sank into a chair in front of Commissaire Tama's desk. "You say the gendarmes caught them ransacking Dubreuil's house, looking for *gold?*" He was frankly incredulous. "You say you'd asked Croisie to stake out Dubreuil's house? What on earth *for?*"

The commissaire shifted his enormous bulk in his chair. "Well, now. . . ." he muttered, and ran a hand through his thick black hair. "It's a good thing I did, isn't it? Those little bastards had Dubreuil trussed up like a chicken and were all ready to start cutting him up to make him tell them where his gold was."

"Hrumph," snorted Inspector Opuu, sounding remarkably like the commissaire himself. "I wonder why they'd think they'd find any . . ." He paused to stare at the gigantic figure on the other side of the desk. "So *that's* it! All that—"

"—blabbing and gossiping I did around the island about this crooked Frenchman and his gold . . ." The commissaire heaved a sigh of mortification. "The coconut radio probably had a garbled version of it to the gang before we were through talking to that old *mutoi* about his wayward daughter."

Inspector Opuu nodded. "So first you put him in peril, and then you rescue him. Very neat. Would you say that you were lucky?"

Alexandre Tama hesitated, then grimaced. "I was lucky," he admitted.

"Hah!" Inspector Opuu grinned. "Speaking of triumphs of detective work, what word from our fine-feathered prosecutor about his missing papers?"

Commissaire Tama raised his round brown face, and to the Inspector's surprise it slowly broke into an enormous smile. "How *kind* of you to remind me, Marcel. You know . . . for an investigation of such great delicacy—I think I'd best be off to Honolulu. But since it's strictly personal: at *his* expense, of course."

THE NATIVE AMERICAN DETECTIVE (Navajo)

THE WITCH, YAZZIE, AND THE NINE OF CLUBS

Tony Hillerman

Although there have been relatively few American Indian detectives in crime fiction, those that have appeared are memorable creations. Manly Wade Wellman's David Re- turn is one; another is Sam Watchman, the Navajo protago- nist of two excellent novels by Brian Garfield, Relentless (1972) *and* The Threeperson Hunt (1974); *a third is Johnny Ortiz, the part Apache (and part Spanish and part Anglo) hero of* Murder in the Walls (1971) *and two other mysteries by Richard Martin Stern. But perhaps the finest series of Native American detective novels are the six (to date) writ- ten by Tony Hillerman and featuring either Joe Leaphorn or Jim Chee of the Navajo Tribal Police.*

Hillerman, who lives in Albuquerque and who numbers many Navajos among his friends, not only provides con- vincing crime puzzles but in-depth studies of Navajo and (and Zuni) culture and folklore and considerable insight into the Indian mind. He is a fine stylist as well; his evoca- tions of the New Mexico landscape are as flawless as his depiction of life on the Navajo Reservation.

His first three detective novels feature Sergeant Joe Leap- horn: The Blessing Way (1970), Dance Hall of the Dead *(which received the Mystery Writers of America Edgar for best novel of 1973), and* Listening Woman *(1978). The subsequent three all feature a younger and less traditional tribal policeman, Jim Chee:* The People of Darkness *(1980),* Dark Wind *(1982), and* The Ghostway *(1984). Hillerman, a former journalist who is presently a Professor of Journalism at the University of New Mexico, has also written books for young readers and a collection of fascinating (and often quite funny) sketches on New Mexico history,* The Great Taos Bank Robbery *and* Other Indian Country Affairs *(1973).*

"The Witch, Yazzie, and the Nine of Clubs" is his only detective short story. It was awarded third prize by the Swedish Academy of Detection in a 1981 worldwide mystery story contest, and subsequently appeared in a British anthology of the Academy's prize-winning stories. This is its first U. S. publication.

·   ·   ·

All summer the witch had been at work on the Rainbow Plateau. It began—although Corporal Jimmy Chee would learn of it only now, at the very last—with the mutilation of the corpse. The rest of it fell pretty much into the pattern of witchcraft gossip one expected in this lonely corner of the Navajo Reservation. Adeline Etcitty's mare had foaled a two-headed colt. Rudolph Bisti's boys lost their best ram while driving their flocks into the high country, and when they found the body werewolf tracks were all around it. The old woman they call Kicks-Her-Horse had actually seen the skinwalker. A man walking down Burnt Water Wash in the twilight had disappeared into a grove of cottonwoods and when the old woman got there, he turned himself into an owl and flew away. The daughter of Rosemary Nakai had seen the witch, too. She shot her .22 rifle at a big dog bothering her horses and the dog turned into a man wearing a wolfskin and she'd run away without seeing what he did.

Corporal Chee heard of the witch now and then and remembered it as he remembered almost everything. But

Chee heard less than most because Chee had been assigned to the Tuba City sub-agency and given the Short Mountain territory only six months ago. He came from the Chuska Mountains on the Arizona-New Mexico border three hundred miles away. His born-to clan was the Slow Talking People, and his paternal clan was the Mud Dinee. Here among the barren canyons along the Utah border the clans were the Standing Rock People, the Many Goats, the Tangle Dinee, the Red Forehead Dinee, the Bitter Waters and the Monster People. Here Chee was still a stranger. To a stranger, Navajos talk cautiously of witches.

Which is perhaps why Jim Chee had learned only now, at this very moment, of the mutilation. Or perhaps it was because he had a preoccupation of his own—the odd, frustrating question of where Taylor Yazzie had gone, and what Yazzie had done with the loot from the Burnt Water Trading Post. Whatever the reason he was late in learning, it was the Cowboy who finally told him.

"Everybody knew there was a skinwalker working way last spring," the Cowboy said. "As soon as they found out the witch killed that guy."

Chee had been leaning against the Cowboy's pickup truck. He was looking past the Emerson Nez hogan, through the thin blue haze of piñon smoke which came from its smokehole, watching a half-dozen Nez kinfolks stacking wood for the Girl Dance fire. He was asking himself for the thousandth time what Taylor Yazzie could have done with $40,000 worth of pawn—rings, belt buckles, bracelets, bulky silver concha belts which must weigh, altogether, 500 pounds. And what had Taylor Yazzie done with himself—another 180 pounds or so, with the bland round face more common among Eastern Navajos than on the Rainbow Plateau, with his thin moustache, with his wire-rimmed sunglasses. Chee had seen Taylor Yazzie only once, the day before he had done the burglary, but since then he had learned him well. Yazzie's world was small, and Yazzie had vanished from it, and since he could hardly speak English there was hardly any place he could go. And just as thoroughly, the silver pawn had vanished from the lives of a hundred families who had turned it over to Ed Yost's trading post to secure their credit until they sold their wool. Through all these thoughts it took a moment for the Cowboy's message to penetrate. When it did, Corporal Chee became very attentive.

"Killed what guy?" Chee asked. Taylor Yazzie, you're dead, he thought. No more mystery.

The Cowboy was sprawled across the front seat of his truck, fishing a transistor radio out of the glovebox. "You remember," he said. "Back last April. That guy you collected on Piute Mesa."

"Oh," Chee said. He remembered. It had been a miserable day's work and the smell of death had lingered in his carryall for weeks. But that had been in May, not April, and it hadn't looked like a homicide. Just too much booze, too much high-altitude cold. An old story on the Reservation. And John Doe wasn't Taylor Yazzie. The coroner had put the death 2 months before the body was recovered. Taylor Yazzie was alive, and well, and walking out of Ed Yost's trading post a lot later than that. Chee had been there and seen him. "You see that son-of-a-bitch," Ed Yost had said. "I just fired his ass. Never comes to work, and I think he's been stealing from me." No, Yost didn't want to file a complaint. Nothing he could prove. But the next morning it had been different. Someone with a key had come in the night, and opened the saferoom where the pawn was kept, and took it. Only Yost and Yazzie had access to the keys, and Yazzie had vanished.

"Why you say a witch killed that guy?" Chee asked.

The Cowboy backed out of the pickup cab. The radio didn't work. He shook it, glancing at Chee. His expression was cautious. The bumper stickers plastering the Ford declared him a member of the Native American Rodeo Cowboys' Assn., and proclaimed that Cowboys Make Better Lovers, and that Cowgirls Have More Fun, and recorded the Cowboy's outdated permit to park on the Arizona State University campus. But Cowboy was still a Many Goats Dinee, and Chee had been his friend for just a few months. Uneasiness warred with modern macho.

"They said all the skin was cut off his hands," the Cowboy said. But he said it in a low voice.

"Ah," Chee said. He needed no more explanation. The ingredients of 'anti'l', the 'corpse-powder' which skinwalkers make to spread sickness, was known to every Navajo. They use the skin of their victim which bears the unique imprint of the individual human identity—the skin of palm, and finger-pads, and the balls of the feet. Dried and pulverized with proper ritual, it became the dreaded reverse-negative of the pollen used for curing and blessing. Chee remembered the corpse as he had seen it. Predators and scavenger birds had left a ragged sack of bones and bits of desiccated flesh. No identification and nothing to show it was anything but routine. And that's how it had gone into the books. "Unidentified male. About forty. Probable death by exposure."

"If somebody saw his palms had been skinned, then somebody saw him a hell of a long time before anybody called us about him," Chee said. Nothing unusual in that, either.

"Somebody found him fresh," the Cowboy said. "That's what I heard. One of the Pinto outfit." Cowboy removed the battery from the radio. By trade, Cowboy was the assistant county agricultural agent. He inspected the battery, which looked exactly like all other batteries, with great care. The Cowboy did not want to talk about witch business.

"Any of the Pinto outfit here?" Chee asked.

"Sure," Cowboy said. He made a sweeping gesture, including the scores of pickups, wagons, old sedans occupying the sagebrush flats around the Nez hogans, the dozens of cooking fires smoking in the autumn twilight, the people everywhere. "All the kinfolks come to this. Everybody comes to this."

This was an Enemy Way. This particular Enemy Way had been prescribed, as Chee understood it, to cure Emerson Nez of whatever ailed him so he could walk again with beauty all around him as Changing Woman had taught when she formed the first Navajos. Family duty would require all kinsmen, and clansmen, of Nez to be here, as Cowboy had said, to share in the curing and the blessing. Everybody would be here, especially tonight. Tonight was the sixth night of the ceremonial when the ritual called for the Girl Dance to be held. Its original purpose was metaphysical—part of the prescribed re-enactment of the deeds of the Holy People. But it was also social. Cowboy called it the Navajo substitute for the singles bar, and came to see if he could connect with a new girl friend. Anthropologists came to study primitive behavior. Whites and Utes and even haughty Hopis came out of curiosity. Bootleggers came to sell illegal whisky. Jim Chee came, in theory, to catch bootleggers. In fact, the elusive, invisible, missing Yazzie drew him. Yazzie and the loot. Sometime, somewhere some of it would have to surface. And when it did, someone would know it. But now to hell with Yazzie and pawn jewellery. He might have an old homicide on his hands. With an unidentified victim and the whole thing six months cold it promised to be as frustrating as the burglary. But he would find some Pinto family members and begin the process.

Cowboy's radio squawked into sudden life and produced the voice of Willie Nelson, singing of abandonment and sorrow. Cowboy turned up the volume.

"Specially everyone would come to this one," Cowboy said toward Chee's departing back. "Nez wasn't the only one bothered by that witch. One way or another it bothered just about everybody on the plateau."

Chee stopped and walked back to the pickup. "You mean Nez was witched?"

"That's what they say," Cowboy said. "Got sick. They took him to the clinic in Tuba City and when that didn't do any good they got themselves a Listener to find out what was wrong with the old man, and he found out Nez had the corpse sickness. He said the witch got on the roof—" (Cowboy paused to point with his lips—a peculiarly Navajo gesture—toward the Nez hogan)—"and dropped anti'l down the smokehole."

"Same witch? Same one that did the killing?"

"That's what the Listener said," Cowboy agreed.

Cowboy was full of information tonight, Chee thought. But was it useful? The fire for the Girl Dance had been started now. It cast a red, wavering light which reflected off windshields, faces and the moving forms of people. The pot drums began a halting pattern of sounds which reflected, like the firelight, off the cliffs of the great mesa which sheltered the Nez place. This was the ritual part of the evening. A shaman named Dillon Keeyani was the signer in charge of curing Nez. Chee could see him, a tall, gaunt man standing beyond the fire, chanting the repetitive poetry of this part of the cure. Nez stood beside him, naked to the waist, his face blackened to make him invisible from the ghosts which haunt the night. Why would the Listener have prescribed an Enemy Way? It puzzled Chee. Usually a witch victim was cured with a Prostitution Way, or the proper chants from the Mountain Way were used. The Enemy Way was ordered for witch cases at times, but it was a broad-spectrum antibiotic—used for that multitude of ills caused by exposure to alien ways and alien cultures. Chee's family had held an Enemy Way for him when he had returned from the University of New Mexico, and in those years when Navajos were coming home from the Viet Nam war it was common every winter. But why use it to cure Emerson Nez of the corpse sickness? There was only one answer. Because the witch was an alien—a Ute, a white, a Hopi perhaps. Chee thought about how the Listener would have worked. Long conversations with Nez and those who knew him, hunting for causes of the malaise, for broken taboos, for causes of depression. And then the Listener would have found a quiet place, and listened to what the silence taught him. How would the Listener have known the witch was alien? There was only one way. Chee was suddenly excited. Someone must have seen the witch. Actually seen the man—not in the doubtful moonlight, or a misty evening when a moving shape could be dog or man—but under circumstances that told the witness that the man was not a Navajo.

254

The Sway Dance had started now. A double line of figures circled the burning pyre, old men and young—even boys too young to have been initiated into the secrets of the Holy People. Among Chee's clans in the Chuskas ritualism was more orthodox and these youngsters would not be allowed to dance until a Yeibichai was held for them, and their eyes had seen through the masks of Black God and Talking God. The fire flared higher as a burning log collapsed with an explosion of sparks. Chee wove through the spectators, asking for Pintos. He found an elderly woman joking with two younger ones. Yes, she was Anna Pinto. Yes, her son had found the body last spring. His name was Walker Pinto. He'd be somewhere playing stick dice. He was wearing a sweatband. Red.

Chee found the game behind Ed Yost's pickup truck. A lantern on the tailgate provided the light, a saddle blanket spread on the ground was the playing surface. Ed Yost was playing with an elderly round-faced Hopi and four Navajos. Chee recognized Pinto among the watchers by the red sweatband and his mother's description. "Skinny," she'd said. "Bony-faced. Sort of ugly-looking." Although his mother hadn't said it, Walker Pinto was also drunk.

"That's right, man," Pinto said. "I found him. Up there getting the old woman's horses together, and I found him." Wine had slurred Pinto's speech and drowned whatever inhibitions he might have felt about talking of witch business to a man he didn't know. He put his hand on the pickup fender to steady himself and began—Navajo fashion—at the very beginning. He'd married a woman in the Poles Together clan and gone over to Rough Rock to live with her, but she was no good, so this winter he'd come back to his mother's outfit, and his mother had wanted him to go up on Piute Mesa to see about her horses. Pinto described the journey up the mesa with his son, his agile hands acting out the journey. Chee watched the stick-dice game. Yost was good at it. He slammed the four painted wooden pieces down on the base stone in the center of the blanket. They bounced two feet into the air and fell in a neat pattern.

He tallied the exposed colors, moved the matchsticks being used as score markers, collected the sticks and passed them to the Hopi in maybe three seconds. Yost had been a magician once, Chee remembered. With a carnival, and his customers had called him Three-Hands. "Bets," Yost said. The Hopi looked at the sticks in his hand, smiling slightly. He threw a crumpled dollar on to the blanket. A middle-aged Navajo wearing wire-rimmed glasses put a folded bill beside it. Two more bills hit the blanket. The lantern light reflected off Wire Rims's lenses and off Yost's bald head.

"About then I heard the truck, way back over the ridge," Pinto was saying. His hands created the ridge and the valley beyond it. "Then the truck it hit something, you see. Bang." Pinto's right hand slammed into his left. "You see, that truck it hit against a rock there. It was turning around in the wash, and the wash is narrow there and it banged up against this rock." Pinto's hands recreated the accident. "I started over there, you see. I walked on over there then to see who it was."

The stick-dice players were listening now; the Hopi's face patient, waiting for the game to resume. The butane lantern made a white light that made Yost's moist eyes sparkle as he looked up at Pinto. There was a pile of bills beside Yost's hand. He took a dollar from it and put it on the blanket without taking his eyes from Pinto.

"But, you see, by the time I got up to the top of the rise, that truck it was driving away. So I went on down there, you see, to find out what had been going on." Pinto's hands re-enacted the journey.

"What kind of truck was it?" Chee asked.

"Already gone," Pinto said. "Bunch of dust hanging in the air, but I didn't see the truck. But when I got down there to the wash, you see, I looked around." Pinto's hands flew here and there, looking around. "There he was, you see, right there shoved under that rabbit brush." The agile hands disposed of the body. The stick-dice game remained in recess. The Hopi still held the sticks, but he watched Pinto. So did the fat man who sat cross-legged beside him.

The lantern light made a point of white in the center of Yost's black pupils. The faces of the Navajo players were rapt, but the Hopi's expression was polite disinterest. The Two-Heart witches of his culture did their evil with more sophistication.

Pinto described what he had seen under the rabbit brush, his voice wavering with the wine but telling a story often repeated. His agile hands were surer. They showed how the flayed hands of the corpse had lain, where the victim's hat had rolled, how Pinto had searched for traces of the witch, how he had studied the tracks. Behind the stick-dice players the chanting chorus of the Sway Dancers rose and fell. The faint night breeze moved the perfume of burning piñon and the aroma of cedar to Chee's nostrils. The lantern light shone through the rear window of Yost's truck, reflecting from the barrels of the rifles in the gun rack across it. A long-barrelled 30.06 and a short saddle carbine, Chee noticed.

"You see, that skinwalker was in a big hurry when he got finished with that body," Pinto was saying. "He backed right over a big chamisa bush and banged that truck all around on the brush and rocks getting it out of there." The hands flew, demonstrating panic.

"But you didn't actually see the truck?" Chee asked.

"Gone," Pinto said. His hands demonstrated the state of goneness.

"Or the witch, either?"

Pinto shook his head. His hands apologized.

On the flat beside the Nez hogan the chanting of the Sway Dance ended with a chorus of shouting. Now the Girl Dance began. Different songs. Different drumbeat. Laughter now, and shouting. The game broke up. Wire-Rims folded his blanket. Yost counted his winnings.

"Tell you what I'll do," Yost said to Wire Rims. "I'll show you how I can control your mind."

Wire Rims grinned.

"Yes, I will," Yost said. "I'll plant a thought in your mind and get you to say it."

257

Wire Rims's grin broadened. "Like what?"

Yost put his hand on the Navajo's shoulder. "Let your mind go blank now," he said. "Don't think about nothing." Yost let ten seconds tick away. He removed the hand. "Now," he said. "It's done. It's in there."

"What?" Wire Rims asked.

"I made you think of a certain card," Yost said. He turned to the spectators, to the Hopi, to Chee. "I always use the same card. Burn it into my mind and keep it there and always use that very same image. That way I can make a stronger impression with it on the other feller's mind." He tapped Wire Rims on the chest with a finger. "He closes his eyes, he sees that certain card."

"Bullshit," Wire Rims said.

"I'll bet you, then," Yost said. "But you got to play fair. You got to name the card you actually see. All right?"

Wire Rims shrugged. "Bullshit. I don't see nothing."

Yost waved his handful of currency. "Yes, you do," Yost insisted. "I got money that says you do. You see that one card I put in your mind. I got $108 here I'll bet you against that belt you're wearing. What's that worth?" It was a belt of heavy conchos hammered out of thick silver. Despite its age and a heavy layer of tarnish it was a beautiful piece of work. Chee guessed it would bring $100 at pawn and sell for maybe $200. But with the skyrocketing price of silver, it might be worth twice that melted down.

"Let's say it would pawn for $300," Yost said. "That gives me three to one odds on the money. But if I'm lying to you, there's just one chance in fifty-two that you'll lose."

"How you going to tell?" Wire Rims asked. "You tell somebody the card in advance?"

"Better than that," Yost said. "I got him here in my pocket sealed up in an envelope. I always use that same card so I keep it sealed up and ready."

"Sealed up in an envelope?" Wire Rims asked.

"That's right," Yost said. He tapped his forefinger to the chest of his khaki bush jacket.

Wire Rims unbuckled the belt and handed it to Chee.

"You hold the money," he said. Yost handed Chee the currency.

"I get to refresh your memory," Yost said. He put his hand on the Navajo's shoulder. "You see a whole deck of cards face down on the table. Now, I turn this one on the end here over." Yost's right hand turned over an invisible card and slapped it emphatically on an invisible table. "You see it. You got it in your mind. Now play fair. Tell me the name of the card."

Wire Rims hesitated. "I don't see nothing," he said.

"Come on. Play fair," Yost said. "Name it."

"Nine of clubs," Wire Rims said.

"Here is an honest man," Yost said to Chee and the Hopi and the rest of them. "He named the nine of clubs." While he said it, Yost's left hand had dipped into the left pocket of the bush jacket. Now it fished out an envelope and delivered it to Chee. "Read it and weep," Yost said.

Chee handed the envelope to Wire Rims. It was a small envelope, just a bit bigger than a poker card. Wire Rims tore it open and extracted the card. It was the nine of clubs. Wire Rims looked from card to Yost, disappointment mixed with admiration. "How you do that?"

"I'm a magician," Yost said. He took the belt and the money from Chee. "Any luck on that burglary?" he asked. "You find that son-of-a-bitch Yazzie yet?"

"Nothing," Chee said.

And then there was a hand on his arm and a pretty face looking up at him. "I've got you," the girl said. She tugged him toward the fire. "You're my partner. Come on, policeman."

"I'd sure like to catch that son-of-a-bitch," Yost said.

The girl danced gracefully. She told Chee she was born to the Standing Rock Dinee and her father was a Bitter Water. With no clan overlap, none of the complex incest taboos of The People prevented their dancing, or whatever else might come to mind. Chee remembered having seen her working behind the registration desk at the Holiday Inn at Shiprock. She was pretty. She was friendly. She was

259

witty. The dance was good. The pot drums tugged at him, and the voices rose in a slightly ribald song about what the old woman and the young man did on the sheepskins away from the firelight. But things nagged at Chee's memory. He wanted to think.

"You don't talk much," the girl said.

"Sorry. Thinking," Chee said.

"But not about me." She frowned at him. "You thinking about arresting somebody?"

"I'm thinking that tomorrow morning when they finish this sing-off with the Scalp Shooting ceremony, they've got to have something to use as the scalp."

The girl shrugged.

"I mean, it has to be something that belonged to the witch. How can they do that unless they know who the witch is? What could it be?"

The girl shrugged again. She was not interested in the subject nor, now, in Jim Chee. "Whyn't you go and ask?" she said. "Big Hat over there is the scalp carrier."

Chee paid his ransom—handing the girl two dollars and then adding two more when the first payment drew a scornful frown. Big Hat was also paying off his partner, with the apparent intention of being immediately recaptured by a plump young woman wearing a wealth of silver necklaces who was waiting at the fringe of the dance. Chee captured him just before the woman did.

"The scalp?" Big Hat asked. "Well, I don't know what you call it. It's a strip of red plastic about this wide," (Big Hat indicated an inch with his fingers) "and maybe half that thick and a foot and a half long."

"What's that got to do with the witch?" Chee asked.

"Broke off the bumper of his truck," Big Hat said. "You know. That strip of rubbery stuff they put on to keep from denting things. It got brittle and some of it broke off."

"At the place where they found the body?"

Big Hat nodded.

"Where you keeping it?" Chee asked. "After you're finished with it tomorrow I'm going to need it." Tomorrow at the final ritual this scalp of the witch would be placed near the Nez hogan. There, after the proper chants were sung, Emerson Nez would attack it with a ceremonial weapon—probably the beak of a raven attached to a stick. Then it would be sprinkled with ashes and shot—probably with a rifle. If all this was properly done, if the minds of all concerned were properly free of lust, anger, avarice— then the witchcraft would be reversed. Emerson Nez would live. The witch would die.

"I got it with my stuff in the tent," Big Hat said. He pointed past the Nez brush arbor. After the ceremony he guessed Chee could have it. Usually anything like that— things touched with witchcraft—would be buried. But he'd ask Dillon Keeyani. Keeyani was the singer. Keeyani was in charge.

And then Jim Chee walked out into the darkness, past the brush arbor and past the little blue nylon tent where Big Hat kept his bedroll and his medicine bundle and what he needed for his role in this seven-day sing. He walked beyond the corral where the Nez outfit kept its horses, out into the sagebrush and the night. He found a rock and sat on it and thought.

While he was dancing he had worked out how Ed Yost had won Wire Rims's belt. A simple matter of illusion and distraction. The easy way it had fooled him made him aware that he must be overlooking other things because of other illusions. But what?

He reviewed what Pinto had told him. Nothing there. He skipped to his own experience with the body. The smell. Checking what was left of the clothing for identification. Moving what was left into the body bag. Hearing the cloth tear. Feeling the bare bone, the rough, dried leather of the boots as he . . .

The boots! Chee slapped both palms against his thighs. The man had his boots on. Why would the witch, the madman, take the skin for corpse powder from the hands and leave the equally essential skin from the feet? He would not, certainly, have replaced the boots. Was the killing not a witch-killing, then? But why the flayed hands? To remove the fingerprints?

Yazzie. Yazzie had a police record. One simple assault. One driving while intoxicated. Printed twice. Identification would have been immediate. But Yazzie was larger than the skinned man, and still alive when the skinned man was dead. John Doe remained John Doe. This only changed John Doe from a random victim to a man whose killer needed to conceal his identity.

The air moved against Chee's face and with the faint breeze came the sound of the pot drums and of laughter. Much closer he heard the fluting cry of a hunting owl. He saw the owl now, a gray shape gliding in the starlight just above the sage, hunting, as Chee's mind hunted, something which eluded it. Something, Chee's instinct told him, as obvious as the nine of clubs.

But what? Chee thought of how adroitly Yost had manipulated Wire Rims into the bet, and into the illusion. Overestimating the value of the man's belt. Causing them all to think of a single specific card, sealed in a single specific envelope, waiting to be specifically named. He smiled slightly, appreciating the cleverness.

The smile lingered, abruptly disappeared, reappeared and suddenly converted itself into an exultant shout of laughter. Jim Chee had found another illusion. In this one, he had been Yost's target. He'd been totally fooled. Yazzie *was* John Doe. Yost had killed him, removed the fingerprints, put the body where it would be found. Then he had performed his magic. Cleverly. Taking advantage of the circumstances—a new policeman who'd never seen Yazzie. Chee recreated the day. The note to call Yost. Yost wanting to see him, suggesting two in the afternoon. Chee had been a few minutes late. The big, round-faced Navajo stalking out of Yost's office. Yost's charade of indignant anger. Who was this ersatz "Yazzie"? The only requirement would be a Navajo from another part of the reservation, whom Chee wouldn't be likely to see again soon. Clever!

That reminded him that he had no time for this now.

He stopped at his own vehicle for his flashlight and then checked Yost's truck. Typical of trucks which live out their lives on the rocky tracks of the reservation, it was battered, scraped and dented. The entire plastic padding strip was missing from the front bumper. From the back one, a piece was missing. About eighteen inches long. What was left fit Big Hat's description of the scalp. His deduction confirmed, Chee stood behind the truck, thinking.

Had Yost disposed of Yazzie to cover up the faked burglary? Or had Yazzie been killed for some unknown motive and the illusion of burglary created to explain his disappearance? Chee decided he preferred the first theory. For months before the crime the price of silver had been skyrocketing, moving from about five dollars an ounce to at least forty dollars. It bothered Yost to know that as soon as they sold their wool, his customers would be paying off their debts and walking away with that sudden wealth.

The Girl Dance had ended now. The drums were quiet. The fire had burned down. People were drifting past him through the darkness on their way back to their bedrolls. Tomorrow at dawn there would be the final sand-painting on the floor of the Nez hogan; Nez would drink the ritual emetic and just as the sun rose would vomit out the sickness. Then the Scalp Shooting would be held. A strip of red plastic molding would be shot and a witch would, eventually, die. Would Yost stay for the finish? And how would he react when he saw the plastic molding?

A split second into that thought, it was followed by another. Yost had heard what Pinto had said. Yost would know this form of the Enemy Way required a ceremonial scalp. Yost wouldn't wait to find out what it was.

Chee snapped on the flashlight. Through the back window of Yost's pickup he saw that the rifle rack now held only the 30.06. The carbine was gone.

Chee ran as fast as the darkness allowed, dodging trucks, wagons, people and camping paraphernalia, toward the tent of Big Hat. Just past the brush arbor he stopped. A light was visible through the taut blue nylon. It moved.

Chee walked toward the tent, quietly now, bringing his labored breathing under control. Through the opening he could see Big Hat's bedroll and the motionless outflung arm of someone wearing a flannel shirt. Chee moved directly in front of the tent door. He had his pistol cocked now. Yost was squatting against the back wall of the tent, illuminated by a battery lantern, sorting through the contents of a blue cloth zipper bag. Big Hat sprawled face down just inside the tent, his hat beside his shoulder. Yost's carbine was across his legs . . .

"Yost," Chee said. "Drop the carbine and . . ."

Yost turned on his heels, swinging the carbine.

Jim Chee, who had never shot anyone, who thought he would never shoot another human, shot Yost through the chest.

Big Hat was dead, the side of his skull dented. Yost had neither pulse nor any sign of breath. Chee fished in the pockets of his bush jacket and retrieved the conco belt. He'd return it to Wire Rims. In the pocket with it were small sealed envelopes. Thirteen of them. Chee opened the first one. The Ace of Hearts. Had Wire Rims guessed the five of hearts, Yost would have handed him the fifth envelope from his pocket. Chee's bullet had gone through the left breast pocket of Yost's jacket—puncturing diamonds or spades.

Behind him Chee could hear the sounds of shouting, of running feet, people gathering at the tent flap. Cowboy was there, staring in at him. "What happened?" Cowboy said.

And Chee said, "The witch is dead."

Mahboob Ahmed Chaudri

THE PAKISTANI/BAHRAINIAN DETECTIVE

THE BEER DRINKERS

Josh Pachter

While Mahboob Ahmed Chaudri is a Pakistani from Kara-
chi, his present bailiwick is the Persian Gulf island of Bah-
rain, where he is attached to the Public Security Force. The
cultural background in the Chaudri stories, therefore, is
Bahrainian—in the present case, modern politics and an-
cient ethnographic treasures in the National Museum. The
"beer drinkers" of the title is the most important relic of
Bahrain's ancient history, a priceless gold medallion which
mysteriously disappears from under Chaudri's very nose
and causes him considerable consternation before he finally
deduces what became of it.

Mahboob Chaudri is one of crime fiction's most delightful
new detectives. "The Beer Drinkers" and several other of
his cases have appeared in Ellery Queen's Mystery Magazine *over the past two years, and more are planned. Hap-*
pily, his creator is also considering a Chaudri novel for
the not too distant future.

A teacher by profession, Josh Pachter has lived in Bahrain
(as well as in Amsterdam, West Germany, and several other
countries in Europe and the Near East) and writes from
first-hand knowledge of the island and its people. He sold

his first short story to EQMM *in 1968, while still a teenager, and followed it with too few others; after a hiatus of several years, he is now writing fiction again on a regular basis. He is also the editor of a recent author's-choice mystery anthology,* Top Crime *(1984), as well as of several other anthologies thus far published only in Europe; and he is presently editing a new series of crime-novel translations for a Dutch publisher.*

. . .

Mahboob Ahmed Chaudri was bored.

I'm a policeman, not a wetnurse, he thought morosely, *and my place is out on the streets, in the sun, where the action is—not stuck here playing nanny to a pack of silly children.*

It was well that Chaudri kept such thoughts to himself. Were he to give them voice, to speak the frustration that was in his heart, it would mean the end of his right to wear the proud uniform of a *mahsool,* the end of his career, the end of his four-year stay in Bahrain.

For these four boys were no ordinary children. They were the eldest sons of four of the most powerful and influential men in the Arabian Gulf—or "Persian" Gulf, as the Western infidels and the damned Iranians insisted on calling it— and one did not call such boys a pack of silly children unless one was eager to give up the respected position that Chaudri had worked so hard to win, and to return in disgrace to the bitter life of a day laborer in Karachi.

It was the third and final day of the second annual meeting of the Gulf Cooperation Council, and the heads of state of the six member nations—the Emirs of Bahrain, Kuwait and Qatar, the Sultan of Oman, the King of Saudi Arabia and the President of the United Arab Emirates—were cloistered away with their prime ministers and defense ministers and aides in a magnificently appointed conference room in Manama's shiniest, most elegant new hotel. They had come together to discuss the coordination of security forces in the region, the establishment of "common market" agreements between their several nations, the Palestinian question, the ramifications of the Iran-Iraq war, the advisability of a joint demand for the withdrawal of Israeli troops from Lebanon, the adoption of uniform passports, and other issues of mutual importance.

Four of the senior ministers had brought their first-born sons to Bahrain with them, and it had fallen to Mahboob Chaudri to take care of the boys while Their Highnesses conferred, to tour them around the island's points of interest and, more important, to keep them away from trouble. And, *most* important, to keep trouble away from them.

It was an important assignment, a vital one, a mark of his superiors' total confidence in his abilities. It was also, thought Chaudri, an incredible bore.

Day 1 of the conference had been filled with arrivals and receptions and parties and dinners; the ministers' children had been a part of all these functions, and Chaudri had been but one small cog in the complex machinery of the security arrangements. By Allah's grace, all had gone well. There had been no incidents of any kind, not at the airport, not during the motorcade into the city center, not at the hotel or the various embassies where the welcoming activities had taken place.

On Day 2, the official meetings had begun; that morning, Chaudri chaperoned the four youngsters on a tramp around the Portuguese Fort and the ruins of the Bronze Age and Stone Age cities, accompanied by a reporter and a photographer from the *Gulf Daily News* and the president of the Historical and Archaeological Society. After a luncheon at the home of the Saudi ambassador, hosted by that dignitary's charming and beautiful wife, they had driven south into the desert for a bus ride through the newly-opened Al-Areen Wildlife Preserve. The children had enjoyed themselves immensely, but Chaudri, of course, had been on duty all day and had not had a chance to eat lunch; by the time they reached Al-Areen he was hot and hungry and tired, and the chatter of the boys and the penetrating stink of the Arabian oryx had given him a headache.

This afternoon, *insh'Allah,* would be the end of it. Another hour or so here at the National Museum and he could herd his charges back across the causeway from Muharraq to the mainland, deliver them safely into their fathers' arms, thank one and all for the honor of having been permitted to serve them, and with a bit of luck catch a ride back to the police barracks in time to take a hot bath before dinner.

Children!

And, to be fair about it, it was not *only* the children. There was also that irritatingly bouncy British reporter with her constant barrage of foolish questions, and her obsequious little Indian photographer constantly shooting off his flashbulbs in Chaudri's eyes, and, this morning, the well-meaning but terribly long-winded assistant curator of the museum, Sheikh Ibrahim al-Samahiji, whose lecture on Bahrain's history had been underway for what felt like the last ten hours, and seemed certain to go on for at *least* the next fifteen.

". . . is one of the earliest hymns known to mankind, written over 4,000 years ago—when the pyramids of Egypt were new!—by a Sumerian in what is today the south of Iraq. It sings the glories of the ancient land of Dilmun, site of the Biblical Garden of Eden, whose capital—as the excavations carried out since 1953 have conclusively proven—was here on the island of Bahrain. 'The land of Dilmun is holy,' the hymn begins, 'the land of Dilmun is pure. In Dilmun the raven does not croak, the lion does not kill. No one says, my eyes are sick, my head is sick. No one says, I am an old man, I am an old woman. . . .' "

The voice droned on and on. Megan McConnell, the reporter, scribbled furiously in her notebook. The Indian photographer snapped exposure after exposure of the assistant curator, the honored guests, the colorful displays of artefacts on the walls. The children themselves, trained since infancy in the art of diplomacy, seemed to be listening attentively, though who knew what thoughts they were thinking as they stood there in their flowing *thobes* and crisp white *ghutras.*

Behind the intent and solemn mask of Mahboob Chaudri's olive face, *he* was thinking that at least the ethnography room had been worth looking at, with its spears and swords and *khunjars*, its models of stilt houses made all of palm fronds and pearl divers's boats rigged out with canvas sails, its mannequins in native dress—especially the bride, in her magnificent gold-embroidered *thobe nashel* with its billowing sleeves that folded upwards to cover her head, the elaborate gold ornaments around her neck, the intricately hennaed hands—its camel saddles and tools and pottery and pearl chests and glassware and porcelain, its orchestra of Arabic instruments—*qanoon, mahsoor, oud, murwass, dirbanka, shaganga* and more—its full-size reproduction of the kitchen of a villager's thatched hut and of the carpets and mirrored walls and silken pillows and curtained four-poster bed of the room in which a well-to-do couple would spend their wedding night.

Shazia, his own dear wife, would enjoy that section of the museum, if no other. Shazia . . . It had been almost two years since his last home leave, since he had last heard her speak his name, last touched a hand to her delicate cheek and kissed her lips and felt the soft caress of her sweet and golden arms. . . .

" 'Let the sun in heaven bring her sweet water from the earth,' " Ibrahim al-Samahiji's monotone pushed the image of his wife to the far edge of Chaudri's consciousness. " 'Let Dilmun drink the water of abundance. Let her springs become springs of sweet water. Let her fields yield their grain. Let her city become the port of all the world.' "

The hymn was over at last, and the assistant curator smiled determinedly and led them off to a small room at the back of the building, a room with a single waist-high display case taking up most of its floor space and old-fashioned black-and-white maps of the Middle East covering its walls.

"About forty years ago," Sheikh Ibrahim told them, "a small number of a previously unknown type of round stamp seal began to be found both in Mesopotamia and in cities of the Indus River valley. Dating to about 2000 BC, they were clearly 'foreign' among the cylinder seals of Mesopotamia and the square seals of the Indus. No one knew where they came from. But the recent discovery of some fifty seals of this type in the Barbar temples and in Cities I and II at Qala'at al-Bahrain, together with debris of seal-cutting workshops, shows us that this seal-type is in fact native to Bahrain. These so-called 'Dilmun seals' are the main evidence for Bahrain's trade connections 4,000 years ago with the whole of the Middle East, and they are this country's greatest, most valuable archaeological treasure."

Chaudri leaned forward to see into the case. It was filled with row upon row of small stone buttons, carved with a confusion of geometric shapes, crude human figures, images of goats and gazelles and flowering trees. Beneath each stone was a square of gray clay bearing the impression of the seal that lay above it. A magnifying panel was set into grooves along the top and bottom edges of the case's surface, so that the seals could be examined more closely.

But that arrangement was not good enough for the four young boys.

"There's so much glare from the overhead lighting," complained Jamil, the fourteen-year-old son of a prime minister. "I can hardly see them."

"And the inside of the case is dim," Mohammed added. He was sixteen, and his father was a minister of defense.

Talal, also sixteen and also a prime minister's child, was the one who came up with the idea. "Open the case and take them out," he proposed, though to Mahboob Chaudri's ears it sounded more like a command than a suggestion.

"Yes, yes," came Rashid's high-pitched agreement. At thirteen, he was the youngest of the boys; he was the most powerful of them all, though, as his father was a Crown Prince and the heir to his country's throne. "I want to hold them, to feel the texture of them in my hand. If these are Bahrain's proudest treasures, I want to learn to know them."

Sheikh Ibrahim looked staggered. Delicately, he began to explain: "That would be very, ah, irregular. You see, the air in this display case is temperature-controlled and dehumidified. If I open the case, the sudden change in temperature and humidity could, ah, could damage the seals. And if you were to touch them, the, ah, oils on your fingertips and palms could—"

"Well, of course," one of the boys interrupted softly, "if you don't want to give us the pleasure of . . ." He allowed his voice to trail off, and turned away from Sheikh Ibrahim.

The assistant curator swallowed nervously. The small room had gone deathly silent—even the photographer had stopped his incessant picture taking—and the atmosphere was thick and stuffy with tension. The dismayed look on Megan McConnell's face was clear: what a story this was, and what a shame that she would never be allowed to publish it! For the first time that day, Mahboob Chaudri found himself truly interested in the events going on around him.

Sheikh Ibrahim took a deep breath, and smiled. "—the oils on your fingertips and palms might counteract the effect of the changes in temperature and humidity," he went on smoothly, "and I would be grateful for the opportunity to investigate that possibility." He pulled a ring of keys from the pocket of his ankle-length *thobe*, selected one of them, and unlocked the back of the display case.

The tightness in the room evaporated, and Chaudri relaxed. He felt that he had at last begun to understand the intricate complexities of statecraft, and the ease with which a simple disagreement between individuals could quickly escalate into an international incident. He tried to feel sorry for Ibrahim al-Samahiji, for the way the distinguished assistant curator had been put in his place by a child, but found himself admiring the Sheikh's tactfulness and diplomacy instead.

He remembered an Arabic saying which he had heard shortly after his arrival in Bahrain: *Both lion and gazelle may be sleeping in one thicket,* a grizzled graybeard in a teashop on the fringes of the *suq* had told him, puffing wisely at the thin stem of his bubbing *narghile,* the crude clay waterpipe no longer smoked by anyone other than old men; *but only the lion is having a restful sleep.* He had not understood that proverb at first, but he knew now what it was like to be a gazelle amongst the lions.

Sheikh Ibrahim had removed several trays of seals from the glass case in the center of the room, and was carefully lifting the stones from their velvet niches and passing them out to the eager boys. Once again the air rang with teenaged chatter, and the photographer's flashbulbs popped almost continuously.

"What's this one?" asked Mohammed, balancing a seal on his upturned palm. "It looks so funny!"

Chaudri was standing close enough to make out the design on the stone: two male figures carved in simple outline, seated on identical chairs or stools, the sun shining above them and, strangely, a star at their feet. He had seen this image before, reproduced on countless T-shirts and wooden plaques and gold medallions; it was the only one of the seals with which he was familiar. What made it funny was that the noses of the two seated men were ludicrously long, and joined in a *V* at the top of a large oval shape which hung between them; each figure held one arm behind him, fingers weirdly misshapen and splayed, and supported his trunk-like nose with his other arm.

"They are called the Beer Drinkers," Sheikh Ibrahim informed them proudly, "and that is the best known and most beloved of all the Dilmun seals. The two men are sharing a skin of mead, drinking it through long spouts or straws— which most people see instead, comically, as enormous noses. Although," he admitted, "there are also those who call this stone 'The Musicians,' and claim that the two figures are playing a primitive sort of bagpipes and not drinking beer at all. In any case, I think I can safely say that that small stone which you hold in your hand is the greatest and most important of Bahrain's ancient treasures."

The children were suitably impressed, and they handled the seal almost with reverence. Megan McConnell made a swift but talented sketch of it in her notebook, and the photographer finished off a roll of film shooting it from all imaginable angles.

"What were these seals used for?" the reporter wanted to know, her drawing complete. "Were they purely decorative, or were they functional as well?"

Her associate was busy changing film, and in the respite from exploding flashbulbs Chaudri glanced surreptitiously at his watch. Another twenty minutes and it would be time to go.

"Oh, absolutely functional, Miss McConnell." Sheikh Ibrahim rubbed his hands with delight at the chance to launch into another lecture. "Each of the seals is different, unique, and four millennia ago they were used as we use our signatures today. A craftsman marked each sample of his handiwork with his own distinctive seal, to show that *he* had produced it and no one else. A scribe used his seal to sign documents, a nobleman to make his decrees official, a merchant to verify transactions. The poor, of course, had no need for such seals, but anyone with valuable property or possessions would identify them as his own by . . ."

The bolts of photographic lightning resumed, and the soliloquy went on.

And then, at last, Sheikh Ibrahim began to fit the Dilmun seals back into their velvet trays, matching each with the clay impression just below its waiting position. Megan McConnell snapped her notebook shut and tucked it away in her shoulder bag. The Indian photographer clicked off a few final shots of the group. The four boys milled about impatiently, ready to be underway. Mahboob Chaudri's stomach growled, and he prayed silently that the rumble had been audible to none but himself.

Then Ibrahim al-Samahiji gasped hoarsely, and when Chaudri looked up there was stark horror etched into the lines of the assistant curator's weathered face. He was pointing a trembling finger at an empty hole in the last velvet tray.

"The Beer Drinkers!" he cried brokenly. "It—it's gone!"

Mahboob Chaudri was no longer bored.

Bahrain's greatest treasure was missing—*stolen* and not lost, as a careful check around the small room quickly revealed. The prime suspects were four young men whose fathers were so high-placed that even to *question* their sons would be the gravest of insults, while the idea of searching the boys for the stone was absolutely unthinkable. And he had less than a quarter of an hour before it would be time to reboard the bus for the brief ride back to the mainland.

No, Mahboob Chaudri was not bored.

But he would have given a great deal to *be* bored once again, instead of mired in this, the most hopeless, desperate situation of his career. Of his *career?* Of his *life!*

Sheikh Ibrahim was gaping at him. Megan McConnell had her notebook out again, and was scribbling in it furiously. The Indian photographer was taking pictures of *him* now, and Chaudri could imagine the caption that would appear in the *Gulf Daily News:* "Mahboob Ahmed Chaudri of the Public Security Force," it would say, "totally baffled by the theft of the most important relic of Bahrain's ancient history."

Luttay gaye, he thought bitterly. *What a disaster!*

The four boys, meanwhile—Jamil, Mohammed, Talal and Rashid—were talking softly amongst themselves, and Chaudri would have sorely liked to have been able to overhear their conversation. The McConnell woman and her photographer had been working all the while that the seals were being handed around; there had been no time for either of them to have pocketed the Beer Drinkers. And it was inconceivable that Sheikh Ibrahim himself had stolen the stone: the thing would be impossible to sell, and if—like certain mad collectors—all he wanted was the knowledge that a unique and priceless piece was in his possession, why, this piece *was* in his possession, safe in its niche in his museum, and he could enjoy it safely and privately whenever he chose.

No, the awful truth was that the only valid suspects in the case were the eldest sons of four of the GCC's strongmen, and there was nothing he could do about it. He could not search them, he could not ask them to turn out the pockets of their *thobes,* he could not ask *any* question which implied that one of the boys was guilty while admitting that he did not already know *which* one. For if the three innocent youngsters saw that their integrity was in doubt, at least one of them would be sure to report the matter to his father, and—

Chaudri didn't really want to think about the consequences.

If only he had been watching more closely, if he had *seen* which of the four had taken the stone.

If only.

If only he had a magic box, like the Grand Vizier in the old fairy tale. It had been one of his favorite stories as a child: the Emperor's wonderful golden ring is stolen, and the Vizier is ordered to uncover the identity of the thief. He gathers the suspects outside one of the palace's smaller apartments, and instructs them to enter the darkened room individually and unaccompanied by guards. In the center of the room they will find the Vizier's magic box, and they are to put one hand into that box as deeply as it will go, then leave the apartment by a second door, where the Vizier himself will be waiting for them. The box will have no effect on the hand of an innocent man, but its magic will stain a criminal's skin a damning black. So, one by one, the courtiers enter the darkened room. One by one, they leave by the opposite door. And one by one, the Grand Vizier examines their hands. At last: "This is the criminal!" he cries. "But my hands are clean!" the accused man protests. "Exactly," smiles the Grand Vizier. For his "magic" box is not magic at all, merely an ordinary wooden box filled to its brim with soot. The innocent suspects, their consciences clear, have obeyed the Vizier's instructions and come out of the room with blackened hands. Only the guilty man, fearful of the box's magic, has disobeyed, and his immaculate hands reveal him to be the thief.

If only I had a magic box, Mahboob Chaudri thought sadly. *If only I had been* watching!

But—but wait. *He* knew that he had seen nothing, but he was the *only* one in the room who possessed that knowledge. And perhaps they *did* have a "magic box" of sorts there with them, after all. If only he could—Yes. Yes. It would be a gamble, but it was all he could think of. And if the Indian photographer was clever enough to catch on and play along, well, then there was even a chance that it might work!

In any case, it was worth a try. Even if it failed, the situation could hardly get any worse than it already was.

Chaudri drew himself up to his full height, calmly projecting an air of what he hoped would pass for confidence. Less than two minutes had passed since Sheikh Ibrahim had announced the disappearance of the treasured seal. The Sheikh, the boys, Megan McConnell, the photographer—they were all turned towards him expectantly, waiting for him to speak.

He spoke. "I saw which one of you took the stone," he lied. "You thought my attention was elsewhere, but you were wrong. I saw you take it, and I saw where you hid it."

He watched their faces hopefully, praying for the guilty boy to give himself away.

But it was not to be that easy.

And it was too late to back away from it, now. He had committed himself, and he could only go forward.

"Your first mistake," he went on, "was coveting that which does not belong to you—a minor sin, true, but a sin all the same. Your second mistake was stealing the stone, repaying Bahrain for her hospitality by robbing her of her dearest treasure—*that*, of course, was a graver sin, and a more serious error. And your third mistake was larger still: you allowed me to see you as you claimed the Beer Drinkers for your own."

The silence in the room was hot and stifling, in spite of the museum's air conditioning.

"But I am only a simple policeman," Chaudri admitted, his voice now humble. "If I accuse you, here or in front of your father, it will be my word against yours. Even if the stone is found in your possession, then perhaps—you will say—I planted it there, in an attempt to discredit you. My word against yours—and your word, obviously, will be worth much more than mine. What I need," said Mahboob Chaudri firmly, "is proof."

Now is the moment, he thought, pausing to let them consider the things he had said. *Understand me, my friend, and give me your help!*

"And I *have* proof," he said, "for you made yet a fourth mistake, and that was the largest error of all." He whirled to face the stocky little photographer, and pointed a finger straight at the man's startled eyes. *"You,"* he intoned dramatically, his mind imploring the other to comprehend, *"you* saw the theft take place as well—not only saw it, but snapped a photograph of it with your camera at the very instant it happened!"

The Indian blinked nervously, clearly confused.

Don't deny it, Chaudri thought fiercely. *You can help me trap the thief. Help me!*

"I—" the man stammered. It was the first sound Chaudri had ever heard him utter.

It's not going to work, he realized. *He doesn't know what I'm talking about.*

And then the swarthy Indian countenance cleared.

"Why, yes, sir," the man said firmly. "That is completely true. I did."

Chaudri flushed with joy. Praise Allah for those beautiful, blessed words! It was working!

"I don't want to cause an embarrassing incident," he told

277

the children confidently. "All I want is for the Beer Drinkers
to be returned. So I have a suggestion to make." He moved
to the panel of light switches by the door, and swung the
door itself—the only entrance to the room—shut. "If all
four of you will gather around the display case, one on
each side of it, I will turn off all the lights in this room.
In the darkness, the boy who took the seal can set it back
down on top of the case without being seen. I will leave
the lights off for one minute. If the stone is there when I
turn them back on, then I will return you all to your hotel,
and nothing further need ever be said about what has happened here today. Sheikh Ibrahim, is that acceptable to
you?"

The assistant curator bobbed his head eagerly. "Yes, of
course," he agreed. "All I want is the seal!"

"Miss McConnell?"

To her credit, the reporter understood him and nodded
her acquiescence immediately. That would mean two marvelous stories lost in a single day, but she was a seasoned
enough journalist to recognize that, in the Gulf, some tales
are better left untold.

"And you, Mr.—?"

"Gogumalla, sir," the Indian supplied. "Solomon Gogumalla."

"Mr. Gogumalla. Will you swear to say nothing about this
incident, and to destroy the incriminating film in your camera without developing and printing it, if the Beer Drinkers
is returned?"

The little photographer swallowed noisily. "Yes, sir," he
promised. "Of course. I won't say a word. You can rely
on me."

"Well, then!" Chaudri rubbed his hands together briskly.
"Another few moments, and all this—unpleasantness will
be over."

The youngsters themselves seemed willing to cooperate,
and Chaudri deferentially arranged them around the sides
of the glass display case. Ibrahim al-Samahiji, Megan
McConnell and Solomon Gogumalla he guided to positions

278

along the wall furthest from the case, so they would be well out of the way.

"Now I will shut off the lights," he repeated, "and I will leave them off for sixty seconds."

With hope and prayer in his heart, he hit the four plastic switches and plunged the room into darkness. . . .

The room was empty, empty of light and of sound. Mahboob Chaudri held his breath and listened for the faint rustle of cloth that would be a hand reaching into a pocket, for the sharp click of stone touching down on glass.

But there was nothing, no rustle, no click, no noise of any kind.

And time floated by, as slow yet intense as one of the Emir's golden peregrine falcons drifting steadily across the sky in search of its prey.

Then the sounds began. There was a cough from the corner of the room, a grating rasp which could have come either from the assistant curator or the photographer. There was the abrupt crack of a joint flexed after too long a time held stiff. There was a shuffle of impatient feet and a long and tired sigh, and, drowning out all of these in Mahboob Chaudri's ears, the rapid pounding of his own anxious heart.

When he judged that a full minute had gone by, "I will now turn on the lights," he announced, and felt for the switches in the darkness and pressed them all at once.

He blinked helplessly at the sudden explosion of light, more disturbing even than Solomon Gogumalla's flashbulbs.

When his eyes had readjusted to the brightness, he looked hopefully to the surface of the display case in the center of the room.

There was nothing there.

His bluff had been called.

Disgrace, dismissal, and banishment back to Pakistan. His children would be ashamed of him, his wife despise him, his friends abandon him.

It was over, all over—his career, his happiness, his life.

279

He would see his assignment through, of course, escort the children back to their hotel, then go straight to the Police Fort and prepare a letter of resignation. If he was going to give up, at least he could do *that* much, and quit before they could throw him out.

If he was going to give up . . .

No! He was Mahboob Ahmed Chaudri—not a quitter, not a coward, but a police officer with a job to do, a case to solve, a criminal to apprehend.

His bluff had failed, true—but before he would admit defeat he would play one more card, the only card that was left to him.

He would bluff again.

"Very well, then," he said, "you have chosen to hold onto the stone, which leaves *me* with no choice at all. I will have that film developed, and I will present the incriminating photograph to your father. Mr. Gogumalla, may I have your camera, please?"

"Certainly, *mahsool,*" the Indian replied. "But may I offer you my services, as well? I have a small darkroom of my own, right here in Muharraq. Allow me to develop the roll for you, and to make a large print of the picture in question, which I can present to you very quickly and with my compliments."

"A kind offer," said Chaudri, pleased, *and a nice touch,* he added silently. "But in a case like this one it would be best to have our own men do that job." He put out his hand for the camera, but the photographer held onto it. "Don't worry about your camera," Chaudri reassured him. "Our specialists will be quite careful with it."

Gogumalla shook his head stubbornly and took a step backwards, and at that moment Mahboob Chaudri finally realized what had really happened to the Beer Drinkers.

. . . *should have seen the truth immediately,* Chaudri wrote to his wife Shazia late that evening. Usually his weekly letters were filled with questions about the children and wistful dreams of the future, when he would have saved enough money from his salary to return to Pakistan for good—as a wealthy man, not a disgraced one. But, this week, he had news to report.

Miss McConnell and the Indian Gogumalla were busy working while the theft was being committed, he wrote, forming the Punjabi words slowly and carefully, *and I was certain that neither of them could possibly have been guilty. Instead of looking only at the fact that they were working, though, I ought to have considered what exactly it was that they were* doing. *The woman was writing and drawing in her notebook all that time, and the photographer was taking pictures. But, at one moment, Gogumalla stopped to put a fresh roll of film into his camera, just after shooting a series of exposures of the Beer Drinkers. And as it turned out, new film was not all that he was loading into the body of his camera—he hid the Dilmun seal there as well, in the hollow cavity inside the lens.*

It was not in his mind to commit a crime when he set out today—he was just a simple photographer on assignment. But when Sheikh Ibrahim explained how valuable the stone was and he saw the opportunity to take it, the temptation was too much for him to resist.

The poor fool! He was too ignorant, Shazia, to know that, for him, the Beer Drinkers had no value at all: unique and instantly recognizable as it is, there is no way he could ever have sold it.

Of course, none of the photos he was taking after the theft were any good, with the Beer Drinkers lodged between his lens and his film. If I had accepted his offer to process and print the roll himself, he would have gone off to his darkroom, taken the seal out of the camera and hid it elsewhere, and come back to me with the sad story that the film had accidentally been ruined. And since he knew that I knew that there really was no incriminating picture, he doubted that—once we had left the museum—I would even bother asking him to do the developing and printing. When I carried my bluff to the extreme, though, and insisted on taking the camera myself, he saw that the game was up and confessed.

He is out on Jiddah now, the prison island, in a cell await-

ing trial, and I have been commended by my superiors for solving the case without insulting or embarrassing the four boys, who by now are back in their home countries and tucked safely away in bed. Sheikh Ibrahim has promised me a golden reproduction of the Beer Drinkers as an expression of his gratitude, and when I receive it I will buy a chain for it and send it to you as a memento of your husband's "triumph."

Not a very satisfying triumph for me—if I hadn't happened to remember that old fairy tale and think of the Indian's camera as a modern-day "magic box," Solomon Gogumalla would now have the seal, and I would be—

Well, the less said about that the better.

It is getting late, dear Shazia, and I must sleep. Kiss the children a hundred times for me, and think ever fondly of your own

Mahboob

Elena Oliverez

THE CHICANA DETECTIVE

THE SANCHEZ SACRAMENTS

Marcia Muller

Chicano detectives have begun to appear with some fre-
quency in contemporary crime fiction, among them Dell
Shannon's Luis Mendoza and Rex Burns' Gabriel Wager.
But to date there is only one Chicana detective: Marcia
Muller's Santa Barbara museum curator and amateur
*sleuth, Elena Oliverez, who is featured in two novels—*The
Tree of Death *(1983) and* Legend of the Slain Soldiers *(to*
be published in 1985)—and in the original novelette which
follows.

Well drawn, with emphasis on her human qualities as
well as her deductive abilities, Elena Oliverez is one of
the best of the new ethnic detectives. Her cases are not only
expertly constructed mysteries but vivid depictions of
museum operation, the world of Mexican art, and the Mexi-
can-American community in general. In "The Sanchez Sac-
raments," she becomes involved in the strange mystery un-
derlying a group of religious pottery figures donated to
the Museum of Mexican Art by the estate of a famous folk
artist—with poignant and memorable results.

In addition to Elena Oliverez, Marcia Muller is the creator
of San Francisco private detective Sharon McCone, whose

adventures are chronicled in such highly successful novels as Edwin of the Iron Shoes (*1977*), Ask the Cards a Question (*1982*), Games to Keep the Dark Away (*1983*), *and* Leave a Message for Willie (*1984*). *She has also coedited several anthologies with Bill Pronzini, as well as coauthored with him a novel and a nonfiction book on mystery and detective fiction,* 1001 Midnights (*to be published in 1985*).

•   •   •

I was in the basement of the museum unpacking the pottery figures Adolfo Sanchez had left us when I began to grow puzzled about the old man and his work. It was the priest figures that bothered me.

Sanchez had been one of Mexico's most outstanding folk artists, living in seclusion near the pottery-making center of Metepec. His work had taken the form of groupings of figures participating in such religious ceremonies as weddings, feast days, and baptisms. The figures we'd received from his estate—actually from the executrix of his estate, his sister, Lucia—represented an entire life cycle in five of the seven Catholic sacraments. They'd arrived by truck only yesterday, along with Sanchez's written instructions about setting them up, and I'd decided to devote this morning to unpacking them so we could place them on display in our special exhibits gallery next week.

The crate I'd started with contained the priests, one for each sacrament, and I'd set the two-foot-tall, highly glazed pottery figures at intervals around the room, waiting to be joined by the other figures that would complete each scene. Four of the five figures represented the same man, his clean-shaven face dour, eyes kindly and wise. The fifth, which belonged to the depiction of Extreme Unction—the last rites—was bearded and haggard, with an expression of great pain. But what was puzzling was that this priest was holding out a communion wafer, presumably to a dying parishoner.

I'm not a practicing Catholic, in spite of the fact I was raised one, but I do remember enough of my Catechism to know that they don't give communion during Extreme

Unction. What they do is anoint the sense organs with holy oil. Adolfo Sanchez certainly should have known that, too, because he was an extremely devout Catholic and devoted his life to portraying religious scenes such as this.

There was a book on the work table that I'd bought on the old man's life and works. I flipped through it to see if there were any pictures of other scenes depicting Extreme Unction, but if he'd done any, they weren't in this particular volume. Disappointed, I skimmed backwards through a section of pictures of the artist and his family and found the biographical sketch at the front of the book.

Adolfo had been born seventy-seven years ago in Metepec. As was natural for a local boy with artistic talent, he'd taken up the potter's trade. He'd married late, in his mid-thirties, to a local girl named Constantina Lopez, and they'd had one child, Rosalinda. Rosalinda had married late also, by Mexican standards—in her early twenties—and had given birth to twin boys two years later. Constantina Sanchez had died shortly after her grandsons' birth, and Rosalinda had followed, after a lingering illness, when the twins were five. Ever since the boys had left home, Adolfo had lived in seclusion with only his sister Lucia as faithful companion. He had devoted himself to his art, even to the point of never attending church.

Maybe, I thought, he'd stayed away long enough that he'd forgotten exactly how things were done in the Catholic faith. But I'd stayed away, and I still remembered.

Senility, then? I flipped to the photograph of the old man at the front of the book and stared into his eyes, clear and alert above his finely chiseled nose and thick beard. No, Sanchez had not been senile. Well, in any event, it was time I got on with unpacking the rest of the figures.

I was cradling one of a baptismal infant when Emily, my secretary, appeared. She stood at the bottom of the steps, one hand on the newel post, her pale-haired head cocked to one side, looking worried.

"Elena?" she said. "There are two . . . gentlemen here to see you."

Something about the way she said "gentlemen" gave me pause. I set the infant's figure down on the work table. "What gentlemen?"

"The Sanchez brothers."

"Who?" For a moment I didn't connect them with the twins I'd just been reading about. Sanchez is a common Mexican name.

"They're here about the pottery." She motioned at the crates. "One is in your office, and Susana has taken the other to the courtyard."

Susana Ibarra was the Museum of Mexican Arts' public relations director—and troubleshooter. If she had elected to take one of the Sanchez twins under her wing, it was because he was either upset or about to cause a scene.

"Is everything all right?"

Emily shrugged. "So far."

"I'll be right up."

"Which one do you want to see first?"

"Can't I see them together?"

"I wouldn't advise it. They almost came to blows in the courtyard before Susana took over."

"Oh." I paused. "Well then, if Susana has the one she's talking to under control, I'll go directly to my office."

Emily nodded and went upstairs.

I moved the infant's figure into the center of the large work table and checked to see if the other figures were securely settled. To break one of them would destroy the effect of the entire work, to say nothing of its value. When I'd assured myself they were safe, I followed Emily upstairs.

Once there, I hurried through the Folk Art gallery, with its Tree of Life and colorful papier-mâché animals, and peered out into the central courtyard. Susana Ibarra and a tall man wearing jeans and a rough cotton shirt stood near the little fountain. The man's arms were folded across his chest and he was frowning down at her. Susana had her hands on her hips and was tossing her thick mane of black hair for emphasis as she spoke. From the aggressive way she balanced on her high heels, I could tell that she was giving the man a lecture. And, knowing Susana, if that didn't work she'd probably dunk him in the fountain. Reassured, I smiled and went to the office wing.

When I stepped into my office, the young man seated in the visitor's chair jumped to his feet. He was as tall as Susana's companion and had the same lean, chiseled features and short black hair. In his light tan suit, conservative tie, and highly polished shoes, he looked excessively formal for the casual atmosphere of Santa Barbara.

I held out my hand and said, "Mr. Sanchez? I'm Elena Oliverez, director of the museum."

"Gilberto Sanchez." His accent told me he was a Mexican national. He paused, then added, "Adolfo Sanchez's grandson."

"Please, sit down." I went around the desk and took my padded leather chair. "I understand you're here about the Sacraments."

For a moment he looked blank. "Oh, the figures from Tía Lucia. Yes."

"You didn't know they're called the Sanchez Sacraments?"

"No. I don't know anything about them. That is why I'm here."

"I don't understand."

He leaned forward, his fine features serious. "Let me explain. My mother died when my brother Eduardo and I were only five—we are fraternal twins. My father had left long before that, so we had only Grandfather and Tía Lucia. But Grandfather wanted us to see more of the world than Metepec. It is a small town, and Grandfather's village is even smaller. So he sent us to school and then university in Mexico City. After college I remained on there."

"So you never saw the Sacraments?"

"No. I knew Grandfather was working on something important the last years of his life, but whenever I went to visit him, he refused to let me see the project. It was the same with Eduardo; we were not even allowed in his workroom."

"Did he tell you anything about it?"

"No. Tía Lucia did not even know. All she said was that
he had told her it was the finish of his life's work. Now
he is gone, and even before Eduardo and I could get to
Metepec for the funeral, Tía Lucia shipped the figures off
to you. She won't talk about them, just says they are better
off in a museum."

"And you . . . ?"

"I want to see them. Surely you can understand that,
Miss Oliverez. I loved my grandfather. Somehow it will
make his death easier to accept if I can see the work of
the last ten years of his life." Gilberto's eyes shone with
emotion as he spoke.

I nodded, tapping my fingers on the arm of my chair.
It was an odd story, and it sounded as if Gilberto's aunt
hadn't wanted him or his twin brother to see the figures.
To give myself time to order my thoughts, I said, "What
do you do in Mexico City, Mr. Sanchez?"

If the abrupt switch in subject surprised him, he didn't
show it. "I am a banker."

That explained his conservative dress. "I see."

He smiled suddenly, a wonderful smile that transformed
his face and showed me what he might be like without
the pall of death hanging over him. "Oh, I am not totally
without the family madness, as my grandfather used to call
the artistic temperament. I paint in my spare time."

"Oils?"

"Yes."

"Are you talented?"

He considered. "Yes, I think so."

I liked his candor, and immediately decided that I also
liked him. "Mr. Sanchez, I understand you and your brother
almost came to blows in our courtyard earlier."

The smile dropped away and he colored slightly. "Yes,
we met as we were both coming in. I had no idea he was
in Santa Barbara."

"What was your argument about?"

"The Sacraments, as you call them. You see, Eduardo

288

also came to Metepec for the funeral. He lives in Chicago now, where he is a film maker—television commercials mainly, but he also does other, more artistic work. The family madness passed down to him, too. Anyway, he was as upset as I was about the Sacraments being gone, but for a different reason."

"And what was that?"

Gilberto laced his long fingers together and looked down at them, frowning. "He thinks Tía Lucia had no right to give them away. He says they should have come down to us. And he wants them back so he can sell them."

"And you don't agree?"

"No, I don't." Quickly he looked up. "We were well provided for in Grandfather's will, but he made Tía Lucia his executrix. She says it was Grandfather's wish that the Sacraments go to a museum. And I feel a man has the right to dispose of his work in any way he chooses."

"Then why are you here?"

"Only because I wish to see the Sacraments."

I decided right then that I had better contact Lucia Sanchez before I went any further with this. "Well, Mr. Sanchez," I said, "the figures just arrived yesterday and haven't been unpacked yet. I plan to have them on exhibit early next week. At that time—"

"Would it be possible to view them privately?"

He looked so eager that I hated to disappoint him, so I said, "I'm sure something can be arranged."

The smile spread across his face again and he got to his feet. "I would appreciate that very much."

Aware that he would not want another run-in with his brother, I showed him the way out through the little patio outside my office, then started out to the central courtyard. Emily was at her desk, doing something to a ditto master with a razor blade.

"Is Susana still talking to Eduardo Sanchez?" I asked her.

"Yes. They seem to have made friends. At least they were sitting on the edge of the fountain laughing when I went past five minutes ago."

"Susana could charm the spots off a leopard." I turned to go, then paused. "Emily, do we have a telephone number for Lucia Sanchez?"

"Yes, I put it in my Rolodex."

"I'll want to talk to her today."

"Then I'd better start trying now. Service to the Metepec area is bound to be poor."

"Right. If I'm not back here by the time the call goes through, come and get me." I turned and went through the doorway to the courtyard.

As Emily had said, Susana and Eduardo Sanchez were sitting on the edge of the blue-tiled fountain, and she appeared to be telling him one of her infamous jokes. Susana loved long jokes, the more complicated the better. The trouble was, she usually forgot the punchlines, or mixed them up with the endings of other jokes. Only her prettiness and girlish charm—she was only seventeen—saved her from mayhem at the hands of her listeners.

When he saw me, Eduardo Sanchez stood up—not as quickly as his brother had, but almost indolently. Up close I could see that his fine features were chiseled more sharply than Gilberto's, as if the sculptor had neglected to smooth off the rough edges. His hair was longer too, artfully blow-dried, and although his attire was casual, I noted his loafers were Guccis.

Eduardo's handshake, when Susana introduced us, was indolent too. His accent was not so pronounced as his twin's, and I thought I caught a faint, incongruous touch of the midwest in the way he said hello.

I said, "It's a pleasure to meet you, Mr. Sanchez. I see Ms. Ibarra has been taking good care of you."

He glanced over at Susana, who was standing, smoothing the pleats of her bright green dress. "Yes, she has been telling me a story about a dog who dresses up as a person in order to get the fire department to 'rescue' a cat he has chased up a tree. We have not reached the ending, however, and I fear we never will."

Susana flashed her brilliant smile. "Can I help it if I forget?

The jokes are all very long, and in this life a person can only keep so much knowledge in her head."

"Don't worry, Susana," I said. "I'd rather you kept the dates of our press releases in there than the punchline to such a silly story."

"Speaking of the press releases . . ." She turned and went toward the door to the office wing.

Eduardo Sanchez's eyes followed her. "An enchanting girl," he said.

"Yes, we're fortunate to have her on staff. And now, what can I do for you? I assume you've come about the Sacraments?"

Unlike his brother, he seemed to know what they were called. "Yes. Has Gilberto filled you in?"

"A little."

Eduardo reclaimed his seat on the edge of the fountain. "He probably painted me as quite the villain, too. But at least you know why I'm here. Those figures should never have been donated to this museum. Rightfully they belong to Gilberto and me. We either want them returned or paid for."

"You say 'we.' It was my impression that all your brother wants is to see them."

He made an impatient gesture with one hand. "For a banker, Gilberto isn't very smart."

"But he does seem to have respect for your grandfather's wishes. He loved him very much, you know."

His eyes flashed angrily. "And do you think I didn't? I worshipped the man. If it wasn't for him and his guidance, I'd be nobody today."

"Then why go against his wishes?"

"For the simple reason that I don't know if donating those pieces to this museum was what he wanted."

"You think your aunt made that up?"

"She may have."

"Why?"

"I don't know!" He got up and began to pace.

I hesitated, then framed my words carefully. "Mr. Sanchez, I think you have come to the wrong person about this. It appears to be a family matter, one you should work out with your aunt and brother."

"I have tried."

"Try again. Because there's really nothing I can do."

His body tensed and he swung around to face me. I tensed too, ready to step back out of his reach. But then he relaxed with a conscious effort, and a lazy smile spread across his face.

"Clever, aren't you?"

"I have to be, Mr. Sanchez. The art world may seem gentle and nonmaterialistic to outsiders, but—as you know from your work in films—art is as cutthroat a business as any other. To run a museum, you have to be clever—and strong-willed."

"I get your message." The smile did not leave his face.

"Then you'll discuss this with your family?"

"Among others. I'll be in touch." He turned and stalked out of the courtyard.

I stood there, surprised he'd given up so easily, and very much on my guard. Eduardo Sanchez was not going to go away. Nor was his brother. As if I didn't have enough to contend with here at the museum, now I would be dragged into a family quarrel. Sighing, I went to see if Emily had been able to put my call through to Metepec.

The following afternoon, Lucia Sanchez sat across my desk from me, her dark eyes focused anxiously on mine. In her cotton dress that was faded from too many washings, her work-roughened hands clutching a shabby leather handbag, she reminded me of the aunts of my childhood who would come from Mexico for family weddings or funerals. They had seemed like people from another century, those silent women who whispered among themselves and otherwise spoke only when spoken to. It had been hard to imagine them as young or impassioned, and it was the same with Miss Sanchez. Only her eyes seemed truly alive.

When I'd spoken to her on the phone the day before,

she'd immediately been alarmed at her great-nephews' presence in Santa Barbara and had decided to come to California to reason with them.

Now she said, "Have you heard anything further from either of the boys?"

"Oh, yes." I nodded. "Gilberto has called twice today asking when the figures will be ready for viewing. Eduardo has also called twice, threatening to retain a lawyer if I don't either return the Sacraments or settle upon a 'mutually acceptable price.'"

Lucia Sanchez made a disgusted sound. "This is what it comes to. After all their grandfather and I did for them."

"I can see where you would be upset by Eduardo's behavior, but what Gilberto is asking seems quite reasonable."

"You do not know the whole story. Tell me, are the figures on display yet?"

"They have been arranged in our special exhibits gallery, yes. But it will not be open to the public until next Monday."

"Good." She nodded and stood, and the calm decisiveness of her manner at once erased all resemblance to my long-departed aunts. "I should like to see the pieces, if I may."

I got up and led her from the office wing and across the courtyard to the gallery that held our special exhibits. I'd worked all the previous afternoon and evening setting up the figures with the help of two student volunteers from my alma mater, the University of California's Santa Barbara campus. This sort of active participation in creating the exhibits was not the usual province of a director, but we were a small museum and since our director had been murdered and I'd been promoted last spring, we'd had yet to find a curator who would work for the equally small salary we could offer. These days I wore two hats—not always comfortably.

Now, as I ushered Lucia Sanchez into the gallery and turned on the overhead spotlights, I had to admit that the late evening I'd put in had been worthwhile. There were five groupings, each on a raised platform, each representing a Sacrament. The two-foot-tall pottery figures were not as primitive in appearance as most folk art; instead, they were highly representational, with perfect proportions and expressive faces. Had they not been fired in an extremely glossy and colorful glaze, they would have seemed almost real.

Lucia Sanchez paused on the threshold of the room, then began moving counterclockwise, studying the figures. I followed.

The first Sacrament was a baptism, the father holding the infant before the priest while the mother and friends and relatives looked on. Next came a confirmation, the same proud parents beaming in the background. The figure of the bride in the wedding ceremony was so carefully crafted that I felt if I reached out and touched her dress it would be the traditional embroidered cotton rather than clay. The father smiled broadly as he gave her away, placing her hand in that of the groom.

The other two groupings were not of joyous occasions. Extreme Unction—the last rites—involved only the figure of the former bride on her deathbed and the priest, oddly offering her the final communion wafer. And the last scene—Penance—was not a grouping either, but merely the figure of a man kneeling in the confessional, the priest's face showing dimly through the grille. Logically, the order of these two scenes should have been reversed, but Sanchez's written instructions for setting them up had indicated it should be done in this order.

Lucia Sanchez circled the room twice, stopping for a long time in front of each of the scenes. Then, looking shaken, she returned to where I stood near the door and pushed past me into the courtyard. She went to the edge of the fountain and stood there for a long moment, hands clasped on her purse, head bowed, staring into the splashing water. Finally I went up beside her and touched her arm.

"Miss Sanchez," I said, "are you all right?"

She continued staring down for about ten seconds, then raised agonized eyes to mine. "Miss Oliverez," she said, "you must help me."

"With the possibility of a lawsuit? Of course—"

"No, not just the lawsuit. That is not really important. But I do ask your help with this: Gilberto and Eduardo must never see those figures. Never, do you understand? Never!"

At nine o'clock that evening, I was sitting in the living room of my little house in Santa Barbara's flatlands, trying to read a fat adventure novel Susana had loaned me. It was hot for late September, and I wore shorts and had the windows open for cross-ventilation. An hour before the sound of the neighbors' kids playing kickball in the street had been driving me crazy; now everything seemed too quiet.

The phone hadn't rung once all evening. My current boyfriend—Dave Kirk, an Anglo homicide cop, of all things—was mad at me for calling off a tentative date the previous evening so I could set up the Sanchez Sacraments. My mother, who usually checked in at least once a day to make sure I was still alive and well, was off on a cruise with her seventy-eight-year-old boyfriend. Although her calls normally made me think a move to Nome, Alaska, would be desirable, now I missed her and would have liked to hear her voice.

I also would have liked to talk out the matter of the Sanchez Sacraments with her. Mama had a keen intelligence and an ability to sometimes see things I'd missed that were right under my nose. And in the case of the Sacraments, I was missing something very important. Namely, why Lucia Sanchez was so adamant that neither of her great-nephews should ever view the figures.

Try as I might, I hadn't been able to extract the reason from her that afternoon. So, perversely, I hadn't promised that I would bar the brothers from the gallery. I honestly didn't see how I could keep them away from a public exhibit, but perhaps had I known Lucia's reason, I might have been more willing to find a way. As it was, I felt trapped between the pleas of this woman, whom I liked very much, and the well-reasoned request of Gilberto. And on top of that, there was the fear of a lawsuit over the Sacraments. I hadn't been able to talk to the museum's attorney—he was on vacation—and I didn't want to do anything, such as refusing the brothers access to the exhibit, that would make Eduardo's claim against us stronger.

I shifted on the couch and propped my feet on the coffee table, crossing them at the ankles. I gave the novel a final cursory glance, sighed, and tossed it aside. Susana and I simply did not have the same taste in fiction. There was a *Sunset* magazine that she had also given me on the end table. Normally I wouldn't have looked at a publication which I considered aimed at trendy, affluent Anglos, but now I picked it up and began to thumb through it. I was reading an article on outdoor decking—ridiculous, because my house needed a paint job far more than backyard beautification—when the phone rang. I jumped for it.

The caller was Lucia Sanchez. "I hope I am not disturbing you by calling so late, Miss Oliverez."

"No, not at all."

"I wanted to tell you that I had dinner with Gilberto and Eduardo. They remain adamant about seeing the Sacraments."

"So Eduardo now wants to see them also?"

"Yes, I assume so he can assess their value." Her tone was weary and bitter.

I was silent.

"Miss Oliverez," she said, "what can we do?"

I felt a prickle of annoyance at her use of the word "we." "I don't suppose there's anything you can do. *I*, however, can merely stall them until I speak with the museum's attorney. But I think he'll merely advise me to let them see the figures."

"That must not be!"

"I don't know what else to do. Perhaps if I knew your reason—"

"We have discussed that before. It is a reason rooted in the past. I wish to let the past die, as my brother died."

"Then there's nothing I can do but follow the advice of our lawyer."

She made a sound that could have been a sob and abruptly hung up. I clutched the receiver, feeling cruel and tactless. The woman obviously had a strong reason for what she was asking, so strong that she could confide in no one. And the reason had to be in those figures. Something I could see but hadn't interpreted . . .

I decided to go to the museum and take a closer look at the Sanchez Sacraments.

The old adobe building which housed the museum gleamed whitely in its floodlights. I drove around and parked my car in the lot, then entered by the loading dock, resetting the alarm system behind me. After switching on the lights, I crossed the courtyard—silent now, the fountain's merry tinkling stilled for the night—and went into the special exhibits gallery.

The figures stood frozen in time—celebrants at three rites and sufferers at two others. I turned up the spots to full beam and began with the baptismal scene.

Father, mother, aunts and uncles and cousins and friends. A babe in arms, white dress trimmed with pink ribbons. Priest, the one with the long jaw and dour lines around his mouth. Father was handsome, with chiseled features reminiscent of the Sanchez brothers. Mother, conventionally pretty. All the participants had the wonderfully expressive faces that had been Adolfo Sanchez's trademark. Many reminded me, as Lucia had initially, of my relatives from Mexico.

Confirmation. Daughter kneeling before the same priest. Conventionally pretty, like her mother, who looked on. Father proud, hand on wife's shoulder. Again, the relatives and friends.

Wedding ceremony. Pretty daughter grown into a young woman. Parents somewhat aged, but prouder than ever. Bridegroom in first flush of manhood. Same family and friends and priest—also slightly aged.

297

So far I saw nothing but the work of an exceptionally talented artist who deserved the international acclaim he had received.

Deathbed scene. Formerly pretty daughter, not so much aged as withered by illness. No family, friends. Priest—the different one, bearded, his features wracked with pain as he offered the communion wafer. The pain was similar to that in the dying woman's eyes. This figure had disturbed me. . . .

I stared at it for a minute, then went on.

Penance. A man, his face in his hands. Leaning on the ledge in the confessional, telling his sins. The priest—the one who had officiated at the first joyful rites—was not easily visible through the grille, but I could make out the look of horror on his face that I had first noted when I unpacked the figure.

I stared at the priest's face for a long time, then went back to the deathbed scene. The other priest knelt by the bed—

There was a sudden, stealthy noise outside. I whirled and listened. It came again, from the entryway. I went out into the courtyard and saw light flickering briefly over the little windows to either side of the door.

I relaxed, smiling a little. I knew who this was. Our ever-vigilant Santa Barbara police had noticed a light on where one should not be and were checking to make sure no one was burglarizing the museum. This had happened so often—because I worked late frequently—that they didn't bother to creep up as softly as they might. If I had been a burglar, by now I could have been in the next county. As it was, I'd seen so much of these particular cops that I was considering offering them an honorary membership in our Museum Society. Still, I appreciated their alertness. With a sigh, I went back and switched out the spots in the gallery, then crossed the courtyard to assure them all was well.

A strong breeze came up around three in the morning. It ruffled the curtains at my bedroom window and made the single sheet covering me inadequate. I pulled it higher on my shoulders and curled myself into a ball, too tired to reach down to the foot of the bed for the blanket. In moments I drifted back into a restless sleep, haunted by images of people at religious ceremonies. Or were they people? They stood too still, their expressions were too fixed. Expressions—of joy, of pain, of horror. Pain . . . horror . . .

Suddenly the dream was gone and I sat up in bed, remembering one thing that had disturbed me about Adolfo Sanchez's deathbed scene—and realizing another. I fumbled for the light, found my robe, and went barefooted into the living room to the bookcase where I kept my art library. Somewhere I had that book on Adolfo's life and works, the one I'd bought when the Sacraments had been donated to the museum. I'd barely had time to glance through it again.

There were six shelves and I scanned each impatiently. Where was the damned book anyway? Then I remembered it was at the museum; I'd looked through it in the basement the other day. As far as I knew, it was still on the worktable.

I stood clutching my robe around me and debated going to the museum to get the book. But it was not a good time to be on the streets alone, even in a relatively crime-free town like Santa Barbara, and besides, I'd already alarmed the police once tonight. Better to look at the book when I went in at the regular time next morning.

I went back to bed, pulling the blanket up, and huddled there, thinking about death and penance.

I arrived at the museum early next morning—at eight o'clock, an hour before my usual time. When I entered the office wing, I could hear a terrific commotion going on in the central courtyard. People were yelling in Spanish, all at once, not bothering to listen to one another. I recognized Susana's voice, and thought I heard Lucia Sanchez. The other voices were male, and I could guess they belonged to the Sanchez brothers. They must have used some ploy to get Susana to let them in this early.

I hurried through the offices and out into the courtyard. Susana turned when she heard my footsteps, her face flushed with anger. "Elena," she said, "you must do something about them!"

The others merely went on yelling. I had been right: It was Gilberto, Eduardo, and Lucia, and they were right in the middle of one of those monumental quarrels that my people are famous for.

". . . contrived to steal our heritage, and I will not allow it!" This from Eduardo.

"You were amply taken care of in your grandfather's will. And now you want more. Greed!" Lucia shook a finger at him.

"I merely want what is mine."

"Yours!" Lucia looked as if she might spit at him.

"Yes, mine."

"What about Gilberto? Have you forgotten him?"

Eduardo glanced at his brother, who was cowering by the fountain. "No, of course not. The proceeds from the Sacraments will be divided equally—"

"I don't want the money!" Gilberto said.

"You be quiet!" Eduardo turned on him. "You are too foolish to know what's good for you. You could help me convince this old witch, but instead you're mooning around here, protesting that you *only want to see* the Sacraments." His voice cruelly mimicked Gilberto.

"But you will receive the money set aside for you in Grandfather's will—"

"It's not enough."

"Not enough for what?"

"I must finish my life's work."

"What work?" Lucia asked.

"My film."

"I thought the film was done."

Eduardo looked away. "We ran over budget."

"Ahah! You've already squandered your inheritance. Before you've received it, it's spent. And now you want more. Greed!"

"My film—"

"Film, film, film! I am tired of hearing about it."

This had all been very interesting, but I decided it was time to intervene. Just as Eduardo gave a howl of wounded indignation, I said in Spanish, "All right! That's enough!"

All three turned to me, as if they hadn't known I was there. At once they looked embarrassed; in their family, as in mine, quarrels should be kept strictly private.

I looked at Lucia. "Miss Sanchez, I want to see you in my office." Then I motioned at the brothers. "You two leave. If I catch you on the premises again without my permission, I'll have you jailed for trespassing."

They grumbled and glowered but moved toward the door. Susana followed, making shooing gestures.

I turned and led Lucia Sanchez to the office wing. When she was seated in my visitor's chair, I said, "Wait here. I'll be back in a few minutes." Then I went downstairs to the basement. The book I'd been looking for the night before was where I'd left it earlier in the week, on the work table. I opened it and leafed through to the section of pictures of the artist and his family.

When young, Adolfo Sanchez had had the same chiseled features as his grandsons; he had, however, been handsome in a way they were not. In his later years, he had sported a beard, and his face had been deeply lined, his eyes sunken with pain.

I turned the page and found photographs of the family members. The wife, Constantina, was conventionally pretty. The daughter, Rosalinda, took after her mother. In a couple of the photographs, Lucia looked on in the background. A final one showed Adolfo with his arms around the two boys, aged about six. Neither the wife nor the daughter was in evidence.

I shut the book with shaky hands, a sick feeling in the pit of my stomach. I should go to the special exhibits gallery and confirm my suspicions, but I didn't have the heart for it. Besides, the Sacraments were as clear in my mind as if I'd been looking at them. I went instead to my office.

Lucia Sanchez sat as she had before, roughened hands gripping her shabby leather bag. When I came in, she looked up and seemed to see the knowledge in my eyes. Wearily, she passed a hand over her face.

"Yes," I said, "I've figured it out."

"Then you understand why the boys must never see those figures."

I sat down on the edge of the desk in front of her. "Why didn't you just tell me?"

"I've told no one, all those years. It was a secret between my brother and myself. But he had to expiate it, and he chose to do so through his work. I never knew what he was doing out there in his studio. The whole time, he refused to tell me. You can imagine my shock after he died, when I went to look and saw he'd told the whole story in his pottery figures."

"Of course, no one would guess, unless–"

"Unless they knew the family history and what the members had looked like."

"Or noticed something was wrong with the figures and then studied photographs, like I just did."

She acknowledged it with a small nod.

"Adolfo and his wife had a daughter, Rosalinda," I said. "She's the daughter in the Sacraments, and the parents are Adolfo and Constantina. The resemblance is easy to spot."

"It's remarkable, isn't it—how Adolfo could make the figures so real. Most folk artists don't, you know." She spoke in a detached tone.

"And remarkable how he could make the scenes reflect real life."

"That too." But now the detachment was gone, and pain crossed her face.

"Rosalinda grew up and married and had the twins. What happened to her husband?"

"He deserted her, even before the boys were born."

"And Constantina died shortly after."

"Yes. That was when I moved in with them, to help Rosalinda with the children. She was ill. . . ."

"Fatally ill. What was it?"

"Cancer."

"A painful illness."

"Yes."

"When did Adolfo decide to end her misery?"

She sat very still, white-knuckled hands clasping her purse.

"Did you know what he had done?" I asked.

Tears came into her eyes and one spilled over. She made no move to wipe it away. "I knew. But it was not as it seems. Rosalinda begged him to help her end her life. She was in such pain. How could Adolfo refuse his child's last request? All her life, she had asked so little of anyone. . . ."

"So he complied with her wishes. What did he give her?"

"An overdose of medicine for the pain. I don't know what kind."

"And then?"

"Gradually he began to fail. He was severely depressed. After a year he sent the boys to boarding school in Mexico City; such a sad household was no place for children, he said. For a while I feared he might take his own life, but then he began to work on those figures, and it saved him. He had a purpose and, I realize now, a penance to perform."

"And when the figures were finished, he died."

"Within days."

I paused, staring at her face, which was now streaked with tears. "He told the whole story in the Sacraments—Rosalinda's baptism, confirmation, and marriage. The same friends and relatives were present, and the same parish priest."

"Father Rivera."

"But in the scene of Extreme Unction—Rosalinda's death—Father Rivera doesn't appear. Instead, the priest is Adolfo, and what he is handing Rosalinda appears to be a communion wafer. I noticed that as soon as I saw the figure and wondered about it, because for the last rites they don't give communion, they use holy oil. And it isn't supposed to be a wafer, either, but a lethal dose of pain medicine. At first I didn't notice the priest's resemblance to the father in the earlier scenes because of the beard. But when I really studied photographs of Adolfo, it all became clear."

"That figure is the least representational of the lot," Lucia said. "I suppose Adolfo felt he couldn't portray his crime openly. He never wanted the boys to know. And he probably didn't want the world to know either. Adolfo was a proud man, with an artist's pride in his work and reputation."

"I understand. If the story came out, it would tarnish the value of his work with sensationalism. He disguised himself in the Penance scene too, by having his hands over his face."

Lucia was weeping into her handkerchief now. Through it she said, "What are we to do? Both of the boys are now determined to see the Sacraments. And when they do they will interpret them as you have and despise Adolfo's memory. That was the one thing he feared; he said so in his will."

I got up, went to the little barred window that overlooked the small patio outside my office, and stood there staring absently at the azalea bushes that our former director had planted. I pictured Gilberto, as he'd spoken of his grandfather the other day, his eyes shining with love. And I heard Eduardo saying, "I worshipped the man. If it wasn't for his guidance, I'd be nobody today." They might understand what had driven Adolfo to his mortal sin, but if they didn't . . .

Finally I said, "Perhaps we can do something after all."

"But what? The figures will be on public display. And the boys are determined."

I felt a tension building inside me. "Let me deal with that problem."

My hands balled into fists, I went through the office wing and across the courtyard to the gallery. Once inside, I stopped, looking around at the figures. They were a perfect series of groupings and they told a tale far more powerful than the simple life cycle I'd first taken them to represent. I wasn't sure I could do what I'd intended. What I was contemplating was—for a curator and an art lover—almost as much of a sin as Adolfo's helping his daughter kill herself.

I went over to the deathbed scene and rested my hand gently on the shoulder of the kneeling man. The figure was so perfect it felt almost real.

I thought of the artist, the man who had concealed his identity under these priestly robes. Wasn't the artist and the life he'd lived as important as his work? Part of my job was to protect those works; couldn't I also interpret that to mean I should also protect the memory of the artist?

I stood there for a long moment—and then I pushed the pottery figure, hard. It toppled backward, off the low platform to the stone floor. Pottery smashes easily, and this piece broke into many fragments. I stared down at them, wanting to cry.

When I came out of the gallery minutes later, Susana was rushing across the courtyard. "Elena, what happened? I heard—" She saw the look on my face and stopped, one hand going to her mouth.

Keeping my voice steady, I said, "There's been an accident, and there's a mess on the floor of the gallery. Please get someone to clean it up. And after that, go to my office and tell Lucia Sanchez she and her great-nephews can view the Sacraments any time. Arrange a private showing, for as long as they want. After all, they're family."

"What about . . . ?" She motioned at the gallery.

"Tell them one of the figures—Father Rivera, in the deathbed scene—was irreparably damaged in transit." I started toward the entryway.

"Elena, where are you going?"

"I'm taking the day off. You're in charge."

I would get away from here, maybe walk on the beach. I was fortunate; mine was only a small murder. I would not have to live with it or atone for it the remainder of my lifetime, as Adolfo Sanchez had.

The 87th Precinct

THE ETHNIC DETECTIVES

"J"

Ed McBain

The ethnic mix in Ed McBain's widely acclaimed 87th Precinct series is the most varied and successful in all of detective fiction: in addition to Italian-American Steve Carella, the central character, there are Richard Genero and Alf Miscolo (also Italian-American), Meyer Meyer (Jew), Arthur Brown (black), Frankie Hernandez (Puerto Rican), and Peter Byrnes (Irish). Each of these characters has a sharply defined ethnic background, and over the course of the series each has been effectively used in conjunction with his own and with other ethnic groups.

"J," one of the few shorter works starring the 87th Squad, features Carella and Meyer Meyer. But it is really Meyer's case, because he is Jewish and because it is about the brutal murder of a rabbi. Its ethnic background is extremely well realized—remarkably so in view of the fact that McBain is not Jewish (nor is he Irish; like Carella, he is of Italian-American origin). A truly heterogenous ethnic mix, after the fashion of the series itself.

There have been close to forty novels and one collection featuring the men (and, recently, women) of the 87th, beginning with Cop Hater *in 1956—in toto comprising what*

306

is surely the finest series of police procedurals ever written. But "Ed McBain" is nothing if not versatile. He has also published four mystery novels about Florida lawyer Matthew Hope, and several other criminous works under the McBain name and such pseudonyms as Richard Marsten, Hunt Collins, Ezra Hannon, and Curt Cannon. And under his real name, Evan Hunter, he has published a score of distinguished mainstream novels and collections, including The Blackboard Jungle *(1954),* Last Summer *(1968),* Sons *(1969), and* Lizzie *(1984).*

.   .   .

It was the first of April, the day for fools.

It was also Saturday, and the day before Easter.

Death should not have come at all, but it had. And, having come, perhaps it was justified in its confusion. Today was the fool's day, the day for practical jokes. Tomorrow was Easter, the day of the bonnet and egg, the day for the spring march of finery and frills. Oh, yes, it was rumored in some quarters of the city that Easter Sunday had something to do with a different sort of march at a place called Calvary, but it had been a long long time since death was vetoed and rendered null and void, and people have short memories, especially where holidays are concerned.

Today, Death was very much in evidence, and plainly confused. Striving as it was to reconcile the trappings of two holidays—or perhaps three—it succeeded in producing only a blended distortion.

The young man who lay on his back in the alley was wearing black, as if in mourning. But over the black, in contradiction, was a fine silken shawl, fringed at both ends. He seemed dressed for spring, but this was the fool's day, and Death could not resist the temptation.

The black was punctuated with red and blue and white. The cobbled floor of the alley followed the same decorative scheme, red and blue and white, splashed about in gay spring abandon. Two overturned buckets of paint, one white, one blue, seemed to have ricocheted off the wall

307

of the building and come to disorderly rest on the alley floor. The man's shoes were spattered with paint. His black garment was covered with paint. His hands were drenched in paint. Blue and white, white and blue, his black garment, his silken shawl, the floor of the alley, the brick wall of the building before which he lay—all were splashed with blue and white.

The third color did not mix well with the others.

The third color was red, a little too primary, a little too bright.

The third color had not come from a paint can. The third color still spilled freely from two dozen open wounds on the man's chest and stomach and neck and face and hands, staining the black, staining the silken shawl, spreading in a bright red pool on the alley floor, suffusing the paint with sunset, mingling with the paint but not mixing well, spreading until it touched the foot of the ladder lying crookedly along the wall, encircling the paintbrush lying at the wall's base. The bristles of the brush were still wet with white paint. The man's blood touched the bristles, and then trickled to the cement line where brick wall touched cobbled alley, flowing in an inching stream downward toward the street.

Someone had signed the wall.

On the wall, someone had painted, in bright, white paint, the single letter J. Nothing more—only J.

The blood trickled down the alley to the city street.

Night was coming.

Detective Cotton Hawes was a tea drinker. He had picked up the habit from his minister father, the man who'd named him after Cotton Mather, the last of the red-hot Puritans. In the afternoons, the good Reverend Jeremiah Hawes had entertained members of his congregation, serving tea and cakes which his wife Matilda baked in the old, iron, kitchen oven. The boy, Cotton Hawes, had been allowed to join the tea-drinking congregation, thus developing a habit which had continued to this day.

At eight o'clock on the night of April first, while a young man lay in an alleyway with two dozen bleeding wounds shrieking in silence to the passersby on the street below, Hawes sat drinking tea. As a boy, he had downed the hot beverage in the book-lined study at the rear of the parish house, a mixture of Oolong and Pekoe which his mother brewed in the kitchen and served in English bone-china cups she had inherited from her grandmother. Tonight, he sat in the grubby, shopworn comfort of the 87th Precinct squadroom and drank, from a cardboard container, the tea Alf Miscolo had prepared in the clerical office. It was hot tea. That was about the most he could say for it.

The open, mesh-covered windows of the squadroom admitted a mild spring breeze from Grover Park across the way, a warm seductive breeze which made him wish he were outside on the street. It was criminal to be watching on a night like this. It was also boring. Aside from one wife-beating squeal, which Steve Carella was out checking this very minute, the telephone had been ominously quiet. In the silence of the squadroom, Hawes had managed to type up three overdue D. D. reports, two chits for gasoline and a bulletin-board notice to the men of the squad reminding them that this was the first of the month and time for them to cough up fifty cents each for the maintenance of Alf Miscolo's improvised kitchen. He had also read a half-dozen FBI flyers, and listed in his little black memo book the license-plate numbers of two more stolen vehicles.

Now he sat drinking insipid tea and wondering why it was so quiet. He supposed the lull had something to do with Easter. Maybe there was going to be an egg-rolling ceremony down South Twelfth Street tomorrow. Maybe all the criminals and potential criminals in the 87th were home dyeing. Eggs, that is. He smiled and took another sip of the tea. From the clerical office beyond the slatted rail divider which separated the squadroom from the corridor, he could hear the rattling of Miscolo's typewriter. Above that, and beyond it, coming from the iron-runged steps which led upstairs, he could hear the ring of footsteps.

He turned toward the corridor just as Steve Carella entered it from the opposite end.

Carella walked easily and nonchalantly toward the railing, a big man who moved with fine-honed athletic precision. He shoved open the gate in the railing, walked to his desk, took off his jacket, pulled down his tie and unbuttoned the top button of his shirt.

"What happened?" Hawes asked.

"The same thing that always happens," Carella said. He sighed heavily and rubbed his hand over his face. "Is there any more coffee?" he asked.

"I'm drinking tea."

"Hey, Miscolo!" Carella yelled. "Any coffee in there?"

"I'll put on some more water!" Miscolo yelled back.

"So what happened?" Hawes asked.

"Oh, the same old jazz," Carella said. "It's a waste of time to even go out on these wife-beating squeals. I've never answered one yet that netted anything."

"She wouldn't press charges," Hawes said knowingly.

"Charges, hell. There wasn't even any beating, according to her. She's got blood running out of her nose, and a shiner the size of a half-dollar, and she's the one who screamed for the patrolman—but the minute I get there, everything's calm and peaceful." Carella shook his head. " 'A beating, officer?' " he mimicked in a high, shrill voice. " 'You must be mistaken, Officer. Why, my husband is a good, kind, sweet man. We've been married for twenty years, and he never lifted a finger to me. You must be mistaken, sir.' "

"Then who yelled for the cop?" Hawes asked.

"That's just what I said to her."

"What'd she answer?"

"She said, 'Oh, we were just having a friendly little family argument.' The guy almost knocked three teeth out of her mouth, but that's just a friendly little family argument. So I asked her how she happened to have a bloody nose and a mouse under her eye and—catch this, Cotton—she said she got them ironing."

"What?"

"Ironing."

"Now, how the hell—"

"She said the ironing board collapsed and the iron jumped up and hit her in the eye, and one of the ironing-board legs clipped her in the nose. By the time I left, she and her husband were ready to go on a second honeymoon. She was hugging him all over the place, and he was sneaking his hand under her dress, so I figured I'd come back here where it isn't so sexy."

"Good idea," Hawes said.

"Hey, Miscolo!" Carella shouted, "Where's that coffee?"

"A watched pot never boils!" Miscolo shouted back cleverly.

"We've got George Bernard Shaw in the clerical office," Carella said. "Anything happen since I left?"

"Nothing. Not a peep."

"The streets are quiet, too," Carella said, suddenly thoughtful.

"Before the storm," Hawes said.

"Mmmm."

The squadroom was silent again. Beyond the meshed window, they could hear the myriad sounds of the city, the auto horns, the muffled cries, the belching of buses, a little girl singing as she walked past the station house.

"Well, I suppose I ought to type up some overdue reports," Carella said.

He wheeled over a typing cart, took three Detective Division reports from his desk, inserted carbon between two of the sheets and began typing.

Hawes stared at the distant lights of Isola's buildings and sucked in a draught of mesh-filtered spring air.

He wondered why it was so quiet.

He wondered just exactly what all those people were doing out there.

Some of those people were playing April Fool's Day pranks. Some of them were getting ready for tomorrow, which was Easter Sunday. And some of them were celebrat-

311

ing a third and ancient holiday known as Passover. Now
that's a coincidence which could cause one to speculate
upon the similarity of dissimilar religions and the existence
of a single, all-powerful God, and all that sort of mystic
stuff, if one were inclined toward speculation. Speculator
or not, it doesn't take a big detective to check a calendar,
and the coincidence was there, take it or leave it. Buddhist,
atheist, or Seventh Day Adventist, you had to admit there
was something very democratic and wholesome about
Easter and Passover coinciding the way they did, something
which gave a festive air to the entire city. Jew and Gentile
alike, because of a chance mating of the Christian and the
Hebrew calendars, were celebrating important holidays at
almost the same time. Passover had officially begun at sunset
on Friday, March thirty-first, another coincidence, since
Passover did not always fall on the Jewish Sabbath; but this
year, it did. And tonight was April first, and the traditional
second *seder* service, the annual re-enactment of the Jews'
liberation from Egyptian bondage, was being observed in
Jewish homes through the city.

Detective Meyer Meyer was a Jew.

Or at least, he thought he was a Jew. Sometimes he wasn't
quite certain. Because if he was a Jew, he sometimes asked
himself, how come he hadn't seen the inside of a synagogue
in twenty years? And if he was a Jew, how come two of
his favorite dishes were roast pork and broiled lobster, both
of which were forbidden by the dietary laws of the religion?
And if he was such a Jew, how come he allowed his son
Alan—who was thirteen and who had been *bar-mitzvahed*
only last month—to play post office with Alice McCarthy,
who was as Irish as a four-leaf clover?

Sometimes, Meyer got confused.

Sitting at the head of the traditional table on this night
of the second *seder,* he didn't know quite how he felt. He
looked at his family, Sarah and the three children, and then
he looked at the *seder* table, festively set with a floral center-
piece and lighted candles and the large platter upon which
were placed the traditional objects—three matzos, a roasted

shankbone, a roasted egg, bitter herbs, charoses, water-cress—and he still didn't know exactly how he felt. He took a deep breath and began the prayer.

"And it was evening," Meyer said, "and it was morning, the sixth day. Thus the heaven and the earth were finished, and all the host of them. And on the seventh day, God had finished his work which He had made: and He rested on the seventh day from his work which He had done. And God blessed the seventh day, and hallowed it, because that in it He rested from all his work, which God had created in order to make it."

There was a certain beauty to the words, and they lingered in his mind as he went through the ceremony, describing the various objects on the table and their symbolic meaning. When he elevated the dish containing the bone and the egg, everyone sitting around the table took hold of the dish, and Meyer said, "This is the bread of affliction which our ancestors ate in the land of Egypt; let all those who are hungry, enter and eat thereof, and all who are in distress, come and celebrate the Passover."

He spoke of his ancestors, but he wondered who he—their descendant—was.

"Wherefore is this night distinguished from all other nights?" he asked. "Any other night, we may eat either leavened or unleavened bread, but on this night only unleavened bread; all other nights, we may eat any species of herbs, but on this night only bitter herbs . . ."

The telephone rang. Meyer stopped speaking and looked at his wife. For a moment, both seemed reluctant to break the spell of the ceremony. And then Meyer gave a slight, barely discernible shrug. Perhaps, as he went to the telephone, he was recalling that he was a cop first, and a Jew only second.

"Hello?" he said.

"Meyer, this is Cotton Hawes."

"What is it, Cotton?"

"Look, I know this is your holiday—"

"What's the trouble?"

"We've got a killing," Hawes said.

Patiently, Meyer said, "We've always got a killing."

"This is different. A patrolman called in about five minutes ago. The guy was stabbed in the alley behind—"

"Cotton, I don't understand," Meyer said. "I switched the duty with Steve. Didn't he show up?"

"What is it, Meyer?" Sarah called from the dining room.

"It's all right, it's all right," Meyer answered. "Isn't Steve there?" he asked Hawes, annoyance in his voice.

"Sure, he's out on the squeal, but that's not the point."

"What *is* the point?" Meyer asked. "I was right in the middle of—"

"We need you on this one," Hawes said. "Look, I'm sorry as hell. But there are aspects to—Meyer, this guy they found in the alley—"

"Well, what about him?" Meyer asked.

"We think he's a rabbi," Hawes said.

2.

The sexton of the Isola Jewish Center was named Yirmiyahu Cohen, and when he introduced himself, he used the Jewish word for sexton, *shamash.* He was a tall, thin man in his late fifties, wearing a somber black suit and donning a skullcap the moment he, Carella and Meyer re-entered the synagogue.

The three had stood in the alley behind the synagogue not a moment before, staring down at the body of the dead rabbi and the trail of mayhem surrounding him. Yirmiyahu had wept openly, his eyes closed, unable to look at the dead man who had been the Jewish community's spiritual leader. Carella and Meyer, who had both been cops for a good long time, did not weep.

There is plenty to weep at if you happen to be looking down at the victim of a homicidal stabbing. The rabbi's black robe and fringed prayer shawl were drenched with blood, but happily, they hid from view the multiple stab wounds in his chest and abdomen, wounds which would later be examined at the morgue for external description, number, location, dimension, form of perforation and direction and depth of penetration. Since twenty-five per cent of all fatal stab wounds are cases of cardiac penetration, and since there was a wild array of slashes and a sodden mass of coagulating blood near or around the rabbi's heart, the two detectives automatically assumed that a cardiac stab wound had been the cause of death, and were grateful for the fact that the rabbi was fully clothed. They had both visited the mortuary and seen naked bodies on naked slabs, no longer bleeding, all blood and all life drained away, but skin torn like the flimsiest cheesecloth, the soft interior of the body deprived of its protective flesh, turned outward, exposed, the ripe wounds gaping and open, had stared at evisceration and wanted to vomit.

The rabbi had owned flesh, too, and at least a part of it had been exposed to his attacker's fury. Looking down at the dead man, neither Carella nor Meyer wanted to weep, but their eyes tightened a little and their throats went peculiarly dry because death by stabbing is a damn frightening thing. Whoever had handled the knife had done so in apparent frenzy. The only exposed areas of the rabbi's body were his hands, his neck, and his face—and these, more than the apparently fatal, hidden incisions beneath the black robe and the prayer shawl, shrieked bloody murder to the night. The rabbi's throat showed two superficial cuts which almost resembled suicidal hesitation cuts. A deeper horizontal slash at the front of his neck had exposed the trachea, carotids and jugular vein, but these did not appear to be severed—at least, not to the layman eyes of Carella and Meyer. There were cuts around the rabbi's eyes and a cut across the bridge of his nose.

But the wounds which caused both Carella and Meyer to turn away from the body were the slashes on the insides of the rabbi's hands. These, they knew, were the defense cuts. These spoke louder than all the others, for they immediately reconstructed the image of a weaponless man struggling to protect himself against the swinging blade of an assassin, raising his hands in hopeless defense, the fingers cut and hanging, the palms slashed to ribbons. At the end of the alley, the patrolman who'd first arrived on the scene was identifying the body to the medical examiner as the one he'd found. Another patrolman was pushing curious bystanders behind the police barricade he'd set up. The laboratory boys and photographers had already begun their work.

Carella and Meyer were happy to be inside the synagogue again.

The room was silent and empty, a house of worship without any worshipers at the moment. They sat on folding chairs in the large, empty room. The eternal light burned over the ark in which the Torah, the five books of Moses, was kept. Forward of the ark, one on each side of it, were the lighted candelabra, the *menorah*, found by tradition in every Jewish house of worship.

Detective Steve Carella began the litany of another tradition. He took out his notebook, poised his pencil over a clean page, turned to Yirmiyahu, and began asking questions in a pattern that had become classic through repeated use.

"What was the rabbi's name?" he asked.

Yirmiyahu blew his nose and said, "Solomon. Rabbi Solomon."

"First name?"

"Yaakov."

"That's Jacob," Meyer said. "Jacob Solomon."

Carella nodded and wrote the name into his book.

"Are you Jewish?" Yirmiyahu asked Meyer.

Meyer paused for an instant, and then said, "Yes."

"Was he married or single?" Carella asked.

"Married," Yirmiyahu said.

"Do you know his wife's name?"

"I'm not sure. I think it's Havah."

"That's Eve," Meyer translated.

"And would you know where the rabbi lived?"

"Yes. The house on the corner."

"What's the address?"

"I don't know. It's the house with the yellow shutters."

"How do you happen to be here right now, Mr. Cohen?" Carella asked. "Did someone call to inform you of the rabbi's death?"

"No. No, I often come past the synagogue. To check the light, you see."

"What light is that, sir?" Carella asked.

"The eternal light. Over the ark. It's supposed to burn at all times. Many synagogues have a small electric bulb in the lamp. We're one of the few synagogues in the city who still use oil in it. And, as *shamash,* I felt it was my duty to make certain the light—"

"Is this an Orthodox congregation?" Meyer asked.

"No. It's Conservative," Yirmiyahu said.

"There are three types of congregation now," Meyer explained to Carella. "Orthodox, Conservative and Reform. It gets a little complicated."

"Yes," Yirmiyahu said emphatically.

"So you were coming to the synagogue to check on the lamp," Carella said. "Is that right?"

"That's correct."

"And what happened?"

"I saw a police car at the side of the synagogue. So I walked over and asked what the trouble was. And they told me."

"I see. When was the last time you saw the rabbi alive, Mr. Cohen?"

"At evening services."

"Services start at sundown, Steve. The Jewish day—"

"Yes, I know," Carella said. "What time did services end, Mr. Cohen?"

"At about seven-thirty."

"And the rabbi was here? Is that right?"

"Well, he stepped outside when services were over."

"And you stayed inside. Was there any special reason?"

"Yes. I was collecting the prayer shawls and the *yarmulkes,* and I was putting—"

"*Yarmulkes* are skullcaps," Meyer said. "Those little black—"

"Yes, I know," Carella said. "Go ahead, Mr. Cohen."

"I was putting the *rimonim* back onto the handles of the scroll."

"Putting the what, sir?" Carella asked.

"Listen to the big Talmudic scholar," Meyer said, grinning. "Doesn't even know what *rimonim* are. They're these decorative silver covers, Steve, shaped like pomegranates. Symbolizing fruitfulness, I guess."

Carella returned the grin. "Thank you," he said.

"A man has been killed," Yirmiyahu said softly.

The detectives were silent for a moment. The banter between them had been of the faintest sort, mild in comparison to some of the grisly humor that homicide detectives passed back and forth over a dead body. Carella and Meyer were accustomed to working together in an easy, friendly manner, and they were accustomed to dealing with the facts of sudden death, but they realized at once that they had offended the dead rabbi's sexton.

"I'm sorry, Mr. Cohen," he said. "We meant no offense, you understand."

The old man nodded stoically, a man who had inherited a legacy of years and years of persecution, a man who automatically concluded that all Gentiles looked upon a Jew's life as a cheap commodity. There was unutterable sadness on his long, thin face, as if he alone were bearing the oppressive weight of the centuries on his narrow shoulders.

The synagogue seemed suddenly smaller. Looking at the old man's face and the sadness there, Meyer wanted to touch it gently and say, "It's all right, *tsadik*, it's all right," the Hebrew word leaping into his mind—*tsadik*, a man possessed of saintly virtues, a person of noble character and simple living.

The silence persisted. Yirmiyahu Cohen began weeping again, and the detectives sat in embarrassment on the folding chairs and waited.

At last Carella said, "Were you still here when the rabbi came inside again?"

"I left while he was gone," Yirmiyahu said. "I wanted

to return home. This is the *Pesach*, the Passover. My family was waiting for me to conduct the *seder.*"

"I see." Carella paused. He glanced at Meyer.

"Did you hear any noise in the alley, Mr. Cohen?" Meyer asked. "When the rabbi was out there?"

"Nothing."

Meyer sighed and took a package of cigarettes from his jacket pocket. He was about to light one when Yirmiyahu said, "Didn't you say you were Jewish?"

"Huh?" Meyer said. He struck the match.

"You are going to *smoke* on the second day of *Pesach*?" Yirmiyahu asked.

"Oh. Oh, well . . ." The cigarette felt suddenly large in Meyer's hand, the fingers clumsy. He shook out the match. "You—uh—you have any other questions, Steve?" he asked.

"No," Carella said.

"Then I guess you can go, Mr. Cohen," Meyer said. "Thank you very much."

"Shalom," Yirmiyahu said, and shuffled dejectedly out of the room.

"You're not supposed to smoke, you see," Meyer explained to Carella, "on the first two days of Passover, and the last two, a good Jew doesn't smoke, or ride, or work, or handle money or—"

"I thought this was a Conservative synagogue," Carella said. "That sounds like Orthodox practice to me."

"Well, he's an old man," Meyer said. "I guess the customs die hard."

"The way the rabbi did," Carella said grimly.

3.

They stood outside in the alley where chalk marks outlined the position of the dead body. The rabbi had been carted away, but his blood still stained the cobblestones, and the rampant paint had been carefully side-stepped by the laboratory boys searching for footprints and fingerprints, searching for anything which would provide a lead to the killer.

"J," the wall read.

"You know, Steve, I feel funny on this case," Meyer told Carella.

"I do, too."

Meyer raised his eyebrows, somewhat surprised. "How come?"

"I don't know. I guess because he was a man of God." Carella shrugged. "There's something unworldly and naïve and—pure, I guess—about rabbis and priests and ministers and I guess I feel they shouldn't be touched by all the dirty things in life." He paused. "Somebody's got to stay untouched, Meyer."

"Maybe so." Meyer paused. "I feel funny because I'm a Jew, Steve." His voice was very soft. He seemed to be confessing something he would not have admitted to another living soul.

"I can understand that," Carella said gently.

"Are you policemen?"

The voice startled them. It came suddenly from the other end of the alley, and they both whirled instantly to face it.

Instinctively, Meyer's hand reached for the service revolver holstered in his right rear pocket.

"Are you policemen?" the voice asked again. It was a woman's voice, thick with a Yiddish accent. The street lamp was behind the owner of the voice. Meyer and Carella saw only a frail figure clothed in black, pale white hands clutched to the breast of the black coat, pinpoints of light burning where the woman's eyes should have been.

"We're policemen," Meyer answered. His hand hovered near the butt of his pistol. Beside him, he could feel Carella tensed for a draw.

"I know who killed the *rov*," the woman said.

"What?" Carella asked.

"She says she knows who killed the rabbi," Meyer whispered in soft astonishment.

His hand dropped to his side. They began walking toward the street end of the alley. The woman stood there motionless, the light behind her, her face in shadow, the pale hands still, her eyes burning.

"Who killed him?" Carella said.

"I know the *rotsayach*," the woman answered. "I know the murderer."

"Who?" Carella said again.

"Him!" the woman shouted, and she pointed to the painted white J on the synagogue wall. "The *sonei Yisroel!* Him!"

"The anti-Semite," Meyer translated. "She says the anti-Semite did it."

They had come abreast of the woman now. The three stood at the end of the alley with the street lamp casting long shadows on the cobbles. They could see her face. Black hair and brown eyes, the classic Jewish face of a woman in her fifties, the beauty stained by age and something else, a fine-drawn tension hidden in her eyes and on her mouth.

"What anti-Semite?" Carella asked. He realized he was whispering. There was something about the woman's face and the blackness of her coat and the paleness of her hands which made whispering a necessity.

"On the next block," she said. Her voice was a voice of judgment and doom. "The one they call Finch."

"You saw him kill the rabbi?" Carella asked. You saw him do it?"

"No." She paused. "But I know in my heart that he's the one . . ."

"What's your name, ma'am?" Meyer asked.

"Hannah Kaufman," she said. "I know it was him. He said he would do it, and now he has started."

"He said he would do what?" Meyer asked the old woman patiently.

"He said he would kill all the Jews."

"You heard him say this?"

"Everyone has heard him."

"His name is Finch?" Meyer asked her. "You're sure?"

"Finch," the woman said. "On the next block. Over the candy store."

"What do you think?" he asked Carella.
Carella nodded. "Let's try him."

4.

If America is a melting pot, the 87th Precinct is a crucible.
Start at the River Harb, the northernmost boundary of the
precinct territory, and the first thing you hit is exclusive
Smoke Rise, where the walled-in residents sit in white-Prot-
estant respectability in houses set a hundred feet back from
private roads, admiring the greatest view the city has to
offer. Come out of Smoke Rise and hit fancy Silvermine
Road where the aristocracy of apartment buildings have
begun to submit to the assault of time and the encroachment
of the surrounding slums. Forty-thousand-dollar-a-year executives still live in these apartment buildings, but people
write on the walls here, too: limericks, prurient slogans,
which industrious doormen try valiantly to erase.

There is nothing so eternal as Anglo-Saxon etched in
graphite.

Silvermine Park is south of the Road, and no one ventures
there at night. During the day, the park is thronged with
governesses idly chatting about the last time they saw Swe-
den, gently rocking shellacked blue baby buggies. But after
sunset, not even lovers will enter the park. The Stem, further south, explodes the moment the sun leaves the sky.
Gaudy and incandescent, it mixes Chinese restaurants with
Jewish delicatessens, pizza joints with Greek cabarets offering belly dancers. Threadbare as a beggar's sleeve, Ainsley
Avenue crosses the center of the precinct, trying to main-
tain a dignity long gone, crowding the sidewalks with
austere but dirty apartment buildings, furnished rooms,
garages and a sprinkling of sawdust saloons. Culver Avenue turns completely Irish with the speed of a leprechaun.
The faces, the bars, even the buildings seem displaced,
seem to have been stolen and transported from the center of Dublin; but no lace curtains hang in the windows.
Poverty turns a naked face to the streets here, setting the
pattern for the rest of the precinct territory. Poverty rakes

the backs of the Culver Avenue Irish, claws its way onto the white and tan and brown and black faces of the Puerto Ricans lining Mason Avenue, flops onto the beds of the whores on *La Vía de Putas*, and then pushes its way into the real crucible, the city side streets where different minority groups live cheek by jowl, as close as lovers, hating each other. It is here that Puerto Rican and Jew, Italian and Negro, Irishman and Cuban are forced by dire economic need to live in a ghetto which, by its very composition, loses definition and becomes a meaningless tangle of unrelated bloodlines.

Rabbi Solomon's synagogue was on the same street as a Catholic church. A Baptist store-front mission was on the avenue leading to the next block. The candy store over which the man named Finch lived was owned by a Puerto Rican whose son had been a cop—a man named Hernandez.

Carella and Meyer paused in the lobby of the building and studied the name plates in the mailboxes. There were eight boxes in the row. Two had name plates. Three had broken locks. The man named Finch lived in apartment thirty-three on the third floor.

The lock on the vestibule door was broken. From behind the stairwell, where the garbage cans were stacked before being put out for collection in the morning, the stink of that evening's dinner remains assailed the nostrils and left the detectives mute until they had gained the first-floor landing.

On the way up to the third floor, Carella said, "This seems too easy, Meyer. It's over before it begins."

On the third-floor landing, both men drew their service revolvers. They found apartment thirty-three and bracketed the door.

"Mr. Finch?" Meyer called.

"Who is it?" a voice answered.

"Police. Open up."

The apartment and the hallway went still.

"Finch?" Meyer said.

There was no answer. Carella backed off against the opposite wall. Meyer nodded. Bracing himself against the wall,

Carella raised his right foot, the leg bent at the knee, then released it like a triggered spring. The flat of his sole collided with the door just below the lock. The door burst inward, and Meyer followed it into the apartment, his gun in his fist.

Finch was a man in his late twenties, with a square crew-cut head and bright green eyes. He was closing the closet door as Meyer burst into the room. He was wearing only trousers and an undershirt, his feet bare. He needed a shave, and the bristles on his chin and face emphasized a white scar that ran from just under his right cheek to the curve of his jaw. He turned from the closet with the air of a man who has satisfactorily completed a mysterious mission.

"Hold it right there," Meyer said.

There's a joke they tell about an old woman on a train who repeatedly asks the man sitting beside her if he's Jewish. The man, trying to read his newspaper, keeps answering, "No, I'm not Jewish." The old lady keeps pestering him, tugging at his sleeve, asking the same question over and over again. Finally the man puts down his newspaper and says, "All right, all right, damn it! I'm Jewish."

And the old lady smiles at him sweetly and says, "You know something? You don't look it."

The joke, of course, relies on a prejudice which assumes that you can tell a man's religion by looking at his face. There was nothing about Meyer Meyer's looks or speech which would indicate that he was Jewish. His face was round and clean-shaven, he was thirty-seven years old and completely bald, and he possessed the bluest eyes this side of Denmark. He was almost six feet tall and perhaps a trifle overweight, and the only conversation he'd had with Finch were the few words he'd spoken through the closed door, and the four words he'd spoken since he entered the apartment, all of which were delivered in big-city English without any noticeable trace of accent.

But when Meyer Meyer said, "Hold it right there," a smile came onto Finch's face, and he answered, "I wasn't going any place, Jewboy."

Well, maybe the sight of the rabbi lying in his own blood had been too much for Meyer. Maybe the words *"sonei Yisroel"* had recalled the days of his childhood when, one of the few Orthodox Jews in a Gentile neighborhood, and bearing the double-barreled name his father had foisted upon him, he was forced to defend himself against every hoodlum who crossed his path, invariably against overwhelming odds. He was normally a very patient man. He had borne his father's practical joke with amazing good will, even though he sometimes grinned mirthlessly through bleeding lips. But tonight, this second night of Passover, after having looked down at the bleeding rabbi, after having heard the tortured sobs of the sexton, after having seen the patiently suffering face of the woman in black, the words hurled at him from the other end of the apartment had a startling effect.

Meyer said nothing. He simply walked to where Finch was standing near the closet, and lifted the .38 high above his head. He flipped the gun up as his arm descended, so that the heavy butt was in striking position as it whipped toward Finch's jaw.

Finch brought up his hands, but not to shield his face in defense. His hands were huge, with big knuckles, the imprimatur of the habitual street fighter. He opened the fingers and caught Meyer's descending arm at the wrist, stopping the gun three inches from his face.

He wasn't dealing with a kid; he was dealing with a cop. He obviously intended to shake that gun out of Meyer's fist and then beat him senseless on the floor of the apartment. But Meyer brought up his right knee and smashed it into Finch's groin, and then, his wrist still pinioned, he bunched his left fist and drove it hard and straight into Finch's gut. That did it. The fingers loosened and Finch backed away a step just as Meyer brought the pistol back across his own body and then unleashed it in a backhand swipe. The butt cracked against Finch's jaw and sent him sprawling against the closet wall.

Miraculously, the jaw did not break. Finch collided with

the closet, grabbed the door behind him with both hands opened wide and flat against the wood, and then shook his head. He blinked his eyes and shook his head again. By what seemed to be sheer will power, he managed to stand erect without falling on his face.

Meyer stood watching him, saying nothing, breathing hard. Carella, who had come into the room, stood at the far end, ready to shoot Finch if he so much as raised a pinky.

"Your name Finch?" Meyer asked.

"I don't talk to Jews," Finch answered.

"Then try *me*," Carella said. "What's your name?"

"Go to hell, you and your Jewboy friend both."

Meyer did not raise his voice. He simply took a step closer to Finch, and very softly said, "Mister, in two minutes, you're gonna be a cripple because you resisted arrest."

He didn't have to say anything else, because his eyes told the full story, and Finch was a fast reader.

"Okay," Finch said, nodding. "That's my name."

"What's in the closet, Finch?" Carella asked.

"My clothes."

"Get away from the door."

"What for?"

Neither of the cops answered. Finch studied them for ten seconds, and quickly moved away from the door. Meyer opened it. The closet was stacked high with piles of tied and bundled pamphlets. The cord on one bundle was untied, the pamphlets spilling onto the closet floor. Apparently, this bundle was the one Finch had thrown into the closet when he'd heard the knock on the door. Meyer stooped and picked up one of the pamphlets. It was badly and cheaply printed, but the intent was unmistakable. The title of the pamphlet was "The Bloodsucker Jew."

"Where'd you get this?" Meyer asked.

"I belong to a book club," Finch answered.

"There are a few laws against this sort of thing," Carella said.

"Yeah?" Finch answered. "Name me one."

"Happy to. Section 1340 of the Penal Law—libel defined."

"Maybe you ought to read Section 1342," Finch said. " *The publication is justified when the matter charged as libelous is true, and was published with good motives and for justifiable ends.' "*

"Then let's try Section 514," Carella said. " *'A person who denies or aids or incites another to deny any person because of race, creed, color or national origin . . .' "*

"I'm not trying to incite anyone," Finch said, grinning.

"Nor am I a lawyer," Carella said. "But we can also try Section 700, which defines discrimination, and Section 1430, which makes it a felony to perform an act of malicious injury to a place of religious worship."

"Huh?" Finch said.

"Yeah," Carella answered.

"What the hell are you talking about?"

"I'm talking about the little paint job you did on the synagogue wall."

"What paint job? What synagogue?"

"Where were you at eight o'clock tonight, Finch?"

"Out."

"Where?"

"I don't remember."

"You better *start* remembering."

"Why? Is there a section of the Penal Law against loss of memory?"

"No," Carella said. "But there's one against homicide."

5.

The team stood around him in the squad room.

The team consisted of Detectives Steve Carella, Meyer Meyer, Cotton Hawes, and Bert Kling. Two detectives from Homicide South had put in a brief appearance to legitimize the action, and then went home to sleep, knowing full well that the investigation of a homicide is always left to the precinct discovering the stiff. The team stood around Finch in a loose semicircle. This wasn't a movie sound stage, so there wasn't a bright light shining in Finch's eyes, nor did any of the cops lay a finger on him. These days, there were too many smart-assed lawyers around who were ready and able to leap upon irregular interrogation methods when and if a case finally came to trial. The detectives simply stood around Finch in a loose, relaxed semicircle, and their only weapons were a thorough familiarity with the interrogation process and with each other, and the mathematical superiority of four minds pitted against one.

"What time did you leave the apartment?" Hawes asked.

"Around seven."

"And what time did you return?" Kling asked.

"Nine, nine-thirty. Something like that."

"Where'd you go?" Carella asked.

"I had to see somebody."

"A rabbi?" Meyer asked.

"No."

"Who?"

"I don't want to get anybody in trouble."

"You're in plenty of trouble yourself," Hawes said. "Where'd you go?"

"No place."

"Okay, suit yourself," Carella said. "You've been shooting your mouth off about killing Jews, haven't you?"

"I never said anything like that."

"Where'd you get these pamphlets?"

"I found them."

"You agree with what they say?"

"Yes."

"You know where the synagogue in this neighborhood is?"

"Yes."

"Were you anywhere near it tonight between seven and nine?"

"No."

"Then where were you?"

"No place."

"Anybody see you there?" Kling asked.

"See me where?"

"The no place you went to."

"Nobody saw me."

"You went no place," Hawes said, "and nobody saw you. Is that right?"

"That's right."

"The invisible man," Kling said.

"That's right."

"When you get around to killing all these Jews," Carella said, "how do you plan to do it?"

"I don't plan to kill anybody," he said defensively.

"Who you gonna start with?"

"Nobody."

"Ben-Gurion?"

"Nobody."

"Or maybe you've already started."

"I didn't kill anybody, and I'm not gonna kill anybody. I want to call a lawyer."

"A Jewish lawyer?"

"I wouldn't have—"

"What wouldn't you have?"

"Nothing."

"You like Jews?"

"No."

"You hate them?"

"No."

"Then you like them."

"No. I didn't say—"

"You either like them or you hate them. Which?"

"That's none of your goddamn business!"

"But you agree with the crap in those hate pamphlets, don't you?"

"They're not hate pamphlets."

"What do you call them?"

"Expressions of opinion."

"Whose opinion?"

"Everybody's opinion!"

"Yours included?"

"Yes, mine included!"

"Do you know Rabbi Solomon?"

"No."

"What do you think of rabbis in general?"

"I never think of rabbis."

"But you think of Jews a lot, don't you?"

"There's no crime against think—"

"If you think of Jews you must think of rabbis. Isn't that right?"

"Why should I waste my time—"

"The rabbi is the spiritual leader of the Jewish people, isn't he?"

"I don't know anything about rabbis."

"But you must know that."

"What if I do?"

"Well, if you said you were going to kill the Jews—"

"I never said—"

"—then a good place to start would be with—"

"I never said anything like that!"

"We've got a witness who heard you! A good place to start would be with a rabbi, isn't that so?"

"Go shove your rabbi—"

"Where were you between seven and nine tonight?"

"No place."

"You were behind that synagogue, weren't you?"

"No."

"You were painting a J on the wall, weren't you?"

"No! No, I wasn't!"

"You were stabbing a rabbi!"

"You were killing a Jew!"

"I wasn't any place near that—"

"Book him, Cotton. Suspicion of murder."

"Suspicion of—I'm telling you I wasn't—"

"Either shut up or start talking, you bastard," Carella said.

Finch shut up.

6.

The girl came to see Meyer Meyer on Easter Sunday.

She had reddish-brown hair and brown eyes, and she wore

a dress of bright persimmon with a sprig of flowers pinned to the left breast. She stood at the railing and none of the detectives in the squadroom even noticed the flowers; they were too busy speculating on the depth and texture of the girl's rich curves.

The girl didn't say a word. She didn't have to. The effect was almost comic, akin to the cocktail-party scene where the voluptuous blonde takes out a cigarette and four hundred men are stampeded in the rush to light it. The first man to reach the slatted rail divider was Cotton Hawes, since he was single and unattached. The second man was Hal Willis, who was also single and a good red-blooded American boy. Meyer Meyer, an old married poop, contented himself with ogling the girl from behind his desk. The word *shtik* crossed Meyer's mind, but he rapidly pushed the thought aside.

"Can I help you, miss?" Hawes and Willis asked simultaneously.

"I'd like to see Detective Meyer," the girl said.

"Meyer?" Hawes asked, as if his manhood had been maligned.

"Meyer?" Willis repeated.

"Is he the man handling the murder of the rabbi?"

"Well we're *all* sort of working on it," Hawes said modestly.

"I'm Artie Finch's girl friend," the girl said. "I want to talk to Detective Meyer."

Meyer rose from his desk with the air of a man who has been singled out from the stag line by the belle of the ball. Using his best radio announcer's voice, and his best company manners, he said, "Yes, miss, I'm Detective Meyer."

He held open the gate in the railing, all but executed a bow, and led the girl to his desk. Hawes and Kling watched as the girl sat and crossed her legs. Meyer moved a pad into place with all the aplomb of a General Motors executive.

"I'm sorry miss," he said. "What was your name?"

"Eleanor," she said. "Eleanor Fay."

"F-A-Y-E?" Meyer asked, writing.

"F-A-Y."

"And you're Arthur Finch's fiancée? Is that right?"

"I'm his girl friend," Eleanor corrected.

"You're not engaged?"

"Not officially, no." She smiled demurely, modestly and sweetly. Across the room, Cotton Hawes rolled his eyes toward the ceiling.

"What did you want to see me about, Miss Fay?" Meyer asked.

"I wanted to see you about Arthur. He's innocent. He didn't kill that man."

"I see. What do you know about it, Miss Fay?"

"Well, I read in the paper that the rabbi was killed sometime between seven-thirty and nine. I think that's right, isn't it?"

"Approximately, yes."

"Well, Arthur couldn't have done it. I know where he was during that time."

"And where was he?" Meyer asked.

He figured he knew just what the girl would say. He had heard the same words from an assortment of molls, mistresses, fiancées, girl friends and just plain acquaintances of men accused of everything from disorderly conduct to first-degree murder. The girl would protest that Finch was with her during that time. After a bit of tooth-pulling, she would admit that—well—they were alone together. After a little more coaxing, the girl would reluctantly state, the reluctance adding credulity to her story, that—well—they were alone in intimate circumstances together. The alibi having been firmly established, she would then wait patiently for her man's deliverance.

"And where was he?" Meyer asked, and waited patiently.

"From seven to eight," Eleanor said, "he was with a man named Bret Loomis in a restaurant called The Gate, on Culver and South Third."

"What?" Meyer said, surprised.

"Yes. From there, Arthur went to see his sister in Riverhead. I can give you the address if you like. He got there at about eight-thirty and stayed a half-hour or so. Then he went straight home."

"What time did he get home?"

"Ten o'clock."

"He told us nine, nine-thirty."

"He was mistaken. I know he got home at ten because he called me the minute he was in the house. It was ten o'clock."

"I see. And he told you he'd just got home?"

"Yes." Eleanor Fay nodded and uncrossed her legs. Willis, at the water cooler, did not miss the sudden revealing glimpse of nylon and thigh.

"Did he also tell you he'd spent all that time with Loomis first and then with his sister?"

"Yes, he did."

"Then why didn't he tell *us?*" Meyer asked.

"I don't know why. Arthur is a person who respects family and friends. I suppose he didn't want to involve them with the police."

"That's very considerate of him," Meyer said dryly, "especially since he's being held on suspicion of murder. What's his sister's name?"

"Irene Granavan. Mrs. Carl Granavan."

"And her address?"

"Nineteen-eleven Morris Road. In Riverhead."

"Know where I can find this Bret Loomis?"

"He lives in a rooming house on Culver Avenue. The address is 3918. It's near Fourth."

"You came pretty well prepared, didn't you, Miss Fay?" Meyer asked.

"If you don't come prepared," Eleanor answered, "why come at all?"

7.

Bret Loomis was thirty-one years old, five feet six inches tall, bearded. When he admitted the detectives to the apartment, he was wearing a bulky black sweater and tight-fitting dungarees. Standing next to Cotton Hawes, he looked like a little boy who had tried on a false beard in an attempt to get a laugh out of his father.

"Sorry to bother you, Mr. Loomis," Meyer said. "We know this is Easter, and—"

"Oh, yeah?" Loomis said. He seemed surprised. "Hey, that's right, ain't it? It's Easter. I'll be damned. Maybe I oughta go out and buy myself a pot of flowers."

"You didn't know it was Easter?" Hawes asked.

"Like, man, who ever reads the newspapers? Gloom, gloom! I'm fed up to here with it. Let's have a beer, celebrate Easter. Okay?"

"Well, thanks," Meyer said, "but—"

"Come on, so it ain't allowed. Who's gonna know besides you, me and the bedpost? Three beers coming up."

Meyer looked at Hawes and shrugged. Hawes shrugged back. Together, they watched Loomis as he went to the refrigerator in one corner of the room and took out three bottles of beer.

"Sit down," he said. "You'll have to drink from the bottle because I'm a little short of glasses. Sit down, sit down."

The detectives glanced around the room, puzzled.

"Oh," Loomis said, "you'd better sit on the floor. I'm a little short of chairs."

The three men squatted around a low table which had obviously been made from a tree stump. Loomis put the bottles on the table top, lifted his own bottle, said "Cheers," and took a long drag at it.

"What do you do for a living, Mr. Loomis?" Meyer asked.

"I live," Loomis said.

"What?"

"I *live* for a living. That's what I do."

"I meant, how do you support yourself?"

"I get payments from my ex-wife."

"*You* get payments?" Hawes asked.

"Yeah. She was so delighted to get rid of me that she made a settlement. A hundred bucks a week. That's pretty good, isn't it?"

"That's very good," Meyer said.

"You think so?" Loomis seemed thoughtful. "I think I coulda boosted it to *two* hundred if I held out a little longer. The bitch was running around with another guy, you see, and was all hot to marry him. He's got plenty of loot. I bet I coulda boosted it to two hundred."

"How long do these payments continue?" Hawes asked, fascinated.

"Until I get married again—which I will never ever do as long as I live. Drink your beer. It's good beer." He took a drag at his bottle and said, "What'd you want to see me about?"

"Do you know a man named Arthur Finch?"

"Sure. He in trouble?"

"Yes."

"What'd he do?"

"Well, let's skip that for the moment, Mr. Loomis," Hawes said. "We'd like you to tell us—"

"Where'd you get that white streak in your hair?" Loomis asked suddenly.

"Huh?" Hawes touched his left temple unconsciously. "Oh, I got knifed once. It grew back this way."

"All you need is a blue streak on the other temple. Then you'll look like the American flag," Loomis said, and laughed.

"Yeah," Hawes said. "Mr. Loomis, can you tell us where you were last night between seven and eight o'clock?"

"Oh, boy," Loomis said, "this is like 'Dragnet,' ain't it? 'Where were you on the night of December twenty-first? All we want are the facts.' "

"Just like 'Dragnet,' " Meyer said dryly. "Where were you, Mr. Loomis?"

"Last night? Seven o'clock?" He thought for a moment. "Oh, sure."

"Where?"

"Olga's pad."

"Who?"

"Olga Trenovich. She's like a sculptress. She does these

crazy little statues in wax. Like she drips the wax all over everything. You dig?"

"And you were with her last night?"

"Yeah. She had like a little session up at her pad. A couple of colored guys on sax and drums and two other kids on trumpet and piano."

"You got there at seven, Mr. Loomis?"

"No. I got there at six-thirty."

"And what time did you leave?"

"Gossssshhhhh, who remembers?" Loomis said. "It was the wee, small hours."

"After midnight, you mean?" Hawes asked.

"Oh, sure. Two, three in the morning," Loomis said.

"You got there at six-thirty and left at two or three in the morning? Is that right?"

"Yeah."

"Was Arthur Finch with you?"

"Hell, no."

"Did you see him at all last night?"

"Nope. Haven't seen him since—let me see—last month sometime."

"You were *not* with Arthur Finch in a restaurant called The Gate?"

"When? Last night, you mean?"

"Yes."

"Nope. I just told you. I haven't seen Artie in almost two weeks." A sudden spark flashed in Loomis' eyes and he looked at Hawes and Meyer guiltily.

"Oh-oh," he said. "What'd I just do? Did I screw up Artie's alibi?"

"You screwed it up fine, Mr. Loomis," Hawes said.

8.

Irene Granavan, Finch's sister, was a twenty-one-year-old girl who had already borne three children and was working on her fourth, in her fifth month of pregnancy. She admitted the detectives to her apartment in a Riverhead housing development, and then immediately sat down.

"You have to forgive me," she said. "My back aches. The doctor thinks maybe it'll be twins. That's all I need is twins." She pressed the palms of her hands into the small of her back, sighed heavily, and said, "I'm always having a baby. I got married when I was seventeen, and I've been pregnant ever since. All my kids think I'm a fat woman. They've never seen me that I wasn't pregnant." She sighed again. "You got any children?" she asked Meyer.

"Three," he answered.

"I sometimes wish . . ." She stopped and pulled a curious face, a face which denied dreams.

"What do you wish, Mrs. Granavan?" Hawes asked.

"That I could go to Bermuda. Alone." She paused. "Have you ever been to Bermuda?"

"No."

"I hear it's very nice there," Irene Granavan said wistfully, and the apartment went still.

"Mrs. Granavan," Meyer said, "we'd like to ask you a few questions about your brother."

"What's he done now?"

"Has he done things before?" Hawes said.

"Well, you know . . ." She shrugged.

"What?" Meyer asked.

"Well, the fuss down at City Hall. And the picketing of that movie. You know."

"We don't know, Mrs. Granavan."

"Well, I hate to say this about my own brother, but I think he's a little nuts on the subject. You know."

"What subject?"

"Well, the movie, for example. It's about Israel, and him and his friends picketed it and all, and handed out pamphlets about Jews, and . . . You remember, don't you? The crowd threw stones at him and all. There were a lot of concentration-camp survivors in the crowd, you know." She paused. "I think he must be a little nuts to do something like that, don't you think?"

"You said something about City Hall, Mrs. Granavan. What did your brother—"

"Well, it was when the mayor invited this Jewish assemblyman—I forget his name—to make a speech with him on the steps of City Hall. My brother went down and— well, the same business. You know."

"You mentioned your brother's friends. What friends?"

"The nuts he hangs out with."

"Would you know their names?" Meyer wanted to know.

"I know only one of them. He was here once with my brother. He's got pimples all over his face. I remember him because I was pregnant with Sean at the time, and he asked if he could put his hands on my stomach to feel the baby kicking. I told him he certainly could not. That shut *him* up, all right."

"What was his name, Mrs. Granavan?"

"Fred. That's short for Frederick. Frederick Schultz."

"He's German?" Meyer asked.

"Yes."

Meyer nodded briefly.

"Mrs. Granavan," Hawes said, "was your brother here last night?"

"Why? Did he say he was?"

"Was he?"

"No."

"Not at all?"

"No. He wasn't here last night. I was home alone last night. My husband bowls on Saturdays." She paused. "I sit home and hug my fat belly, and he bowls. You know what I wish sometimes?"

"What?" Meyer asked.

And, as if she had not said it once before, Irene Granavan said, "I wish I could go to Bermuda sometime. Alone."

"The thing is," the house painter said to Carella, "I'd like my ladder back."

"I can understand that," Carella said.

"The brushes they can keep, although some of them are very expensive brushes. But the ladder I absolutely need. I'm losing a day's work already because of those guys down at your lab."

"Well, you see—"

"I go back to the synagogue this morning, and my ladder and my brushes and even my paints are all gone. And what a mess somebody made of that alley! So this old guy who's sexton of the place, he tells me the priest was killed Saturday night, and the cops took all the stuff away with them. I wanted to know what cops, and he said he didn't know. So I called headquarters this morning, and I got a runaround from six different cops who finally put me through to some guy named Grossman at the lab."

"Yes, Lieutenant Grossman," Carella said.

"That's right. And he tells me I can't have my goddamn ladder back until they finish their tests on it. Now what the hell do they expect to find on my ladder, would you mind telling me?"

"I don't know, Mr. Cabot. Fingerprints, perhaps."

"Yeah, *my* fingerprints! Am I gonna get involved in murder *besides* losing a day's work?"

"I don't think so," Carella said, smiling.

"I shouldn't have taken that job, anyway," Cabot said. "I shouldn't have even bothered with it."

"Who hired you for the job, Mr. Cabot?"

"The priest did."

"The rabbi, you mean?" Carella asked.

"Yeah, the priest, the rabbi, whatever the hell you call him." Cabot shrugged.

"And what were you supposed to do, Mr. Cabot?"

"I was supposed to paint. What do you think I was supposed to do?"

"Paint what?"

"The trim. Around the windows and the roof."

"White and blue?"

"White around the windows, and blue for the roof trim."

"The colors of Israel," Carella said.

"Yeah," the painter agreed. Then he said, "What?"

"Nothing. Why did you say you shouldn't have taken the job, Mr. Cabot?"

"Well, because of all the arguing first. He wanted it done

339

for Peaceable, he said, and Peaceable fell on the first. But I couldn't—"

"Peaceable? You mean Passover?"

"Yeah, Peaceable, Passover, whatever the hell you call it." He shrugged again.

"You were about to say?"

"I was about to say we had a little argument about it. I was working on another job, and I couldn't get to his job until Friday, the thirty-first. I figured I'd work late into the night, you know, but the priest told me I couldn't work after sundown. So I said why can't I work after sundown, so he said the Sabbath began at sundown, not to mention the first day of Peace—Passover, and that work wasn't allowed on the first two days of Passover, nor on the Sabbath neither, for that matter. Because the Lord rested on the Sabbath, you see. The seventh day."

"Yes, I see."

"Sure. So I said, 'Father, I'm not of the Jewish faith,' is what I said, 'and I can work any day of the week I like.' Besides, I got a big job to start on Monday, and I figured I could knock off the church all day Friday and Friday night or, if worse came to worse, Saturday, for which I usually get time and a half. So we compromised."

"How did you compromise?"

"Well, this priest was of what you call the Conservative crowd, not the Reformers, which are very advanced, but still these Conservatives don't follow all the old rules of the religion is what I gather. So he said I could work during the day Friday, and then I could come back and work Saturday, provided I knocked off at sundown. Don't ask me what kind of crazy compromise it was. I think he had in mind that he holds mass at sundown and it would be a mortal sin if I was outside painting while everybody was inside praying, and on a very special high holy day, at that."

"I see. So you painted until sundown Friday?"

"Right."

"And then you came back Saturday morning?"

"Right. But what it was, the windows needed a lot of putty, and the sills needed scraping and sanding, so by sundown Saturday, I still wasn't finished with the job. I had a talk with the priest, who said he was about to go inside and pray, and could I come back after services to finish off the job? I told him I had a better idea. I would come back Monday morning and knock off the little bit that had to be done before I went on to this very big job I got in Majesta—it's painting a whole factory; that's a big job. So I left everything right where it was in back of the church. I figured, who'd steal anything from right behind a church. Am I right?"

"Right," Carella said.

"Yeah. Well, you know who'd steal them from right behind a church?"

"Who?"

"The cops!" Cabot shouted. "That's who! Now how the hell do I get my ladder back, would you please tell me? I got a call from the factory today. They said if I don't start work tomorrow, at the latest, I can forget all about the job. And me without a ladder!"

"Maybe we've got a ladder downstairs you can borrow," Carella said.

"Mister, I need a tall painter's ladder. This is a very high factory. Can you call this Captain Grossman and ask him to please let me have my ladder back? I got mouths to feed."

"I'll talk to him, Mr. Cabot," Carella said. "Leave me your number, will you?"

"I tried to borrow my brother-in-law's ladder—he's a paper hanger—but he's papering this movie star's apartment, downtown on Jefferson. So just try to get *his* ladder. Just try."

"Well, I'll call Grossman," Carella said.

"The other day, what she done, this movie actress, she marched into the living room wearing only this towel, you see? She wanted to know what—"

"I'll call Grossman," Carella said.

As it turned out, he didn't have to call Grossman, because a lab report arrived late that afternoon, together with Cabot's ladder and the rest of his working equipment, including his brushes, his putty knife, several cans of linseed oil and turpentine, a pair of paint-stained gloves and two dropcloths. At about the same time the report arrived, Grossman called from downtown, saving Carella a dime.

"Did you get my report?" Grossman asked.

"I was just reading it."

"What do you make of it?"

"I don't know," Carella said.

"Want my guess?"

"Sure. I'm always interested in what the layman thinks," Carella answered him.

"Layman, I'll give you a hit in the head!" Grossman answered, laughing. "You notice the rabbi's prints were on those paint-can lids, and also on the ladder?"

"Yes, I did."

"The ones on the lids were thumb prints, so I imagine the rabbi put those lids back onto the paint cans or, if they were already on the cans, pushed down on them to make sure they were secure."

"Why would he want to do that?"

"Maybe he was moving the stuff. There's a tool shed behind the synagogue. Had you noticed that?"

"No, I hadn't."

"Tch-tch, big detective. Yeah, there's one there, all right, about fifty yards behind the building. So I figure the painter rushed off, leaving his junk all over the back yard, and the rabbi was moving it to the tool shed when he was surprised by the killer."

"Well, the painter did leave his stuff there, that's true. He expected to come back Monday morning."

"Today, yeah," Grossman said. "But maybe the rabbi figured he didn't want his back yard looking like a pigsty, especially since this is Passover. So he took it into his head to move the stuff over to the tool shed. This is just speculation, you understand."

"No kidding?" Carella said. "I thought it was sound, scientific deduction."

"Go to hell. Those *are* thumb prints on the lids, so it's

logical to conclude he pressed down on them. And the prints on the ladder seem to indicate he was carrying it."

"This report said you didn't find any prints but the rabbi's," Carella said. "Isn't that just a little unusual?"

"You didn't read it right," Grossman said. "We found a portion of a print on one of the paintbrushes. And we also—"

"Oh, yeah," Carella said, "here it is. This doesn't say much, Sam."

"What do you want me to do? It seems to be a tented-arch pattern, like the rabbi's, but there's too little to tell. The print could have been left on that brush by someone else."

"Like the painter?"

"No. We've pretty much decided the painter used gloves while he worked. Otherwise, we'd have found a flock of similar prints on all the tools."

"Then who left that print on the brush? The killer?"

"Maybe."

"But the portion isn't enough to get anything positive on?"

"Sorry, Steve."

"So your guess on what happened is that the rabbi went outside after services to clean up the mess. The killer surprised him, knifed him, made a mess of the alley, and then painted that J on the wall. Is that it?"

"I guess so, though—"

"What?"

"Well, there was a lot of blood leading right over to that wall, Steve. As if the rabbi had crawled there after he'd been stabbed."

"Probably trying to get to the back door of the synagogue."

"Maybe," Grossman said. "One thing I can tell you. Whoever killed him must have been pretty much of a mess when he got home. No doubt about that."

"Why do you say that?"

"That spattered paint all over the alley," Grossman said. "It's my guess the rabbi threw those paint cans at his attacker."

"You're a pretty good guesser, Sam," Carella told him, grinning.

"Thanks," Grossman said.

"Tell me something."

"Yeah?"

"You ever solve any murders?"

"Go to hell," Grossman said, and he hung up.

9.

Alone with his wife that night in the living room of their apartment, Meyer tried to keep his attention *off* a television series about cops and *on* the various documents he had collected from Rabbi Solomon's study in the synagogue. The cops on television were shooting up a storm, blank bullets flying all over the place and killing hoodlums by the score. It almost made a working man like Meyer Meyer wish for an exciting life of romantic adventure.

The romantic adventure of *his* life, Sarah Lipkin Meyer, sat in an easy chair opposite the television screen, her legs crossed, absorbed in the fictional derring-do of the policemen.

"Ooooh, *get* him!" Sarah screamed at one point, and Meyer turned to look at her curiously, and then went back to the rabbi's books.

The rabbi kept a ledger of expenses, all of which had to do with the synagogue and his duties there. The ledger did not make interesting reading, and told Meyer nothing he wanted to know. The rabbi also kept a calendar of synagogue events and Meyer glanced through them reminiscently, remembering his own youth and the busy Jewish life centering around the synagogue in the neighborhood adjacent to his own. *March twelfth,* the calendar read, *regular Sunday breakfast of the Men's Club. Speaker, Harry Pine, director of Commission on International Affairs of American Jewish Congress. Topic: The Eichmann Case.*

Meyer's eye ran down the list of events itemized in Rabbi Solomon's book:

March 12, 7:15 P.M.
Youth Group meeting.
March 18, 9:30 A.M.
Bar Mitzvah services for Nathan Rothman. Kiddush after services. Open invitation to Center membership.
March 22, 8:45 P.M.
Clinton Samuels, Assistant Professor of Philosophy in Education, Brandeis University, will lead discussion in "The Matter of Identity for the Jews in Modern America."
March 26
Eternal Light Radio. "The Search" by Virginia Mazer, biographical script on Lillian Wald, founder of Henry Street Settlement in New York.

Meyer looked up from the calendar. "Sarah?" he said.

"Shhh, shhh, just a minute," Sarah answered. She was nibbling furiously at her thumb, her eyes glued to the silent television screen. An ear-shattering volley of shots suddenly erupted, all but smashing the picture tube. The theme music came up, and Sarah let out a deep sigh and turned to her husband.

Meyer looked at her curiously, as if seeing her for the first time, remembering the Sarah Lipkin of long, long ago and wondering if the Sarah Meyer of today was very much different from that initial exciting image. "Nobody's lips kin like Sarah's lips kin," the fraternity boys had chanted, and Meyer had memorized the chant, and investigated the possibilities, learning for the first time in his life that every cliché bears a kernel of folklore. He looked at her mouth now, pursed in puzzlement as she studied his face. Her eyes were blue, and her hair was brown, and she had a damn good figure and splendid legs, and he nodded in agreement with his youthful judgment.

"Sarah, do you feel any identity as a Jew in modern America?" he asked.

"What?" Sarah said.

"I said—"

"Oh, boy," Sarah said. "What brought *that* on?"

345

"The rabbi, I guess." Meyer scratched his bald pate. "I guess I haven't felt so much like a Jew since—since I was confirmed, I guess. It's a funny thing."

"Don't let it trouble you," Sarah said gently. "You *are* a Jew."

"Am I?" he asked, and he looked straight into her eyes.

She returned the gaze. "You have to answer that one for yourself," she said.

"I know I—well, I get mad as hell thinking about this guy Finch. Which isn't good, you know. After all, maybe he's innocent."

"Do you think so?"

"No. I think he did it. But is it *me* who thinks that, Meyer Meyer, Detective Second Grade? Or is it Meyer Meyer who got beat up by the *goyim* when he was a kid, and Meyer Meyer who heard his grandfather tell stories about pogroms, or who listened to the radio and heard what Hitler was doing in Germany, or who nearly strangled a German colonel with his bare hands just outside—"

"You can't separate the two, darling," Sarah said.

"Maybe you can't. I'm only trying to say I never much felt like a Jew until this case came along. Now, all of a sudden . . ." He shrugged.

"Shall I get your prayer shawl?" Sarah said smiling.

"Wise guy," Meyer said. He closed the rabbi's calendar, and opened the next book on the desk. The book was a personal diary. He unlocked it, and began leafing through it.

Friday, January 6

Shabbat, Parshat Shemot. I lighted the candles at 4:24. Evening services were at 6:15. It has been a hundred years since the Civil War. We discussed the Jewish Community of the South, then and now.

January 18

It seems odd to me that I should have to familiarize the membership about the proper blessings over the Sabbath candles. Have we come so far toward forgetfulness?

Baruch ata adonai elohenu melech haolam asher kid-shanu b'mitzvotav vitzivanu l'hadlick ner shel shabbat.

Blessed are Thou O Lord our God, King of the universe who hast sanctified us by Thy laws and commanded us to kindle the Sabbath Light.

Perhaps he is right. Perhaps the Jews are doomed.

January 20

I had hoped that the Maccabean festival would make us realize the hardships borne by the Jews 2,000 years ago in comparison to our good and easy lives today in a democracy. Today, we have the freedom to worship as we desire, but this should impose upon us the responsibility of enjoying that freedom. And yet, Hanukkah has come and gone, and it seems to me The Feast of Lights taught us nothing, gave us nothing more than a joyous holiday to celebrate.

The Jews will die, he says.

February 2

I believe I am beginning to fear him. He shouted threats at me today, said that I, of all the Jews, would lead the way to destruction. I was tempted to call the police, but I understand he has done this before. There are those in the membership who have suffered his harangues and who seem to feel he is harmless. But he rants with the fervor of a fanatic, and his eyes frighten me.

February 12

A member called today to ask me something about the dietary laws. I was forced to call the local butcher because I did not know the prescribed length of the *hallaf,* the slaughtering knife. Even the butcher, in jest, said to me that a real rabbi would know these things. I *am* a real rabbi. I believe in the Lord, my God, I teach His will and His law to His people. What need a rabbi know about *shehitah,* the art of slaughtering animals? Is it important to know that the slaughtering knife must be twice the width of the throat of the slaughtered animal, and no more than fourteen finger-breadths in length? The butcher told me that the knife must be sharp and smooth, with no perceptible notches. It is examined by passing finger and fingernail over both edges of the blade before and after slaughtering. If a notch is found, the animal is then unfit. Now I know. But is it necessary to know this? Is it not enough to love God, and to teach His ways?

His anger continues to frighten me.

February 14

I found a knife in the ark today, at the rear of the cabinet behind the Torah.

March 8

We had no further use of the Bibles we replaced, and since they were old and tattered, but nonetheless ritual articles containing the name of God, we buried them in the backyard, near the tool shed.

March 22

I must see about contacting a painter to do the outside of the synagogue. Someone suggested a Mr. Frank Cabot who lives in the neighborhood. I will call him tomorrow, perhaps. Passover will be coming soon, and I would like the temple to look nice.

The mystery is solved. It is kept for trimming the wick in the oil lamp over the ark.

The telephone rang. Meyer, absorbed in the diary, didn't even hear it. Sarah went to the phone and lifted it from the cradle.

"Hello?" she said. "Oh, hello, Steve. How are you?" She laughed and said, "No, I was watching television. That's right." She laughed again. "Yes, just a minute, I'll get him." She put the phone down and walked to where Meyer was working. "It's Steve," she said. "He wants to speak to you."

"Huh?"

"The phone. Steve."

"Oh." Meyer nodded. "Thanks." He walked over to the phone and lifted the receiver. "Hello, Steve," he said.

"Hi. Can you get down here right away?"

"Why? What's the matter?"

"Finch," Carella said. "He's broken jail."

10.

Finch had been kept in the detention cells of the precinct house all day Sunday where, it being Easter, he had been served turkey for his midday meal. On Monday morning, he'd been transported by van to Headquarters downtown on High Street where, as a felony offender, he participated in that quaint police custom known simply as "the line-up." He had been mugged and printed afterward in the basement of the building, and then led across the street to the Criminal Courts Building where he had been arraigned for first-degree murder and, over his lawyer's protest, ordered to be held without bail until trial. The police van had then transported him crosstown to the house of detention on Canopy Avenue where he'd remained all day Monday, until after the evening meal. At that time, those offenders who had committed, or who were alleged to have committed, the most serious crimes, were once more shackled and put into the van, which carried them uptown and south to the edge of the River Dix for transportation by ferry to the prison on Walker Island.

He'd made his break, Carella reported, while he was being moved from the van to the ferry. According to what the harbor police said, Finch was still handcuffed and wearing prison garb. The break had taken place at about ten P.M. It was assumed that it had been witnessed by several dozen hospital attendants waiting for the ferry which would take them to Dix Sanitarium, a city-owned-and-operated hospital for drug addicts, situated in the middle of the river about a mile and a half from the prison. It was also assumed that the break had been witnessed by a dozen or more water rats who leaped among the dock pilings and who, because of their size, were sometimes mistaken for pussy cats by neighborhood kids who played near the river's edge. Considering the fact that Finch was dressed in drab gray

uniform and handcuffs—a dazzling display of sartorial ele-
gance, to be sure, but not likely to be seen on any other
male walking the city streets—it was amazing that he hadn't
yet been picked up. They had, of course, checked his apartment first, finding nothing there but the four walls and
the furniture. One of the unmarried detectives on the
squad, probably hoping for an invitation to go along, suggested that they look up Eleanor Fay, Finch's girl. Wasn't
it likely he'd head for her pad? Carella and Meyer agreed
that it was entirely likely, clipped their holsters on, neglected to offer the invitation to their colleague, and went
out into the night.

It was a nice night, and Eleanor Fay lived in a nice neighborhood of old brownstones wedged in between new, all-
glass apartment houses with garages below the sidewalk.
April had danced across the city and left her subtle warmth
in the air. The two men drove in one of the squad's sedans,
the windows rolled down. They did not say much to each
other; April had robbed them of speech. The police radio
droned its calls endlessly; radio motor patrolmen all over
the city acknowledged violence and mayhem.

"There it is," Meyer said. "Just up ahead."

"Now try to find a parking spot," Carella complained.

They circled the block twice before finding an opening
in front of a drugstore on the avenue. They got out of the
car, left it unlocked, and walked briskly in the balmy night.
The brownstone was in the middle of the block. They
climbed the twelve steps to the vestibule, and studied the
name plates alongside the buzzers. Eleanor Fay was in
apartment 2B. Without hesitation, Carella pressed the buz-
zer for apartment 5A. Meyer took the doorknob in his hand
and waited. When the answering cl   came, he twisted
the knob, and silently they headed fo   e steps to the second floor.

Kicking in a door is an essentially rude practice. Neither
Carella nor Meyer was particularly lacking in good manners,
but they were looking for a man accused of murder, and
a man who had successfully broken jail. It was not unnatural
to assume this was a desperate man, and so they didn't

even discuss whether or not they would kick in the door. They aligned themselves in the corridor outside apartment 2B. The wall opposite the door was too far away to serve as a springboard. Meyer, the heavier of the two men, backed away from the door, then hit it with his shoulder. He hit it hard and close to the lock. He wasn't attempting to shatter the door itself, an all but impossible feat. All he wanted to do was spring the lock. All the weight of his body concentrated in the padded spot of arm and shoulder which collided with the door just above the lock. The lock itself remained locked, but the screws holding it to the jamb could not resist the force of Meyer's fleshy battering ram. The wood around the screws splintered, the threads lost their friction grip, the door shot inward and Meyer followed it into the room. Carella, like a quarterback carrying the ball behind powerful interference, followed Meyer.

It's rare that a cop encounters raw sex in his daily routine. The naked bodies he sees are generally cold and covered with caked blood. Even vice-squad cops find the act of love sordid rather than enticing. Eleanor Fay was lying full length on the living-room couch with a man. The television set in front of the couch was going, but nobody was watching either the news or the weather.

When the two men with drawn guns piled into the room behind the imploding door, Eleanor Fay sat bolt upright on the couch, her eyes wide in surprise. She was naked to the waist. She was wearing tight-fitting black tapered slacks and black high-heeled pumps. Her hair was disarranged and her lipstick had been kissed from her mouth, and she tried to cover her exposed breasts with her hands the moment the cops entered, realized the task was impossible, and grabbed the nearest article of clothing, which happened to be the man's suit jacket. She held it up in front of her like the classic, surprised heroine in a pirate movie. The man beside her sat up with equal suddenness, turned toward the cops, then turned back to Eleanor, puzzled, as if seeking an explanation from her.

The man was not Arthur Finch.

He was a man in his late twenties. He had a lot of pimples on his face, and a lot of lipstick stains. His white shirt was open to the waist. He wore no undershirt.

"Hello, Miss Fay," Meyer said.

"I didn't hear you knock," Eleanor answered. She seemed to recover instantly from her initial surprise and embarrassment. With total disdain for the two detectives, she threw the jacket aside, rose and walked like a burlesque queen to a hard-backed chair over which her missing clothing was draped. She lifted a brassière, shrugged into it, clasped it, all as if she were alone in the room. Then she pulled a black, long-sleeved sweater over her head, shook out her hair, lighted a cigarette, and said, "Is breaking and entering only a crime for criminals?"

"We're sorry, miss," Carella said. "We're looking for your boy friend."

"Me?" the man on the couch asked. "What'd *I* do?"

A glance of puzzlement passed between Meyer and Carella. Something like understanding, faint and none too clear, touched Carella's face.

"Who are you?" he said.

"You don't have to tell them anything," Eleanor cautioned. "They're not allowed to break in like this. Private citizens have rights, too."

"That's right, Miss Fay," Meyer said. "Why'd you lie to us?"

"I didn't lie to anybody."

"You gave us false information about Finch's whereabouts on—"

"I wasn't aware I was under oath at the time."

"You weren't. But you were damn well maliciously impeding the progress of an investigation."

"The hell with you *and* your investigation. You horny bastards bust in here like—"

"We're sorry we spoiled your party," Carella said. "Why'd you lie about Finch?"

"I thought I was helping you," Eleanor said. "Now get the hell out of here."

"We're staying a while, Miss Fay," Meyer said, "so get off your high horse. How'd you figure you were helping us? By sending us on a wild-goose chase confirming alibis you knew were false?"

"I didn't know anything. I told you just what Arthur told me."

"That's a lie."

"Why don't you get out?" Eleanor said. "Or are you hoping I'll take off my sweater again?"

"What you've got, we've already seen, lady," Carella said. He turned to the man. "What's your name?"

"Don't tell him," Eleanor said.

"Here or uptown, take your choice," Carella said. "Arthur Finch has broken jail, and we're trying to find him. If you want to be accessories to—"

"Broken jail?" Eleanor went a trifle pale. She glanced at the man on the couch, and their eyes met.

"Wh—when did this happen?" the man asked.

"About ten o'clock tonight."

The man was silent for several moments. "That's not so good," he said at last.

"How about telling us who you are," Carella suggested.

"Frederick Schultz," the man said.

"That makes it all very cozy, doesn't it?" Meyer said.

"Get your mind out of the gutter," Eleanor said. "I'm not Finch's girl, and I never was."

"Then why'd you say you were?"

"I didn't want Freddie to get involved in this thing."

"How could he possibly get involved?"

Eleanor shrugged.

"What is it? Was Finch with Freddie on Saturday night?"

Eleanor nodded reluctantly.

"From what time to what time?"

"From seven to ten," Freddie said.

"Then he couldn't have killed the rabbi."

"Who said he did?" Freddie answered.

"Why didn't you tell us this?"

"Because . . ." Eleanor started, and then stopped dead.

"Because they had something to hide," Carella said. "Why'd he come to see you, Freddie?"

Freddie did not answer.

"Hold it," Meyer said. "This is the other Jewhater, Steve. The one Finch's sister told me about. Isn't that right, Freddie?"

Freddie did not answer.

"Why'd he come to see you, Freddie? To pick up those pamphlets we found in his closet?"

"You the guy who prints that crap, Freddie?"

What's the matter, Freddie? Weren't you sure how much of a crime was involved?"

"Did you figure he'd tell us where he got the stuff, Freddie?"

"You're a real good pal, aren't you, Freddie? You'd send your friend to the chair rather than—"

"I don't owe him anything!" Freddie said.

"Maybe you owe him a lot. He was facing a murder rap, but he never once mentioned your name. You went to all that trouble for nothing, Miss Fay."

"It was no trouble," Eleanor said thinly.

"No," Meyer said. "You marched into the precinct with a tight dress and a cockamamie bunch of alibis that you knew we'd check. You figured once we found those to be phony, we wouldn't believe anything else Finch said. Even if he told us where he *really* was, we wouldn't believe it. That's right, isn't it?"

"You finished?" Eleanor asked.

"No, but I think you are," Meyer answered.

"You had no right to bust in here. There's no law against making love."

"Sister," Carella said, "*you* were making hate."

11.

Arthur Finch wasn't making anything when they found him.

They found him at ten minutes past two, on the morning

of April fourth. They found him in his apartment because a patrolman had been sent there to pick up the pamphlets in his closet. They found him lying in front of the kitchen table. He was still handcuffed. A file and rasp were on the table top, and there were metal filings covering the enamel and a spot on the linoleum floor, but Finch had made only a small dent in the manacles. The filings on the floor were floating in a red, sticky substance.

Finch's throat was open from ear to ear.

The patrolman, expecting to make a routine pickup, found the body and had the presence of mind to call his patrol-car partner before he panicked. His partner went down to the car and radioed the homicide to Headquarters, who informed Homicide South and the detectives of the 87th Squad.

The patrolmen were busy that night. At three A.M., a citizen called in to report what he thought was a leak in a water main on South Fifth. The radio dispatcher at Headquarters sent a car to investigate, and the patrolman found that nothing was wrong with the water main, but something was interfering with the city's fine sewage system.

The men were not members of the Department of Sanitation, but they nonetheless climbed down a manhole into the stink and garbage, and located a man's black suit caught on an orange crate and blocking a pipe, causing the water to back up into the street. The man's suit was spattered with white and blue paint. The patrolmen were ready to throw it into the nearest garbage can when one of them noticed it was also spattered with something that could have been dried blood. Being conscientious law-enforcement officers, they combed the garbage out of their hair and delivered the garment to their precinct house—which happened to be the 87th.

Meyer and Carella were delighted to receive the suit.

It didn't tell them a goddamned thing about who owned it, but it nonetheless indicated to them that whoever had killed the rabbi was now busily engaged in covering his tracks and this, in turn, indicated a high state of anxiety.

Somebody had heard the news broadcast announcing Finch's escape. Somebody had been worried about Finch establishing an alibi for himself that would doubtless clear him.

With twisted reasoning somebody figured the best way to cover one homicide was to commit another. And somebody had hastily decided to get rid of the garments he'd worn while disposing of the rabbi.

The detectives weren't psychologists, but two mistakes had been committed in the same early morning, and they figured their prey was getting slightly desperate.

"It has to be another of Finch's crowd," Carella said. "Whoever killed Solomon painted a J on the wall. If he'd had time, he probably would have drawn a swastika as well."

"But why would he do that?" Meyer asked. "He'd automatically be telling us that an anti-Semite killed the rabbi."

"So? How many anti-Semites do you suppose there are in this city?"

"How many?" Meyer asked.

"I wouldn't want to count them," Carella said. "Whoever killed Yaakov Solomon was bold enough to—"

"Jacob," Meyer corrected.

"Yaakov, Jacob, what's the difference? The killer was bold enough to presume there were plenty of people who felt *exactly* the way he did. He painted that J on the wall and dared us to find *which* Jewhater had done the job." Carella paused. "Does this bother you very much, Meyer?"

"Sure, it bothers me."

"I mean, my saying—"

"Don't be a boob, Steve."

"Okay. I think we ought to look up this woman again. What was her name? Hannah something. Maybe she knows—"

"I don't think that'll help us. Maybe we ought to talk to the rabbi's wife. There's indication in his diary that he knew the killer, that he'd had threats. Maybe she knows who was baiting him."

"It's four o'clock in the morning," Carella said. "I don't think it's a good idea right now."

"We'll go after breakfast."

"It won't hurt to talk to Yirmiyahu again, either. If the rabbi was threatened, maybe—"

"Jeremiah," Meyer corrected.

"What?"

"Jeremiah. Yirmiyahu is Hebrew for Jeremiah."

"Oh. Well, anyway, him. It's possible the rabbi took him into his confidence, mentioned this—"

"Jeremiah," Meyer said again.

"What?"

"No." Meyer shook his head. "That's impossible. He's a holy man. And if there's anything a really good Jew despises, it's—"

"What are you talking about?" Carella said.

"—it's killing. Judaism teaches that you don't murder, unless in self-defense." His brow suddenly furrowed into a frown. "Still, remember when I was about to light that cigarette? He asked me if I was Jewish—remember? He was shocked that I would smoke on the second day of Passover."

"Meyer, I'm a little sleepy. Who are you talking about?" Carella wanted to know.

"Yirmiyahu. Jeremiah. Steve, you don't think—"

"I'm just not following you, Meyer."

"You don't think . . . you don't think the rabbi painted that wall *himself*, do you?"

"Why would . . . what do you mean?"

"To tell us who'd stabbed him? To tell us who the killer was?"

"How would—"

"Jeremiah," Meyer said.

Carella looked at Meyer silently for a full thirty seconds. Then he nodded and said, "J."

12.

He was burying something in the backyard behind the synagogue when they found him. They had gone to his home first and awakened his wife. She was an old Jewish woman, her head shaved in keeping with the Orthodox tradition. She covered her head with a shawl, and she sat in the kitchen of her ground-floor apartment and tried to remember what had happened on the second night of Passover. Yes, her husband had gone to the synagogue for evening services. Yes, he had come home directly after services.

"Did you see him when he came in?" Meyer asked.

"I was in the kitchen," Mrs. Cohen answered. "I was preparing the *seder*. I heard the door open, and he went in the bedroom."

"Did you see what he was wearing?"

"No."

"What was he wearing during the *seder?*"

"I don't remember."

"Had he changed his clothes, Mrs. Cohen? Would you remember that?"

"I think so, yes. He had on a black suit when he went to temple. I think he wore a different suit after." The old woman looked bewildered. She didn't know why they were asking these questions. Nonetheless, she answered them.

"Did you smell anything strange in the house, Mrs. Cohen?"

"Smell?"

"Yes. Did you smell paint?"

"Paint? No. I smelled nothing strange."

They found him in the yard behind the synagogue.

He was an old man with sorrow in his eyes and in the stoop of his posture. He had a shovel in his hands, and he was patting the earth with the blade. He nodded, as if he knew why they were there. They faced each other across the small mound of freshly turned earth at Yirmiyahu's feet.

Carella did not say a solitary word during the questioning and arrest. He stood next to Meyer Meyer, and he felt only an odd sort of pain.

"What did you bury, Mr. Cohen?" Meyer asked. He spoke very softly. It was five o'clock in the morning, and night was fleeing the sky. There was a slight chill on the air. The wind seemed to penetrate to the sexton's marrow. He seemed on the verge of shivering. "What did you bury, Mr. Cohen? Tell me."

"A ritual object," the sexton answered.

"*What*, Mr. Cohen?"

"I have no further use for it. It is a ritual object. I am sure it had to be buried. I must ask the *rov*. I must ask him what the Talmud says." Yirmiyahu fell silent. He looked at the mound of earth at his feet. "The *rov* is dead, isn't he?" he said, almost to himself. "He is dead." He looked sadly into Meyer's eyes.

"Yes," Meyer answered.

"*Baruch dayyan haemet,*" Yirmiyahu said. "You are Jewish?"

"Yes," Meyer answered.

"Blessed be God the true judge," Yirmiyahu translated, as if he had not heard Meyer.

"What did you bury, Mr. Cohen?"

"The knife," Yirmiyahu said. "The knife I use to trim the wick. It *is* a ritual object, don't you think? It should be buried, don't you think?" He paused. "You see . . ." His shoulders began to shake. He began weeping suddenly. "I killed," he said. The sobs started somewhere deep within the man, started wherever his roots were, started in the soul of the man, in the knowledge that he had committed the unspeakable crime—thou shalt not kill, thou shalt not kill. "I killed," he said again, but this time there were only tears, no sobs.

"Did you kill Arthur Finch?" Meyer asked.

The sexton nodded.

"Did you kill Rabbi Solomon?"

"He . . . you see . . . he was working. It was the second day of Passover, and he was working. I was inside when I heard the noise. I went to look and . . . he was carrying paints, paint cans in one hand, and . . . and a ladder in the other. He was *working*. I . . . took the knife from the ark, the knife I use to trim the wick. I had told him before this. I had told him he was not a *real* Jew, that his new . . . his new ways would be the end of the Jewish people.

And this, *this!* To work on the second day of Passover!"

"What happened, Mr. Cohen?" Meyer asked gently.

"I—the knife was in my hand. I went at him with the knife. He—he tried to stop me. He threw paint at me. I—I—" The sexton's right hand came up as if clasped around a knife. The hand trembled as it unconsciously re-enacted the events of that night. "I cut him. I cut him. . . . I killed him."

Yirmiyahu stood in the alley with the sun intimidating the peaks of the buildings now. He stood with his head bent, staring down at the mound of earth which covered the buried knife. His face was thin and gaunt, a face tormented by the centuries. The tears still spilled from his eyes and coursed down his cheeks. His shoulders shook with the sobs that came from somewhere deep in his guts. Carella turned away because it seemed to him in that moment that he was watching the disintegration of a man, and he did not want to see it.

Meyer put his arm around the sexton's shoulder.

"Come, *tsadik,*" he said. "Come. You must come with me now."

The old man said nothing. His hands hung loosely at his sides.

They began walking slowly out of the alley. As they passed the painted J on the synagogue wall, the sexton said, *"Olov ha-shalom."*

"What did he say?" Carella asked.

"He said, 'Peace be upon him.' "

"Amen," Carella said.

They walked silently out of the alley together.